PRAISE FOR THE NOVELS OF
JANICE KAY JOHNSON

"Janice Kay Johnson wins our hearts with appealing characters in this poignant tale of sacrifice, healing, and family relationships."
—*Romantic Times*

"Well-written characters living through complex situations that are neither glossed over nor magically solved. . . . A lovely romance with strong, likable characters."
—Her Hands, My Hands

"Johnson writes in a way that conveys real life very well and, at the same time, makes romance seem possible for normal people in everyday places."
—All About Romance

"Believable characters that demonstrate admirable growth and sensitivity. Remarkable in scope, beautifully realized with plot and characterizations . . . very highly recommended."
—Word Weaving

Turning Home

❋

Janice Kay Johnson

JOVE
New York

A JOVE BOOK
Published by Berkley
An imprint of Penguin Random House LLC
penguinrandomhouse.com

Copyright © 2020 by Janice Kay Johnson
Scripture taken from the New King James Version®. Copyright © 1982 by Thomas Nelson.
Used by permission. All rights reserved.
A JOVE BOOK, BERKLEY, and the BERKLEY & B colophon are
registered trademarks of Penguin Random House LLC.

ISBN: 9780593197967

First Edition: September 2020

Printed in the United States of America
1   3   5   7   9   10   8   6   4   2

Cover art by PixelWorks
Cover design by Katie Anderson
Book design by Gaelyn Galbreath

This is a work of fiction. Names, characters, places, and incidents either are the product
of the author's imagination or are used fictitiously, and any resemblance to actual persons,
living or dead, business establishments, events, or locales is entirely coincidental.

Without Jill Marsal, my wonderful literary agent, this book, the start of a new direction for me, wouldn't have happened. Thank you, Jill!

Chapter One

❖◆❖

JULIA DURANT WASN'T a very good liar. Lying to her brother, in particular, was chancy, because his years in law enforcement seemed to have honed his ability to catch untruths. And, heaven help her, all he'd asked was what her plans were for today.

The fact that Nick stood with his back to her as he poured himself another cup of coffee bought her a few seconds.

She had to say something.

"Oh, I'll probably keep exploring." *That's good,* she congratulated herself. Casual. "I haven't driven out to see that covered bridge yet, and I'm told there's another fabric store in Dunnington."

"Seen one, seen 'em all." His teasing grin relieved her.

Somehow, she doubted the greater public had ever seen police chief Nicholas Durant anything but stern. He'd developed that guarded cop look into an art form, which did *not* deter the women who chased him.

She rolled her eyes at his teasing. "Should I wait to start

dinner until you call?" He'd cut back his hours the first week of her visit, but when she continued to leave her departure date open, he'd reverted to his usual working habits.

"Probably best."

Two minutes later, he went out the door.

Once she was positive he was gone, she hurried to clean up, check her appearance in the mirror, and rush out to her rental car in the driveway. She did have plans that both scared and exhilarated her.

She was looking for a job . . . and if she found one, her stay in Tompkin's Mill, Missouri, would no longer be a vacation. It would be a new start for her.

FINGERS CROSSED, JULIA asked first at the Stitch in Time Quilt Shop. A quilter herself, she'd already gone in twice, once to pick up fabric and then again for a new packet of tiny needles and some thread. Today, she had brought in a quilt in hopes the owner would admire it enough to agree to sell it on consignment. She'd had a store back home that did that. The moment she'd laid out the quilt today, the two women working at the store had touched it with pleasure and immediately suggested a sale price. That, at least, felt like a triumph. She felt at home among the women she'd seen there, although many were Amish. It didn't seem to matter, since quilters spoke their own language.

But when she asked if there were any job openings at the store, she was met with a regretful headshake. The younger Amishwoman brightened immediately, however. "My *daad* needs to hire someone to answer phones and show his furniture. His place, it's only a block away."

Outside, reflecting off the sidewalk, the June sun felt blistering. This was far and away the hottest day since she arrived twelve days ago. Given that July through September was reputed to be far hotter, she'd better toughen up. Julia blinked away a salty bead of sweat that stung one eye. She could learn to like—or at least endure—the heat and humidity if she had the chance to stay here.

She loved the fact that Tompkin's Mill had a thriving downtown, and no big-box stores on the outskirts. The town, while good-sized, was also old-fashioned in some ways, with few stoplights and no buildings over two stories except for the combined city hall and police station. Originally established on the banks of Tompkin's Creek—beginning with a gristmill—the town was built on land that was flat as a pancake, surrounded by the rolling, wooded hills typical of much of northern Missouri.

Hurrying along, Julia skipped all the businesses on the block between the quilt shop and her destination. A few others appeared to be Amish-owned, as well, including a cabinetmaker's shop and the bakery. She could come back to them. Last week, she'd peered wistfully in the window of Bowman & Son's Handcrafted Furniture. The sign itself had letters etched into polished wood. It was handsome, but not fancy. The Amish didn't do fancy.

And yet, every piece she'd seen on the sales floor was exquisite: gorgeous woods gleaming with hand-rubbed finishes, the lines of the chests and tables and cupboards distinctive, inlays of secondary woods seamless. She hadn't needed to see price tags to know she probably couldn't afford a quilt rack.

Now, she didn't let herself so much as hesitate. If Mr. Bowman hired her, she could admire the furniture to her heart's content.

Clutching her handbag, she pushed her way inside. A bell on the door rang, but there was nobody behind the counter or in the display room. Neither Mr. Bowman nor his son popped out immediately to greet what might be a customer, either.

Temptation beckoned. Julia paused to slide her fingers over the silky top of the most beautiful chest of drawers she'd ever seen. Ebony inlay contrasted with the rich color of what she thought must be cherry. The sides curved subtly between the floor and top. She instantly coveted the chest—until she saw the price tag and winced. *Hands off.*

"Gute mariye." A man's voice startled her. He switched to English, probably once he saw her. "May I help you?"

Julia's head came up and she flushed. "The chest is beautiful. I was just admiring it."

A strongly built man who was likely in his late fifties or early sixties smiled at her from behind the long wooden counter. Silver strands threaded his brown hair and dominated in the beard that reached the middle of his chest. Of medium height, he wore a blue chambray long-sleeved shirt with suspenders, as the local Amishmen all did. He'd rolled up his sleeves, she saw, and didn't wear a hat, though the line where it usually compressed his hair was very visible. Amusement in his eyes, he said solemnly, "You are *wilkom* to do that as long as it pleases you."

She was afraid she could spend all day stroking the furniture in here.

He felt safe to her, allowing her to relax.

"I . . . thank you. *Denke*." She knew that much *Deitsh*, or Pennsylvania Dutch, as the language was commonly known to most Americans. She squared her shoulders. "Are you Mr. Bowman?"

"Eli Bowman, *ja*," he agreed.

"Your daughter . . . Miriam, who works in the quilt shop"—as if he didn't know his own daughter's name or where she worked—"she told me you have a job opening." It was all she could do not to rattle on and detail what kind of job he was supposed to have open, too.

"Ah." He smiled again. "You're a quilter?"

"Yes." She knotted her fingers together in front of her. "I went there first, because I know more about quilting than I do about furniture making. But I can answer phones and do the bookkeeping for any business. Oh—my name is Julia Durant."

He studied her keenly for a moment, then said, "Come sit down, please."

A dining room table as gorgeous as the chest held a heap of binders, one open to show photographs of pieces of furniture that presumably were stored elsewhere, or had been sold but could be replicated for a customer.

As she nervously pulled up a chair, a second man appeared in the open doorway leading to the back. Likely in his thirties, he had shoulders wide enough to block her view into the back, which she guessed was a workroom. A fleeting glance at him triggered her alarms. She lifted her chin in response, refusing to let either man see to her fearful core.

"Daad?" His eyes, a vivid blue, settled on her, narrowing slightly at whatever he saw on her face. To his father, he continued in *Deitsh*. Unfortunately, she couldn't understand a word he said in a slow, deep voice.

The senior Bowman—for the second man had to be the son—shook his head. "No. Julia Durant is not here to buy furniture. She would like to work for us."

A flicker of something she absolutely could not interpret crossed the younger man's face. Dislike? Concern, at least.

He had to be six inches taller than his father, as much as six foot one or two, Julia guessed. His hair had started out about the same shade as his father's, but the sun had glazed it with gold. The fact that his angular jaw was clean-shaven signaled his unmarried state. Curiously, he had shaggy hair not quite long enough to be cut in the typical Amish style. Yet he, too, wore a light blue shirt, broadfall trousers, and suspenders that she knew, from seeing men on the street, stretched in a Y across what had to be a broad, powerful back.

"My son," Eli said, pride in his voice. "Luke works here with me in the shop. Sometimes we have another helper, to sweep or do small jobs, but mostly we work alone."

Her disappointment was greater than it should have been, especially given her complicated reaction to Luke

Bowman. She could apply at other businesses. "Oh. So you don't have a job available." She started to push back the chair. "I'm sorry to have bothered you."

"No, no. A *bodderation* you are not."

Eli's slip back into *Deitsh* surprised her. His English was considerably more fluent than most Amishmen or -women spoke, probably because he dealt every day with customers from the outside world. *Englischers*, as the Amish would say.

Cheeks flushed, she said, "Well, I'm wasting your time."

"No, Luke and I agree we do need someone to answer the phone and talk to people who come in the door. We are too busy to make the furniture *and* sell it. This 'bookkeeping' would be *gut*, too. I have ignored it too much and now it's a mess." He was the one to twine his fingers together this time, as if demonstrating a knot.

Julia laughed. "I like numbers."

Luke's eyes sharpened on her face. She couldn't imagine why.

"I don't speak your language," she admitted, "but I can learn."

"Most people who call or come in are *Englischers*. And we all speak some English."

She nodded and slid her résumé across the table.

"Durant," the son said unexpectedly. "The police chief is also named Durant. Are you related?"

He had no accent at all.

"Yes, he's my brother." She hesitated. "I came for a visit, but I like Tompkin's Mill. To stay, I need a job."

"Your brother doesn't like it when we won't talk to him."

"He understands," Julia countered. Nick had expressed his frustration about the Amish refusing to report crimes or testify in court, choosing instead to forgive someone who had wronged them. He reluctantly, she thought, also admired them for that same determination. "At least they're mostly law-abiding," he'd grumbled at the dinner table a few evenings before.

Eli looked up from the résumé. "The pay will not be as much as you have made."

Since she hadn't listed her pay on the résumé, he was betraying some knowledge of the outside world.

"I don't expect that. It's not as expensive to live here. I can stay with my brother until I find a small apartment."

"We don't offer health insurance, either." Luke's face, seemingly all sharp angles and planes, didn't quite show hostility, but she sensed it just below the surface. "Or pay government taxes. You have to do that yourself."

"I can manage." She smiled again at the father. "Like I said, I'm good with numbers."

"And people?" the son demanded.

She forced herself to meet blue eyes that appeared cold. "When they're friendly." That she could challenge him and keep her voice from trembling told her how far she'd come.

Eli turned his head to look at his son. He didn't say anything, but Luke's mouth tightened.

"Give us a minute," Eli said, suddenly formal.

She summoned her best smile. "Yes, of course."

They disappeared into what was indeed a workroom. Through the half-open doorway, she could see a table saw and part of a wall of cubbies that held small tools and scraps of wood in various sizes and colors. Sawdust lay beneath the table saw, as it had clung to the gold hairs on Luke Bowman's powerful forearms as well as the front of his shirt. The pleasing scent of fresh-cut wood would always cling to him, too, along with sweat and soap.

Thinking about how he smelled made her stomach tighten. She *shouldn't* think about any such thing, not if there was a chance she'd be working here. Though Amish, he didn't have his father's air of serenity. He was a man; a big, muscular, domineering man, if she was any judge. She didn't dare let any part of that draw her. It would only end in disaster.

Julia bent her head and stared at her hands, hearing the

men's voices but unable to understand what they were saying. They weren't quite arguing, but she'd bet Luke didn't want his father to hire her. Maybe he was uncomfortable with a woman here all the time who wasn't of his faith . . . but that didn't seem like the right explanation.

Their voices stopped. She braced herself. Eli smiled as he returned to the table.

"We would like you to work for us."

Julia blew out a breath she hadn't realized she was holding. He explained what they could pay and the hours, which she barely took in. She wanted this job. She might even have accepted ludicrously low pay—but what he offered was acceptable.

She beamed at him. "That sounds fine. I can start anytime."

His smile was equally broad. "Tomorrow, then. In the morning, we will show you what needs to be done, *ja*?"

"Yes, please." A moment later, without having caught even a glimpse of the younger Bowman, she was back out in the heat, hurrying down the sidewalk to her car. She was both excited and a little frightened. This would be a huge change . . . and she had to explain it to Nick.

And tomorrow . . . no, she wouldn't think about Luke Bowman. Julia suspected he would avoid her as much as he could, and she'd avoid him, too. That should work fine.

"WHY HAVE YOU been so quiet this afternoon?" Eli asked as he adjusted the breast strap between the mare's forelegs.

From long practice Luke checked the crupper beneath Polly's tail before patting her brown rump. It gave him a moment to switch mentally from English to *Deitsh*. Even after six months home, he still tended to think in English.

"No reason," he lied, in the language he had grown up speaking.

His father saw through him, of course, but didn't call

him on it. "You will have dinner with your *mamm* and me?" he asked.

Luke had fallen into eating too often with his parents and sister. Feeding him made his mother happy. But he was too old to go home as if he were the same boy who had left. He no longer fit in the narrow, too-short bed upstairs in his parents' home. He had stayed only for a few weeks when he first arrived, until he was able to buy a house on three acres just outside of town. He had never wanted to farm, but once he married, he expected to keep a flock of chickens, perhaps a milk cow, and have an extensive vegetable garden, pasture for several horses as well as the cow, and an orchard. The orchard already on the property was the only part he did have, but for a pasture half-covered by the snarl of blackberry vines run amok. He had no prospects for a wife yet, either, but that would happen. He was already a decade older than the average Amishman when he married.

"*Denke*, but not tonight," he replied. "I'm in the mood to cook."

His father laughed. "You need a wife."

Yes, Eli too often knew what his son was thinking.

Luke said nothing, settling on the front bench seat, waiting until his father joined him and had picked up the reins. Luke had bought a buggy big enough to haul furniture right away as well as a retired harness racehorse, a big gelding. Half of the days or more, though, Eli came by for him in the morning. There was no sense in making two horses spend the day confined to a small paddock beneath the sycamore behind their building. Polly was older and seemed not to mind drowsing away the heat of the day as long as she had water and a feedbag.

"I saw the way Rebecca King watched you Sunday," Eli continued. "November is not so far away."

That was a not-so-subtle nudge. November was the traditional month for Amish weddings.

Luke had seen the way she looked at him, too, and done

his best to steer clear of Rebecca. She was pretty enough, but too young, too . . . He didn't know. He couldn't put whatever it was that he craved into words yet. Yes, he had chosen this life, but he wasn't the same man he would have been if he had never left it. He was careful not to look at *Englisch* women, however, like the one who had come in today to apply for the job.

The one his father had hired despite Luke's wishes.

He was disturbed that he could so easily picture her. Although only medium height, she was long legged. He had thought she was too thin, and had dressed to hide any curves, not show them off. Her hair was a dark auburn, drawn back into some kind of bun at her nape. The severe style, much like the way Amishwomen wore their hair, only emphasized high cheekbones and a sharp chin. He'd only been so aware of the rich color because she didn't wear a *kapp*. Creamy white skin would suffer under the Missouri sun, he had thought, bothered that he would care. Even more bothered to have been so aware of her astonishing eyes, a velvety brown lit with gold striations. Her eyelashes—

Luke shook his head hard.

The *Leit*, the people, lived apart from others. The separation was an essential tenet of their faith. They had neighbors and good customers among the *Englischers*, might even have some they called friends, but that wasn't the same as being drawn to a woman. The temptation could pull a man away from his faith and deepest beliefs. Luke didn't imagine it happening, but this Julia had undeniably disturbed him. Best not to have her around, he had thought, but his father disagreed. Although he might not have if Luke had admitted to his momentary weakness.

This brief attraction wouldn't matter. He would soon find that she was shallow or selfish or vain, and she would no longer appear so beautiful.

He was relieved when his father stopped to let him off at

the foot of the long driveway leading to the old house he'd bought. He waved goodbye and enjoyed the walk and surveying his own property.

Charlie, his Standardbred buggy horse, trotted toward the fence to meet him. A brown so dark he was almost black, Charlie had perfect conformation. He had been gelded, Luke was told, because he had been too difficult to handle as a stallion. His later success on the racecourse made his owner deeply regret the necessity, but it was Luke's good fortune that Charlie couldn't be sent to stud.

Luke stopped to scratch the horse's poll and slide a hand over his neck and shoulder. "Does dinner sound good to you, too?" he asked.

Charlie snorted, and bobbed his head. He stuck close to Luke until the fence stopped him short of the house. Watching his person walking away, he looked forlorn. As herd animals, horses needed a companion.

A sound escaped Luke's throat. He was lonely, too, but not for just anyone.

Once he married, he'd need a second buggy and horse.

The next church Sunday, he could attend the worship in a different district. No one would mind, and he could meet other people his age. He wondered if he would be happier with a widow. Most never-married Amishwomen were in their late teens or early twenties. A ten-to-twelve-year gap between man and wife felt too much like an abyss to him. But would a widow have any more interesting conversation than an eighteen-year-old girl did?

Irritated with himself, he shook his head. Amishwomen were homebodies. That was exactly what he needed. He had made the decision to forsake the outside world, and that included pretty *auslanders*.

He let himself into his oppressively hot house and indulged in a brief fantasy. *Englisch* women he didn't miss, but air-conditioning, that was something else again.

Chapter Two

❖◆❖

JULIA CALLED HELLO from the kitchen when Nick arrived home from work. She had only a glimpse of him in his daunting, dark green uniform and badge, with the big black pistol on his hip, before he headed upstairs to change clothes. It was easier to think of him as her big brother once he returned in faded jeans, athletic shoes, and a ragged T-shirt.

"Mom would throw that away if she saw it go through *her* laundry," Julia pointed out.

He laughed. "Over my dead body. Man, that smells good. I'm starved."

She'd put together a meatloaf, sautéed small red potatoes, and green beans, fresh from the garden. She knew, because she'd seen the neighbor picking them. An elderly man, he'd immediately offered her some and wouldn't take a polite no for an answer.

Once they were seated and dishing up, Nick asked, "Good day?"

She knew his question wasn't entirely casual. He'd always been protective of her. He had suffered because he hadn't been there to keep her safe the one time that really mattered. Since then, she was never sure if he was capable of turning off his worry for her.

Nonetheless, she'd missed him when he left the Cleveland PD for this job in a relatively small Missouri town. The change was so drastic, she knew something had gone wrong, either on his job or in his personal life. Of course, he'd never been willing to talk about it. She hated knowing he believed she was too frail to be asked to bear anyone else's burdens.

Having hoped to save her news until after dinner, she said, "Your day has to have been more exciting than mine. Fair's fair. Your turn to go first."

He raised his eyebrows. "I barely left my office today. Figured out who could take vacation when, talked to an officer about losing his temper with a group of admittedly provocative teenagers, took a dozen calls, and pored over the budget trying to find a few extra dollars to pay for training courses my officers urgently need. That pretty well sums it up. The lack of catastrophes explains why I made it home before six."

"Oh. Um . . . what kind of training?"

He proved willing to talk. She'd cleaned her plate and he was dishing up seconds when he said, "Okay, out with it."

Julia carefully set down her fork. This was *her* life. Much as she loved him, he had no say.

"I applied for a job today. I've decided to stay in Tompkin's Mill."

Nick froze with a full serving spoon halfway between the bowl and his plate. "Why?"

"I like it here." She hesitated. "It's peaceful. Quiet. You're here. I think I've already begun to make friends at the quilt shop."

"We have crime."

"But not like Cleveland."

"No, this isn't a big city." He finally dumped the potatoes onto his plate. "What job?"

When she told him, lines deepened in his forehead and he stayed quiet long enough to send her nerves skittering.

"Is this about the Amish?" he asked at last. "You're not kidding yourself that they're saintly, are you? They have domestic violence and drunkenness, like any other group. It just stays below the radar because they refuse to report it to authorities."

"It's not about the Amish," Julia retorted . . . and didn't know whether that was another lie or truth.

LUKE WANTED TO start a new project, but he had stained several almost-completed pieces of furniture late yesterday. It would make sense to apply the first layer of finish, except if he did that, he shouldn't operate a saw. The fine particles of wood floated throughout the workroom. Feeling disgruntled, he decided to work on the finish. This was good timing, since his father intended to spend a couple of hours with their new sales assistant.

That was the title *Daad* had decided to give the *Englisch* woman.

Later, he could hand-saw dovetail joints for drawers if he stayed well away from the drying finishes—or even worked in the alley.

A timid knock on the back door brought his head up. It had to be her. Had *Daad* told her to park back there? He hoped she hadn't scared Charlie, who was still somewhat jumpy around noisy cars.

"It's open. Come in," he called. It would be interesting to see what she thought was appropriate to wear. Something about her yesterday had scraped at his skin like sandpaper, but today she would be just another woman. Not interesting at all.

The door opened, the sunlight so bright for a moment he saw her only as a dark shape with a halo. He had to blink a few times even once she shut the door behind her.

She hovered just inside. And no, he decided after scanning her, those weren't the same clothes she'd worn yesterday, but they were very similar. A khaki skirt instead of pants, sandals with thin straps she must consider dressier than yesterday's, and a white shirt. It was just oversize enough to serve as a disguise, except that she had tucked it in, allowing him to see how slender her waist was. His hands would nearly span it. His fingers twitched at his side as he had the thought.

Maybe she had been sick or suffered some trauma that led to a significant weight loss. That would explain a wardrobe of too-large garments.

She offered a smile as tentative as her knock had been. "Good morning."

"*Gute mariye.*" He could be polite while using language as a barrier.

"That means good morning, doesn't it?"

"*Ja.*" Blast it, she knew he spoke English fluently. "Yes."

"I do want to learn *Deitsh.*"

He corrected her pronunciation. Her lips curved again, more naturally. Had she not had reason to smile often? He'd wondered yesterday. This smile was better than the first, or any of yesterday's. It was gentle and beautiful. She looked . . . hopeful.

That they would become good friends? She'd quickly learn that wasn't happening. He'd be civil, that's all. Help her on the job when she needed it.

Having his gut tighten only because she'd walked into the room wasn't really about her so much as his discomfort with having to work at all closely with a young, unmarried woman who was not Amish. He hadn't expected this to happen after he returned home. He had accepted baptism six months ago, after Bishop Amos had become convinced

Luke was sincere in his repentance and desire to embrace the faith.

The sound of steel-rimmed buggy wheels crunching on gravel stopped right behind the store. Thank the good Lord, his father had arrived to rescue him.

While they waited for *Daad* to remove the harness from Polly and set her up in an enclosure near Charlie's, Julia walked around the workroom, studying tools and pieces of furniture at various stages of completion. She asked questions, which Luke had to answer. He would get this over with, he decided. She needed to know these things if she was to represent them to the public.

Careful to maintain a distance so that they never brushed against each other, Luke led her into the temperature-controlled lumber room, pointed out different woods, showed her samples of various stains on each kind of wood.

He also led her into the alley to show her the shed-roof extension that housed the diesel generator that powered their tools and lights. *Daad* had gotten permission to jog the alley around the extension.

Of course, his father was out there beneath the shed that offered their horses protection from the sun and rain. Apparently in no hurry, he added water to the trough, although he also called a cheerful *"Gute mariye."* Julia repeated the words, echoing their intonation.

Daad beamed. "You will speak like us soon."

Luke's glare apparently bounced off his father.

The sun lit fire in Julia's hair, including the heavy mass at her nape. How long was it? Was it wavy, as he suspected? His fingers did some more twitching, although he pushed back before he speculated on what her hair would feel like slipping through his fingers. The gold shimmered in her eyes, too, defying his attempt to block out awareness of her as a woman.

Escorting their new employee back inside, Luke began a lecture. Better if he pretended he was a tour leader, speaking to people whose faces he'd forget as soon as the tour was done.

As pedantically as he could manage, he described how the Amish lit and powered homes and businesses. "Kerosene is fine for lighting in homes, but not here," he explained. "It can be dangerous when there is sawdust and fumes from finishes in the air. The generator also powers the overhead lights in the workroom, and the skylights give us natural light." Large skylights studded the ceiling in the showroom out front, too, reducing the need for artificial lights.

"I suppose I pictured only hand tools," she said thoughtfully.

"We do use those. Saws, hammers, chisels." He showed her a hand plane. "Without powered saws and sanders, creating something like this desk"—he indicated one he had stained yesterday afternoon—"would take so long, we'd have to price it beyond most people's means. And if you're thinking of the name of our business, we are still making every cut ourselves."

She wrinkled her nose at him. "Your furniture is already beyond *my* means."

Luke held back a smile, grateful when his father came in the back door just then.

"I've heard the phone ringing," Luke said, earning a surprised look from Julia.

"You should have said. It isn't good business not to answer."

"That will be your job." He didn't mind answering specific inquiries about their furniture, but callers often liked to talk and ask stupid questions. "What's your furniture like?" He'd hung up on that caller. His least favorite part was wasting time in the front room with *auslanders* who had wandered in off the street and only pretended they could afford to buy anything.

Maybe having Julia here wouldn't be so bad, if she'd stay in front and leave him peacefully alone in back.

* * *

JULIA HAD TWO personal visitors that afternoon. The first
was Miriam from the quilt shop, a cheerful young woman
with a curvaceous figure, curly blond hair, and a gently
rounded face that might lead some people to describe her as
placid. Julia had recognized flickers of sadness in her eyes,
and guessed Miriam saw the same in her. She appeared to
be in her early- to midtwenties, but still lived at home.

Wearing a lavender dress that reached midcalf with an
apron of a slightly darker shade, she also wore the standard
white organdy prayer *kapp* with ties that flew around her
shoulders with her quick movements.

"I'm so happy that *Daad* hired you!" she exclaimed.
"Maybe we can have lunch together soon."

"I'd like that." Julia had been feeling like a fraud, sitting
behind the counter and pretending to callers and the two
couples who had wandered into the showroom during the
day that she knew what she was talking about. It was always like this, starting a new job, though; a week from
now, she'd feel much more confident. "I could use help
learning to speak your language."

Miriam bent forward, speaking in a hushed tone. "I've
heard people say there is a vocabulary online, and maybe
more. I don't *know*, but you could look. That might help."

Julia knew that the owner of the quilt shop might have
dispensation from the bishop to maintain a web page just as
the Bowmans had for this store, but that wouldn't necessarily apply to Amish employees—nor did it mean they were
permitted to browse the internet. The unwritten *Ordnung*,
or rules, by which they lived their lives, was known by all
Amish, or so Julia had read. There must be a delicate bal-
ance in living in the modern world yet holding to many
practices two centuries out of date.

Miriam went on cheerily, "But I would love to help you.
If business is slow and Ruth doesn't need me, I'll come over

here. Monday we're having a frolic—a quilting bee, as you would call it, to finish a wedding quilt. It will be at our house. Would you like to come?"

"I'd love to." Bowman's was open Tuesday through Saturday. "If . . . well, others don't mind me."

"Mind you?" Miriam sounded puzzled.

"Not being Amish, I mean."

"Oh! No one will mind that. You are a good quilter, that's all anyone will think about." Suddenly she aimed her smile past Julia. "Ain't so, Luke?"

"For quilting, I don't know," he said, voice repressive. Even Miriam's smile dimmed.

Julia refused to turn around. Luke Bowman hadn't said a word to her since this morning's brief tutelage. She'd felt his reluctance. She resented his poorly hidden dislike, even as she knew it was best if they stayed away from each other. The hairs on the back of her neck prickled only because of this awareness that he was behind her. Not standing in the workshop door, but closer.

How close?

Rearing over her. Huge, with meaty fists, a snarl baring his teeth. *He's going to kill me.* There was nobody to hear, nobody to see. If she'd locked her door—

Miriam softly saying her name interrupted the scene playing in her head. There were triggers that sent her to another place and time. She would have fought a touch, but the gentle voice was different. Even so, it took her a minute to compose herself, to see Miriam leaning against the counter, her worry evident.

"Julia? *Was der schinner is letz?*"

"Speak English," her brother said from right behind Julia. He'd come forward silently.

Now, he towered over her. Unable to bear it, Julia leaped to her feet, whirling at the same time and backing away from him. She felt herself shaking. At least she kept the mewling sound from escaping.

The complete astonishment on his face told her how dreadfully she'd embarrassed herself. This hadn't happened in a long time. Why now? She wanted this job! She loved it! Now they'd think she was crazy. *Ab im kopf*, that's how they'd describe her. Off in the head. And maybe she was.

"I . . . I'm all right," she said with difficulty. Swallowed. "I'm sorry. I was . . . dizzy for a minute, and you startled me."

Dizzy. Now they'd ship her off to the ER, in case she was prone to mini-seizures.

Miriam's face had softened. She might buy the explanation, but Luke didn't.

Julia hurried to add, "I'm not used to the heat. I probably haven't been drinking enough water."

"Oh! Didn't Luke or *Daad* show you the refrigerator? There is always water in there."

Luke, in fact, disappeared into the workshop, returning immediately with a bottle of water. Droplets beaded on the chilled metal bottle. He approached cautiously—*looming . . . no, no*—to hold it out.

Julia made sure not to brush his fingers with hers when she accepted it. "Thank you. I am sorry. This . . . isn't like me."

"It makes no trouble," Miriam said, her accent more pronounced than it had been. *"Sehr gut."*

Was that the equivalent of "it's all good"? Julia smiled shakily at her. *"Denke."* She tried not to look at Luke, standing well away now, but watchful, suspicious.

Well, that hadn't changed.

She took a long drink of the icy cold water, pulled herself together enough to reassure both sister and brother, and pounced on the phone when it providentially rang.

"Yes, Mr. Russell. I understand. I'll tell Mr. Bowman that you're running late. I'm sure that'll be fine." The warmth she'd injected into her voice seemed to reassure both Bowmans.

Miriam smiled and waved and then hustled out the front

door and down the sidewalk. Luke faded away when Julia wasn't looking.

Phone call over, Julia bent forward until her forehead rested on the smooth wooden surface of the counter, and moaned.

Of course, that's when the bell over the door rang and she looked up to see Nick entering.

ELI DIDN'T SEEM to mind shaking the police chief's hand, but Luke was less happy. Chief Durant had stopped by to check out his sister's employers, and he didn't make any bones about it. He wanted a tour. He wanted to scrutinize father and son. He did wait until she was out of earshot before he asked about their expectations for her. Luke thought Julia had enough pride not to appreciate her brother acting like a stern, overprotective father.

Luke was annoyed enough to abandon his *daad* to the man and go back to work—or, at least, pretend to work. This was one of the moments that still came too frequently, when he struggled with what God expected of him. Not perfection, no, but although he was at peace with his decision to come home, his own moodiness was unexpected. He needed to cut himself some slack, though; even after a year back home, he felt the worldly side of him still dominated too often. The bishop had been right in wanting him to wait before being baptized. If he had known that Luke still struggled, he might have insisted on a longer probationary period before allowing Luke to make the irrevocable commitment. Yet it was done.

Shifting his thoughts, he considered what was behind that scene in the office. Julia had sprung from him as if she were terrified. That didn't look like any dizzy spell he'd ever seen.

He rubbed his jaw, unsettled on a deep level. Had something bad happened to her? He'd read the newspapers while he was out in the world. Violence seemed to be the norm. Perhaps his increasing awareness partially explained his decision to return to the fold.

No matter what, he felt guilty for allowing her to see that he didn't want her here. What if she'd misjudged him and thought him capable of the violence that was on the television news every night? What could he say to let her know he would never hurt her? Or would he only make matters worse? Luke had no idea.

He was still brooding when he became aware the police chief had stopped at his side.

"You don't have much to say, do you?" the man said.

Luke raised his eyebrows. "I don't know you. I'm not good at meaningless talk."

Nicholas Durant's jaw muscles bulged, and if Luke was any judge, that was an angry glint in his brown eyes. He muttered something under his breath and stalked away.

Listening to his voice in the office, followed by Julia's softer voice, Luke understood that if something bad—he didn't want to define what—had happened to either of his sisters, he would feel protective, too. That was natural.

What did upset Luke was the knowledge that now he, too, would worry about Julia. She worked for him, as much as for his father. Wasn't it his responsibility to make sure she felt safe here?

Yes. But how was that compatible with his determination to keep his distance? He greatly feared it wasn't, although the fact that it seemed *he* was the one who scared her might help.

Conflicted and not liking the feeling, he was grateful to see that it was almost five. He needed to get away.

Chapter Three

❧◆❧

LUKE DIDN'T UNDERSTAND what drove him, but in the absence of his father—and where *was* he?—he felt the need to check on Julia, to . . . reassure her, maybe.

Frustrated to be compelled to do exactly what he'd told himself he wouldn't, Luke opened the door into the front office. Julia was shutting down the computer his father had reluctantly purchased and not tried very hard to learn how to use. *Daad* had tried to convince Luke to take over the inventory and bookkeeping because he was good on computers, but Luke had dug in his heels. If he'd wanted to do that with his life, he wouldn't have come home to Tompkin's Mill.

Julia raised her head and saw him. Her lips firmed. "I'm sorry. I mean, about my brother coming by. I can't believe he did that! I'm twenty-nine years old, and he's acting as if I'm a sixteen-year-old with her first job."

Luke leaned his shoulder against the doorframe. "Big brothers are like that. Even Amish ones."

She let out a huff. "Well, I'm going to chew him out when I get home!"

A chuckle rose from Luke's chest. "Miriam and Rose have chewed me out before. I told them they were wasting their breath."

The impulse to humor died as he felt the jagged edges of another piece of guilt he carried because he hadn't been here when Miriam's come-calling friend had died in a logging accident. She'd had the rest of the family's support, but not his. Nobody had known how to reach him. That was nothing he could change. Every decision a man or woman made had consequences. He had to live with his own.

Julia watched him, her extraordinary eyes troubled. "I've wondered about Miriam." She sounded hesitant. "Aren't most Amishwomen her age already married? I didn't like to ask . . ."

Only an hour or two ago, he wouldn't have expected to have this kind of conversation with her, but he sensed her concern rose from compassion. "They are," he agreed. "Not all. Some teach school for a few years, or hold a job like she's doing. Miriam would have been married by now, though. The man she loved was crushed when a tree he and his partner were felling landed on him. That was five years ago. She seems happy, but hasn't become interested in any other man."

"It takes time to work through grief. It should, don't you think?"

"I do, although it helps to know God had a purpose calling Levi home when He did." He paused. "I wanted to say I'm sorry if I startled you earlier. If you didn't know I was there . . ." He purposely left it open-ended.

She tried to smile. "Thank you, but it wasn't anything to do with you. It was just . . . nothing important."

Luke discovered how much he disliked smiles produced only to cover sadness. He wasn't much happier with her discounting herself and her reactions as unimportant. But he didn't know her well enough to argue, and didn't *want* to know her that well. So he only nodded and said, "Good night, Julia. We'll see you tomorrow."

This smile was a little better. "Tomorrow."

JULIA SAW REMARKABLY little of Luke during the rest of the short week beyond the occasional glimpses when she went back to the workshop to ask Eli a question. Luke's glance in her direction always appeared disinterested before he returned his focus to the wood he was cutting or oil he applied. Fortunately, Eli didn't alarm her at all. His warmth and kindness were almost tangible. She couldn't imagine this man losing his temper.

Luke was something else. It was as if the father were a placid pool, the son a deep river with a shimmering surface hiding powerful currents beneath. Yet he couldn't be Amish without believing wholeheartedly in forgiveness while rejecting violence. She found herself wanting to ask him about his faith in an effort to understand him.

Truthfully, Julia thought about Luke Bowman entirely too much.

By Saturday, she felt increasingly confident on the job, although the showroom was much busier on the weekend and she had to ask a lot of questions. Still, she made it through the day, and one couple bought a gorgeous dining room table with a set of eight chairs and the matching buffet. She did a private victory dance before she opened the workshop door to tell Eli and Luke. Both came to see which dining room set had sold.

"Ach, we need to fill that place," Eli said.

"You have more in storage?"

"*Ja*, a part of my barn. We built a wall and put the insulation in. The temperature must be kept the same all the time, you understand."

She grinned at him. "*Ja*."

"When is it to be shipped?" Eli asked.

"Wednesday. The buyers arranged it while they were here. I should have asked—"

"No, no, that is *gut*."

Luke didn't say a single word.

That evening, Nick found her curled up comfortably on the sofa, scouring Craigslist.

"Rentals?" he asked. He seemed reconciled to her having a job, which was something.

"Yes, there are more available in town than I expected. Did you know someone is converting that really cool brick building on Elm Street into apartments?" Gorgeous ones, from what she could see, with refinished hardwood floors, high ceilings, and distinctive woodwork echoing the original moldings and casings.

Another thing she loved about Tompkin's Mill and the surrounding area was the sense of history. So many of the farmhouses dated to the early twentieth century, and she often saw primitive stone structures that were likely pre–Civil War. Even here in town, little was really *new*.

Julia thought her fascination with quilting had begun with a Log Cabin quilt her mother kept tucked away in a cedar chest at home. It had been made by Julia's maternal great-grandmother. As a girl, she'd often opened the chest to study the stitches and finger the many different fabrics. According to her mother, they'd have been scraps left over from dresses or shirts made by family members. She'd touch one and wonder. Was that from a dress made for her grandmother as a little girl?

Even now, Julia loved the traditional patterns best, because they'd been handed down by women from other generations. Knowing she was a part of the whole that flowed from past to future felt comforting. That the old buildings here still stood and were protected gave her the same feeling.

Watching her, Nick unsnapped his holster from his belt

and unbuttoned his cuffs. "That used to be a school. Built in about 1920, from what I gather. I heard it's being renovated." Nick sounded surprisingly reasonable, until he added with a hint of smugness, "The apartments aren't ready for tenants yet, are they?"

"They're pre-leasing. The second-floor apartments will be available starting July 1." She smiled at him. "That's only two weeks away."

He grunted. "What's wrong with living here? It's free." Then he played dirty. "It's safe."

She stiffened her spine. "I've had my own place for years, Nick. You know that. If I cling to you, I'd be taking a step backwards. That's not what I want to do."

"You think I'm trying to make you dependent on me?" Frustration turned his face grim.

Julia softened her voice. "I think you don't want to have to worry about me."

He held her eyes for a good twenty seconds before bowing his head and rubbing the back of his neck. "You're right."

"Ha! I wish I'd recorded that! I'm sure it's a first."

Rueful acceptance on his face, Nick said, "Where you're concerned, probably. Enjoy it. The words will never cross my lips again."

Julia laughed, jumped up, and kissed his cheek. He hugged her. For a moment, she savored the closeness. Despite their four-year age difference, they had been best friends growing up. Just knowing he was here in town gave her a sense of security she still needed.

Not that she'd tell *him* that. Why give her brother, the control freak, any added ammunition?

She wouldn't be able to look at apartments until Monday. No, not even then, she realized, unless she did it first thing in the morning. Miriam had invited her to the midday meal on Monday to be followed by the quilt frolic. And truthfully, she wasn't in that big a hurry to move out. She did take pleasure in cooking for Nick, who had probably eaten a lot of microwave meals until her arrival.

Maybe *that's* why he wanted her to stay.

SUNDAY, SHE AND Nick attended the service at a Congregational church in Tompkin's Mill. Her first Sunday here, she'd expected to have to go alone. Nick hadn't been a churchgoer back in Cleveland, which she'd regretted but understood. His job would turn anyone into a cynic, or worse. How could even the most devout see God's hand in a vicious crime scene or head-on collision that killed an entire family?

For her, it was different. After the attack and her eventual release from the hospital, she hadn't gone back to her church for nearly three months, but when she did, she found desperately needed comfort. *Delusion*, Nick had said once, then apologized.

Seeing her surprise that first week here, he admitted that he had joined the church because it was expected of him as a public official. Amish or *Englischer*, people in this town attended worship every Sunday. He faced enough doubt among townsfolk already by virtue of being a northerner.

This Sunday, Julia found her mind wandering during the service, either because of her eventful week or because the sermon was uninspiring. The heat in the church didn't help either. She dabbed surreptitiously at sweat on her forehead and throat several times.

She had to turn in her rental car soon. Keeping it ate briskly away at her savings—but without it, she'd take twice as long on a bus to get to work, and would be otherwise stranded until she bought a car. Back to Craigslist and the newspaper tonight.

She'd email Mom tonight and ask her to sell her aging Volkswagen right away. Lucky she'd left it at her parents' house. The apartment was paid through July, so the rest of her stuff could stay where it was until she had rented a place here.

Blinking away the sting of sweat, Julia had the fleeting image of herself in a buggy, holding the reins close behind the powerful rump of a horse.

Her brother shot her a look that made her wonder if she was smiling at a particularly inappropriate part of the sermon.

Okay, given that she'd never even sat atop a horse before, she'd settle for a *ride* in a buggy.

This was an off-church Sunday for the local Amish, she knew. They held services every other Sunday, using the intervening one for visiting and time with family. What would their services be like? Trying to imagine one held in a barn or kitchen, she decided they must have dull ministers, too, mixed with inspirational ones. Even if she became fluent in *Deitsh*, she wouldn't understand the hymns or their Bibles, as she'd read that they were in an archaic form of German.

Luke would certainly attend with the rest of his family, including Miriam. The other sister as well, unless she had married a man from another church district. Were there other boys in the family? Surely there were. It must be rare among them to have only three children.

Julia's heart squeezed, just as her hand would into a fist. She had always assumed she'd have children. Now, she didn't see how that was possible, unless she went to a sperm bank. But her dream had included a husband who was also a good father. Was she able and willing to raise a child alone?

Nick's elbow poked her side. The congregation was rising to sing a hymn. In fact, he'd already opened the book, probably because he'd forgotten the words even to the hymns he had known well as a child.

And she had sat here for almost two hours while giving no thought at all to God, which was not like her. She sent a single apology wrapped in a prayer winging upward even as she remembered the last thing Eli had said to her at closing yesterday.

"Da Herr sei mit du." The Lord be with you.

She prayed that He was.

LUKE GENTLY TUGGED at the top of a strip of wallpaper in his dining room. One corner already peeling, it came loose easily, but seeing what was beneath it, he groaned. Another layer of wallpaper. The second layer looked much older, which meant it would be more difficult to remove. Strippable wallpaper had not been a concept when this house was built in 1904. There was no saying he wouldn't find a third layer beneath.

When he bought the house, he'd known he was taking on a great deal of work. At his request, the power company came out right away and removed the wire feeding electricity to the house. He had had to replace an aging stove, refrigerator, and hot-water heater immediately with propane-powered appliances, and have a propane tank installed. The people who lived here must have loved wallpaper. Luke hadn't realized how difficult it could be to strip from the walls.

The Amish had plain walls in their homes. They didn't decorate with wallpaper or artwork, any more than the women wore makeup or jewelry, or the men built or purchased buggies painted bright colors. They accepted the *Ordnung* as the bishop interpreted it.

A knock on his front door was followed by a voice before he could climb down.

"Luke? Are you here? *Mamm* said you need help."

"I'm in the dining room," he called back. "The job is fun."

His brother, just turned twenty-five, appeared in the

arched opening to the hall. "No-o," he moaned. "She didn't say what you were working on."

"Come on! You're an expert after helping me with the kitchen. With two of us working, this will be nothing."

Elam's gaze went to the corner where Luke had peeled the first strip. "There's more under there!"

"The house was built a hundred and fifteen years ago. There might be many layers."

Elam whimpered but said, "I'll get another ladder."

Luke called after him. "You know where the scrapers are."

Truly the work did go faster after that. It helped to have someone to talk to. Elam had been twelve when Luke left, only a boy. Now they had to get to know each other all over again. Initially sulky and uncommunicative, Elam had warmed to the brother who had repented of his sins. When Luke first came home, Elam had been working in their father's furniture-making business, but that's not what he wanted to do with his life, so he had been grateful rather than resentful to be replaced. He now worked for a relatively prosperous Amish farmer, and hoped to buy his own land someday.

Three hours later, they had removed the first layer, and dampened one wall with a vinegar and hot-water mixture before scraping it. The last part had been by far the hardest, but there hadn't been a third layer. Luke studied the blotchy wall, satisfied with the progress. Once it dried, he'd still have to sand it before painting, but it was good that plaster underlay the wallpaper. He liked the look of it better than wallboard.

Of course, there were three more walls to go, not to mention three bedrooms and two bathrooms still wallpapered. There was no great hurry, fortunately; Bishop Amos understood that progress would be slow. In every room, Luke had to remove light switches and electrical outlets, filling the holes with wallboard to which he would add a thin sheet of plaster. The floors should be refinished, too, and the exterior painted.

Then there were the blackberries.

"Let's go home to eat," Elam suggested. "*Mamm* and Miriam will have been cooking all morning. They're holding a quilt frolic this afternoon."

Luke's stomach growled. He had stuffed himself yesterday, staying for two meals. He still hadn't readjusted to the enormous meals his mother put on the table, but eating all his childhood favorites had been a pleasure. That Julia would be there caused him to feel disquiet, but he had to get used to her in his life, however small a part that was.

"*Schnitz und knepp?*" he asked. He'd found good shoofly pie and butter cookies in cafés and bakeries, but never dried-apple dumplings like his *mamm*'s.

Elam laughed. "Come on! You know *Mamm*."

SITTING IN THE busy kitchen, at the table where she'd been consigned after her offer to help with the meal was refused, Julia kept a smile on her mouth even though she felt as if she didn't belong. And perhaps uncomfortable because she wasn't accustomed to this kind of crowd.

Women paused to speak to her, but she could tell what an effort it was for them to speak English. Luke and Eli were so fluent, they'd spoiled her.

She'd immediately noticed all the usual appliances in the kitchen, although presumably these were powered by propane rather than electricity. Earlier, Luke's mother had used a hand-cranked blender that obviously worked fine. None of this should have surprised her after seeing the workshop behind the store; just as the men had made adaptations to allow them to use the same tools *Englischers* did, so had the women in their kitchens.

She smiled stiffly at another strongly accented greeting.

What really felt odd was to look so different than everyone else here. She was dressed wrong, her hair was exposed, and she didn't even recognize the smell of some of the dishes being placed in big crockery bowls on the table.

A young man came in the back door just then and said something to Deborah Bowman, who had to be his mother. He looked like a younger version of Luke.

What she hadn't expected was to see Luke come in the back door with his father.

His gaze went right to her. Of course he'd known about the invitation. Anyway, he would have seen her car when he arrived. Mixed emotions showed on his face: resignation, reluctance, and more she couldn't identify. It stung to know he didn't want her here, but she kept her chin high and her shoulders squared. She'd been invited, and he could stuff it if he wasn't happy. She knew from Miriam that he had his own house, so why was he here?

"Sitz! Sitz!" his mother called, setting the crowd into motion. It was rather like a dance, everyone finding seats even as a few of the women were still putting food on the table.

Miriam pulled out a chair next to Julia, to her relief. They exchanged smiles before she turned her head. To her shock, Luke had taken the seat on her other side. He bent his head in acknowledgment.

She wasn't sure she even did that before she fumbled with her napkin and thanked a woman whose name she couldn't remember for the coffee she was pouring.

Within moments, everyone was seated. When Eli murmured, *"Händt nunna,"* they bowed their heads and she followed suit for the ensuing silent prayer. Not until cutlery clattered did Julia dare raise her head. Eli had lifted his hands to his cutlery. Had he said *Hands down?*

"Do you pray before meals?" Luke asked in that quiet, deep voice.

"Yes, my family always has." She smiled weakly. "At home, we say the words aloud, though."

"We each pray in our own way. Many of us say the Lord's Prayer." He recited it to her, and she drank in the familiar words.

"Thank you," she said, hoping for a smile, but his expression remained reserved, grave.

Miriam chattered as the serving bowls began to circulate, but eventually turned to her other brother. For all that Julia suspected Luke didn't want her here, he quietly identified many of the dishes as he handed them to her.

There were pickled beets, scalloped tomatoes, ham, pork with sauerkraut, hot potato salad, applesauce, and home-baked bread. The variety of choices was astonishing. She didn't want to offend anyone, but she couldn't possibly eat even a sample of every dish that went past.

"Save some room for dessert," he suggested at one point.

Her expression brought a glimmer of humor to his blue eyes.

The moment the meal was over, the men rose together and went out the back door. Luke didn't even say goodbye.

Julia's offer to help clear the table was declined.

"No, no! You're a guest. Just"—that sounded more like *chust*—"relax."

Miriam rescued her, taking her to the living room where the quilt, batting, and backing were already stretched in a quilt rack. Eight chairs surrounded the quilt.

"Oh, my," Julia said, reaching out to touch. The Double Wedding Ring pattern had been beautifully hand-pieced in soft, buttery-yellow and white fabrics. It was simple, graceful, and lovely. Julia's tight grip on her longing slipped. This wasn't a quilt made to cover the bed of a single woman. "Who made this?"

"I helped with it, but *Mamm* and my *aenti* Mary did most of the work. It's for my cousin Ruthie, who is marrying a man from Iowa. We'll miss her, but this will remind her of us."

Suddenly glad to be here after all, Julia guessed that the recipient would never know some stitches had been set in place by a strange *auslander*. But that was all right. Maybe . . . maybe those stitches would let her belong, if only a little bit.

Chapter Four

❖◆❖

JULIA CHECKED MESSAGES as soon as she arrived at work each morning. With today being Tuesday, it was especially important. The *Englisch*—yes, only two weeks into her job with the Bowmans, she already thought of the majority of their customers that way—expected to be able to shop on Sundays, and had trouble understanding why the store might be closed on a weekend day.

Seeing that Eli hadn't yet arrived, Julia had barely nodded at Luke when she passed him in the workshop on her way in. Smoothly sliding the blade of the table saw through a dense dark wood, he hadn't glanced up through his eye protection, although she was sure he'd seen her. Of course he couldn't afford to be distracted when using such a dangerous tool, but he made such a point of being occupied whenever she was near, Julia never knew which times he truly couldn't allow so much as a thin fracture in his concentration and which were excuses to avoid interacting with her.

She wanted to be relieved. She did. The uneasiness she felt around him hadn't relented at all. In retrospect, she recognized that she'd turned down what would have been a good job at a construction firm back in Cleveland not because of the commute or hours, but because the majority of the employees were male, and several of those men were big and muscular.

Luke disturbed her more, but she was determined to overcome her reaction. She had made a new start, and she wouldn't let cowardice derail it.

Yes, it was just as well Luke Bowman kept his distance—but privately she could admit that it also stung. She hadn't done anything to *him*, so why did he dislike her?

A beep in her ear told her she'd tuned out an entire lengthy message while she brooded. She replayed it and made notes. A truck due to pick up a bedroom set had broken down. Julia already knew that Bowman & Son's Handcrafted Furniture often used the company and would understand an occasional delay. The man leaving the message promised to call later today to reschedule.

Beep.

The bell attached to the front door tinkled, and she lifted her head with an automatic smile even as she set the phone back in its cradle. Two couples likely in their thirties entered, tourists at a guess. The door swinging closed behind them, the men strutted in front. One of the two wore Hawaiian-print board shorts, the other cargo shorts. Both had bulging biceps emphasized by too-tight T-shirts. The women trailed behind.

Instinct told her these people wouldn't be buying furniture, although she understood the desire to look and covet.

"May I help you?" Julia asked, rising to her feet. A light startled her. The man in the loud shorts held up a smartphone. He'd set off the flash. Why would he want a photo of her?

"You're not Amish." He scanned what he could see of her over the counter, his mouth curling into a sneer. "It's not Amish furniture if it's people like *you* working here."

The woman behind him tugged at his arm. "Ken—"

He shook her off and advanced on Julia. "Well?"

"The furniture is made by Amish craftsmen, father and son, just as the sign says. I'm the receptionist."

"So where are they?" His head swung.

What was this about? The two women both looked embarrassed, but the other guy smirked as he watched his friend.

"The Amish don't like to be photographed, you know. Please respect their wishes when you do see anyone of their faith."

"Faith!" he scoffed. "Weirdos is what they are." His eye fell on the door labeled Employees Only. "They back there?"

To her horror, he headed toward the door leading to the workshop. Julia dashed to intercept him. "Can't you read? You're not permitted back there! You could be injured—"

He grabbed her by the upper arms and lifted her to the side. Old panic flared, but so did anger. She slid between him and the door, pressing her back against it.

"No! You can't go in here! Now, I'm asking you to leave the store or I'll call the police."

"Just want to see this Amish furniture being made so I know it's not some scam. That a crime?"

Dizzy from the speed of her heartbeat, she still snapped, "Yes. If you try to go in there, you'll be trespassing. You've already assaulted me, but I'll let it go if you leave. *Now.*"

"What the—" Dark color flushed his face. At the ugly look he gave her, she'd have shrunk back if the door hadn't been holding her up.

The door that suddenly opened. She'd have fallen if she hadn't stumbled against the solid wall of a man.

"What is the problem?" Luke. Of course it was Luke.

"This man. He wants—"

He had already lifted his smartphone again. Julia lunged for it, snatching it away.

He cursed and grabbed for it, crushing her hand.

Another big hand closed around the man's wrist, tightening. "You can have the phone once you leave the store," Luke said, voice polite but implacable.

"You ain't Amish neither," the creep snarled. "You talk English just like me. Dressing up to fake out the tourists, that's what you're doing! I just might stop by the police station to report fraud. What d'ya think of *that*?"

Luke's knuckles turned white briefly before he released the other man and deftly removed the phone from her hand. "I think you need to go. Julia." He spoke so close to her ear, she felt the warmth of his breath. "Call 9-1-1."

"Are you sure?" Surprised, she started to turn, but he nudged her toward the reception area. Released from the awful tension, she hustled for the protection of the counter.

She ostentatiously lifted the phone but didn't yet dial.

"I'm asking you to leave," Luke said.

"Yeah, get the cops here! Let's see what *they* have to say, you stealing my phone."

If he meant it . . . She pressed 9.

He shot a look at her.

Half a head taller than either man, Luke stepped forward. Despite a stolid expression, he exuded menace. Mr. Hawaiian Board Shorts backed up.

"Ken," the same woman entreated. The flush on her cheeks was surely from humiliation.

Julia hoped for the woman's sake that she wasn't married to this jerk.

Luke took another long stride.

"Fine! But you'll hear about this!"

Luke stalked him all the way to the front door. One of the women had already opened it. Once both couples were out on the sidewalk, Luke handed over the phone. The creep yanked it away so aggressively, he stumbled back.

"We ask that you do not take photographs of us, particularly our faces."

Julia had a feeling he was talking to the women, but by this time the group was hurrying away.

Bell tinkling, the door swung shut. To her shock, Luke locked it and turned the sign beside it to Closed. Then he came directly to her, gaze steady on her.

Stopping just on the other side of the counter, he said gently, "You can hang up."

"Hang up—?" She looked down to find herself still clutching the receiver. "Oh!" She almost dropped it, but it fell into the cradle with a clunk.

"You didn't call the police."

"No. I . . . knew that's not what you'd want. I would have if he hit you."

Luke smiled. "He was a coward, the kind who bullies women."

Feeling an odd thump in her chest, Julia stared. That smile had changed his hard face, warmed the usually chilly blue of his eyes.

The smile slowly faded. "Are you all right?"

She gave her head a small shake. "Yes. Well, my hand is a little sore, but I'm sure it's fine."

"You could have called for me."

She squared her shoulders. "I thought I could handle him. They weren't interested in furniture. All they wanted was to take photographs of Amish."

His mouth twisted. "Even after the years I spent out in the world, I don't understand that. Why would you want pictures of strangers only because they are dressed differently from you?"

"People are curious."

He made a disgusted sound.

"Also . . . I think he didn't like being told no. He already knew the Amish ask not to be photographed. That's why he did it quickly, before I could cover my face."

"He took a picture of *you*?"

Luke didn't like that, she could tell. Or else he was surprised because she was so plain and uninteresting. She couldn't regret that, she reminded herself; she had worked hard to fade into the background.

"He didn't wait to see what I looked like. He was mad when I stood up and he saw from my clothes that I was *Englisch*."

"He scared you." Those eyes, cooler now, were too perceptive.

"Mostly, he made me mad."

His mouth curved, not quite a smile but close. "I could tell. You weren't going to let him through that door, were you?"

"I didn't want him to surprise you." Her voice shook, just a little. Adrenaline, she told herself. "You might have hurt yourself if you were using a saw."

For a moment, he only looked at her. Shy, she let her own gaze lower to her hands.

"Thank you," Luke said. *"Denke."*

"Gern schehne."

He openly grinned. "You are learning our language."

Julia wrinkled her nose. "I'm trying. It's not easy. I had a year of German in college, but you don't pronounce letters the way I remember."

"No, *Deitsh* started as a German dialect with its own idiosyncrasies, but has changed through the years. You notice how many English words find their way in."

"Ja. Like pizza." She bit her lip. Would he retreat from a question? He certainly didn't invite them. "You don't speak English as if it's a second language for you."

And . . . bang. He might as well have lowered a steel helmet over his head, so impassive had his face become.

"I've been away enough years to be fluent." He stepped back from the counter. "I have work waiting."

The phone was ringing and she hadn't even noticed. "I do, too." She reached for the phone, but it fell silent before she could lift it. He'd turned to walk away, so she spoke to his back. "Thank you."

Luke stopped where he was, finally turning slowly. "No, Julia. I thank you." A tip of his head, and within a few strides, he disappeared into the workshop.

Employees Only. She wished she felt more like a real employee, one who wouldn't need to mumble an explanation for her intrusion every time she stepped through that doorway.

FOR ALL THE work waiting for him, Luke was doing nothing when his father came in the back door.

"Are you thinking deep thoughts?" *Daad* asked with humor.

Heat crept over Luke's cheeks. He couldn't remember the last time he had felt self-conscious enough to flush. It didn't help that he required too long to reset his brain to *Deitsh* from the English he used with Julia.

"*Ja*, certain sure." He shrugged, looking down to see a marker in one hand, a measuring tape in the other. He lifted it. "I'm measuring." As if that wasn't obvious.

"Except you haven't started." Crinkles had formed beside his father's eyes.

Luke gusted a sigh. He'd never been good at lying to his father. "I need to go choose some wood for the inlay on that desk."

Daad nodded.

"But something happened a few minutes ago, and I wanted to be sure I was near enough to hear voices in front." He nodded toward the sturdy door separating them from the display area.

Any hint of amusement left his father's face.

Luke told him as much as he knew about what had occurred.

Daad listened in frowning silence. "Lucky we are to have so little trouble from the *moderns*."

"Ours is not the kind of business that attracts troublemakers," Luke said.

Pursuing his own thoughts, *Daad* said, "Sometimes our picture is taken." He shrugged. "It's disrespectful, but preventing that happening isn't worth getting hurt." He paused. "Or hurting anyone else."

"The only one hurt was Julia." Luke's jaw tightened. "She said she was fine, but I saw red marks on her arms." He gestured at his own to indicate where those incipient bruises in the shape of fingerprints had been.

"You don't like having her here," his father said unexpectedly.

Shame might not show in heightened color this time, but Luke felt it. "I was wrong. She tries hard to do a good job. She frees us up to make furniture. I no longer have to waste time talking to foolish people."

Eli's gravity relaxed into a smile. "Glad I am to hear you say that. I think this job is good for her, too."

"Ja," Luke agreed, if reluctantly. Why couldn't they have hired an Amish *maidal* who needed work that would help her gain confidence?

Because that *maidal* wouldn't have been computer literate, or so fluent in English.

"Was she frightened?"

"I'm sure she was." Luke hesitated. "More angry, she said."

His father nodded, as if Luke had confirmed a suspicion of his. "She wanted to take care of us."

But she wasn't Amish. Aloud, he said, "Perhaps she is more like her brother than she knows."

His father's eyebrows rose. "Did she strike that man?"

"No. She stood against the door so he couldn't open it and take a picture."

"As one of us might have done."

It was true. The police chief would have threatened, perhaps even gotten physical. Julia had been trying to protect him, Luke, for all that she was outmuscled by a mean excuse for a human being.

Whom Luke needed to forgive. The flip side of his too-ready temper, his ability to forgive was stunted. Perhaps forgiveness depended on his understanding that *aesel* more than forgiving him. *Ja*, "jackass" was a good word for that fellow, but it was also true that nobody who had been raised with kindness, patience, and a good example would turn out like that. He might have been hit or belittled as a child and now felt a need to puff himself up like one of those creatures in nature frightening off a predator.

But Luke saw in his mind's eye what would surely be black marks on Julia's creamy skin by tomorrow, and any sympathy he had tried to make himself feel for the man who'd dug his fingers into her flesh dissipated.

He became aware of his father's stare. Bishop Amos at his most unnerving had nothing on *Daad*, who relented enough to say, "I'll go speak to her."

Luke murmured something, he didn't know what, dropped the marker, and started toward the lumber room. Once he was caught up in his work, he'd quit thinking about the *Englisch* woman. For all the fine motives *Daad* wanted to ascribe to her, Julia Durant wasn't Amish.

HEARING A CLATTER in the kitchen, Julia winced. Why was Nick home so early, today of all days? She'd intended to dash upstairs and change to a shirt with longer sleeves so her brother wouldn't see the bruises. In his need to keep her safe, he was likely to blow up an unpleasant episode into the crime of the century.

She paused to marvel that she could think of what happened that way. Why wasn't she shaken to her core? Afraid to go back to the store for fear that man would return? Was she truly healing?

The water in the kitchen came on, drawing her back to her present problem. Maybe she could slip by . . .

The minute she opened the back door, her brother turned to face her. Of course, his gaze went straight to the bruises.

Eyes narrowed, he began, "What the—"

"It's nothing," she said hastily. "I tripped and—"

He cut her off. "Was it that big brute of a carpenter?"

"If you're talking about Luke, he's Amish. He would never hurt me." If only she could convince her subconscious so that she quit shrinking in his presence. "And he's a fine craftsman, not a carpenter."

"You're trying to distract me. It won't work. Who did that to you?"

She sighed. "A man came into the store determined to take pictures of Amishmen and -women. He was mad because I'm not one, and went straight for the employees-only door. I told him that would be trespassing, but he didn't care. I stepped between him and the door, because I was afraid if he went in using the flash on his phone, Eli or Luke might be startled enough to hurt themselves with a saw or other tool."

Nick was steaming. "He assaulted you?"

"He moved me to one side."

Her brother muttered some profanities. "Then what?"

"Luke must have heard us, because he came out and insisted the man and his friends leave."

Sounding disbelieving, Nick said, "He let them take pictures."

"No." She explained how she'd taken the phone, and that Luke promised to return it as soon as those people left the store. "I was a little nervous that they'd come back, but they didn't."

"Why didn't you call me?"

"You know that's not the Bowmans' way. Anyway, the guy was a jerk, but he didn't break the law."

"If he laid his hands on you without your permission, he did."

"Nick, I can get bruises in a crowd watching the Fourth of July fireworks. These"—she touched one lightly—"will fade in no time."

It took a minute, but he finally gusted out a sigh. "I guess I have to accept your judgment."

Julia burst into laughter. "That was almost as hard as admitting I'm right and you're wrong, wasn't it?"

Had she been anyone but Nick's sister, she'd have found his grin as devastatingly appealing as Luke Bowman's. Tipping her head to one side, she asked, "Why aren't you married?"

Though the smile still lingered on his face, his brown eyes became as devoid of expression as Luke's entire face had when she asked a question that was too personal.

"Too many fish in the sea," Nick said lightly.

Unconvinced, she could only scrunch up her nose and say, "Dinner won't take me long."

He put an arm around her shoulders. "Why don't we go out for once?"

"That sounds good," she admitted, then hesitated. "We can drive by a couple of places for rent that I'm considering. I'd like your opinion."

"I think you can guess—"

Julia laughed again. "Since you've already made up your mind, we don't have to bother."

Her brother mock glowered.

She rose on tiptoe to kiss his cheek. "I'm hoping you'll help me look for a used car, too. I asked Mom to sell my Volkswagen."

"Good riddance," he muttered. "It's been ready to be put out to pasture for years."

She just laughed at him. "At least I'm not going back to Cleveland."

He offered a twisted smile. "You win. I'll look."

She had won in many ways today. Proud that she had scraped up enough of her tiny sum of courage to stand up to an aggressive man, Julia felt light as air. The Amish would say God had been with her. She'd never felt as though she had such a personal relationship with the Lord, but . . . was it possible?

Luke and Nick both had secrets, or at least tender places; she'd seen the walls they used to protect themselves. She understood, because her own walls were higher yet, thicker. Necessary, she had always believed.

Had she lowered them enough today to hear a voice long shut out?

Chapter Five

⤖ ◆ ⤖

THE MOVING TRUCK was two days late. She'd planned to move in on Monday since that wasn't a working day, but no. Now it was Wednesday, and already the eighth of July. Julia would have feared losing all her volunteers with the delays, except she really didn't need that much help. Of course it didn't work that way. No one, and especially the Amish, quite believed the moving company workers would bring furniture and boxes into her second-story apartment and put them down wherever she told them to.

Standing on the sidewalk outside the building, clutching her phone, she watched two buggies proceed down the street toward her, their steel tires a drone on the pavement that had become a familiar sound to her. The first buggy drew to a stop at the curb so close to her, she could stroke a hand down the horse's sleek brown neck. Polly's lips quivered and she leaned into the caress, making Julia smile.

Offering a chorus of cheerful greetings, a good part of the Bowman family spilled out of this buggy and the second one, which belonged to Luke and was pulled by his black gelding. The fact that both men were here meant they'd closed the store to help her, which was astonishing.

Eli's wife, Deborah, was joined by Miriam, of course, and another young woman who looked enough like Miriam that she had to be a cousin. Carrying a stepladder, Elam appeared less enthused but obedient. Two other women were introduced as Deborah's sister Barbara and a young cousin on Eli's side of the family named Jane.

"It's so nice to meet you," Julia said helplessly. "Thank you. I don't think there'll be that much to do, but—"

"Ach, windows are never clean," exclaimed Barbara. "And the cupboards, you'll need shelf paper." She brandished a roll from the hefty bag she carried.

"Oh, but—"

The women told her of the many things that would have to be done for this apartment to be livable, as Eli grinned and even Luke smiled.

"It's brand new!" she pointed out.

Deborah only shook her head. "Workers won't have cleaned up the way they should have. They never do."

Luke cleared his throat.

She sniffed. "Amish workmen might, but *Englischers*? No."

"Oh! Here comes the moving truck."

Indeed, it lumbered around the corner, aiming for the very spot occupied by the two buggies.

"Are there hitching posts in back?" Eli asked, seeming unconcerned by the approaching behemoth with wheezing air brakes. "Or a shed for the horses?"

She should have thought to look. "I . . . don't know."

"Ach, we'll find someplace." He lifted the reins and clucked to Polly, who started forward.

Luke's gelding laid his ears back, bunched his muscles, and shifted those huge hooves until the harness creaked and the wheels of the buggy rolled a few inches forward and then back. Luke murmured to him in *Deitsh* and persuaded him, too, to start forward without kicking the buggy to pieces.

Watching, his aunt Barbara said, "Not so trustworthy, that one. It's like Luke to take him on."

Julia couldn't decide if that was said disapprovingly or not.

"You know Charlie was on a racetrack not so long ago," Miriam reminded her. "He'll settle down." She flashed a grin. "Luke has, ain't so?"

Nobody else commented. In fact, there was an odd moment of silence until the enormous truck stopped right in front of them. The uniformed driver hopped out, scanned the crowd of Amish on the sidewalk with incredulity or even alarm, and then focused on her. "Julia Durant?"

She stepped forward. "That's me."

Obviously relieved, he gave her a brisk smile. This was undoubtedly only one stop among many for him today. "Tell us where to take everything, and we'll start unloading." In fact, his partner was already heaving up the heavy metal door at the back of the truck.

"Second story. Number 204." She pointed up at the converted old school behind them.

"Elevator?"

"Yes. I don't think it's big enough for the sofa, though."

"Hardly ever is. At least you don't have a piano."

If she had, she'd have rented a ground-floor apartment, or even that small house on Sycamore Street, like it or not. She felt safer knowing no one could break a window and climb in, so she'd allowed her fears to make her decision for her. As she always did.

Not always, she reminded herself, thinking again of the scene at Bowman & Son's Handcrafted Furniture. Every time she did, she felt a tinge of hope.

She unlocked the lobby door and braced it open, then went upstairs to unlock the apartment door. The women all trooped after her.

She'd fallen in love with the apartment at first sight. It had gleaming, wide-plank wood floors that had to have been original to the school, high ceilings, and white-painted woodwork to set off the cream color of the walls. Whoever had chosen the kitchen cabinets had done so wisely; they were designed to be simple, with rectangular inset panels, and also painted white.

"Ach!" Deborah exclaimed, looking around. "This is very nice. Except for the electrics, it could be one of our houses."

Julia hadn't thought of it that way, but Luke's mother was right. With no wallpaper, no fancy flourishes on the mantel or woodwork, the apartment would be comfortable for any of them. Except, of course, for the refrigerator, microwave, and dishwasher, all hooked up to the electric grid. The stove was gas. And she intended to hang artwork on the walls, something they never did. Or display family pictures on the mantel, as she would.

Twittering like birds, the women stayed in a clump as they inspected the two bedrooms, walk-in closets, large bathroom, and linen closet. There was even a pantry closet here in the kitchen.

Within minutes, Deborah had them organized, scrubbing shelves and countertops whether they needed it or not, measuring for shelf paper—white, of course, no flowers or fancy designs for them—and directing the men from the moving company as well as Luke and his father, who brought up boxes with the help of a wheeled dolly.

"Bathroom." Barbara would point. "Linen closet—set that here so it doesn't block the hall."

Luke rolled his eyes when his *aenti* wouldn't see him, but set down the box where ordered.

All that was left to Julia was to decide where she wanted her sofa and upholstered rocking chair, which lamps went where, what wall would be best for her bookcases.

Luke paused beside her. "I didn't see a TV."

"The one I had was practically an antique, so I threw it out. I suppose I'll buy a flat-screen one to hang on the wall."

She'd sounded unsure, presumably the reason for the odd look he gave her. Truthfully, she hardly ever bothered turning the thing on. She read a daily newspaper, and intended to subscribe to either the *Kansas City Star* or the *St. Louis Post-Dispatch* now that she had an address.

She directed the bed to be set up in the larger of the two bedrooms. The quilt frame would go in the smaller bedroom, rather than the middle of her living room as it had been in her last apartment in Cleveland.

Knowing the women had brought food, Julia popped into the kitchen. Not sure if they'd want to use her electrical appliances, she asked permission to warm fried chicken in her microwave.

"Knock knock," a deep voice said. She peeked into the living room. The door having been left open, her brother walked in, official in his uniform, star pinned on his chest, big black gun at his hip.

She beamed. "Isn't it beautiful?"

After a glance around, he grinned ruefully. "It's better than my house. Sorry to be late, but you don't seem to be hurting for help."

Deborah and Miriam stole wide-eyed looks at him from the kitchen. He nodded and smiled at them.

Julia had begun introducing everyone he hadn't already met—specifically, the women and Elam—when the moving company man thrust a clipboard at her.

"Looks like we have everything. I need a signature, and we'll be on our way."

Flustered, she said, "Wait. Let me take a quick look around."

The dresser and bedside stand had gone by without her noticing, and yes, her small dining set was in place right where sunlight poured in tall windows.

"Unless a box is missing—"

"We're careful, ma'am," he assured her. "Here's the phone number if you have any problems. We'll be back through the Kansas City area in about a week."

"Oh. Okay." She signed and handed him the clipboard. Was she supposed to tip him? He didn't act as if he expected any such thing. In fact, he departed with such dispatch, Eli had to step hastily out of his way.

The wonderful aroma of fried chicken came to her.

"The Bowman women brought food." Lots of food, including German potato salad, cornbread, and several different desserts.

Standing beside her, Nick said, "Apparently. I was going to take off since you obviously don't need me, but now I think I'll hang around."

Julia ventured into the kitchen to find Deborah and Jane had begun warming what was bound to be a generous meal in the microwave and oven. The food didn't surprise her as much as their practical willingness to use electrical appliances when there wasn't an alternative.

Seeing her expression, Miriam said, "How can we have a work frolic without food?" She opened a cupboard to show unpacked dishes. "I can move them if you'd rather, or you can later. I thought this was closest to the sink and dishwasher."

"That's perfect." Julia looked around, dazed. Laughter came from one of the bedrooms. Elam and Luke were inserting the metal pins in the sides of her bookcases so that they could install the shelves. In another half hour, her possessions would all be put away, the boxes flattened, and she'd be moved in. "This is . . . is *wunderbaar*."

LUKE HADN'T ARGUED with his *mamm*'s suggestion that they must help Julia move into her new apartment. He even agreed that this was the right thing for them to do. She was too new to town to have made *Englisch* friends, and her

brother could be called away by his job even if he offered
to help. As had happened.

Luke had guessed, as his womenfolk hadn't, that Julia
could have done without a horde of assistants. Once he set
eyes on the fresh paint, gleaming wood floors, and shiny
new appliances and fixtures of this apartment, he had been
sure she could have managed alone, if not so quickly. But no
Amishman or -woman would ever make a move like this
alone, and even *moderns* had what they called "housewarm-
ing" parties, which might be more about bringing food, like
the women of Luke's family had, and gifts the new home-
owner might need than about offering manual labor.

He'd enjoyed seeing *Mamm*, *Aenti* Barbara and the others sweep authority from Julia's hands while still asking her
preferences. He could also concede that the apartment
smelled better now than it had. That "new house" smell was
all very well, but now he caught scents of lavender so real,
he almost turned his head in search of a clump of the deep
purple flowers. Lemon, too, *ja*, it made the best cleaning
products, if his mother was to be believed. And, of course,
there was the food. Nobody was a better cook than Deborah
Bowman, although since coming home he'd learned Rose
had a fine touch with pies, and Miriam might make the best
cookies he'd ever had, especially her snickerdoodles.

Thanks to the moving men, he and his *daad* didn't have
much to do. Elam was summoned and used shamelessly by
the women to put boxes on upper shelves in closets and the
like. He cast an occasional beseeching look at his father
and brother. Luke grinned each time like a Cheshire cat, a
reference nobody here but Julia would understand.

That disturbed him, when he thought about it. He'd
come back to his faith, his family, but a much larger part of
him than his family understood was still worldly. Along
with getting a college education, he'd read voraciously. He
would make his choices of reading material more cautiously

now, but didn't intend to give up something he enjoyed so much.

Here he was thinking that, while standing out of the way beside one of the four tall bookcases he had helped put together. After eating, he would help empty the cartons of books stacked close by onto the shelves. It would be interesting to see what Julia liked to read. They were unlikely to have tastes in common, but he didn't know her well enough yet to guess what she did read.

Except even today she wore chinos and a loose brown T-shirt. Dull. The Amishwomen wore brighter colors than he'd yet seen Julia in. Their dresses and aprons were more formfitting, too. He couldn't help noticing how hard she tried to deflect attention from men. The reason for that— no, this was a bad time to speculate on that.

He wanted to shake his head. What was he thinking? An *Englisch* woman, employee or not, was none of his business.

Wouldn't you know, she emerged from the kitchen just then, laughing at something Miriam called after her. Luke froze. That laughter lit her fine-boned face to true beauty, and she needed none of the paints *modern* women used. *Happiness*, he thought; that was what she needed, and must be seeking with this move to Tompkin's Mill.

Seeing her happy stirred feelings too dangerous for him to acknowledge. Yet at that moment her eyes sought his, and for seconds—minutes—their gazes remained locked. Luke couldn't have looked away if Bishop Amos Troyer had laid a firm hand on him. Luke knew for the first time what a fish felt like, the hook embedded deep.

Color warmed her pale skin. Her lips parted, softened. Gold shimmered in her warm brown eyes. His chest ached. He couldn't remember last breathing.

A deep voice sounded in his ear. *Daad*, he realized, so stunned he hadn't parsed the words. But Julia blinked hard several times, as if also hearing his father, or perhaps his mother in the kitchen, and spun away. Luke's brain played back what his father said. Another saying most of his people wouldn't understand.

"Your *mamm* is calling us. Time to eat!"

"Ja, gut," Luke got out, hoping his voice wasn't as guttural to his father's ears as it was to his own. Praying no one else had seen the way he and Julia had looked at each other.

But when he turned his head, he saw that his prayer had not been answered. For all the jovial words, *Daad* watched Julia hurry down the hall, before transferring the same worried gaze on his son. Oh, *ja. Daad* had seen.

All Luke could do was strive to act natural, to keep as many of his relatives between him and Julia as possible, to not so much as look her way. He was afraid his hope that *Daad* wouldn't talk to him about this was futile. Lying to his father would be a sin. Yet what if *Daad* decided they shouldn't keep Julia working for them? That might be best for Luke, but he feared what the rejection would do to a woman who anyone could see had suffered, who had begun to blossom.

No, he couldn't let his father do such a thing. The problem was his, and she should not suffer for it. He had to put her out of his mind. It would be best if he started to court a faithful Amishwoman . . . if only he could find one who stirred a fraction of the interest in him that this *Englischer* did.

No, he was overreacting, he told himself. Although the bishop had been convinced that his commitment was sincere, had baptized him, Luke had known all along that he couldn't slam the door shut on the past ten years and never give any of it a thought. There had to be an adjustment, the gradual letting go of that other way of life, forgetting emotions and actions wrong for an Amishman. These inappropriate feelings were part of that, surely. It wasn't as if he'd been drawn to an Amishwoman but distracted by Julia. The part of him that responded to women simply hadn't made that adjustment yet. A year ago, he would have wanted Julia

Durant, not a kind, domestic girl with only an eighth-grade education and no interest in the wider world, though she would be the right wife for him, for the life he'd chosen.

Satisfied by his rationalization, he carried dishes and duffels filled with what cleaning supplies were left to the buggies while his father and Elam put Julia's books on the shelves. Luke took his time, not hurrying back up to the apartment.

When they left shortly thereafter, he only nodded at Julia's thanks without quite meeting her eyes.

JULIA TRIED TO cling to the precious sense of belonging the Bowman family had given her when they chose to treat her as their own even though she discovered barely an hour into the following morning that she had also lost something that day. The friendship, or at least helpfulness, that Luke had begun to extend to her was no more. If he had to focus on her, his eyes were cool, his responses to her questions as brief as he could make them.

By closing on Thursday, she had resolved to go to Eli whenever possible with those questions raised by customers. On Friday, after he explained what a catalyzed conversion varnish was and why he and Luke preferred to use it to finish most of their furniture pieces—durability and resistance to water damage—she asked a bit timidly if she had offended Luke during the moving party.

Eli surprised her by going silent for a moment, his gaze on the traffic outside the front windows of the store. "No offense," he said at last, slowly, "but he is a single man and you are unmarried, too. It's best for both of you if you avoid being alone or too friendly."

She wanted to argue, to say, *What you're afraid might happen never will*, but given the lump in her throat, she could only nod.

"You understand?" he asked kindly.

She lifted her chin, schooled her face to show nothing but polite surprise. "Of course I do. If I was too friendly, I apologize."

Creases formed between his eyebrows, but he said, "It's not that. Just . . . Luke being careful. As he must be, still new to the faith."

How she smiled, she didn't know, any more than she understood why Luke's attitude and his father's approval of it stung. More than stung. It *hurt*, even though she hadn't wanted a closer relationship with Luke. Especially not physically closer. That wasn't possible for her, would never be possible. Maybe it was only that he'd made her feel safe in a way that gave her courage, too. But she couldn't explain that to his father, could never admit to the terrifying thing that had happened to her, or the shame that still lived in her.

"I won't pester him," she said, still holding on to that smile. "I promise."

The front door opened and a middle-aged couple entered, the woman already exclaiming about the beautiful furniture and reaching out to run a finger over the satin finish.

Julia wondered if Eli was as grateful as she was for the interruption.

Chapter Six

❖◆❖

LIKE A BOY, Luke resisted the need to fidget with a painful effort. Then, he'd been ever conscious of his father's stern gaze. His father wasn't here today, and he wasn't ten years old and too restless to sit still for three hours straight, but it seemed that boy was still in residence. Consisting of hard benches with no backs, the seating for worship wasn't designed for comfort, but that didn't normally bother him. Unfortunately, the minister currently speaking had a delivery that was dry as a cornfield in a drought, interrupted by long pauses.

Not his fault, Luke reminded himself; the bishop, ministers, and deacon for each church district were chosen by lot, not by a popular vote because of their charismatic speaking or wisdom. The most ordinary of men might be chosen, and would accept God's will. That man was offered no formal training and spoke not from notes but from the heart. Yet, most often, he would grow into the position, earning the trust of his district. This fellow was young; he had time.

Luke had no business comparing him to Bishop Amos and the minister in Luke's own church district, who were both powerful speakers. They had a way of choosing a topic that struck him like an arrow, helping him understand his weaknesses as well as his strengths.

Today, however, he'd decided to attend worship at a neighboring district, hardly more than a fifteen-minute buggy ride farther than the Ropp home, where his own family would be listening to a sermon right this minute.

It had to be coincidence that this boring young minister had chosen, of all things, to talk about 2 Corinthians 6:14: *Do not be unequally yoked together with unbelievers. For what fellowship has righteousness with lawlessness? And what communion has light with darkness?*

If Luke's own bishop had chosen the same scripture, he would have suspected his father of putting a bug in Bishop Troyer's ear. But here, where he'd never attended worship . . . no, it must be chance. Unless, of course, God had whispered in the minister's ear. If so, Luke ought to pay the closest of attention. He needed this reminder.

Julia was not an unbeliever, nor was she wicked, but she was not Amish. She was forbidden to him.

Letting his thoughts stray to her as often as he did was wrong.

Despite his resolve to open himself to God, his mind kept wandering. Today, he felt as if he didn't belong. If he'd sat among the unmarried men, he would likely have been the oldest by ten years. These men his own age, some of whom had been boyhood playmates, had beards that reached their chests, wives, and as many as five or six children already. They had followed the path of good Amish boys instead of taking a lengthy detour. Now, he was a fish out of water.

No—he'd come home to take his proper place. He had no doubt at all about that decision. He would never let himself stray from his choice, once made. A wife was what he needed next. It was past time he married. That was the very reason he was attending worship in a neighboring church district rather than his own.

He'd seen a few pretty *maidals* earlier, met saucy gazes and shyly downcast eyes. His presence had caused a noticeable stir among the young women.

The next time the sermon became only a mumble, background noise, Luke reminded himself that *pretty* was not so important. He should study the unmarried women who might be plain but have other fine qualities, or be plump and a fine cook. He didn't laugh often enough; a wife with a sense of humor would suit him fine.

Or a wife who loved to read, who wanted most to care for her husband and children, who would place her duty as an Amish wife and mother before all else, but who also liked to stretch her mind, take flights of imagination, understand people who didn't think like the Amish.

No, no, that was dangerous territory for many reasons.

Annoyed with himself, he considered other qualities in a woman that would draw him. Her cooking, for sure; his mother had spoiled him growing up. A loving heart. Patience with his sometimes dark moods. An understanding that he had knowledge and experiences beyond that of the other men she knew. A pleasant voice. Beautiful eyes even if her face was plain. Complexities that would keep him from becoming bored.

Movement all around shook him from his brooding. He sent a silent apology to God for his inattention and wondered if it would be heard, but took comfort in knowing that Christ accepted the fallibility of His followers. Luke had dedicated himself to striving to be better, devoted, accepting in his turn the failings of their neighbors and friends. A perfect man would have no need to strive.

Anyway, in thinking about taking a wife from among the faithful, wasn't he heeding the message God had sent to him today? Or was he excusing himself?

"Luke Bowman!" A man clapped a hand to Luke's back. "It's good to see you."

Luke said with pleasure, "Jake Kemp. So long it's been."

His old friend chuckled. "I meant to stop at the store to say welcome, but, ach, you know what spring and summer are like on a farm!"

"It's a busy time for us, too. In winter, there aren't so many tourists looking at our furniture."

"*Ja*, I can see that might be."

The two joined the other men in carrying the backless benches out to the lawn and converting them into tables for the fellowship meal. Later, they would be stacked on the bench wagon, which would then be moved to the home where the next service would be held.

Looking around, Luke saw that women had already begun to carry out dishes and pitchers of lemonade. As much as the worship, he had come to think, the time spent together afterward cemented the bonds that made this community. Friendship, fun, the pleasure of sampling food from different households, the games that would be played, the gossip, those were all a big part of what, out in the world, he had missed. Here, the gatherings weren't an excuse to overindulge in spirits. The Amish were wise to keep each church district small enough to allow them to gather in each other's homes and barns like this, while maintaining ties to the groups that broke away to form new districts.

Yet, disturbingly, Luke continued to feel a distance even as he exchanged stories with boyhood friends, watched them with their children, met their wives, and was introduced to the unmarried women, one after another.

"I worked one summer with your father," he told one, feeling as old as Methuselah. "Mark was a slave driver, I remember that. More than your *grossdaadi*, who hired me." Like most boys, he'd had a period of doubting whether he wanted to do the same work as his father. Harvesting corn late that summer had cured him of any desire to devote his life to the land.

Becky Brenneman wrinkled her nose. "*Daadi* is still so stern. I don't think he was ever young."

"Never wild, I think."

"He said you were."

"*Ja*, I can't deny that." He could only be grateful God and his family had forgiven him for his transgressions, that he had a chance to begin again. Becky Brenneman might have appealed to him long ago, before he'd broken from his people. Even now, maybe, if he had been newly hatched as an eighteen- or twenty-year-old.

But he hadn't been, and to his eyes she and the others he was meeting were girls. Too young to marry, he thought, even knowing that was an *auslander* belief he wouldn't express among his people.

The men ate in the first shift, as always. There wasn't seating for everyone to sit down together.

He was served by a slender, calm woman named Hannah Beiler. She laid a gentle hand on his shoulder twice as she bent to refill his glass or set down a plate holding a generous slice of rhubarb crunch in front of him. He didn't see her touch any of the other men.

When Hannah was out of earshot, a cousin sitting nearby told Luke that she had moved home after being widowed. She belonged to the host family. Lowering his voice, Luke said, "Lost her husband, she did. Two years ago?"

He looked around, nodding when several voices said, "More like three."

"*Ja*, that's more like it. Sad day it was. Their boy, Timothy, five years old, knew better than to go in the pasture, but you know what boys are like. He didn't see the bull and thought he must be in the barn. Perry saw what was happening and got the boy out, but not himself. Thrown up in the air and impaled by the horns. The boy's screaming brought Hannah out to see Perry die."

There was a collective moment of silence. That would have been bad. After the others resumed eating and talking, Luke found himself watching her more closely. He expected to see shadows, but her air of serenity never cracked.

Not so much as a shadow in her eyes made him think her calm might not be more than skin-deep. But that was their way, he had to remind himself; she would accept that God had called her husband home for a purpose she wasn't expected to understand.

When the men had finished eating, another childhood friend, Lloyd Wagler, called to him to meet his sister.

"A widow," he murmured out of her hearing. "Even though my brother Matthew has taken over keeping her dairy farm going, we worry about her. Our hope once she remarries is that he and his wife can buy the farm from her."

Emma Fisher was sturdy, with a bright smile for Luke. "Your family must be rejoicing to have you home."

"I think they are," Luke agreed, a truth that was tempered by the more complicated emotions felt by individual members of his family, from Elam's initial resentment of the prodigal son to his mother's bouts of tears and the loss of the trust Miriam had once felt for him.

This Emma seemed a sensible woman, as she had to be with three children ranging from a two-year-old up to a girl who might be eight. The two-year-old sat on her lap, and her attention kept darting to the two others to be sure they hadn't gotten into trouble in the scant minutes since she'd last checked on them.

Luke grappled with the idea of taking on three children that he would need to raise as his own. For some reason, he hadn't considered that possibility, although most widows would come with children. His first reaction of near horror shamed him. If he loved a woman, surely he could love her children, too.

Was that God's will?

If so, Luke thought later as he located his buggy among a line of them, all black, he might need a nudge from Him, because none of the unmarried women he had met today called to him.

He wouldn't want to admit to anyone he felt relief rather than disappointment.

HAVING SURVIVED ANOTHER week of work, aware always that Luke pretended she wasn't there, Julia appreciated having this Monday entirely to herself.

She gathered stitches on her tiny needle and pulled the thread through the layers of fabric and batting basted together and secured in her quilt frame. Her current project was based on a nineteenth-century pattern called Checkers and Rails, starkly geometrical using plain navy blue fabric against white. It allowed her substantial white spaces for the hand quilting she loved to do.

She'd experimented along the way with appliqué and even what were called art quilts, but her true love was the traditional patterns. The idea that a woman a hundred and fifty years ago might have pieced and stitched a quilt very like this one to keep her children warm, or for a wedding gift, gave Julia a sense of continuity, of comfort. She liked knowing, too, that her new Amish friends would approve of her choice of plain fabrics. Like any other skilled quilters, they admired work of all kinds, but never used printed fabrics themselves any more than the women would wear dresses or aprons printed with tiny flowers or a paisley design. Fancy, they called those fabrics. It was only an extension of their refusal to wear jewelry or hang artwork in their homes that had no purpose but to look pretty.

Julia thought she might have been influenced in her fabric selections for this quilt by the stunning Amish-made quilts offered for sale at A Stitch in Time here in town. And why not? She'd increasingly come to admire the *Leit*, as they called themselves. The people. Not that she'd say so to Nick, who still wasn't happy that she was working for Amish employers. His tolerance only went so far; it was clear he feared that, like a cult, they might brainwash her and steal her away.

"You do know the Amish don't proselytize," she'd pointed out just yesterday, when she'd made a big Sunday dinner at Nick's house after they attended church together. "From what I've read, they never try to convert an outsider."

He'd grunted. "They wouldn't turn someone away."

Julia laughed at him. "Trust me."

"I do," he muttered, but she'd be willing to bet he had his fingers crossed under the table. If he'd thought he could get away with it, he'd probably install a spy camera in her apartment.

Hmm. She'd lost sight of him several times on moving-in day, although his primary interest had been in stuffing his face. It seemed he did approve of Amish cooking, which had delighted the Bowman women.

Now, she paused with more stitches gathered on her needle. So what if Nick was spying on her? He'd get bored in no time. She loved her new apartment, but since that first day, no one but her had stepped foot in it. She'd hoped to make friends at church, but while the women were cordial, they also seemed wary. She was a northerner, and from a big city besides. Julia couldn't decide if they were afraid she'd look down on them, or whether they imagined she'd contaminate them with the sinful ways she had to have absorbed.

In fact, the Amish she'd met were far more accepting of her than her fellow *Englischers*.

The pang under her breastbone reminded her that Amish acceptance only went so far. An unmarried man couldn't be sullied by too much contact with her. She had a suspicion her friendship with Miriam would go only so far, too. Neither her family nor her bishop would approve of Miriam coming over here very often to hang out with Julia.

After a minute, she resumed quilting. It was too hot to go out right now, and what would she do anyway? A few cafés would be open in town, but the library was closed on

Sundays and Mondays. There was no multiplex, not that she had ever been a big moviegoer. No shopping mall, as if she had the slightest interest in buying clothes. The young woman she'd once been had loved bright colors even though she'd always been too shy to choose extremes of fashion. Now, well . . . Even her sleep tees and shorts were drab colored. If something happened, she wouldn't want people to think—

Mad at herself, she cut off the thought. On a conscious level, she knew better than to blame herself in any way for the horrific attack, yet deep inside, that voice still whispered, *If you hadn't worn such a short skirt, or smiled at guys you didn't know.* Most of all, if she hadn't left her apartment door unlocked. That was practically an invitation, or so the investigating police officers had seemed to imply.

She'd never told Nick how shamed she'd been by the questions they'd asked. Attitudes had to be changing in law enforcement, but not fast enough.

And why was she thinking about this anyway? It was long past, and she was supposed to be enjoying her day off. Her own company. She couldn't possibly be lonely. Deep friendships required a trust and willingness to be vulnerable that was impossible for her.

Be satisfied with the changes you've made in your life, she told herself, with having a job she liked, closeness with the brother she had missed, and a new circle of fellow quilters who, Amish and *Englisch* alike, had accepted her with open arms.

She checked to be sure her troubled thoughts hadn't caused her to add too much tension on the thread and pucker the quilt layers, but her hands knew what to do even when she didn't.

AS LUKE SETTLED Charlie in the paddock across the alley from the back of the store, scantily shaded by the enormous old sycamore, he tried to remember when he'd last worked a day at Bowman's without his father here for at least a few hours of that day. Certainly not since they'd hired Julia in June. Now, August was only ten days away.

Elam had brought the message today that *Mamm* didn't feel well, so *Daad* was staying home with her. "Miriam offered to take care of *Mamm* instead," he added, "but this week is a big sale at the quilt shop and she might be needed. Besides"—he'd smirked—"I think *Mamm* is only trying to make *Daad* take a day off. You know how he is."

Not as young and feckless as his brother, Luke was quicker to worry that his mother might really be ill. It was true she never seemed to get sick, even this spring when that flu went around. Still, at her age, heart conditions became more likely. She worked so hard, never slowing down, and didn't like even admitting she needed to get off her feet for a minute.

On the other hand, Elam was right; *Mamm* got exasperated with their *daad*, who worked even when the store was closed. Since Luke had come home, and it was clear he was here to stay and built furniture that satisfied even Eli, she had hinted that he should take it a little easier.

Luke chuckled at the thought. That was the pot calling the kettle black, for sure.

Once in the workshop, the rising heat of the morning shut out along with the bright sunlight, he immediately began evaluating the work from Saturday and planning where to begin this morning. Only the first sounds in front broke his concentration. Maybe he should tell Julia that *Daad* wouldn't be here today, that if she had questions, she would need to come to him. He'd noticed in the past week and a half that she tried not to bother him. While he was grateful, · he didn't like thinking she was still afraid of him.

He let himself through the door into the store proper. Julia was just flipping the sign in the window to Open, turning when she heard him.

A crisp white, sleeveless blouse bared long slender arms with only a faint hint of a tan. The blouse was more formfitting than her usual attire, momentarily pulling his attention to feminine curves he didn't want to think about.

Stiffly, he said, "*Daad* won't be here today, so if you have any questions, you'll have to come to me."

Like all the women of his family, her first reaction was concern. "Is he all right?"

"It's my mother not feeling good, according to my brother, who let me know. Elam thinks *Mamm* is exaggerating to make *Daad* take a day off."

Julia smiled. "I hope that's true. Your mother usually has so much energy."

That's what he'd been thinking, too, without using that word.

He should go to work, but had trouble looking away from her. This was why none of the young women he'd met on the last church Sunday had appealed to him. He had to resist a wish for something that was impossible, and not only because he was Amish and she was not. There was also that fear, the drab colors she wore, the way she so carefully kept distance between herself and any men who came into the store.

Caught up in her despite himself, he jerked when the bell over the door rang. A customer. He wasn't the only one who needed to go to work.

But once he focused on the woman and child who had entered the store, he knew they weren't customers. The woman, perhaps in her early forties, wore a pin-striped gray suit, the skirt knee-length, her shoes sturdy to suit her stocky body. Lips pressed together to form a thin line, she scowled at him. Since he'd never seen her in his life, he couldn't imagine how he'd offended her.

In one hand she clutched a briefcase, while with the other she gripped the very small hand of a little girl whose pale blond hair slithered free of a ponytail. Brown dribbles on her faded pink top might be syrup. Beneath it . . . was that a unicorn? Both her pink sneakers trailed dirty shoe-laces. Had no one helped clean her or tied her shoes this morning?

She tried to shuffle behind the woman, who tugged her forward.

"Are you Mr. Luke Bowman?" the woman demanded.

Tempted to pretend he didn't speak English, he responded politely. "I am."

"Do you know how hard you were to find?" She made no effort to hide her annoyance.

"I have worked in the same place for over a year." Why was he defending himself? "Who are you?"

"I'm Melissa Tanner, with the Missouri Department of Social Services, Children's Division. We have been searching for you for two months while this child waited in a foster home. None of the contact information we had for you was good."

Suddenly wary, he asked, "I don't understand why you looked for me, or who told you how to find me."

She must have had the address for his last apartment, he supposed, and the number for the mobile phone he had given up even before he spoke to Bishop Amos about his desire to be belatedly baptized.

Melissa Tanner's eyes sparked. "You didn't think you were obligated to stay in touch with the mother of your child?"

Chapter Seven

LUKE COULD ONLY gape at the woman. The mother of his child? What was she talking about?

"I don't have any children." Although he'd had sexual relations with several women during his years away. Confessing that to Bishop Amos had not been among his happiest moments.

Was there any chance—? No, he'd always been careful. And why wouldn't a woman have told him?

"You're denying paternity of this child?" Melissa Tanner looked and sounded even angrier. She had made up her mind, although based on what evidence, he didn't know.

Julia spoke up, startling Luke with the reminder that she was present and hearing all this. "I think she's scared. I can keep an eye on her while the two of you speak privately."

Wincing, Luke saw that the girl seemed to be trying to shrink, as if she thought she could disappear. That disturbed him enough that he nodded and said, "Please." He hesitated. "If you'd come back to my workshop, Ms. Tanner."

The social worker did glance down at the child, and he

saw a reflection of his chagrin. Despite her hostility, she might not be a bad woman. In his years away, he had heard divorced men complaining because they had to help support their own children, and he knew from the newspapers that many men and probably some women hid from the legal authorities so they didn't have to pay anything. He'd found that kind of thinking and behavior unimaginable. He had never met a man or woman of his faith who didn't want children, and love and value each and every one. To simply walk away—no. To deal constantly with such people would make a good person angry.

After a moment, Ms. Tanner led the child to Julia and said, "Please stay with this nice lady, Abby. Okay?"

Expression blank even as she continued to make herself as small as possible, she didn't protest, although she didn't look at Julia, either. She especially didn't look at him.

Julia, though, crouched to her level and smiled. Holding out a hand, she coaxed, "I have lemonade and cookies."

The girl stole a furtive look out of eyes as blue as Luke's own, and finally, timidly, let Julia take her hand.

Reassured, he led this social worker into the part of the business where he felt most comfortable. Inhaling the sharp scent of sawdust and finishes helped.

Ms. Tanner took in her surroundings, appearing surprised. Did she think of the Amish as so primitive, they barely used tools?

He must learn not to jump to unkind conclusions.

"Have a seat." He pulled up a stool to a workbench. Grateful for a minor errand to hide his turmoil, he found his father's and carried it over for himself.

"How old is . . . Abby?"

"Three. Almost four," Ms. Tanner told him. "As you ought to know." She sounded less certain now.

He had to know.

"Who is the mother?" He braced himself.

"Elizabeth Miller."

A stampede of emotions trampled atop his initial reaction. Understanding came last. Yes, he'd known Beth, as she called herself. Calculating, he counted back. Six or even seven years back, she had taken to panhandling near his bus stop in St. Louis. He had given her money, sometimes brought her breakfast. Come early enough to sit and talk to her for a few minutes before his bus arrived. Beth had been pathetically grateful for any kindness.

He'd noticed her first because of the trace of an accent she retained. She'd grown up Amish, there was no mistaking it. Of course he'd been interested. Sometimes he'd felt so lonely, he hungered for that hint of home.

She refused to talk about her roots, but her thin face and haunted blue eyes told him she hadn't grown up surrounded by love, faith, and security as he had. There were Amish groups far more conservative than his, judgmental and even repressive. It might have been only that . . . but he thought her pain had a different cause.

Now and again, she would disappear for a few weeks or as much as a couple of months when she found a job or a new boyfriend. Yet she never seemed able to keep either for long. Barely skin and bones, she'd been like a bundle of live electrical wires. Luke had wondered about drugs but never been sure. She had talked about the men, an ever-changing roster of them. He took it as a desperate need for love. His attempts to help her see that she would never find anything meaningful or lasting that way had been futile.

Once he'd graduated from college and gotten a good job, Luke had moved to a safer neighborhood in St. Louis. He'd tried to find Beth to let her know she could always come to him, but when he asked around about her, head shakes were his answer. In the following months, he'd gone back several times, hoping to see her by the bus stop. He was making good money now, and could help her, but she was never there. Eventually, she had faded from his thoughts.

He had cared for Elizabeth Miller, pitied her . . . but he

had never gone to wherever she lived, or had her to his apartment. He had held her when she cried, but not so much as kissed her. That wasn't how he felt about her.

That girl with her mother's eyes could not be his daughter.

"You obviously knew her," Ms. Tanner said in accusation.

"I did. I haven't—" He cut himself off, needing a moment to think. "What happened to her?"

"She died. She left a letter naming you as Abby's father." Her voice stayed firm. "Your name is on Abby's birth certificate. She wanted us to find you."

Had he been the only safe person that Beth, in her extremity, had been able to think of?

"Abby must have grandparents. Aunts and uncles, cousins . . ." None of whom Beth trusted with her daughter.

He wouldn't have said he'd looked that closely at the little girl, but he pictured her now, seeing her mother in the shape of her face and eyes, the color of those eyes. Even in what he had guessed was her late twenties, Beth still had the rare pale blond hair. Abby's hair had curls that might have come from her father.

Luke found himself fiercely glad that Beth had not named the true father, even if she'd known who he was, on her baby's birth certificate. Then the Missouri Department of Social Services would have hunted *him* down, and if they had been foolish enough to leave this frail girl with him, Abby might well have been condemned to a childhood as terrible as her mother's.

Luke frowned. If they knew the truth, would they allow him to foster her? Or another Amish family in his church district? John and Sarah Beiler had not been able to have children and would joyfully take Abby to raise. He could tell Ms. Tanner that he knew Beth had been raised Amish.

But he held his tongue, too aware of the contempt and even anger bureaucrats in government institutions felt for the Amish. Without her certainty that he was the father, this social worker would never have brought Abby to him. Thinking that, she'd have had no other choice however she felt about his religion and lifestyle.

In that instant, he made a decision. This was one last thing he could do for the young woman he had tried to help. It was a big thing, one that would start with a lie, but God must want him to accept Abby Miller as his daughter, or He wouldn't have brought her to Luke's doorstep.

He realized Ms. Tanner had been talking. While thinking, he hadn't really listened to what she'd said, but the gist wasn't unexpected. She had had no success tracing other family. If he didn't take in Abby, she would go permanently into foster care. At her age, it was possible she'd be adopted, but he recognized that she might have problems that would reduce her appeal to couples shopping for the ideal child of their dreams.

"Yes," he said quietly. "I knew Beth was pregnant, but she took off. She was . . ." He stopped.

The social worker nodded, accepting what he didn't say.

Glancing uneasily toward the closed door separating them from Julia and the child, he asked, "Does Abby have any toys?"

Ms. Tanner pushed the file folder toward him before she went out to the car to get a suitcase that apparently held Abby's few possessions. While she was gone, he opened the file. On top was the birth certificate. As he had guessed, Abby was really named Abigail, a popular name among the Amish. Beth had fled her upbringing, yet held enough regret at least to want this tiny girl to be raised by a man who had shared that faith. Or had she guessed that, in the end, he would return to his roots?

Below the birth certificate but atop other paperwork was an envelope with his name on it, written by hand. Picking it up, he was surprised to find it still sealed. Under the circumstances, he would have understood if the social worker had opened it. Not knowing what Beth had needed to say to him, he found himself grateful Ms. Tanner had considered the letter private.

No matter what, while writing to him, Beth would have prayed it found him. This would be the last time he'd hear her voice. Now wasn't the time. He took the letter and placed it facedown on the high workbench before he followed the social worker back out to the front of the store.

He'd barely had a chance to wonder where Julia and Abby were when a toilet flushed and then water ran. Julia carried Abby from the bathroom available to employees and customers. Seeing him, Abby buried her face against Julia's neck.

Panic struck Luke hard. Did a three-year-old need help to get on the toilet? He'd never had such responsibilities, even for his youngest sister. Miriam had had *Mamm*, and Luke's older sister had still been home then. *Grossmammi*, too. Luke had done more for Elam, but he was a boy.

Julia mouthed, "Where is she?" a second before Melissa Tanner appeared on the sidewalk outside the front window of the store carrying a small, battered suitcase.

He smiled at Abby. "Did you have a cookie?"

She hunched her shoulders, her arms visibly tightening on her protector.

Julia glanced down at her, furrows between her brows, but said cheerfully, "She did. They were good, weren't they, honey? Miriam brought them yesterday."

She had to let Ms. Tanner back in and he realized she'd thought to turn the sign back to Closed and lock the door so they weren't interrupted. Smart and good-hearted, both.

He wouldn't like seeing contempt in her eyes if she believed he'd knowingly abandoned his own child, but he was nonetheless grateful she was here.

The small suitcase, unzipped atop the reception counter, held only a skimpy collection of clothing as well as a few toys that appeared new. Purchased by the Missouri Department of

Social Services? He thought not. Either the foster mother had spent her own money, or this bulldog of a woman had.

Julia chose a simple puzzle and sat behind the desk with Abby on her lap, nodding gently to Luke. He didn't think Abby had actually looked at him yet, but she had relaxed with Julia, showing no inclination to rush back to Melissa. Having Julia to take charge allowed him to take deeper breaths.

He needed more information, and Ms. Tanner returned willingly with him to the workshop. She didn't know as much as he'd hoped she would. Nothing of what Ms. Tanner did tell him came as a surprise. Beth had died of a drug overdose, track marks up and down her arms.

"She didn't have those when I knew her," he said, "but she was . . . jittery. I wondered about drugs."

Ms. Tanner nodded. "I doubt she turned to heroin until after Abby was born. Thank God."

Their eyes met briefly. He thought she'd meant that sincerely, not as the throwaway *auslanders* sometimes used the name of the Lord.

"She's had a physical and been given immunizations," she told him. "We had no way of knowing if she'd had vaccines as an infant, so the pediatrician started her at the beginning."

"I don't know if Beth would have allowed her to be vaccinated or not," he said. "My impression is that she grew up in an ultra-conservative group of Amish. They might not have allowed them." He thought she had been torn every day between what she'd been taught and believed, and the determination to destroy that very thing, which turned out to be herself.

The social worker's eyes narrowed in renewed suspicion. "Abby needs the next round in six weeks. Will you see to it that she gets her vaccines?"

"Yes. I promise. We know the shots are important. I had them myself."

After a moment, she nodded. "Abby was also evaluated

by a psychologist. Although she is a little behind her age group in physical development and play, we think that's because of neglect, not prenatal damage."

"I'm glad to hear that." The Beth he'd known would have tried not to use drugs while she was pregnant. She might have hated herself, but never an innocent child.

"It's been hard to judge her speech, because she doesn't talk."

"At all?" he asked, alarmed.

"Her foster mother reports hearing her quietly singing, but I haven't. Otherwise . . . no. Even if a test hadn't confirmed that she hears fine, it's obvious she understands what's said to her. Whether she was punished for being loud—"

He frowned. "Beth wouldn't have done that."

"A man she lived with might have. As her mother's . . . health deteriorated, we can't know what kind of care Abby got."

As Beth sank deeper into addiction, she meant. He had to nod. Melissa was right. Even when he knew Beth, she'd lacked the patience and maturity to be a mother. Later . . . he didn't like to think what this child had endured.

"You're willing to accept responsibility for your daughter?"

He pushed back renewed panic. What did he know about being a parent?

"Ja." Why had that slipped out? "Yes, of course I am." So many lies, but for a good cause, he told himself. And this one wasn't such a big lie, only saying that the little girl was his daughter. The responsibility part was truth.

Sounding sharp again, the social worker said, "In most instances, I wouldn't be enthusiastic about placing a child on my caseload with an Amish family."

He tried not to take offense. "We raise our children with love. She will have fewer toys than she would in an *Englisch* home, and there will be no television or electronic games, but I'll read her stories and she'll have fun. I have a large family, Ms. Tanner. They'll welcome her with open arms. My parents live nearby, and I have a younger brother and sister who both still live at home. Here in the area I have a married sister, aunts, uncles and cousins." So many, he couldn't count them. He didn't lack for family.

Her face might have softened, but the doubt still remained. "I'll be frank. One of my biggest reservations about people of your faith is your refusal to allow your children more than eight years of education."

"More education would pull our children away from their families and church." He understood that, even as he had mixed feelings. "Some young men and women do take technical courses beyond what our schools offer, and many become apprentices." He hesitated. "Others leave to continue their education. You probably know that I did."

"I might not be here if I hadn't learned that, Mr. Bowman."

He dipped his head in acknowledgment. "Our young people are allowed a few years to run a little wild, sample some of what the outside world offers. Abby will have that chance before she chooses to be baptized. Should she long for a college education, I will be afraid she is turning her back on her upbringing, as my parents were afraid, but I'll support her anyway." And pray, as *Mamm* and *Daad* had for him, that what she'd lost would come to outweigh the excitement and challenges outside their faith.

This nod seemed decisive. "I know you're not prepared for her to stay today. I can give you time to—"

"You don't need to do that. I have a second bedroom set up for my brother, who sometimes spends the night. I can take her home right now, get her settled."

"You're not married?"

"Not yet, but I will be. Abby needs to have sisters and brothers." And a mother, perhaps most of all. Seeing Melissa's continued reluctance, he asked, "Is she especially attached to her foster parents . . . ?"

"No, she seems happiest with her own company. Are you *sure*, Mr. Bowman? This is a *huge* commitment."

"I'm sure." Yet another lie. His conscience writhed, but he felt something already for a little girl who needed love and family more than anybody he had ever seen. "She will enjoy riding in a buggy on the way home."

"I'll want to check on her a few times."

He expected that, was even glad she cared enough to make sure Abby was all right.

"You are welcome," he said simply. He gave her his home address and the phone number for the telephone that sat out in a shanty on the road. Four neighbors shared it.

She went through papers with him, including the medical records, and had him sign in several places. Of course, she was momentarily frustrated that he could show her no official identification, but by this time she'd become resigned to the fact that, as an Amishman, he couldn't comply with her usual requirements.

In what seemed like no time, he watched as she said goodbye to Abby, who scarcely acknowledged her. In fact, she squeezed closer to Julia. After a last brisk nod, Melissa left. When the door closed behind her, Luke's stomach stirred unpleasantly, and his eyes didn't quite want to focus. This dizziness felt as if he'd turned too many somersaults.

He didn't ask God if he had done the right thing, because he couldn't have turned away this child. What Luke did was pray that Beth could know that her precious daughter was with him. Safe. Sure to be loved.

What would happen if he touched her? Crouched to her level and tried to make her meet his eyes? Was she afraid of men, or just shy? He dreaded finding out.

His first thought had been to take her directly to his parents' house, but then he remembered *Mamm* didn't feel well. What if she had a contagious sickness?

Now he faced the dilemma of what to do next.

Better to take her home, just the two of them . . . except that the long day yawned ahead, with him having no idea of the real needs of a child this age. Especially one already afraid to cry or scream or say what she wanted. He needed help. Elam would be long since at work, and probably useless anyway. And male, if Abby feared men. Rose . . . but he hated the idea of abandoning Abby with yet another stranger.

SEEING PERTURBED LINES on Luke's face, Julia had a good idea where his thoughts had taken him. Still grappling with how this had happened, she didn't want to believe he'd known he had a child out there and just abandoned her with her mother, but Julia sympathized no matter what. At least having come from a big family, he'd be a better instant parent than many men—or than she would be, for that matter.

So quickly, though, she felt tenderness for this child. Julia had been much older when bad things happened to her, but she had shut down, too. She recognized what Abby was experiencing, and wondered if Abby hadn't instinctively recognized the same in this woman she didn't know. She hadn't protested being left with her, and had allowed herself to relax in Julia's arms.

"You can't take her to your parents," she blurted.

He tore his gaze from Abby and looked at Julia, visibly shaken. "I know. I think I have to take her home. It might be best if we close for the day, once you've listened to messages to be sure there's nothing urgent."

Feeling more timid, she said, "It's not that busy out here. I can keep her with me while you get at least a little work done, and . . . maybe you could go out and buy us lunch. Or watch her while I do. She'll probably nap later. I'm . . . enjoying having her."

"She's not your responsibility."

Julia bit her lip. "I'm offering. But . . . you'd probably rather take her to family. I just thought, well, that you'd have a few hours to think."

His laugh was a harsh sound. No, painful. "I want to believe God will guide me, but I was one man when I got out of bed this morning and am now another."

She could see that he didn't like feeling out of his element. What strong man did, Amish or not?

Quietly, she said, "We know that all things work together for good to those who love God, to those who are called according to His purpose."

He looked sharply at her, no doubt recognizing the passage from Romans, probably surprised that she would know her Bible.

Summoning another small moment of courage to say what she thought he needed to hear, Julia made sure to hold his gaze. "Haven't you been called to be a father? Don't you think most men fear at some point that they'll fail their child? I'll bet your *daad* would say the same." She glanced down; Abby was listening, although Julia couldn't imagine that she fully understand what they were talking about.

Luke didn't hide his indecision.

Stung, although she had no reason to be, Julia suggested, "I can go down to the quilt shop and offer to take Miriam's place so that she can help you with Abby."

He stared at her with those unnervingly blue eyes for so long, she was ready to thrust his daughter at him and bolt. But then he shook his head, one side of his mouth curving up.

"No," he said softly. "My daughter trusts *you*." He paused. "I trust you."

Chapter Eight

❖

HEARING LUKE'S BUGGY the next morning, Elam emerged from the chicken coop. Any excuse to escape a chore he hated.

Luke reined in Charlie and said in *Deitsh*, "I can smell you from here." After a harrowing night, he'd made the decision to find out if his mother was recovered, leaving the house extra early to catch his father still home, too. He couldn't keep depending on a young unmarried *Englisch* woman, especially one who already disturbed him.

His brother grimaced. "I stepped in—" He spotted Abby. "Who is this, *bruder*? Did you find her by the road?"

"*Nein*, in Charlie's manger."

Elam chuckled. "What is your name?"

Abby peered through her unkempt hair at him. This morning, when Luke had approached her with his comb, all he had, she'd scuttled backwards as if he held a whip. He'd left it alone, just as he'd accepted the mismatched leggings and shirt she had put on herself, along with her one pair of shoes on the wrong feet—laces dangling. The first word that would come to his mother's mind at seeing her would be *strubly*. Disheveled, in English. He couldn't be bothered with embarrassment, saving his worry for the fact that Abby had barely nibbled at the eggs he cooked for breakfast.

Worst of all, she hadn't yet spoken a word to him. He wished he'd thought to ask Julia when they closed yesterday whether Abby was talking to her at all.

Unless her *mamm* had spoken to her in Pennsylvania Dutch, she wouldn't understand what he and Elam were saying now. Luke switched to English. "Her name is Abigail Miller. She goes by Abby. I don't think she speaks our language."

Elam's expression changed, puzzlement replacing amusement. "I don't understand. What are you doing here so early? Why do you have an *Englisch* girl?"

"I came to see if *Mamm* is better." Luke drew a deep breath. On the way here, as the buggy swayed and the wheels droned their song on the pavement, as he kept reaching out to ensure Abby didn't lean so hard against the door that she fell out, he had made a decision. Another decision. This one might be wrong, but he would rather Abby was accepted as his from the beginning. "She's my daughter," he said. "A daughter I didn't know I had."

Elam's mouth fell open.

Unexpectedly enjoying the sight, Luke waited.

"*Mamm* doesn't seem sick at all. She made a huge breakfast for us."

Luke nodded, flicked the reins, and clicked to Charlie, who started forward toward a hitching post. He'd tie him up until they were ready to leave. *Daad* could ride with him to work.

Walking beside the buggy, Elam said, "I'll take care of Charlie. You need to talk to *Mamm* and *Daad*."

"That's true. *Denke*." Luke hopped down and lifted Abby out, hating that her body went rigid as a board only because he was touching her. He'd almost rather she cried.

Setting her down and laying a hand on top of her head, he said, "Abby, this is my brother. His name is Elam. He's your uncle."

She stuck her thumb in her mouth. Not so good at three years old, if Luke remembered right, but understandable given the loss of her mother and being cared for by strangers ever since. And, in his case, a male stranger. He wondered if she even understood what a father was. Had she ever heard the word *Daddy*?

If not, she would learn it.

His greater fear was that Beth had called each of the men who came and went *Daddy*.

He took Abby's hand and they walked slowly down the packed dirt lane to the sprawling farmhouse where he'd grown up. He had to catch her several times when she stepped on loose laces and tripped.

His father had always leased out much of the land to someone else. The fields of corn were a perfect place for boys to play, although spooky at night. *Mamm* maintained a large garden, though, as well as an orchard of old fruit trees that bore cherries, apples, and peaches. The cherries had already been picked and canned, but this was peach season, and the apples would be ripe soon.

Smiling down at Abby, he asked, "Have you ever eaten a peach?"

She remained silent and solemn, although he knew from her reactions that her hearing was fine.

Tension rode his shoulders when he reached the back door. His parents would never let Abby see anything but love and acceptance. That was their way. They would be disappointed in him, fathering a child out of wedlock, not even knowing she existed. Because it could have happened with one of those other women he'd known, he had to accept the reminder that he had violated his parents' values. He wanted to believe his mistakes had led to him being the person this sad girl needed.

86 JANICE KAY JOHNSON

He sighed and murmured, "Face the music," which Abby heard with no more visible comprehension than for anything else he'd said. He opened the door and walked into the kitchen.

Which was filled with the rich, sweet aroma of cooking peaches, and women working at the table, counter, and stove. Why hadn't Elam said? *Mamm* and the others must have wanted to start their canning early, before the house became too hot. Luke felt the impulse to run—but it was too late.

Mamm was the first to turn, *Aenti* Barbara next. Something in their stillness and the way they stared had his cousin Katie turning to look, too. Miriam wouldn't be happy to have missed this scene. His sister had been snoopy from the time she was Abby's age, always in the middle of everything.

His mother beamed at Abby. "And who is this?"

He took in the other two women, wishing he could say this first to his parents, but knowing word would spread like wildfire anyway. Ach—*Daad* appeared in the doorway from the living room.

For the first time, Abby huddled close to him.

He remembered an *Englisch* saying: *Better the devil you know.*

"This is my daughter, Abigail Miller. Abby is the name she knows."

Three mouths fell open at once. His father's, he thought, tightened instead. Abby buried her face against his thigh. Feeling her terror like a silent scream, he crouched and picked her up. She grabbed onto his shirt and shook. It seemed instinct to bend and kiss the top of her head lightly.

Something sizzled fiercely on the stove, and *Aenti* Barbara cried, "Ach, it's boiling over! We're *ferhoodled* for sure, forgetting what we're doing!"

Katie and his aunt leaped into action. His *mamm* advanced on him, smile restored. "A new *kinskind*! And such a *blabbermaul, ja*?"

Luke laughed. "I can't get her to stop talking, can't you tell?" He lowered his voice, spoke gently in Abby's ear. "This is your grandmother. My mom. My *mammi*, your *grossmammi*."

Abby tried to scrunch herself even smaller.

He met his mother's eyes over the top of the curly blond hair. In *Deitsh*, he said, "Her *mamm* died not so long ago. Nobody knew how to find me."

"Will she let me hold her?"

"Why don't I sit down with her instead? She can watch you all work." He forced a smile. "She didn't eat much breakfast, but she does like her sweets. Yesterday she ate two of Miriam's snickerdoodles without stopping."

"I'll cut up a fresh peach for her. *Ja*, that's a good start."

Nodding, he sat in a straight-backed wooden chair at the table, settling Abby's slight weight on his thigh, holding her securely with an arm around her. The other two women stole glances at him and his little girl—his *dochder*, he thought in renewed shock—even as they lifted sterilized jars from an enormous pot full of boiling water, or cored and sliced peaches. Now Abby was refusing to look at anyone.

A moment later, his mother set down a plastic cup of milk and a plate with a sliced peach in front of them, followed by a cup of coffee for him.

"*Denke, Mamm.*" He lifted a slice for Abby. "Try this, little one. You'll like it."

She shook her head hard and continued to burrow into him.

Sad and scared for her, he set down the piece, wiped his fingers, and said, "In a minute." He didn't know her, this little girl, and already he would do anything to keep her safe. If only he could go back, find her before life had stolen the optimism a *kind* should feel. Luke had to remind himself that she was only three. Memories of those first years faded and, most often, were forgotten. He had to trust God would be so merciful.

His father gestured toward the living room, and Luke

nodded. He carried her on one hip, the plate with the peach in his free hand. His *mamm* brought the cup of milk and followed. He had no doubt his aunt and cousin would burst into whispered speculation the minute he was out of earshot.

In the living room, he chose one end of the sofa, beside an end table and the propane-fueled lamp that allowed his mother to do her mending or hand quilting in the evening, his father to read passages from the Bible to his family. As a teenager, Luke had grown impatient, sure he'd go mad if he had to sit here while his parents did the exact same thing they had done every other night of his life. Now he felt a pang. He wanted to give Abby the same. The bedrock that had brought him home after his long absence.

Mamm took the recliner, *Daad* the rocking chair that he had made himself.

Daad frowned. "Where is Elam?"

"He met Abby. He's taking care of Charlie." Gently rubbing Abby's thin back, he thought she was relaxing some. Continuing to speak in *Deitsh*, he said, "The social worker brought her yesterday. I didn't ask how she found me. She said it wasn't easy, me without a phone or a driver's license anymore."

His parents both nodded in understanding.

"She came to the store. We had just opened. I would have closed and brought her here then, but Elam had told me you were sick, *Mamm*."

"Only tired, I think."

Was that evasive? He couldn't decide. If it happened again, he would push her to see a doctor.

"Abby liked Julia."

The little girl's head lifted at the familiar name. He smiled at her and switched to English. "Will you drink some milk?"

She didn't bury her face again, so he held out the cup. She wrapped her tiny hands around it and sipped as he tipped it up slightly.

Luke's mother wanted to snatch this new grandchild from him and cuddle her, he could tell. It was all she could do to stay seated, her hands folded on her lap.

Back to their language, he continued, "She has been afraid of me. Maybe of all men. Julia offered to watch her yesterday, so I worked some. We had lunch together, all three of us. I hoped Abby was getting used to me, but once we were on our own . . ." He shook his head. "We didn't have a very good night. Now, she's thinking at least she knows me."

"She'll know all of us soon," *Mamm* said.

He tried a slice of peach again. This time, Abby touched her tongue to it and then took a big bite. To his satisfaction, she ate the first slice and reached for another herself.

"This was a good choice," he said to his mother.

They said little as Abby ate, drank more milk, and then curled up comfortably in his arms. He watched as her eyelids drooped. She probably hadn't slept any better than he had. Thumb in the mouth—no, he wouldn't pull it out—and with a child's astonishing ability to fall asleep anywhere, she sagged. When her thumb slipped out, he laid her on the sofa beside him, keeping a hand on her.

That gave him a chance to tell his parents about the woman he had considered a friend and how she died. In Amish society, men pretended not to notice that women were pregnant. He was blunt, though. "I never knew she was pregnant. She . . . disappeared. Beth was a troubled woman. She was raised Amish, but I think her father or someone else hurt her." He didn't know if *hurt* was a euphemism either of his parents would understand, but it wasn't as if he could be sure what had been done to Beth to cause such deep despair.

"At least she did the right thing for her daughter," Eli said.

"It's . . . a little frightening, becoming a father this way."

As he could have predicted, his mother said immediately, "Glad I'll be to take care of her during the day. Miriam can help. Work fewer hours at the quilt shop, maybe."

Knowing how much his sister loved her job, he hoped to find another solution. She wasn't like most *maidals*, working only until she married. He couldn't tell whether she was interested at all in marriage since her come-calling friend died. Even their parents hadn't pushed her, thinking she needed time but probably not guessing that years would pass.

Luke wished Miriam would talk to him, but regaining her trust would take time, too.

Perhaps he could hire Katie or another young woman in their church group. Even that worried him, though, because Abby had drawn so deep inside herself. He wished he knew if she'd been like this before her *mamm* died, or whether this was temporary, a reaction to the bewildering circumstances. Until he knew how the next few days would go, he was reluctant to leave her at all.

"The bad choices you made could have led to even worse consequences for Abby," his father said sternly.

True humility didn't come easily to Luke. He had to unclench his jaw to say, "They're already bad enough. I wish Beth had looked for me."

"Did she try?" his mother asked. "Do you know?"

He shook his head. "If so, she didn't find me. The social worker had her computer and all the government records." Beth might have been afraid he wouldn't be willing to take Abby. Had she kept putting it off, until it was too late?

She might have answered his questions in the letter he hadn't yet read. He wasn't sure why he was so reluctant to hear those last words. Her hopes or regrets.

He couldn't tell his parents how long it had been since he'd seen Beth, or they'd know she wasn't his child. He was already second-guessing his decision not to be honest, but what if they felt he had no right to keep a little girl who must have other family out there somewhere? He could almost hear his mother saying, *They lost their daughter. Having their grandchild could fill the hole left by grief.*

Luke wouldn't call them naive. Perhaps his mother more

than his father. But he would never let Beth's family have her daughter. She'd wanted him to raise Abby. He wished she had come to him before she died and asked him in person. His agreement might have given her peace.

He had to trust she was in heaven, happy in her faith that the time would come when she and her daughter would be reunited.

"How old is she?" his mother asked.

"Three. Her birthday is in November."

"I see. Tiny even for that age, ain't so?"

"I don't know. You're the one who had daughters."

Deborah said, "At this age, Miriam made two of her."

He chuckled. Hearing that, Miriam would have been indignant. "Saying she was fat, are you?"

Mamm laughed. "Roly-poly."

Luke smiled. "I remember."

Funny that now his little sister was slim and not very tall, either, only five foot three.

Mamm insisted, "We need to feed this one up until she has a chin that jiggles, too."

Looking down at Abby's delicate features, he couldn't quite imagine that happening.

He told them about the doctor visits and the evaluation by a psychologist. "I think—I hope—she is mostly scared right now. That social worker says her foster mother heard her singing, but she hasn't said a word to me yet."

"Give her time," *Mamm* said comfortably. "Shy, and with reason."

With good reason indeed.

Already he and his father would be late to the store, although he knew Julia would guess why and wouldn't be alarmed. A part of him wished he were taking Abby with him, knowing she'd be happy with Julia. He had to push back at that wish. He'd be taking advantage of a woman who had been hired to do an entirely different job. Privately, he knew that was the least of his reasons. Yesterday, seeing Julia's ease with his little girl, her warmth and tenderness and something he could only call grief, had awakened complicated feelings in him.

Feelings he could allow to go nowhere.

Abby would be safe here. His mother was beloved by her grandchildren, always ready with a smile and a comfortable lap, a story and good food.

He thought of waking Abby to say goodbye and reassure her that he'd be back to get her at dinnertime, but decided to slip away. By the time he came back for her, she'd likely be clinging to the women of his family and afraid of him again.

Mouth twisting at that image, he took a last look at this small, vulnerable girl, and left her.

JULIA WAS THE first to arrive at the store again. She'd fussed all night about Abby and Luke, worried that the little girl was terrified, wondering if he'd gotten Miriam or another sister or cousin to spend the night. She had hated hugging Abby yesterday and saying goodbye, knowing she'd be lucky to see her again. Then it would only be in passing when—if—she was invited to another quilting frolic or the like.

Even as she checked phone messages now, she kept an ear tuned for any sound from the back. The first message ended with a beep; a second began, Julia realizing she hadn't taken in the first.

It was stupid to feel this ache in her chest, as if . . . Abby should be hers.

The phone dropped out of her hand and landed with a clunk on the counter. A small, distant voice continued to talk as she dealt with her shock.

She'd begun to hunger to have a baby of her own, that's what was wrong with her. Abby had reached out and touched that increasingly sensitive place inside Julia. She'd enjoyed playing with friends' kids, but that was usually only for a few minutes at a time. Their parents were there, firmly in possession. Some of those children had probably been too old to trigger this primal need. But Abby . . . Abby had *needed* her. Clung as if she never wanted to let go.

I didn't want to let go, either.

Before making this move to Tompkin's Mill, Julia had thought about ways to start a family. She couldn't imagine ever marrying. If she'd made more money on her own, she might have gone ahead, one way or the other. She just wasn't sure she could afford all the costs that came with having a child. Her parents would help, she knew they would, but their love and worry had begun to feel suffocating.

Thus the move. She was determined to prove she could be independent—if you could call it that when she'd run to her big, tough cop brother. Having him five minutes away should she need him made all the difference.

Officially feeling pathetic, she picked up the receiver and set it back on the cradle. She'd have to start all over with voice mail.

That's when she heard the door from the workshop open, and everything inside her went still.

Chapter Nine

FORCING A SMILE, Julia swiveled in her desk chair, expecting Eli but seeing that both men had walked in.

Neither held a small blond child.

"Gute mariye," she said. Or croaked.

Eli smiled. "You sound like one of us now."

Apparently her accent was acceptable when she used one of the couple of dozen sentences she'd learned.

"I wanted to join my son in saying thank you for your help yesterday," he added. "It was good you were here."

She clasped her hands in front of her. "How is Abby?"

"Well. She is home with her *grossmammi.* Fun, they'll have today."

Of course they would. Abby wouldn't give Julia another thought. Soon, she would be swallowed by her huge, loving Amish family, who would give her everything she needed.

Julia—she was an outsider. An *auslander*, and always would be.

And she hated herself for the stab of envy that felt as if it could be fatal.

Somehow she kept a smile on her face. "I'm sure they will. I'll bet there will happen to be some cookies around."

"Ja!" Eli gave a belly laugh. "Ach, I need to get to work. Unless there are messages I should hear?"

"No, not yet. I haven't finished." Or really started.

"If Jason Warren calls, tell him his dining room table and chairs will be ready by the end of next week."

"I'll do that."

He glanced at his son, who had neither said a word nor smiled. Without comment, Eli went back through the door that had been left standing open.

Luke stayed where he was. Lines in his face and dark shadows beneath his eyes told her he hadn't slept well. Discomfort was apparent, too, and more that she couldn't read.

"You look tired," she said, barely above a whisper.

"I don't think Abby slept at all. She was scared by herself, scared of me."

"Oh, no. I hoped . . ."

"She was a mess when I took her to *Mamm*. This morning she wouldn't let me help her dress or brush her hair or even tie her shoelaces."

Compassion pierced her heart. "She'll learn to trust you."

"When?" He huffed out a breath and let his head fall back, exposing his strong throat. "I thought she'd go happily to my mother, but that's when she decided to grab onto me." Now he rubbed the back of his neck, as if it hurt.

"You were familiar."

"Yes." He studied her with somber eyes. "But she went right to you. Why you, and not *Mamm*?"

Was that an accusation of some sort? No, she decided. His mother was so warmly maternal, Julia would have readily gone to her. "Was it just your mother?"

"No, my aunt Barbara and cousin Katie were there also. They were canning peaches."

"So the kitchen was busy."

"Yes, but *Mamm* and *Daad* and I went to the living room to talk. Abby wouldn't let go of me."

"Could it be because their clothes are so unfamiliar to her? What you wear isn't so different, but the long dresses and *kapps* . . ."

He shifted uncomfortably, the movement unusual for a man so confident. "That could be. They have an accent, too, more so than *Daad*'s."

"That's true." She wanted to magically know the right thing to say so that he could go to work reassured that all would be well. It *would* be, she knew it would—eventually. But tonight might be no better. "There's just been so much change. It'll take Abby time to feel secure. Know that you'll be there for her forever, that you'll come for her every single day after work." She heard her voice growing more and more passionate. "That she has her own room, a routine she can trust will stay the same. It's . . . not realistic to expect her to adjust so fast."

He didn't blink once during that speech. After staring at her long enough for her to feel nerves jumping, Luke nodded. "She must trust that nobody will hurt her."

Julia felt tears at the backs of her eyes at the idea that anyone could have hurt that precious, fragile child, but her instincts said it had happened. Luke obviously guessed the same.

"You're right," he said abruptly. "Patience is what I need."

Absurdly, given her tangle of emotions, she found herself smiling. "You're endlessly patient with wood. I believe you're very capable of all the patience you'll need."

A light flickered in his blue eyes, and he nodded. "My father will wonder what I'm doing, wasting time talking."

Julia didn't say anything.

One side of his mouth turned up. "Thank you. For yesterday, and for saying what I need to hear this morning."

The sting she'd felt instantly smoothed, she smiled back. "You're welcome."

He walked away without another word, the door closing behind him. Left alone, Julia took entirely too long to collect herself enough to call up voice mail once again, and actually listen to the messages this time.

APPREHENSION GREW IN Luke with every thud of Charlie's hooves. He paid little attention to the passing landscape, none of which was new to him. He knew the bushy tops of potatoes, the tangled vines decorated with still-green squash.

He should have taken a break midday and gone to check on Abby. All day, he'd struggled to concentrate, battling guilt because he'd left while she slept. He should have woken her up, explained that he had to go to his job but his *mamm* and *aenti* would watch over her until he came back for her.

With a sound like a gunshot, a covey of quail exploded from the long grass at the edge of a cornfield. Charlie briefly broke into a canter, but Luke controlled him with firm hands on the reins. Luke's brooding was scarcely interrupted.

He prayed his little girl hadn't been too frightened when she awakened to find him gone. Why hadn't his mother suggested that?

Luke shook off that annoyed thought. The responsibility for Abby was his, not his mother's. He needed to listen to his instincts.

Except for the instinct that told him Abby would be happiest with Julia. Who should not be expected to be a child minder on top of the rest of her job. He'd liked being able to check on Abby frequently, though, watch her play or snuggle with Julia, give her a chance to grow more comfortable with his presence.

He wished his father would say something to take his mind off the tenderness he'd felt yesterday watching his new daughter with the *Englisch* woman. Tenderness he could not afford to feel, when it wasn't all for the child.

"You will want to speak to the bishop soon," his father said, out of the blue.

Luke managed not to wince. That was not quite what he'd had in mind, although it certainly distracted him from thoughts of Julia. His father was right; he'd better see Bishop Amos soon. The Amish grapevine was lightning fast despite the lack of telephones, email, and instant messaging. Even if he could trust his sister, brother, and parents to keep quiet, Katie would have eagerly told her friends and siblings. Luke wasn't at all sure that Elam wouldn't have blabbed, too. And any other men at the farm would hurry home to tell *their* wives, who would tell . . .

Yes, perhaps he should stop to talk to Amos this evening on his way home. It wouldn't be far out of the way, and Abby might soften the bishop's heart.

He nodded in agreement as he turned Charlie up the lane to his parents' home.

"You will stay for dinner, *ja*?"

"*Ja*, if *Mamm* isn't too tired."

"She'd be hurt if you didn't stay."

Luke grimaced. Of course she would be.

He let his father off by the house and continued on to the barn, where he unharnessed his gelding and turned him loose in a large stall, aware of the buzzing of cicadas, a sound he often tuned out. Charlie trumpeted a challenge answered by one of the three horses outside in the pasture.

"Just for an hour or two," Luke told him, scratching behind his ears. "Then we'll go home."

Charlie's dark head bobbed as if he understood. He was already lipping up hay as Luke turned to leave the barn.

Luke reached the back doorstep, where he hesitated with his hand on the knob. *Coward,* he accused himself, for the second time today, and opened the door.

At first sight of his mother and Miriam bustling to put

dinner on the table, he was reassured. But the worried look his sister cast him stirred up the apprehension, like sludge at the bottom of a pot.

"Where is Abby?"

His *mamm* turned. "Asleep, at last," she said tautly.

At last? She'd been asleep when he left that morning.

"You were barely gone when she opened her eyes to find only strangers," his mother continued. "She scrambled off the couch and ran. We found her hiding behind the toilet, squeezed in."

"*Mamm* says she didn't cry or scream," Miriam contributed. "She just . . . shook. Even after I got home, she wouldn't eat or drink, and if any of us touched her, she became as rigid as a board."

"She was terrified," he said flatly, sick to find his worst fears had come true.

"I'm afraid so," his mother said, her face crumpled in distress. "I rocked her and sang to her, but nothing worked. A troubled child, she is."

Immediately feeling defensive, he argued, "Just scared after so much change. I shouldn't have left her."

"You think you shouldn't have gone to work?"

"If necessary."

"There was no reason to expect—"

"There was all the reason in the world." Heart heavy, he asked, "Where is she? I need to wake her up for dinner. If she sleeps too much now, there'll be no chance of her sleeping tonight."

His mother wasn't happy to admit as much, but she directed him to the small downstairs bedroom used only on occasion for a sick child or for a visitor.

For a panicky moment he didn't see her. Then his eye settled on a lump halfway down the bed. It was no bigger than a pillow. Either *Mamm* had pulled the covers over Abby, or she'd crawled under them herself. He hoped she was able to breathe.

Thankful that none of his family had followed him, he sat on the side of the bed and laid a hand on the bump, gently bouncing the child.

"Abby, it's your father. I'm sorry I left this morning without telling you where I was going or when I'd be back. I will never do that again."

She had gone very still at his touch.

"Time to come out," he said softly. "We'll eat dinner here with my family and then go home." He peeled back the covers, saddened anew to see her lying facedown, her knees drawn up under her, her elbows pressed to her sides, as if she were enclosed in an egg. Again he rubbed her back. "You must be hungry. I know I am."

When she didn't move, he thought of what Julia had said. *Patience.* So he waited. At last Abby slowly uncoiled and sat up. The sheer misery and desperation in her eyes hurt more than any harsh words could have.

"I'm sorry." He held out his arm. "Come here."

Still wary, she did crawl inside the circle formed by his arm. Hugging her with care, he said, "I'm sorry you had such a bad day. Would you like to see Julia tomorrow?"

Her head lifted. Yes, that was hope to replace the terrible unhappiness. He truly didn't think Julia would mind. Was it such a bad thing to do, just for a day or two? Or until the end of the week? By then he wanted to believe Abby would have become more accustomed to this new life.

He carried her to the kitchen, keeping her on his lap when he sat down. Once the rest of the family was seated, he bowed his head and held her hands together between his own as he prayed in earnest.

O Lord God, heavenly Father, bless us and these Thy gifts, which we accept from Thy tender goodness. Give us food and drink also for our souls until life eternal, that we may share at Thy heavenly table, through Jesus Christ.

Please. Teach me how to help this little girl.

Amen.

* * *

JULIA SLEPT POORLY that night, waking several times to the sound of a crying child. Once awake, no matter how hard she strained, she didn't hear so much as a peep to suggest she had a new neighbor with a young child in the apartment building. In fact, so far as she knew, she didn't yet have a neighbor above or below her unit, and she'd barely met the man renting the apartment beside hers. If he had any children, they lived with an ex-wife and had yet to visit.

For the first time, she was late to work. Turning into the alley, she saw a buggy, but didn't know Eli's from Luke's. Their horses, though, she did know. As she parked to one side of the shed, it was a black horse that poked his head out to identify her. Charlie, Luke's gelding. Had the two men come together, as they sometimes did?

Probably, she thought, depressed. Luke would have to drop his daughter at his parents' house every day before coming to work, then return there to pick her up. It wouldn't make any sense for them to drive separately and make both horses spend a hot day penned in such close quarters.

After locking her car, she stopped to pet Charlie's sleek, still sweat-damp neck. He blew out a breath, his lips vibrating, and she laughed.

"Hold on." He waited as she dug in her brown paper lunch bag and produced two carrot sticks. Having seen Luke give his horse treats, Julia gingerly held out the first carrot stick on her palm. He lipped it off her hand so carefully, all she felt was the tickle of whiskers.

Chuckling, she gave him the second carrot stick, patted him again, and let herself into the workroom.

It was empty. Surprised, she hurried toward the front. Wouldn't you know, the one day she was late, someone must have needed help, requiring Luke or Eli to do *her* job.

Pushing through the door, she saw Luke immediately. Abby rode on his hip. Head bent toward her, he was talking softly. As Julia came to a stop, watching, he leaned over, took Abby's tiny hand, and stroked it over the satiny finish on top of a maple wood dresser. When he let go, Abby tentatively touched the wood again and then stroked it like her daddy had.

Julia must have made a sound, because Luke turned. Two sets of blue eyes examined her. Even though her own eyes burned, she smiled.

"Luke! Abby, I'm so glad to see you."

The little girl squirmed. When Luke crouched to set her on her feet, she ran to Julia, who went down on her knees to wrap her in her arms.

"Oh, sweetheart! Oh, my. Look at your hair."

Rising to his feet, Luke grimaced. "It has knots. I think she hasn't let anyone brush it in a long time. We didn't get very far with it."

"Oh, dear." She smiled at Abby. "I bet it hurts, doesn't it?"

The blond head bobbed. A rush of pleasure filled Julia at a response as clear as words.

"Will you let me try? I have a brush in my purse. Or," she teased, "I'll bet your daddy could let us borrow the comb he uses for Charlie's mane and tail."

A tiny quiver of her lips betrayed the mute girl's amusement.

Julia looked up to see an aching kind of hope in Luke's eyes as they rested on his daughter. Then they met hers and he took a deep breath.

"I shouldn't even ask you, but I'm going to anyway. Abby wasn't happy yesterday, with—" He didn't want to say. "I pushed for too much, too fast. I can tell she likes you. If you could watch her today and maybe tomorrow . . ."

"Of course I will." She, too, stood, the child's small hand captured in her own. "I would love to have Abby help me today. We'll have fun, won't we, sweetheart? And I bet your daddy wants to have lunch with you, doesn't he?"

"I do." Expression suddenly rueful, he said, "I'll have to

buy our lunch at the café, but Miriam is bound to show up with cookies again sometime this morning."

"She's working?"

"Yes, but she got home before me yesterday and met Abby."

Julia tipped her head. "Why doesn't she work for you here?"

"She did a few years back, when Elam was helping *Daad*. The store wasn't so busy, and I think she was bored." His mouth quirked. "Elam lived to annoy her, she says. And she loves to quilt, and to work with other women who feel the same."

"I understand." Julia smiled. "I applied there first, you know."

Luke laughed, the skin beside his eyes crinkling in the way that gave her such a funny feeling in her belly. But then, as his smile faded, he said something that touched her even more deeply. "*Daad* and I got lucky." His voice grew husky. "Thank you for coming here next."

"I'm . . . glad I did." The idea, she suddenly knew, of never having met Luke, or of seeing him only in passing, a tall, handsome Amishman who momentarily caught her eye, seemed unbearable.

Oh, she was in such trouble.

LUKE HADN'T EVEN gotten started when his father let himself in the back.

"Was it a good idea to bring Abby with you today?" Eli asked. "You disappointed your mother."

Luke seriously doubted that. His mother would have gladly taken on the care of his daughter again, because that's what a *grossmammi* did, but she'd been shaken yesterday to be rejected so completely, and to have to see Abby withdraw.

"I couldn't put her through another day like that," he

told his father. "She'll get to know *Mamm* and you and the rest of the family, and then it will be different. But she took to Julia right away. This morning, she ran to her as soon as Julia came in."

"What if she gets busy?"

"Then she can always call for help."

"She's not one of us."

"No, she's not, but she's a kind, devout woman who is good with Abby. Abby was raised *Englisch* and does not speak our language. You saw what happened when I forced too much change on her."

His *daad* didn't like it, but finally nodded.

"Come, let's see how they're doing," Luke suggested.

Upon opening the door, the first thing he heard was "What pretty hair you have!"

Pretty was not how he'd describe the tangled mess.

His father raised his eyebrows just a little. He must be thinking the same.

"Oops!" Julia exclaimed, a smile in her voice. "I pulled too hard. Now it's your turn."

Your turn?

Sitting on the counter with her lower legs dangling, Abby reached out and gave a lock of Julia's hair a tug. They both laughed. So—they had made a bargain.

And Abby laughing! What a wonder that was!

As Luke and his *daad* watched, unnoticed, Julia gently worked at a mat near the ends of Abby's long hair. To Luke's astonishment, most of her hair already lay smooth, wavy instead of lumpy.

"Pigtails," Julia mused aloud. "I think that's what we'll do with your hair. Have you ever worn it that way?"

Abby's thin shoulders lifted in a shrug.

"I'll bet your dad knows how to braid hair. Or we can teach him. What do you think?"

Abby's head bobbed.

She *wanted* him to do her hair? The squeeze of happiness

in Luke's chest took him by surprise. He would have told anyone he was happy, once he had confessed his sins before the members of his church and received unhesitating forgiveness. Now he knew: contentment was not quite the same thing.

Thank you, Lord.

Eli touched his arm. The two men silently withdrew.

Once they were closeted in the workroom, Luke's father said, "That is not the same little girl I saw yesterday."

"No."

"Bishop Amos will not like it," his *daad* said thoughtfully, "but this was best for Abby. Wean her away from Julia, we must do, as soon as possible."

"But not too quickly," Luke agreed, because his father was right. *Do not be unequally yoked together with unbelievers,* he reminded himself, even as he felt a flicker of rebellion he knew to be wrong.

Chapter Ten

❖❖❖

JULIA FOUND PURE joy in a day spent entertaining Abby while also managing the phones and talking to the tourists who wandered into the store, all of whom beamed at the cute little girl. Julia had once considered becoming a teacher, but hadn't finished the coursework. Now, she wondered if she could go back to school, perhaps even online, and finish the requirements. But she also feared that this craving wasn't to spend time with any child, but specifically Abby.

At the end of the day when Luke came in to get Abby, he smiled first at his daughter and then at Julia. "You two look as if you had a good day."

"We did."

The pigtails had come and gone. Abby's hair was now in an elaborate French braid that wrapped her head before releasing a side ponytail. When Julia took her to the bathroom and lifted her so she could see in the mirror, Abby glowed with delight.

Watching as Luke studied his daughter, Julia remembered how the Amish felt about anything they regarded as "fancy" and knew she shouldn't have introduced Abby to a hairstyle that definitely qualified as such.

"I'm sorry," she murmured. "I didn't think."

His blue eyes met hers. "Right now, if she had fun, that's what matters. I'll explain to my parents."

She nodded. A lump in her throat, she asked, "Will you leave her with your mother tomorrow?"

"No. She's happy. Do you know what a gift that is?"

All Julia could do was nod again. Yes, she of all people marveled at true happiness. *I want to steal his child,* she thought in shame, but . . . he had been part of what made the day special. Every hour or so, he'd come out front to see what they were doing, and he'd insisted on bringing lunch for all of them, eating with them. Julia saw how much progress Luke and Abby had made; he spoke naturally to her, and she responded readily, albeit still without words. And now, she took his hand without any sign of fear.

"If you don't mind . . ." he added.

"Of course I don't."

"Then we'll see you in the morning. Right, little one?"

Abby broke away from him to rush to Julia for a last hug, which she reciprocated fervently. *Don't cry, don't cry.* Not until they were gone. She was able to hold back her tears since Luke waited while she locked the front door and got her purse. The three walked out together. Eli, she was relieved to discover, had already left.

She itched to ask whether his father disapproved of having her care for his new granddaughter, but couldn't in front of Abby. She knew it really wasn't her business, anyway. In fact, did she even need to ask? Of course Eli wouldn't be happy to depend on an *Englischer,* the kind of woman who would unthinkingly encourage his granddaughter to think of herself as pretty. The Amish had chosen to be of the world, but separate. She wasn't one of them.

Luke held Abby so that she could pet Charlie's sleek cheek and giggle when he blew bubbles from his lips.

"I gave him carrot sticks this morning," Julia said. "I think he likes them better than Abby does."

Abby wrinkled her nose, and both adults laughed.

Julia held her while he harnessed the gelding and was ready to place her on the seat. Then Julia backed away, digging in her purse for her keys.

"Well, goodbye. I'll see you tomorrow." She waved even as she wondered what Luke was thinking as he stood watching her in turn while she hurried the few feet down the alley to her car. But by the time she started it, the buggy had reached the end of the alley and was turning to circle the block and go north out of town.

Hoping the air-conditioning would kick in soon, Julia took out her phone and called her brother.

"Will you be home if I come over and make dinner?" she asked.

A smile in his voice, he said, "You think I'm stupid enough to say no?"

His obvious pleasure lifted her spirits as she headed for the grocery store to pick up some ingredients for a favorite casserole.

THE MOMENT HIS mother set eyes on Abby's hairstyle, she said, "How did *that* happen? Let me take her hair down, now." *Schnell*, was what she said. Fast.

As *Mamm* advanced on his daughter, she scuttled behind him.

"Won't you like having your hair brushed?" *Mamm* coaxed, circling him.

Abby shook her head vehemently, gripping his trousers in both hands. He found himself rotating to stay between her and his mother. Out of the corner of his eye, he saw Miriam working at the kitchen counter. She'd turned to watch.

"*Mamm*, let it go," he said.

"She must learn to be Amish. You know that. In fact, I

need to measure her so I can make her first dresses. She can't keep going around like this." Her forehead puckered. "I can ask Rose if she has any the right size packed away."

"She has her own family."

Her mouth tightened, but she understood what he meant. Amishmen pretended not to notice when a woman was pregnant, but his sister definitely was. The new baby could be a girl.

Frustrated that his usually warmhearted mother thought Abby could be fixed instantly, turned into a proper Amish girl overnight, he said firmly, "There's no hurry. We must take slow steps."

Miriam opened her mouth but closed it without saying a word when their father laid his hand on his wife's arm. Startled, she turned her head and saw his slight headshake, then sighed and said, "*Ja, ja.* But I can start sewing, can't I?"

"Tomorrow, I'll bring one of Abby's dresses. You can use that for her size." Did she have one? So far, she had picked out her own clothes, pink leggings and one of a couple of faded T-shirts festooned with glitter that was falling off.

Just to improve the evening, a knock on the back door announced the arrival of a visitor. Luke couldn't help noticing that his mother didn't look surprised. When she let in none other than Bishop Amos Troyer, he knew why she'd wanted to transform Abby instantly.

Greeting the family, the bishop studied the little girl hiding behind her *daadi.*

His bushy, graying eyebrows rose.

Luke braced himself. "Bishop Amos."

Force of personality made Amos more imposing than he was physically. In fact, he stood maybe five foot eight inches and was thin. His hair was still mostly brown, but, like his eyebrows, his long wiry beard was well threaded with steel gray. Luke had seen him stern more than a few times, but he was loved by his church members for his kindness as well as his wisdom.

"Ach," he said mildly, "so this is the child I've heard so much about."

Now, *that* was pointed. Luke hoped his wince wasn't visible. He really should have made time to stop to talk to the bishop.

"This is my Abby," he agreed, hearing pride in his voice. "She's a sweet girl, isn't that so, *Daad*?"

"She is," his father said with a smile. "Come, sit down, Amos! Deborah, he'll surely want a cup of coffee."

She beamed. "Can you stay for dinner? It won't be half an hour."

"No, no, Nancy will be expecting me. I shouldn't stay long."

"A slice of peach pie, then. I'll send you home with a pie."

"How can I refuse?" He moved to take a chair at one side of the table. "Luke, sit with me, will you?"

Luke nodded and bent to pick up Abby, resting her on his hip. He sat across the table from the bishop, settling her on his lap, enclosed in his arms with her face buried against his chest.

"Abby, I'd like you to meet Amos Troyer. He has at least one granddaughter your age who I bet will be a good friend for you."

She stiffened.

With a soundless sigh, he lifted his head. "Too much has changed for Abby. She's still shy."

"*Ja*, so I see." He softened his voice. "I'm glad to meet you, Abby. Your *daadi* is right, I have a granddaughter named Leah who is three years old. She'd like to have a friend like you."

No response, but Luke hadn't expected one.

"She's getting used to us," he explained. "I don't want to hurry her." He prayed that the bishop wouldn't hear a challenge in that.

Amos smiled his thanks to Luke's mother, who set a cup of coffee and a slice of pie in front of him. Eli took a seat as well, accepting coffee but shook his head at the offer of pie, as did Luke. They could both smell the sourdough biscuits in the oven and the hot potato salad. Behind him, Luke heard the sizzle as his mother put chicken into a cast-iron skillet to fry. On her way to the cellar, Miriam gave him a wink once she was far enough past the bishop to be sure he wouldn't see her.

Miriam understood, he knew. She had stopped by today, both to bring cookies and to visit with Abby and Julia. Luke had cracked the door once and heard her quizzing Julia on Pennsylvania Dutch vocabulary. He wasn't sure why Julia was so determined to learn his language, but he liked the idea.

After eating a few bites, Amos said, "We need to talk another time, I think." When Abby wasn't listening, he meant. "Sunday after worship?"

Luke nodded.

"Sarah will be glad for Leah to find a new friend." Sarah was Amos's daughter.

Sunday would be ideal, Luke thought; he and the bishop could walk away from the others for a talk, but if Abby panicked, he'd be nearby.

"That will be good," Luke agreed. Truthfully, he dreaded having to get Abby through a three-hour worship service, of which she wouldn't understand a word, or the need to sit still and attentive. Had her mother even talked to her about their heavenly Father? Perhaps three was too young to expect much. Well, they had to start, so why not this week? Sarah would be a good one to advise him, without the friction he sometimes had with his own married sister, it occurred to him.

Once the bishop had departed and only family sat down to eat dinner, Abby gradually relaxed enough to nibble at her own serving. When Miriam spoke to her, she even peeked at her and once shook her head.

Good, Luke told himself in relief. First Miriam, then *Mamm.* It wouldn't be that long before he could leave Abby with family while he worked.

But not yet.

That acknowledgment brought a different kind of relief. Only because Julia had such a way with Abby, as if they had always known each other.

He didn't look forward to separating them permanently.

AFTER HE WAS certain Abby slept, Luke took the envelope from the drawer where he had hidden it and sat down at his kitchen table. His reluctance to read Beth's last words to him hadn't lessened, and he scarcely knew why. This was important; he shouldn't have put it off. Perhaps he feared a surprise, like the names and address of her parents or a sister or brother she'd prefer to raise her little girl. No—he knew better. If she'd trusted any family member, she wouldn't have put his name on the birth certificate. What he truly feared was that reading the final words she had to say to him would be a sharp reminder that she really was dead—and he hadn't done all he could to help her.

He did believe that she was now with God, perhaps even watching over Abby, and yet he felt the tragedy of her life. The gentle, sweet young woman he'd known had deserved to find happiness in this life, too.

He bowed his head and prayed.

And those who know Your name will put their trust in You; for You, Lord, have not forsaken those who seek You.

The hard part was accepting that he would never know God's purpose, that his trust must be blind.

"Help me quiet my anger, these doubts," he murmured.

He turned to a passage from Psalms that had spoken powerfully to him when he realized his dissatisfaction with the outside world, seeing that, for him, the greed and unrelenting ambition, the need to rush through life without appreciating any single moment, the desire to take that was more common than the wish to give, all outweighed the satisfaction he had gained from using his talent for understanding numbers and patterns.

Aloud but softly, so as not to awaken Abby, he said, *"As for me, I will call upon God, and the Lord shall save me. Evening and morning and at noon I will pray, and cry aloud, and He shall hear my voice. He has redeemed my soul in peace from the battle that was against me. What had He to fear, with the Lord His light and salvation?"*

Luke tore open the envelope and slowly read the childishly printed letter.

Dear Luke,

I'm real sick, but today is good so I'm writing this. I feel as if death is tapping me on the shoulder. I'd like to think God is summoning me, although He'll have stern things to say, for sure. I deserve them all. Don't feel sad for me. You almost convinced me that God's forgiveness is absolute and I don't have to be afraid.

I know you understand why I never told you about Abby. I wish so much I had. I should have looked for you sooner. I hope so much this letter finds you, although I fear only He can accomplish that. If He does . . . I'm begging you to keep Abby with you and be the daddy she needs so much. Raise her the way you were raised—with love and laughter and faith. If you've married, I pray your wife is willing and will love Abby as much as she deserves. I have no doubt at all that you will.

I love her, I do, but I look at her and know how I've failed her. You're not a man who would ever fail anyone who depends on you. I wish I could have trusted myself to you.

With what faith I have left,
Beth

She'd been more eloquent than he could have imagined.

She'd told him she liked to read, so maybe in her own way Beth had continued her education.

Mostly, the letter wrung his heart and stiffened his resolve. Whatever came, he would live up to her faith in him—as God would offer her both forgiveness and a warm welcome.

HIS FATHER HAD begun looking askance at Luke when he took breaks every couple of hours to check on Abby. Luke understood why but felt resentment anyway.

Dismayed by the emotion, he realized anew that he hadn't won the battle between his deep faith and the fierce need for independence that had driven him away from his church and community all those years ago. He'd genuinely believed he had returned home a humble man, accepting that the path his life took was God's will. From time to time, he worried that he took too much pride in his craftsmanship and in the finished furniture. *Hochmut*—pride—was not a quality the Amish admired. It helped that he considered the pieces his father had made as well as the products of several other area furniture makers equal to his own work. Taking pleasure from a job well done couldn't be wrong, he had mostly convinced himself.

But Abby's arrival had triggered something in him. Surrendering himself to God's will as interpreted by the bishop was one thing; giving up his right to make decisions for this troubled girl was another.

His child in the ways that counted.

He knew his father and Bishop Amos would call his belief that he knew best *hochmut*. They were right, he had no doubt. And yet . . .

The sound of the saw his father was using drowned out his groan.

Driven by the same need to be sure his *dochder* was safe and well that had plagued him since he'd accepted responsibility for her, he set down the chisel that he'd been using and pushed through the door into the front of his store without looking back at his father.

The quiet had him frowning. Abby usually napped right after lunch, not close to the end of the day. When he came in sight of the office, he found Julia on the computer. She had assumed responsibility not only for bookkeeping but for taking photographs of furniture and uploading them to their website. Business had taken a distinct uptick since, now that the site was truly current.

He must have made a sound, because her head turned. Smiling, she lifted her finger to her lips. Luke stepped close enough to see Abby sound asleep, curled on a nest of quilts beneath the counter. He went to her and crouched, studying in astonishment every line of her face, the perfection of her tiny fingers, the delicate knobs of vertebrae on the back of her neck.

God was truly wonderful, he couldn't help thinking.

He swiveled on his heels to see that Julia, too, watched Abby, her expression betraying everything he felt and more. It was the *more* that worried him. He didn't like the sadness and even grief mixed with her pleasure and, yes, astonishment like his.

Standing, he gestured toward the showroom. Although clearly startled, Julia rose to her feet and followed him. In one corner, several rocking chairs were arranged around a coffee table crafted of cherry with inlaid walnut. As she sat, she stroked the wide arms of the rocker she'd chosen, then gave a wriggle.

"It's shaped perfectly," she said quietly.

He had worked very hard to ensure it was as comfortable as he could make it. Walnut was a hard wood that didn't readily yield to planes and sandpaper.

"For you," he agreed. "Not for everyone."

She looked thoughtful. "I guess you're right. We do come in all sizes and shapes."

Luke smiled. "We do."

The seat of the chair he'd chosen fit him well. He rocked a few times before saying, "She didn't nap earlier?"

"No, she was antsy. I wouldn't have let her nap twice, knowing you'd never get her to sleep tonight if I did."

"I wasn't criticizing," he said mildly.

Julia's gaze slid from his and she nodded. After a minute, she asked, "Is she getting used to your mother and sister?"

"Yeah, some. Miriam more than *Mamm*, who still alarms her, I think."

"I wonder . . ." Julia hesitated. "Does Abby look like her mother? If so, Miriam may remind her of her mother."

Which flew in the face of the truth that Abby had chosen instantly to trust a thin woman with brown eyes and a mass of deep auburn hair, Luke couldn't help thinking.

"Beth—Elizabeth—was blond and blue-eyed," he agreed. "Petite, too, but you may have noticed that most Amishwomen aren't tall."

"The men, either, although you're the exception. Well, Elam, too."

"My grandfather on *Mamm*'s side was a big man. We took after him."

It felt odd to be talking to her like this, but he understood her curiosity. Because of the quilt frolic and the help his family gave her to move, she wasn't entirely on the outskirts of their lives the way their *Englisch* clients were.

"Will you tell me a little about Abby's mother?" she asked, sounding timid.

How could it hurt? Thanks to her presence when the social worker showed up, Julia already knew more even than his parents did about Abby's sad upbringing. With them, he had skimmed over Beth's drug use.

Luke started talking, telling Julia about the equally sad young woman he'd met, the one so desperate for love, to belong, she'd let herself be abused.

"I wondered if she was using drugs," he said finally, "but I didn't know for sure."

"You think she was raised Amish, too?"

Like him. He nodded. "I know so. She still had an accent."

"Did you . . . love her?" Then Julia's cheeks flushed. "I'm sorry. That's none of my business. It's just . . ."

"Just?"

"You accepted Abby with such joy."

"Shock and fear are closer to the truth," he said ruefully. "And no, I pitied Beth more than anything. I wanted to help her, but she wouldn't accept anything but an occasional meal or a few dollars."

Julia's forehead, usually smooth, crinkled, and he realized how intently she was watching him. The shyness she felt around him was in abeyance, perhaps because of her need to help Abby. He had no trouble guessing what Julia was thinking.

If you didn't love her, if she wouldn't accept anything meaningful from you, how is it that you shared her bed? And, *How could you never have suspected she was carrying your child?*

Or worse, she shared Melissa Tanner's suspicion that he'd chosen to walk away from his child.

In that moment, he felt the weight of the lie, something that had seemed an easy decision but would be with him for a lifetime. Telling somebody, anybody at all, might ease that weight.

He trusted this woman.

Compelled by other forces he couldn't acknowledge, he said, "She's not my daughter."

Julia stared, her eyes shimmering with gold. "What?" she said faintly.

"I didn't have that kind of relationship with Beth. Even if I'd been tempted, she was so vulnerable, I would never have taken advantage of her."

"But then—"

"I haven't told my family," he said with sudden urgency. "Please keep this to yourself. I want them all to accept her as my child."

"But . . ."

"I was afraid the bishop would insist we search for Beth's family. She had to be desperate to put my name on the birth certificate. I think she was terrified of them."

"Because she was abused."

"That's what I believe. She wouldn't talk about them. Even in the letter she left for me, she didn't say anything about her family. But how else was it that she considered a life on the streets as better than what she'd run from? And she was so hungry to be loved. There was one man after another."

"If she was abused, that might explain why," she said, almost inaudibly.

He shook his head. "I don't understand that."

Her hands had left the smooth arms of the rocker to writhe together on her lap. He'd seen that darkness in her eyes before, too.

"I've . . . read about it. For rape victims, it's different. I mean, ones who survived a single attack."

He nodded, battling his need to stand and pull her to her feet, too. To grasp her arms and demand to know what happened to her. He'd lose this oddly intimate, painful moment if he did that, though. She was still wary of him, and she knew as well as he did that touching her was forbidden to him. Nor was she likely to welcome his hands on her, not given the fear he'd seen in her eyes.

"But from what I've heard, people who have been sexually abused as children often react the way you described," she continued. "As if they think their bodies are the only thing of value they have to give."

He let his head fall back. To think of Beth suffering like that . . . Why hadn't he done more for her?

When he first knew Beth, he'd had very little to offer, he reminded himself. That wasn't an excuse, but truth. Leaving the Amish, going into the world with only an eighth-grade education, wasn't easy. He'd been scraping his way toward a college degree by then, living in a small rented room, eating some meals at the mission. He'd given what he could. And yet . . .

And yet.

"Are you ever going to tell Abby?" Julia asked after a minute.

He hadn't thought that far ahead. His throat felt tight. "I don't know."

Riveted by the compassion on her face, it took him a moment to notice that her hand lay on his forearm. That she'd given a gentle squeeze to comfort him.

This, from a woman who was always sure to keep ample space between them. A woman who had certainly been afraid of him, and probably still was.

Her gaze followed his to where her slim, long-fingered hand rested on his muscular, much darker arm. Shock transformed her expression.

Chapter Eleven

JULIA SNATCHED BACK her hand. What had she been *thinking*? To touch any man so carelessly, and this one in particular?

"I'm sorry," she mumbled.

With small creases between his eyebrows, he looked perturbed, but he also shook his head. "There is never a reason to apologize for kindness."

"Your father spoke to me—"

"Did he?" Luke sounded annoyed.

"Just . . . just making sure I knew that, being unmarried, you had to be . . . circumspect around me. He didn't mean any harm by it." She did understand, as much as an outsider could, but the warning still stung.

"*Daad* still acts as if he thinks I'm a teenager," he growled.

Wrinkling her nose, she said, "Do parents ever see their children as adults? Anyway, you were away for a lot of years."

Luke gusted out a sigh. "I was. I hurt them. Now—" He broke off.

"Now?" This was probably something else that wasn't

her business, but maybe he had no one else to talk to who might understand without being hurt anew.

"I think they fear I'll stumble and fall. They want the part of me that lived in the world to be obliterated. It's as if I came home covered with tattoos. They see them every time they look at me."

Living under the glare of suspicion, however loving the welcome had been, that would be hard. Frowning, she said, "Those years had to have been part of the path God led you to walk, don't you think?"

Luke's vivid blue eyes held hers. He didn't move, not to so much as breathe, as he stared at her. At last he shook his head, as if trying to rattle his brains. "I . . . never thought of it that way."

Her hand lifted from her lap, as if she needed to touch him again. She subdued it with her left hand.

"If you hadn't left the faith for a while," she pointed out, "you'd never have met Beth. Then what would have happened to Abby?"

"You're saying that her coming to me was God's will."

The lump in her throat almost kept Julia from answering. "Yes."

"I want to believe that." He stared for another unnerving minute before nodding and saying huskily, "Thank you. I needed to be reminded."

"You're welcome." She jumped to her feet. "I should get back to work."

"Me, too." He rose more slowly.

They were still looking at each other when Julia heard the door from the workroom open behind her. In an instant, Luke wiped all expression from his face.

"*Daad,*" he said evenly.

Somehow she summoned a smile for his father. "Come and see Abby. She thinks she's a kitten when she naps."

Eli did follow her once she scuttled behind the counter, leaving the rocker swaying gently back and forth on the display floor. He gazed down at his granddaughter and then smiled. "Or a squirrel."

Julia covered her mouth to quiet her laugh, but sadness came in its wake, as it too often did. "I'd like to hear her voice."

"*Ja,*" Eli agreed. "We all would."

"And we will," Luke said softly. "Sooner if we're patient than if we demand too much."

This time when their eyes met, she understood him to be offering silent thanks for her earlier advice.

Her heart ached as she remembered she'd be lucky to have one more day with Abby. After that . . . she'd revert to being an employee again. An *Englischer*. There'd be no more reason for her and Luke to talk, and she might never hear Abby's voice or laugh.

Swallowing, she said to both men, "I've been thinking. If you have completed furniture stored elsewhere, maybe I should come and take pictures so I can put those up on the website, too. You might sell pieces without ever having to find room here."

Eli blinked a couple of times. "That's smart thinking. We did well hiring Julia, ain't so, Luke?"

His son chuckled, shaking his head. "You mean, *you* did well hiring Julia. Bragging is not in keeping with our faith, or so you've always taught me."

His father's laugh was deep and hearty . . . and woke up Abby, who stared at her grandfather with an expression of wonder.

Pain squeezed Julia's chest even as she thought how lucky this little girl was to have been claimed by such a wonderful family.

JULIA GRABBED HER phone that evening to see her parents' number. Knowing she owed them a call, she answered hastily. "Mom?"

A quiet man, her father wouldn't be the one to make the call unless something terrible were wrong.

"Sweetie, how are you?" her mother asked. "We worry when we don't hear from you. I wish you weren't so far away."

"I know," she said, feeling a pang. "But just think, Nick and I are in the same place if you want to come for a visit."

"We were thinking this might be a good time."

"I . . . actually don't recommend it." A part of Julia reveled in being too far away for her mother to stop by her apartment frequently, always with an upbeat smile and an excuse but her deeper worry and guilt visible. "It's awfully hot. *And* humid. Why don't you wait until early fall?"

"It was eighty-four degrees here today, and humid."

"According to the bank clock, it was ninety-four here," Julia retorted. August was bound to be hotter yet, and from what she'd heard, September would be no better. "And the forecast calls for it to get up to a hundred by Sunday. You know Dad doesn't do well in hot weather."

"That does sound daunting," her mother admitted. "How are *you* surviving?"

"Air-conditioning, what else?" She was a little ashamed that she hadn't spent much time outside these past weeks. This week, Abby was the reason, of course, but she hadn't told her parents that she had been caring for a little girl. "You got the pictures of my apartment."

Her mother had already exclaimed over them via email.

"Yes, but you work for some Amish. Do they use modern improvements like air-conditioning?"

"Not usually." She thought. "Maybe if they can power it by propane. They get a sort of dispensation if the heat might put someone's health at risk. But the shop is cooled, because fine woods have to be kept from drastic temperature changes."

"I didn't know that."

She'd already shared the Bowman & Son's Handcrafted Furniture website so her parents could see some of what she did, and read what made this furniture distinct from what could be bought in any department store.

She heard muffled voices, and then her father came on. "Aren't tornadoes a risk in your area at this time of year?"

"Yes, the farmers especially worry, but the building where I work is really solid, and so is the apartment building." Both were built of brick, not so good in an earthquake, but resistant to high winds, even ones spinning with lethal force. "Have you asked Nick about it?"

"He blows me off," Dad said, clearly disgruntled.

"That's because he's too big and tough to be afraid of anything."

Her father grunted, making her laugh.

After the call ended, though, she remembered the expression on her brother's face when he assured her he hadn't married because there were too many fish in the sea. Julia had no doubt Nick had been hurt, although how and by whom she had no idea. And she hated knowing he'd likely never confide in her, fragile and damaged as she was.

She had a very bad feeling Luke recognized those same qualities in her, and yet . . . today, he *had* confided in her.

Only, she reminded herself, because she was there, available, and not Amish.

Sometimes she thought she should consider looking for another job. Maybe not now—she wouldn't want to let down Eli and Luke—but once tourist season was past and traffic at the store slowed down. Before she suffered another wound, this one stupidly self-inflicted.

Or maybe she should take this unexpected attachment to Abby and use it to motivate herself to pursue another path.

Maybe . . . God had brought Abby into her life for a reason.

It wouldn't hurt to do some research online to find out what it would take for her to earn a teaching certificate, would it?

* * *

CARRYING THE LUNCH his mother had packed with enough for him, his father, Julia, and Abby, Luke had just reached the showroom when the bell over the front door tinkled as Miriam hurried in.

"Oh, good!" She beamed. "I'm in time to eat with you."

"*Ja. Daad* will be right out." He smiled and lifted the bags. Out of the corner of his eye, he saw Julia rise from her chair, Abby on her hip as if that were her natural resting place.

Julia bent her head. "Abby, look who's here. Your *aenti* Miriam. And what do you think she might have with her?"

Abby's face lit. Luke prayed she might cry, *Cookies!* but of course she didn't. She did wriggle to get down and came around the corner on her own.

"Hmm." Miriam pretended to look worried. "Did I remember the cookies?"

Julia laughed.

Something twisted in Luke's chest, as happened too often around this *Englisch* woman. He hadn't yet told her that he intended to start leaving Abby daytimes with his *mamm* next week, but felt sure she'd guessed. Her smiles were still there, but too many of them looked forced.

Julia had fallen in love with his little girl, as much as he had. She'd be a good mother, but he wondered if she'd ever marry. Of course, *Englisch* women had babies in other ways, but raising one alone would be a struggle. Her current salary wasn't high enough to add childcare to other bills, although *Daad* and he had agreed that, on the first of August, they would give her a raise. She had more than earned it—but it still wouldn't be that much money. This was small-town Missouri. Even salaries for teachers, police officers, and medical professionals lagged behind most of the rest of the country. He had speculated more than once about why her brother had moved from a big northern city to Tompkin's Mill.

Soon his father had emerged to join them. He and *Daad* pulled up stools to the counter, while the two women sat on the other side in the desk chairs, Abby on Julia's lap.

Miriam chattered about how successful the sale at the quilt shop had been, and how they were having to order many more bolts of fabric and notions—whatever notions were—than usual to refill their stock.

She turned to look at Julia. "Oh! Your Flying Geese quilt sold this morning. I meant to say that first thing! I have the money for you right here." She produced an envelope from her lunch bag and handed it over. "Ruth says she'll be happy to take any other quilts you want to sell on commission."

"That's good news." Looking quietly pleased, Julia opened a drawer where she kept her handbag and dropped the envelope in. "I do have others I can bring. I thought she might have a harder time selling mine, since most people who come in are probably looking for Amish quilts."

"But your work is beautiful. Anyway, sometimes people don't even ask about the maker."

Her brow creased. "I wouldn't want them misled."

Daad nodded his approval of her integrity.

"Oh, Ruth would never do that. But you know we sell quilts from several other non-Amish quilt makers. It's never been a problem."

"Okay." This smile seemed to be a shadow of its usual self. "Tell Ruth how much I appreciate her giving me the opportunity. I love to quilt, but I think my parents or brother would run the other way if I tried to give them another one."

They all laughed.

Clearly listening, Abby ate in her tidy, birdlike way. Luke wanted to see her appetite grow, but perhaps she was meant to stay tiny. He liked the way Julia encouraged her with smiles and touches even as she seemed engaged in the conversation.

By the time he and his father returned to work, leaving the two women talking—actually, practicing *Deitsh*—he regretted that he hadn't been able to have lunch just with Julia and Abby.

Next week, he'd have no excuse to take breaks out front with Julia. By then, he'd have heard what Bishop Amos had to say, from disappointment in Luke for having allowed his own child to grow up in deplorable circumstances to his duty now to raise her within the faith—and without leaning on an *Englisch* woman, however well-meaning.

His father quit work, tidied his space, and swept, finishing a good ten minutes early. Since they had arrived separately today, he nodded at Luke and said, "I'll see you in the morning, *ja*? Lucky we are to worship in the Klines' barn, where it will be cool."

Ninety degrees instead of ninety-eight, maybe, but Luke agreed.

His father's last glance held a clear message, but also kindness. *Daad* had to have guessed how much Julia would miss Abby.

Luke found himself moving slower and slower as he, too, cleaned up, making sure no sawdust lurked on the table saw or floor, that each and every tool was in the place designed to hold it. Finally, he could delay no longer.

He slid his thumbs beneath his suspenders, smoothing out wrinkles in his shirt, before heading out front to fetch Abby. The sign on the front door was already turned to Closed. Julia was waiting, hand in hand with his *dochder*. As though nothing at all was wrong, she handed him a bag that he could tell, from the odd bumps, held all of Abby's toys.

"Her change of clothes is in here, too," she assured him.

"Thank you." He took the bag. "Walk out with us?"

"Sure." As he'd done a minute ago, she glanced around as if to be sure she hadn't left anything undone, or out when it shouldn't be. Then she grabbed her purse and, still holding Abby's hand, came out from behind the counter.

Outside, she waited while he locked the back door. They might as well have stepped into an oven. It had to be around a hundred degrees, unless it was his mood making the heat more oppressive. Charlie stood hipshot, barely flicking his ears at their appearance.

Julia followed Luke to the buggy, watching as he set the bag inside on the floor. Then she lifted Abby into her arms and held her tight, cheek pressed to the top of her head, as he harnessed his gelding, taking unnecessary time to check the fit of the collar and slide his fingers beneath the breast strap to smooth the lie of Charlie's coat, before he backed him into place.

When he turned to take Abby, he saw the tears that streaked Julia's cheeks. He hesitated, heard her choked whisper.

"Goodbye, little one."

Clenching his teeth, he reached for his daughter. Julia surrendered her while averting her face. By the time Abby latched onto him, Julia was hurrying away.

Even as he stood there, she leapt into her car, started the engine and drove down the alley. If she so much as glanced in the rearview mirror, he didn't see it.

A burn at the back of his eyes told him how deeply he had wounded her. He wanted to think unwittingly, but knew better. He'd always seen the hurt she carried behind outward confidence and bright smiles. He'd known, *known*, that from the first moment, Abby had touched her heart. And still, he'd taken advantage of her.

For Abby, a terrified, equally damaged child.

How could he have made any other choice?

Chapter Twelve

❖◆❖

"THIS *DOCHDER* COULD serve as a link to your past away from our faith," the bishop observed. "Might she remind you often of those times, people you knew? Even if she doesn't pull you away from the *Leit* in the flesh, she might turn your heart away."

He and Luke strolled in a circle around the vegetable garden at the Kline home. The garden was undoubtedly watered daily, but the corn in an adjoining field looked drier than it should, Luke noted with a small part of his attention. After a dry late spring and early summer, the leaves on apple, plum, and peach trees hung limp.

A rabbit hopped behind the tomato plants. A rabbit lucky that Katie-Ann hadn't see it. She might be chasing it with her shovel already.

High above, the distinctive shape of a chimney swift soared.

Luke was taking care to allow himself a moment before he answered. He must fight any hint of temper or even defensiveness. Bishop Amos was a wise man, chosen over twenty years ago to guide his brethren to faith in the Lord and His teachings.

"No," Luke said at last, calmly. "Abby's mother is dead. She would have been the only tie that meant anything. In making sure that social worker found me, she made her wishes clear. Despite whatever drove her away from her own family and church, she asked that I raise our daughter to walk with God. She spoke of the faith that I had been raised with. I believe she'd be glad to know that Abby has the same chance to rejoice in the fellowship among us."

Clasping his hands behind him, Amos nodded. "You relieve my mind, Luke. I believe you came home humbled, genuinely changed from the headstrong boy I remember. It's a blessing indeed that this child was brought to you, and now, when you're ready for her."

"I think so, too," he agreed. "Although jumping into being a father like this is a little like discovering the pond is so deep, I don't know if I can make it to the surface or ever breathe again."

Amos chuckled. "Every new father feels that way. You must trust in God to guide you. This may be the Lord's way of hinting that you find a helpmeet."

"I have that in mind," he said simply.

"I'm told you've been taking Abigail with you to work each day."

Having expected this, Luke said, "Just for this week. I tried leaving her with *Mamm* on Wednesday, but she was so frightened she squeezed behind the toilet and shook all over. I knew that she liked and trusted Julia, who is *Daad*'s and my employee. She was kind enough to watch over Abby."

Bishop Amos said nothing, which drove Luke to continue. "I've been eating dinner with my parents every night to give Abby a chance to get to know *Mamm* and Miriam, especially. Miriam has stopped by at the store daily, too, bringing cookies. Abby has gotten so she's really happy to see her."

Another laugh. "I confess to searching for your sister's cookies at our fellowship meals. They are very fine."

Luke smiled. "They are."

"Abby speaks no *Deitsh*?"

"She doesn't speak at all."

Amos shook his head. "*Ja*, I had not forgotten. I misspoke."

Luke answered the real question. "It seems clear she doesn't understand our language. Her mother must not have used it with her, even though *Deitsh* was Beth's first language. That doesn't help, of course."

His gaze on a bluebird perched on the gnarly limb of an old apple tree, watching them with head tilted, Amos was quiet for a moment. "But why so frightened?"

"I don't know. I don't know why she won't speak, either. It's not just speech—she doesn't laugh aloud, or cry out if she's afraid or falls and skins a knee." Troubled, Luke continued, "Julia suggested that the clothing our women wear might have scared a girl used to *Englisch* garments. But now she is becoming accustomed to *Mamm*, so it's my intention to have her watch over Abby starting Tuesday. I think *Mamm* is eager to get to know her new granddaughter better."

"That seems like the wise course," Amos agreed, his keen gaze turned now to Luke.

"It was always my intention."

"Deborah says Abby refused to wear the new dress."

Luke grimaced. "So far, Abby refuses to wear anything but what she picks out in the morning. If she puts her shoes on the wrong feet, she throws a silent fit if I try to take them off and put them back on. I have trouble standing up to her tears. We have a ways to go."

"Your *mamm* is a good one to guide her."

Luke heard what wasn't said: *You must not let an* Englisch *woman influence your child.*

One who had transformed Abby with the fancy hairdo that had so offended *Mamm* and probably Bishop Amos.

And yet, Julia's advice to him could have been given by his mother, or even Amos himself. No, she didn't speak their language and worshipped at a different church, but she had been everything good to a vulnerable child. After his own experiences, Luke agreed that the decision his people had made to live separate lives was wise. How better to keep God first and families close without all that would tear them apart in the outside world?

It wasn't as if the Amish were blind to what was happening around them. How could they be, when the challenge to keep families intact became greater and greater? Their young now experimented with modern music, mobile phones, electronic games, and alcohol during the *rumspringa* time they were all permitted. These days, more of those kids made the decision Luke had, to leave the plain ways for more education or an indefinable something they saw as greater—but most still chose to be baptized and stay within a faith and community that offered a rich if simpler life, one that followed their Lord's admonitions.

Luke felt in accord with the bishop as they returned to the gathering, but no more settled in his mind about the woman he would see again Tuesday morning.

JULIA SLID INTO the pew, sandwiched between Nick's solid bulk and a hefty fellow she knew to be a plumbing contractor. He nodded pleasantly at her, as did his wife when she looked to see who'd joined them. Nick greeted them by name, no surprise; he seemed to know everyone in town.

Light fell through stained glass windows to each side of the altar in this beautiful old church. When a few minutes later the doors were closed and the minister stepped behind the lectern, she reached for hope. Today, she needed the comfort of the service. She wanted to feel God's presence so she could let go of this painful, unreasonable sense of loss.

Five minutes later, she glanced sidelong at her neighbor, who seemed unable to sit still. He arched his back, rolled his shoulders, and gazed at the pastor only briefly between studying his feet or scanning the congregation. His wife wasn't much better; a minute ago, she'd reached for her purse and was rooting inside it. Paper rustled. Was she secretly checking her phone?

Although, honestly, Julia's attention wandered, too. The sermon concerned the parable of the Pharisee and the tax collector. It might be aimed at those who felt smug only because they went to church every Sunday and tithed, yet didn't live their faith. Was it too pointed for the contractor and his wife? Or were they paying attention at all?

The pews were half-empty. All she had to do was turn her head to see several people checking their smartphones, texting, or, who knows, maybe playing a computer game.

The church she'd attended in Cleveland had some of the same problems. Attendance had been falling for years. Churches were being shuttered across the country, grand buildings torn down to be replaced by condominiums. People gave lip service to being Christian but didn't live their faith in the way she tried to do. In fact, dearly though she loved her brother, she could feel his restlessness like electricity in the air even when he didn't so much as twitch a muscle.

Her dissatisfaction had strengthened since moving to Tompkin's Mill, maybe because of the time she was spending with the Amish. Their devotion to God was a living thing, central to every decision they made, expressed without apology. She admired that, felt more in common with them in that respect than she did with the members of this church.

Besides, she couldn't imagine someone new arriving to join a local Amish church district not being welcomed wholeheartedly. Hardly anyone here had even expressed curiosity about her, far less invited her to join a committee or to help with a volunteer project. The few young women who had come up to talk to her so blatantly had their eyes on Nick, it was hard to work up a glow at their friendliness.

And, ugh, maybe the sermon was aimed at *her*. Wasn't she being smug, criticizing others for a lack of Christian acceptance and forgiveness when she hadn't exactly gone out of her way to get to know people?

Still, there might be a local church with a more fervent and faithful congregation. She made a mental note to ask Nick if he'd tried others before settling on this one.

Realizing she'd missed the concluding minutes of the sermon entirely, she felt shame creeping up her neck to her cheeks. No, she couldn't brag about her own attentiveness to God's word on this day of worship.

Nick nudged her, and she rose to her feet. As she preceded him down the aisle, he spoke to half the people here, relaxed, friendly. A politician. Which, in a way, he was. In Cleveland, he'd been a lieutenant in charge of a homicide unit, with several layers of men and women above him to deal with the city council, mayor, and irate citizens. Here, he had to do it all.

By the time the two of them got out to their roasting hot car, opening the doors and waiting until the air-conditioning kicked in before they dared slide onto the seats, Julia was downright chagrined. Some of the whispers she'd heard during the sermon were probably parents chiding or hushing their children. There might have been elderly who had trouble sitting still. What if the plumbing contractor had a bad back? Some of the people texting could have been doctors staying in touch with staff at the hospital, or young mothers worrying about sick children, or—?

Really, she'd been as judgmental as an intolerant, cranky old woman. Her life was relatively simple; *she* had so few other people to worry about, because she'd closed herself off even from old friends.

If she'd left Abby with a sitter instead of bringing her

along to church, her attention would have been split down the middle, too.

In fact . . . it already was.

"Why the awful face?" Nick asked.

She rolled her eyes at him. "I'm scolding myself for uncharitable thoughts."

He flashed a grin at her. "No, you?"

Dismayed, she asked, "Am I that much of a prig?"

"What's a prig?" He oinked.

This time, she stuck out her tongue.

Nick only laughed. "Of course you're not." The smile disappeared. "You are more thoughtful than most people, in both meanings of the word. When you do something, you give yourself wholeheartedly to it, but you also guard yourself, if that isn't a contradiction. What's wrong with that?"

She knew he was thinking that she had reason to be guarded. It was true, but also crippling. When was the last time she'd really opened her heart to anyone?

But that answer she knew.

Less than a week ago, to a frightened, mute, young girl, Julia realized in dismay. The stab of pain came out of nowhere, yet didn't surprise her. It was foolish to have become invested in a child she'd always known would be in her life for only a matter of days—but downplaying what she felt didn't reduce it.

"I'm thinking of going back to school," she heard herself say, even though she was far from sure she actually wanted to. As she'd browsed university websites last night, a small voice inside questioned her motivation. What if she was trying to fill a deep need in herself for the kind of connections other people had? A husband, children, dear friends.

The kind of life fear had stolen from her.

Well, as Nick put it, what was wrong with that? If helping other people's children filled even a fraction of that hollow space in her, that was better than nothing.

"There's a lot to consider about that," her brother said, his very neutrality making her suspect he saw right through her—or doubted she'd be able to move to a strange city, alone, to do the coursework and student teaching.

Looking out the side window, she closed her eyes against the brightness. What were Abby and Luke doing?

But she knew. They were surrounded by their congregation, worshipping God more attentively than she had—and most of all, they were enveloped by loving family that would heal Abby.

All she could do was pray that was so.

ON MONDAY, MIRIAM came over so that Luke could work on his house. He'd found virtually no time to continue stripping wallpaper in the past week, since Abby came into his life. Of course, Bishop Amos would understand if the multiple jobs he needed to complete took longer than he'd originally estimated, but Luke felt a restless need to make progress.

To his greater surprise, Elam arrived barely an hour later and set to work in the dining room, where they'd left off. Luke decided to tackle the small bathroom beneath the stairs—a powder room, *Englischers* would call it.

As he tore off the first strip, Elam called, "It will be good not to feel I'm being suffocated by flowers when I need to use the toilet."

"I think this room will still give me claustrophobia even when I'm done," Luke responded. It had not been designed for a man his size, for certain sure. His shoulders almost spanned the space, and the ceiling slanted over the pedestal sink. Why someone had thought giant cabbage roses entwined with fern fronds on the walls and ceiling would be an improvement, he couldn't imagine.

He and Elam talked desultorily. Good smells came from the kitchen, where Miriam had apparently determined both to cook and bake so he'd have meals ready. It also overrode the powerful chemical stench of the stripper he was forced to use.

Every now and again, he needed to stretch, and checked on Abby. The first time, she was sitting at the kitchen table coloring, but she jumped down and ran to him, throwing her arms around his leg.

Glad that she wanted him, he scooped her up and carried her back to the table so that he could see her artwork. A black figure—he assumed a horse—faced away from a black rectangle that might have wheels. Her black crayon was worn down compared to the others scattered on the table.

"A black horse," he said. "That must be Charlie."

Abby nodded.

"Your drawing is *sehr gut*." He had taken to throwing in words in *Deitsh*, even simple sentences where the meaning was clear. "We'll hang it on the refrigerator when you're done."

If she was pleased, he couldn't tell, but once he set her back on the chair, she reached for another sheet of paper.

Miriam gave him a wry look over her shoulder. "You stink, *bruder*."

He grinned. "*Denke*. Perhaps we should trade places. Little as you are, you'd fit in the bathroom better than I do."

"But my cooking is so much better than yours."

He shook his head in pretend dismay. "*Hochmut*. Be careful not to say such things where others might hear."

"I heard!" Elam called from the dining room.

His sister stuck her tongue out, no doubt aiming at both brothers.

As the day went on, Luke had to contort himself to reach the spaces behind the porcelain pedestal sink and the toilet. While he was on his knees, face all but in the toilet bowl, he saw that the linoleum curled up in the corner. Did that mean a leak, and possible rotting floorboards?

Experimentally, he tugged. He couldn't pull much up

without removing the toilet, but he saw wide boards beneath rather than plywood, as befitted the age of the house. Good wood, he thought, pleased. Sycamore, maybe, or maple, but not oak.

He hadn't meant to tackle the flooring in the house until later. He didn't like the carpet, especially on the stairs, or the kitchen linoleum, but they were serviceable. Now, sinking back to his heels, he decided to work on flooring as well as walls, room by room. People might think he should finish one job before he started another, but he loved working with wood. Gleaming wood floors would satisfy him and give a better sense of how the house would look eventually.

Ja, and once the toilet and sink were removed, he wouldn't have to try to squeeze his arm into spaces his sister's skinny arm might better fit. Or Julia's. She hardly ate more than Abby, and he didn't like it.

Had she once been softer, more overtly feminine? Perhaps wearing drab clothing wasn't enough for her, although paring that softness away might not have been a conscious decision.

He tried to picture her at a happier time in her life, as he had too often.

Elam's voice drifted to him. "You're too quiet. Are you hiding out while we do all the work?"

He grimaced. That wasn't what he'd been doing, but squatting here brooding about a woman who was taboo for him wasn't any better.

"I'm thinking. A little of that makes work go better, you know."

His brother snorted and, a moment later, appeared in the doorway. "There's more wallpaper under there."

"Of course there is." The next layer had been tiny sprigs of flowers—he guessed lavender, although because of the discoloration of aging and the glue on the back of the latest paper, it was hard to tell. He stood aside so Elam could look at the wood floor beneath the linoleum, then announced his intention to remove the fixtures before he continued stripping wallpaper and ripped up the ugly linoleum that had been probably laid in the 1950s.

"*Ja,*" Elam conceded, "that sounds smart. If I think long enough, maybe I can find a better way to finish the dining room."

They teased each other as Luke checked his brother's progress, let everyone use the bathroom, then turned off the water behind the toilet and removed the anchor bolts. He carried the toilet out to the back porch, studied it, and made another decision: he would buy a new one.

He had a quick lunch with his brother, sister, and daughter before going back to work with a will, sternly keeping his thoughts from Julia. But his dread of morning, when he would first see her, hovered. He had no doubt she'd have shored up her walls again. He might never again see the glorious smile that had greeted Abby and, yes, him this week.

Better if I don't, he told himself. Better if he stayed in the workshop and went back to avoiding a woman who drew him in more than was advisable.

Chapter Thirteen

THE PRACTICE SHE'D had in hiding her feelings came in useful when Julia arrived for work Tuesday morning and saw that Luke and Eli had just arrived. She couldn't beat them inside. Having already noticed her, Eli was opening the back door while Luke removed his gelding's harness and turned him loose in the small paddock.

She got out of her car and locked it, pride stiffening her spine. No way would she let either man think she'd become too attached to Abby—or Luke.

Casting a casual "Hello" toward Luke, she smiled at Eli. *"Gute mariye."* Hoping her grammar was somewhere near correct, she continued in *Deitsh*, asking how his weekend had been.

Holding the door open for her, he grinned in delight. *"Gut.* And yours?"

"Quiet but also good." The big workroom felt shadowy. She lapsed back into English. "I always attend church with Nick, and then cook a big Sunday dinner at his house. I think he lives on microwave meals the rest of the time, or eats out."

He, too, used English, turning on lights. "I might do the same if cooking at the end of a long day was the only other choice."

Julia made a face. "I need a wife."

He laughed, even slapping his thigh. "*Ja, ja*, I will tell Deborah that."

Uneasily aware Luke had come in behind her and shut the door, Julia could feel the back of her neck prickling. Not being able to see him, wondering how close he stood, she took a few more steps. She didn't like having anyone standing behind her, but with him it was worse. He was such a big man.

Refusing to turn, she said, "I need to check messages," and hustled for the door leading into the showroom and small, open office.

Neither man spoke, but surely she'd fooled them. Eli, for certain. Luke had that way of looking right through her, but how could he from the back?

She was doing fine until she went behind the counter and saw the two quilts heaped beneath it, the imprint of Abby's small body still visible. Suddenly unable to breathe, she froze.

How could she have forgotten the quilts? If she'd shaken them out right away, taken them home with her, she wouldn't be devastated now.

Except, of course, she knew better.

The pain slowly subsided, allowing her to pick them up one by one and fold them. She looked around for someplace to set them out of sight, but the space was too small for that. At last, resigned, she piled them to one side of the desk, where she wouldn't forget them at the end of the day.

Not until midmorning did either man appear, and then it was Luke. Seeing she was with potential customers, he hesitated, but she told them, "Luke Bowman is one of our two furniture makers."

"'Son,' presumably," the man said, holding out a hand.

They shook, something Luke must have become accustomed to in his years away. "Yes, I have no sons of my own yet."

"I suppose you'd never teach furniture making to a daughter," the man remarked. Not quite critically, more thoughtfully, but Luke's jaw noticeably tightened.

"Not usually, but if I had a daughter who was especially interested, I would. Why not? Young women often hold a job outside the home for a few years or, later, work beside their husbands in a business. My sister Miriam works now at the quilt shop down the street."

"Oh!" The wife's face lit. "I think I might sign up for a class there. I've always wanted to give quilting a try, and this seems like the time now that Jim has retired and we've moved here. We have a daughter living in Tompkin's Mill," she added as an aside.

"Julia here is a very fine quilter." Luke tipped his head at her. "If you have questions, she'd be a good one to ask." He turned his gaze to the man, asking politely, "What work did you do?"

"Software design." He chuckled. "Not something you'd be familiar with. You folks don't use computers at all, do you?"

A flicker of something showed on Luke's face. "We do in our businesses." He nodded toward the one behind the counter. "Many of our sales come from our website. But before I was baptized, I spent some years working on algorithms."

Julia gaped along with both *Englischers*. As reserved as he was, why had he said that? Had his pride been pricked? But the Amish eschewed pride, in the sense she'd imagined. Anyway, Luke was so confident, he'd never feel the need to put a man in his place.

Had he wanted *her* to know he had skills beyond the craftsmanship that was acceptable among the Amish?

Luke raised his eyebrows, no doubt at their expressions. "Furniture making involves mathematics, too, you know. Angles, for example. Measurements must be precise—

although quilters know that, as well." He shook himself. "Can I answer any questions about the furniture?"

It turned out they were shopping for a new bedroom set. The wife had already gravitated toward one of Luke's, made of bird's-eye maple with a warm stain, inlaid with paler, smooth-grained ash. More than his father, he liked to do inlays, Julia had learned. Now she wondered if it was the mathematician in him, enjoying the precision. Or did contrast please him?

This pair of dressers and headboard and footboard used subtle curves in an unmistakably modern way that would still mix beautifully with antiques.

Luke made his excuses and disappeared in back, leaving her wondering why he'd come out in the first place. To tell her about Abby? Julia didn't know how that would make her feel.

She concentrated on the customers, who indeed decided to buy the entire bedroom set. Bowman's delivered free of charge locally. And why not? The total price was huge. While running their credit card, Julia encouraged the wife to visit the quilt shop and sign up for a class.

"That way you'll get to know other local quilters, too."

"I'll do that." She looked past Julia. "Are those quilts your work? May I see them?"

She couldn't refuse. "Yes, both are twin-bed-size. I'm afraid I'm overwhelmed with my own quilts. Thank goodness, I'm able to consign some to A Stitch in Time to sell. These . . ." Would Luke accept one from Julia for Abby's bed, if she offered it?

Probably not—it would only remind his daughter of the *Englisch* woman who could not be an important part of her life.

The woman, who introduced herself as Evelyn Williams, examined both quilts minutely, savoring the texture much as she had the silky surface of the fine woods. "These are lovely. That's what I'd like to make—quilts for my grandchildren."

"That's a good place to start," Julia told her. Bed-size might be too ambitious, but not necessarily if she chose a relatively simple pattern.

"Well, I'll hope to see you at the quilt store." Evelyn's gaze became speculative. "You're not Amish, are you?"

No, but I wish I were. Shocked by the thought, Julia pushed it away. It was ridiculous.

Gathering herself, she said, "No, but both Amish and *Englisch*—er, everyone else—shop at A Stitch in Time. Quilters understand each other."

Evelyn was beaming by the time they left. Julia made herself call the local trucking company and arrange the delivery before she opened the door into the workroom.

"They bought the set!" she announced.

Holding a handsaw, Eli looked up. "Set?"

"The inlaid maple bedroom set. I won't be surprised if they come back for a dining room table and chairs, too."

Luke watched her with what she'd swear was a faint smile in his eyes. "That was a big sale. You enjoy this, don't you?"

"Yes!" She hesitated, looking from father to son. "Is there something wrong with that?"

Eli answered. "No. We wouldn't brag because our sales were better than Yoder's Heritage Furniture's, because competition isn't our way. We send customers to them when we think their furniture might be more what they're looking for, and they do the same for us. But this is how we support our families, so a big sale is something to celebrate."

Luke contributed in his deep, calm voice. "Also, we spend so many hours on each piece, knowing it has sold to people who will appreciate it is a good feeling."

"I understand that." She felt the same way when she let one of her quilts go. Speaking of . . . "I had an idea." Her best ideas invariably came when she was trying to outrun depression or panic.

The two men waited, expressions inquiring.

"Well, what if you made a deal with Ruth at the quilt

shop? She could have a couple of your quilt racks there, and maybe a rocking chair or two. They'd be great for displaying quilts for sale. Here, we could do the same, showing a few quilts for sale. Customers might be more likely to go back and forth to choose just the right quilt or rack, and you'd both be able to display more of your product than you can now."

They stared at her. Maybe there was a downside to the idea that she hadn't thought of, or she was just plain over-stepping, considering she was nothing but a receptionist and bookkeeper here.

But Eli began to nod slowly as he turned to his son. "It wonders me why we didn't think of this. Why *I* didn't think of it. You've only been working with the furniture for a year."

"This summer we did something like that during special sales, remember?" To Julia, Luke said, "We'd put smaller pieces out on the sidewalk. All the stores did the same. The police closed the street so people could wander across and back. Anyway, Miriam carried a few quilts to us, and they had already borrowed some of our racks to show the quilts. Inside . . . it would make our display room more colorful, feel like home."

Julia relaxed. They'd listened to her suggestions before without slapping her down, so she didn't know why she'd expected any different.

"You'll talk to Ruth, then?"

"*Ja*—or why don't you do that. *Daad?*"

"Certain sure." Eli smiled at her. "Ruth will be glad, I think. She's a good businesswoman."

Which was apparently fine only because she was a widow, if Julia understood right. But that made sense. Miriam said Ruth had opened the shop after her youngest daughter got married and Ruth's husband died only six months later.

"We could take a few larger quilts to display on the beds, too," Julia said.

Luke raised his eyebrows. "Does she have a bed of some

kind in the store? What kind of headboard and footboard does it have?"

"It's an antique, or at least it looks like one. White-painted metal, sort of lacy."

He shrugged. "Ach, that might be best with the quilts."

This was one of the times when she could hear the Pennsylvania Dutch accent in his voice. Unhappy to be focused on how much she liked his voice, however he chose to speak, she said hastily, "When I take my lunch break—"

"Why don't you go now?" Eli said. "Catch Ruth when she's certain sure to be there, *ja*? If you leave the door open, Luke or I can help anyone who comes in."

With a grin, Luke contributed, "Strike while the iron is hot."

"That's really a strange saying, you know? I've never hit anybody with *my* iron."

Luke's grin deepened the creases in his cheeks. Eli roared with laughter.

Feeling better about herself, glad to have had such a natural discussion with the men, Julia propped open the door as they'd suggested, and hurried out into the heat of the day without even grabbing her purse.

LUKE WAS GLAD for Julia that Ruth immediately liked her idea. Although why wouldn't she? Ruth and Julia had brought armfuls of quilts back to the furniture store with them, and at their request, he'd made two trips to carry two rocking chairs while they each took a quilt rack the other direction.

At the end of the day, Luke and his father went to see what Julia had done with the quilts. He stopped only a few feet into the room, startled by the change but impressed right away.

"The quilts look at home here," he said, turning his head to take in the sight of one draped casually over the back of a rocker, another smoothed to cover a bedstead. Quilt racks held several crib- or wall-hanging-size ones.

"*Ja*, they look fine, ain't so?" *Daad* said from just behind him.

Julia smiled at them, although not the smile that lit her entire face and warmed Luke's heart. "*Denke*. And I'll have you know, I've already sold a crib quilt. A woman was walking past, stopped dead on the sidewalk to look at it through the window, then hurried in."

Eli chuckled. "I hope she wasn't truly dead. Perhaps she would be wrapped in the quilt for the funeral."

Julia blinked at him. "Why—? Oh. That's just a saying. I mean, stopping dead."

Luke's father patted her arm and said in *Deitsh*, "*Ja*, I know. Ach, having fun with you, I am."

"That's certain sure," she shot back, also in his language.

Eli beamed. "My daughter is teaching you, *ja*?"

"*Ja*, and I listen."

More than any of them had realized, Luke couldn't help thinking. For the first time, he speculated on why she was so determined to learn to speak his native language. Many people in the area knew common phrases, but unless they'd grown up having a close friendship with an Amish boy or girl, not so common, they were hardly fluent. *Determined* was a good description of Julia, he decided. For whatever reason, she had set the goal of becoming fluent in *Deitsh*, and was progressing with surprising speed. He wondered if she'd confided her motivation to his sister—and whether Miriam would tell him if he asked.

They locked the door, turned the sign to Closed, and all walked out the back together. Under his father's eye, Luke pretended to pay no mind to her departure. During the trip, he and *Daad* did discuss this new change, with Luke pointing out that the quilt shop might benefit financially more than they did, but not disputing that the sale of an occasional extra rocking chair would be worthwhile.

"We may be surprised," Eli commented. "Having Julia putting so much more on the website has brought more sales, and this will bring different people into our store. Maybe *Englisch* visitors who wouldn't have thought of buying furniture while they travel, but who will like what they see and discover that we can ship to their door."

Luke inclined his head. It was another ten minutes down the road before he said, "We could let Julia sell her quilts in our store, too, if it's clear that they are not Amish made."

His *daad* gave that some thought before nodding. "*Ja*, I think we could do that. It seems fair, ain't so?"

Luke didn't remark further.

He had already decided not to stay at his parents' house for dinner tonight, but he tied up Charlie so he could go in with his father. In the kitchen, Luke greeted his *mamm*, then looked around.

"Did Abby have a good day? Where is she?"

He could tell from her expression that *good* was too positive a word.

"Not afraid today, she wasn't," *Mamm* said, "but quiet. She keeps to herself." She nodded toward the front of the house. "She's in the living room."

Hiding his dismay, he kissed her cheek. "*Denke, Mamm.*"

A tuneless humming caught his attention as he approached the living room. Was this what the foster mother had described as singing? Thrilled to hear Abby's voice, he was still disappointed at the lack of words.

He paused in the doorway, watching her.

Abby sat cross-legged on the sofa, feet bare, still wearing the saggy pink leggings and threadbare unicorn shirt she'd chosen that morning, as she did whenever it reappeared in her drawer. She'd permitted him to do two pigtails, lopsided because of his inexperience. Now, wisps of blond hair straggled out of the braids. Luke knew without asking that *Mamm* would have tried to convince Abby to change into one of the dresses she'd made for this new *kins-kind*, but to no avail.

Abby held two of the faceless cloth dolls the Amish made for their children, one in each hand. If he had to guess, they were dancing. *Or maybe two boxers warming up,* he thought wryly.

The moment she lifted her head and saw him, she quit humming. She did slide off the sofa and come to him as he crouched to greet her. She held up the dolls.

"Your *grossmammi* gave you these? Do you like them?"

One wore a lilac dress, the other green. White aprons and white *kapps* seemed to be sewed on, or Abby would have figured out how to get them off.

Not answering in any recognizable way, she let the dolls drop as if she'd lost interest, and leaned against him. With a tight feeling in his chest, Luke closed his eyes and gave thanks to the Lord for her increasing trust.

Amusement threaded through his other emotions. For a traumatized child, this new daughter of his was amazingly stubborn, willful. The *Deitsh* word *agasinish* suited her perfectly.

"I missed you today," he murmured against the top of her head, only then realizing how true that was. He'd missed being able to wander out front and see what his daughter was up to, her impish smile, and hear Julia's laughter. He missed eating lunch with them. Much as he loved his father, having lunch in the workshop where his *daad* might want to talk hadn't held any appeal, and he couldn't join Julia. It did occur to him that today he could have used the excuse of talking to her about her clever idea, but an excuse was what it would have been.

No, spending unnecessary time with her wasn't a good idea. He didn't need his father to chide him.

And no, there'd been nothing wrong with the food he'd packed from Miriam's flurry of cooking, but it seemed tasteless eaten while he baked in the sun leaning against the paddock fence out back. Hiding out. Charlie seemed pleased to keep him company and share a few bites, but it wasn't the same.

Yes, he missed spending time with Julia *and* Abby.

"Shall we go home, little one?" he asked, and Abby tugged away to search his eyes, although what she looked for he didn't know. She didn't protest their departure or seem to notice that her new grandmother was sad. He regretted this child's resistance to the loving mother who'd raised him, but didn't know what he could do differently.

And he could see all too clearly that Abby wasn't ready to welcome a new *mamm* were he to marry in the near future. Waiting seemed sensible. Luke told himself that, in her own way, Abby would let him know when she was ready.

It wasn't as if he felt any urgency, given that he had yet to meet a suitable woman he could imagine waking to every morning for the rest of his life.

Chapter Fourteen

JULIA LIFTED HER head at the sound of the bell, surprised to see an older Amishman walking in. His iron-gray, somewhat stringy beard reached the middle of his chest. He seemed an unlikely customer, although she had sold quilt racks to a couple of Amishwomen and, once, a handsome wood chest to a young man just growing a beard. He had blushed during the entire transaction.

She smiled and came around the end of the counter. "May I help you?"

He studied her with unexpected care. "You must be Julia?"

"Yes."

"You do *gut* work, so I'm told."

"I do my best. Thank you. *Denke.*"

He nodded. "I am here to speak to Eli and Luke."

"They're both in the workshop, this way—" She felt her cheeks color. "You must know that."

"*Ja.*" His smile was sweet. "But you were being helpful." With a nod at her, he rapped on the door and entered the workroom.

The door didn't quite close behind him, the gap only a few inches, but a temptation to her. If she walked just a little closer . . .

Who he was and what they were saying were none of her business. And besides, what if one of the men came out unexpectedly and caught her eavesdropping?

She wrinkled her nose. So much for personal integrity. Only the risk of being humiliated kept her from inexcusable nosiness.

Business had so far been slow today, so this would be a good chance to take some new photographs of the display room now that the furniture was accented by colorful quilts. They would liven up the website, which had been in the doldrums when she arrived.

Julia didn't quite understand why. If Luke had worked in a computer field before returning to his faith, why hadn't he taken over jobs like the website? He'd no doubt be faster and more efficient than she was. She was lucky, because whoever had set up the site in the first place had planned for changes to be made with an ease that was almost insulting.

As if that person had envisioned her ineptitude.

She surprised herself with a smile. No, that person had envisioned Eli fumbling to upload a photograph or change the posted hours. Yes, she fit in perfectly here at Bowman & Son's Handcrafted Furniture—in all but one way. And that was a big one. The Berlin Wall, choked with twisted barbed wire and impregnated with mines.

No, it was wrong to use such a violent image to define the separation the Amish maintained from the modern world around them. They wouldn't wish anyone to be hurt trying to draw too close. Better to picture a crevasse too deep to jump from her side, although they did occasionally make the leap from their side.

As Luke had done. But for those like him, a bridge existed, allowing a return trip. Julia wondered if it ever happened that outsiders sought to join the Amish. She didn't suppose it was common, given how large the sacrifices the Amish made to live as they believed God asked them.

Her forehead wrinkled as she stood unmoving.

Were the lifestyle choices made by the Amish really sacrifices? Or did they only choose to concentrate on the things in life that truly mattered? It was true the women rarely had careers, but they had the joy of caring for the people they loved most. Many did essentially have part-time jobs as well, baking goods for sale or selling quilts or other crafts. And women like Ruth and Miriam weren't discouraged from working, either. Julia had been told that, more unusually, an Amishwoman in a settlement near Jamestown was much admired for her skill in training buggy horses.

Shaking off useless thoughts, Julia fetched the digital camera and began snapping pictures, trying for angles that would captivate the eye. She had crouched to capture the sheen on the spindles of a rocking chair, when voices drifted through the open door to her.

She'd moved farther to the back of the store than she'd intended.

The men were speaking in *Deitsh*, of course, but she made out enough to get a sinking sensation in her stomach. Something *arig*—bad—had happened at a *greitsweg*. She knew that word, but had to grope for the meaning. Crossroad, that was it. A *waegli* was involved, a buggy. And if she was understanding right, the horse had been killed and maybe a person, too? They must all pray for Sol.

The voices became louder and she realized the visitor was emerging, accompanied by at least one of the men. Eli, who was saying that, *ja*, they would help for certain sure.

She stood, the camera in her hand. Hesitating to use her clumsy *Deitsh* with a stranger, she said in English, but timidly, "Is something wrong?"

Both men looked at her in surprise. No, all three men, because Luke had followed the others through the doorway, too.

He was the one to say, "Yes, an *Englisch* teenager with friends in his car hit a buggy this morning." Of course, he sounded grim. "An older boy was killed, the younger boy was injured but will be okay, and their father is in bad shape. Not conscious yet, and has so many broken bones he'll probably be in the hospital and then rehab for months, at least, before he can walk again." Pause. "A girl in the car wasn't wearing a seat belt and is in critical condition, too."

They would all pray for her as they would for their brethren, she knew. And *that* was one of the things she most admired about them.

Meeting the older man's eyes, she said, "I'm so sorry. If . . . if there's anything I can do . . . Give a ride to anyone, or help if you'll be doing a fundraiser . . ." She stumbled to a stop and looked to Luke for help. "Was this anyone I've met?"

"I don't think—" He visibly changed his mind. "The man's name is Sol Graber. His wife Lydia quilts, I know. She might have been at that quilt frolic, or you could know her from the shop."

A picture formed in her mind, the woman short and plump, and encouraging to the newer quilters.

"I have met her. The boy who died—?"

"Was her oldest, yes."

Julia closed her eyes. "I can't imagine."

"Evenings, it would be a help if you could drive Lydia to the hospital or home sometimes. She has two younger children who will need her, too."

"After work, I don't do anything important. I can be available anytime."

His keen blue eyes softened. The man who had brought the horrible news studied her quizzically and said, "That is good of you. I will give your name and phone number to the family."

Eli stepped forward. "Did you meet Bishop Amos Troyer, Julia? He owns Troyer Bulk Foods."

"Oh, I've been in there!" She smiled weakly. "I'm glad to meet you, even at such a dreadful time."

"What happened, it is *Gotte's wille*," he told her gravely. "Always hard to understand, but we must believe *Gott* has a reason."

She took an involuntary step back, but swallowed and nodded even though she thought, *Hard to understand?* That was the understatement of the year. The decade, in her case. What possible purpose would God have had in allowing the vicious attack on her? She didn't believe she'd become a better person, only one who lived in fear. The man who'd assaulted her hadn't been caught because of her.

How many times had she reminded herself of Romans 12:19?

Beloved, do not avenge yourselves, but rather give place to wrath; for it is written, "Vengeance is Mine, I will repay," says the Lord.

Nick believed no such thing, she knew. He yearned to take vengeance into his own hands. Either way, she took no comfort; she wanted that monster *stopped* so he couldn't hurt other women.

She wanted to find some sort of silver lining to the painful dark event that had forever divided her life into a before and an after, yet she'd never achieved even that small comfort.

WITH DAYLIGHT STILL lasting well into the evening, Luke decided on Saturday to visit Sol in the hospital. Sol had regained consciousness on Thursday, Luke had heard. They'd been more casual friends than close; Sol—short for Solomon, of course—had been a placid boy who never questioned the rules. He'd apparently grown into an equally easygoing man who would never have dreamed of leaving the Amish life or questioning any part of the *Ordnung*, the unspoken rules that governed the lives of all Amish. Still,

as children they'd gone to school together, and played base-
ball together during breaks and after the worship service.
His father, Abram, was a close friend of Luke's father's.

Luke brought Abby along both because he wanted to
include her in community events and because in her re-
strained way she still clung to him. She wouldn't want to be
left for additional hours at her grandparents' house, however kind *Grossmammi* and *Grossdaadi* were to her. He
had no intention of taking her into Sol's room, however; he
didn't know what she'd seen or experienced when her
mother died, but it had to have been bad. The waiting room
would be full of Amish, because they always gathered in
support of any members of their church who might be in
need. Any of them would be happy to keep an eye on Abby
for a few minutes.

He left Charlie still hitched to the buggy at the end of a
row of other buggies and patiently waiting horses, then entered the hospital through a rear entrance, holding Abby's
small hand.

Following directions, he took an elevator up two floors
and went down a hall until he saw a waiting room filled
with Amishmen and -women. If asked, he couldn't have
named one of them. All he saw was the one *Englischer*
seated among them: Julia. He should have anticipated this;
when she'd offered to drive Sol's wife back and forth as
needed, she had meant it. Julia was a woman who would
keep promises, he knew.

She still wore her working attire of a drab skirt and white
shirt, but the deep fire of her auburn hair stood out like a
beacon.

Luke bent to pick up Abby, but the little girl stiffened,
her eyes fixed ahead. Wrenching her hand from his, she
cried, "Julia!" and raced toward her before he could do anything to stop her.

Julia saw her at the same moment and stood, taking a
step, then another, until they collided. Abby hugged Julia's

legs until the woman Luke secretly wanted to hug, too, bent to squeeze his tiny daughter in her arms.

When he reached them, it was to find Abby crying even as tears streamed down Julia's cheeks. Everyone else in the waiting room gaped. All were members of his church district, and all knew that his traumatized little girl didn't speak.

Until now, for an *Englischer*.

A rock in his throat, he stood above the pair, unable to look away from the face of the beautiful woman his small daughter had chosen.

He was petty enough to feel a stab of hurt because Abby had said Julia's name before calling him *Daadi*. But that hurt tumbled in a confusion of other emotions. He wanted to be able to take them both in his arms but couldn't. He wanted *not* to feel so much for this woman who was forbidden to him. He wanted not to be standing here with no idea what he should do or say.

He identified the second person he knew of the many people in the waiting room when Bishop Amos rose to his feet and came to him. Neither Julia nor Abby so much as raised their heads.

"Why her?" he murmured.

Luke could only shake his head. "Abby trusted Julia immediately."

Keen brown eyes studied him. "But she loves and trusts you."

"*Ja*, sure, but not the same."

"This is the first time she's spoken."

"It is." He heard how choked he sounded.

"She still won't wear a dress?"

"Not without a battle that would hurt our relationship. She'll get there." Or so he'd told himself. It would have been better if she hadn't seen Julia again.

Except he was so moved by the sight of the joy and pain exhibited by Julia and Abby both, he couldn't regret this moment, not as he should. He'd been blind not to see how much they both had hidden from him since he separated them.

"What should I do?" he asked helplessly.

Now the older man's expression was pitying. "You must keep weaning her away. You know that. If Abby holds tight to the outside world, you will have a foot in it, too, ain't so?"

Luke unclenched his teeth. "I committed myself to my faith."

"Yet I think you still hold back a part of yourself." The bishop paused, now watching as Julia wiped at her wet cheeks with her hand and stood. "She is not for you."

Startled, Luke glanced at him. Had he been so obvious? It would seem so.

His "no" was gruff. He'd known when returning home how much he would be giving up, starting with the career he'd worked so hard to achieve. His heart and, he wanted to believe, his Lord, had led him to turn his back on all that, and he hadn't regretted his decision for a minute.

Until he became so tangled up about the child he'd claimed—and the woman he would have courted if that were in any way possible.

To Julia, he said, "Will you watch her for a minute while I visit with Sol?"

Her smile for him shook. "Of course I will."

Two people came out of the room just as he approached. One was Sol's wife, Lydia. Despite the strain on her face, she said, "So good of you to come, Luke! Sol will be so glad to see you. You go in now, shoo."

"If there is anything I can do . . ."

"The bishop said you and your *daad* are donating beautiful furniture to be auctioned to pay the hospital bills. That is a big something, *ja*?"

"It doesn't seem enough." She had lost so much weight in a matter of days. Was she eating at all? "You should go to the cafeteria. There are plenty of people here to watch out for Sol."

"Julia has been waiting for me—" She broke off, seeing Abby.

"She won't mind staying longer." He hated knowing how wrenching this goodbye between her and his *dochder* would be.

But it must be.

He walked into the room to find a man he wouldn't have recognized, so heavily bandaged and covered in casts was much of his body. One leg was in traction, one arm raised by a pulley system, too. Even Sol's head was engulfed in a white turban. Reaching the bed, Luke laid a hand on his boyhood friend's shoulder, one of the few places on the wounded body that might feel his touch.

Sol had survived. God had been with him, knew he was still needed here. What Luke hadn't thought to ask was whether anyone had told Sol about his oldest boy.

But then the swollen eyes raised to him, and a fat tear formed in each. He knew, all right—and however powerful his faith and humility, he grieved and had to be railing against God's decision.

Luke sat in the chair pulled up to the bed and said bluntly, "We were never promised an easy life."

Sol's swollen lips barely moved. "Gone, my David. Hard to accept, that is. My fault not to hear that car coming, so fast."

Luke gently gripped his shoulder again. "Not your fault. You know better. What could you have done, with it happening so fast? You are a careful man, and a good father."

Sol cried in what would have been racking sobs, if he had been able. Luke kept a hand on him, and felt his own eyes sting with tears.

JULIA HADN'T BEEN able to resist lifting Abby onto her lap. Other women would have been glad to watch over Luke's daughter, but she wouldn't give them a chance. These few stolen minutes were too precious.

Smile tremulous, she looked down into that sweet, thin face. "You said my name."

Abby wrinkled her nose.

Despite the tears that still stung her eyes, Julia laughed. "You gave yourself away. You might as well talk."

The little girl's lips pinched together, but a smile seemed to dance in her blue eyes.

"I'll tell you a secret." Julia bent her head and whispered in Abby's ear. "If you ask out loud for what you want, you're more likely to get it. People won't have to guess what you're trying to say. And think how happy your *daadi* will be. How can he say no to you then?"

Abby shrank into herself.

"What is it, sweetheart? Why don't you want to talk?"

Abby whispered, too. "I'm s'posed to shut up."

The nasty edge in the "shut up" part had to be pure mimicry. Julia rarely felt violent impulses, but right now was an exception. Betraying her anger would only scare Abby, though.

Instead, she said, "Bah, humbug. Most of us like *loud* little girls. Ones who can shout, 'Cookie!'" The two women sitting closest to them had tilted their heads as they eavesdropped without apology. Julia looked at them. "That's so, isn't it?"

The younger of the two grinned. "*Ja.* When we get older, we learn to ask in a nice voice, but making noise, small children should."

Bishop Amos was near enough to hear, too, she suddenly realized. Heat crept onto her cheeks as she met his eyes. A nod of approval astonished her.

He spoke directly to Abby. "Yes, little one. Our children are precious to us. We love to hear their voices."

Julia smiled tenderly at Abby. "What do you say?"

For a moment, nothing. Then she said, "Cookie!" but cringed.

It was obvious that the someone who'd told her to shut up had also hit her.

Julia hid this burst of anger, too, and hugged Abby harder. "That's wonderful. Say it again, so loud everyone hears you."

"Cookie!"

Several of the women clapped for her. *"Wunderbaar!"* exclaimed an older woman.

Abby looked around in such astonishment, she broke Julia's heart all over again. She kissed the top of Abby's head. "You *are* wonderful." Then movement snagged her attention. "Here comes your *daadi*. Can you surprise him?"

Had Luke heard the to-do out here? But creases furrowed his forehead, and he held his mouth and jaw tightly. His eyes met hers, a kind of desperation in them that awakened an ache beneath her breastbone.

Abby stirred on her lap. Her face lit up and she wriggled until Julia let her slide to her feet. Then she said, almost loudly, *"Daadi!"*

His stare left Julia and settled on his daughter. He didn't so much lower himself to his knees as collapse. He swallowed, held out his arms . . . and Abby flew into them.

Julia cried again. Then, knowing she couldn't bear another goodbye, she fled, determined to find Lydia in the cafeteria and take her home.

Chapter Fifteen

HOPING NO ONE noticed how close to tears he was again, Luke accepted hugs from several women and nodded when Bishop Amos told him firmly, "I'll walk with you."

Abby rode on Luke's hip. He didn't like the idea of letting her go even as far as the bench seat beside him in the buggy. Face buried against his chest, she had his shirt gripped in two small fists.

They had paced nearly the length of the institutional hallway, passing other patient rooms, before Amos said anything.

Then his tone was odd. "She's a *gut* woman, Julia. Her instincts are right."

Luke could only nod again. He'd been stunned to look up from Abby, wanting to share the moment, only to see Julia's back as she hurried down the hall. Abby had turned her head at the same moment.

A thread of panic in her voice, she asked, "Where's Julia?"

"I think she had to go. She's here at the hospital to help someone. I guess they needed her."

That's when she pressed her face against him so she couldn't see anyone else.

"Even so," Amos continued, "forget she's not one of us, you can't let yourself do."

Luke just looked at him, knowing his eyes must be red-rimmed, that the punch of too many emotions had to show on his face.

Amos reached out and gripped his arm for only a moment, much as Luke had squeezed Sol's. A way of connecting that men, Amish or *Englisch*, could allow themselves. He offered sympathy, Luke supposed, which allowed him to say only, "I must get Abby home."

"*Ja*, you probably haven't had dinner yet."

"No." His appetite was nonexistent, but this too-frail child needed something more to eat than the half of an apple, sliced, he'd given her as a snack before they came. She'd poked at him until he gave most of the rest to Charlie, who'd crunched the treat so vigorously, bits of apple and flecks of foam flew. Luke had managed to get only one slice in his mouth, and pretended to eat with as much messy enthusiasm, Abby's silent giggle his reward.

But now, now, he knew her voice.

Having said what he meant to, the bishop turned back. Once out in the warm evening, dusk softening the surroundings, a bat darting above, Luke set Abby in the buggy. He had to gently pry her fingers from him. Taking up the reins, he backed Charlie out from between two other buggies, then clicked for him to start for home.

He'd stayed too long at the hospital. Since coming home, he'd driven after dark only a few times. Seeing Sol's grief had raised his awareness of how unsafe it could be on country roads that often had no shoulder. Even though full night was a half hour away, Luke turned on the battery-operated lights that would make the buggy visible to anyone behind the wheel of a car who was driving with enough care to react in time.

"Did Julia tell you to talk to me?" he asked.

Abby had never looked tinier. She kicked her feet in those tattered athletic shoes and finally whispered, "She said I could surprise you."

Luke smiled down at her. "You did."

"She wanted me to yell." She sneaked a peek at him, then yell she did. "'Cookie!'"

Luke jumped and the gelding swiveled his ears back. "Why did she want you to yell?"

So softly, he just barely heard her, Abby said, "'Cuz . . . 'cuz I said I'm s'posed to shut up."

Luke controlled his rage. "Your mother didn't tell you that, did she?"

Abby's sagging pigtails whipped from side to side as she shook her head vehemently. "Uh-uh. It was Ron. Or maybe Justin. Or . . . or . . ."

Maybe both. Maybe yet another man Beth had allowed into their lives.

He would forgive her eventually for putting her vulnerable daughter at risk, over and over, but he hadn't gotten there yet. If only she'd mounted a serious search for him.

But he knew she'd been past being able to do any such thing. He couldn't forget that some of the guilt was his to bear. He'd thought about her, worried, but only occasionally. The truth was, he'd let her go as incidental to his life. He'd been more important to her than she was to him, although he hadn't known *how* important.

He prayed she knew that he had Abby now, that she would be safe and loved.

"You must miss your mom," he said.

The resounding silence made him wish he hadn't asked. Either the answer was yes . . . or Beth had been in a stupor most of the time for months or even the past couple of years. She must have played with her tiny daughter, once upon a time, loved her and despaired for an answer on how to give her a better life, but maybe she'd passed beyond that, too.

Abby reverted to one-word answers once they were home, but even that was an important step forward. Luke didn't have to interpret every twitch of her shoulders or crinkle of her nose.

Not long after dinner, bathed and tucked into bed, she dropped off to sleep as if exhausted.

He stroked her hair one more time, turned off the kerosene bedside lamp, and went out of the room, leaving the door open so he'd hear her. Then he stopped there in the hall, feeling exhausted himself.

Not in body. If any muscle in his body ached, it was his heart. He'd felt too much today. More than he could remember in years. Unexpectedly seeing Julia had hit him hard, despite the fact that he'd parted from her barely an hour before, as they closed the store. Hearing Abby's voice for the first time. Her emotional reunion with Julia. Then, in trying to take on some of Sol's pain, he hadn't been able to evade understanding the devastation that could happen with no warning, in no more time than it took to snap his fingers. And finally, hearing, *"Daadi!"* as his daughter flew into his arms.

He turned to face the wall, flattening both hands on it, allowing his head to fall forward. *Finally?* No. The last blow had been seeing Julia run away. He couldn't escape knowing he had hurt her again. He'd never meant to, but that was a flimsy excuse.

A muffled groan escaped him. The bishop's warning had been pointed. Luke had to keep his distance . . . or betray everything he believed in.

JULIA CONTINUED TO drive Lydia to the hospital, at least every other evening. Apparently, a neighbor did the same on alternate evenings. Julia had become acquainted with Sol and Lydia's two young daughters and even the boy who, like his father, was still hospitalized. What she didn't do was go anywhere near Sol's room. Luke was sure to visit, and if he didn't, his mother or father might, bringing Abby along as he'd done.

Thursday of the same week, Julia walked down the street after closing to join Miriam, Ruth, and several other Amishwomen in the room at the back of the quilt shop. Two she already knew, including Miriam's *aenti* Barbara, and the others seemed friendly.

"I'm Sarah Yoder," said one. "Sol's cousin."

The other, taller than most Amish, holding herself with graceful dignity, bent her head in greeting. "Susanna Fisher."

She didn't mention a relationship, but didn't really need to. Within any local Amish group, almost any two people could trace some blood connection.

"Julia is a very fine quilter, uh-huh," Ruth assured them, "and works with Eli and Luke at the furniture store."

The two women Julia hadn't met before nodded acknowledgment.

Miriam added, "She's learning to speak our language." She surely hadn't meant to let pride sound in her voice, but she had to know she was a good teacher.

Ruth declared, "I think we should hold the quilt auction the afternoon before the other one. More people might come to town because they could go to both."

The evening auction would include fine furniture, antiques, other Amish crafts, and just about anything else that had been donated. Some were unexpected to Julia, at least, including a promised large doghouse and a decorative bridge. An Amishman made sundials out of stone, while a local soap maker had already donated a basket full of bars and shampoos. Of course there'd be rag rugs, leather products, and hand-thrown pottery. The evening would be divided into two, starting with a silent auction of lower-cost items, followed by the live auction that would bring in the most money.

Julia had taken responsibility for ensuring that the Bowmans' donations would be delivered when and where they needed to be. It was scheduled for Saturday, three weeks away. They would have preferred sooner, but to make good money, they needed time for publicity, to attract *Englisch* bidders from out of the area.

Yet another auction would be held on the Saturday only a little over a week away, this one of donated farm equipment and tools as well as miscellaneous household items. Only locals were expected to be interested.

The plans were ambitious, donations so far generous, but Julia worried that the amount raised would fall far short of allowing the bills to be paid for the two Grabers' hospital stay. She'd spent two weeks herself in the hospital after the attack and another week in rehab to get intensive physical therapy, and she'd seen the appalling bills that resulted. In the intervening years, the cost of medical care had only risen.

She couldn't call these women naive, however; the Amish always paid their bills even if it required other church districts to chip in—which they would willingly do. Besides, if the auctions were well attended, she knew the prices the Bowmans' furniture would bring, and the finest of the quilts donated so far could each go for as much as three thousand dollars.

Glancing around, she saw only one rocking chair. Already, the quilt store had sold two.

Seeing where she looked, Ruth nodded. "*Ja*, today. A cherrywood rocker *and* a quilt rack."

"A quilt, too," Miriam chimed in. "The yellow-and-cream Tumbling Blocks. The woman is pregnant. The buyers wanted a crib, too, so we sent them to Yoder's." She looked reproachful. "It's too bad *Daad* and Luke don't make them."

"They say it's good to specialize." Also, now they'd feel as if they were being unacceptably competitive if they edged into an area that had formerly belonged solely to the other store.

Miriam only nodded her understanding. That was their way.

Then the group got down to business. Out of deference to Julia, the women continued to speak in English with only occasional resorts to *Deitsh* words. Julia soaked those in.

By common consensus, she took notes. Susanna was to arrange for the grange hall and the frames used to display large quilts. One of Barbara's sons was an auctioneer, and Barbara had already asked him to give his time and that of his two assistants, which he had gladly promised to do.

Knowing all local quilters as she did, Ruth had already begun soliciting donations, and would continue to do so.

They all agreed that they should also hold a bake sale outside the grange hall. "The money we make from that isn't so much, but every bit helps, *ja*?" Sarah asked. "It's a *gut* way for everyone to contribute."

Julia made a silent vow to finish her current quilt and donate it on top of the others she'd already offered.

Once they were satisfied that the plans were well in hand, they talked about Sol's progress—slow—and that of his boy.

"Noah is set to go home by the weekend," Sarah told them. "More work for Lydia, but many of us plan to take turns sitting with him and taking the girls." She flashed a smile at Julia. "You've given so much time to drive her. Such a help that has been!"

"It's a small thing to do. Since I don't have a family, my evenings aren't as busy as most of you must have."

The barest flicker of some raw emotion on Miriam's face made Julia regret her words. Although they'd become good friends, Miriam had yet to tell her about the come-calling friend who'd died in the logging accident. But Miriam's expression wiped clean so fast, Julia wondered if she'd imagined seeing the pain.

Or had she seen a reflection of her own, as if she'd looked in a mirror?

When the meeting broke up and the women separated, chattering, to go to their buggies parked in the alley out back, Julia found herself beside Miriam. She couldn't resist asking.

"You must see Abby. Is she still talking?"

Miriam chuckled. "She's no *blabbermaul*, but talk, she does. Still quiet, except when she wants a cookie."

A burn in her chest, but Julia chuckled. "Then she yells, does she?"

"*Ja*, because Julia told her that's what she should do." Mischievously, the other woman added, "When she makes trouble in school yelling, we'll know whom to blame."

"I'll happily accept that blame."

Miriam saw her expression and gave her a quick hug. "Go, I must, with *Aenti* Barbara and Susanna waiting."

The cadence of Amish speech, the reversal of subjects and objects, all had come to sound natural to Julia. A few times she'd caught herself echoing the patterns, even in her own language.

"Nick and I are meeting at Salvatore's for pizza." *See?* she knew herself to be saying. *I have someone waiting for me, too.* Ashamed, she said, "See you."

Her Amish friend apparently bought her act, because she grinned and echoed, "See you."

Julia walked down the alley to her car, still behind Bowman's, and got in. Alone, doors locked, she felt her energy drain away. She tried to convince herself it would be good to see Nick. She'd made excuses the last time he'd suggested dinner. After all, she'd just seen him Sunday.

Unfortunately, she knew what her problem was. She was changing until she hardly recognized herself. She had lost her hard-achieved resignation, and the acceptance of what her life could be. Around Nick, she was increasingly having to bite her tongue. The qualities that made him a good cop had always been a sharp contrast to her personality, but there'd been a time she understood him as no one else did, not even their parents. *She* was the reason he'd done a one-eighty and changed his major in college from premed to criminology.

She couldn't help wondering whether he regretted the drastic turn his life had taken after her rape. She especially wondered after he had abruptly resigned from the Cleveland PD, even though he'd risen to lieutenant in major crimes, and taken this job in what his friends back there no doubt considered a Podunk town. Something had happened, but he wouldn't tell her what. Julia was supposed to lean on him, but not the other way around.

Abby was the closest she'd come to having somebody need *her*, and look how that had turned out.

Julia made herself take a deep breath, then another and another. Straighten her shoulders and reach for the key in the ignition. She'd vowed many years ago not to give in to self-pity, and she wouldn't let herself stumble now. Maybe God had known Abby would need her, and that Julia was strong enough to let her go, as if this precious child had been an injured wild creature that couldn't stay with her.

With resolve, she told herself that a little hurt was nothing if she'd made a difference to that sad little girl. The fact that she'd foolishly begun to love her . . . well, maybe her own vulnerability was *why* Abby was able to trust her enough to finally speak again.

Tonight before sleep, she'd ask God to allow Abby to wholeheartedly join a family who could give her so much more than a single woman could. Right now, though, she had to brace herself for Nick's reaction to her too-deep involvement in helping the wife of an injured Amishman and his son—and now participating in the fundraiser to pay their hospital bills, too.

The first thing he'd do was shrug and say, *They should carry insurance.*

The second? *You're not Amish, Julia, and don't forget it.*

As if she could.

* * *

THAT EVENING, LUKE and Abby stayed for dinner at his parents' house. *Mamm*'s fried chicken and hot potato salad were not to be missed. If he were lucky, she'd send leftovers home with him.

As they settled around the table, there was the usual flurry of talk.

"Oh, ach! I almost forgot the sauerbraten. Miriam, will you—"

"Certain sure, *Mamm*."

"No need to hurry, Deborah," his father said.

"No need?" That was Elam, teasing. Always teasing. "I'm hungry."

Mamm leveled a reproving stare at him.

"Shut your trap," *Daad* said mildly.

Luke glanced down to see that Abby's forehead had crinkled.

"Was ist letz?" he asked her quietly. He'd seen that she had absorbed the beginnings of *Deitsh,* and encouraged it whenever possible.

"You said she's *grossmammi*, but *he* says she's Deborah," Abby said indignantly. *"You* don't say either word."

"Grossmammi means 'grandmother,' and *grossdaadi* is 'grandfather.' I don't call them that because they aren't my grandparents. They're my *mamm* and *daad.*"

"What's a grandparent?"

His mouth fell open at her perplexity. It had never occurred to him that the entire concept was a mystery to this child.

At the same time, he saw that the rest of his family had been struck silent and unmoving. His mother was bent with a bowl in her hand, held only inches from the tabletop, as she stared at Abby. Miriam, midturn from the counter, had frozen with another dish in her hand. *Daad* and Elam only gaped as Luke did.

He thanked his God that Abby apparently hadn't noticed. "I'm your *daadi*, *ja*?"

Face turned up to his, she nodded.

Did she really understand what that was? he suddenly wondered. After all, she might have called other men *Daddy*.

Shaking that off, he said, "This—Eli—is my *daadi*. Deborah is my *mammi*. Because they are my parents, they love you, too. You are related." Familiar guilt needled him. What if she—or his parents—ever learned they weren't in fact related at all? "Did your mommy ever talk about her *mamm* and *daad*?"

Forehead furrowed, she shook her head. "Mommy didn't have a *mamm* and *daad*."

Movement in the kitchen had resumed, but not conversation. All were listening.

"She did have parents." He smoothed a hand over Abby's downy blond hair. "We all do. She just didn't talk about them." He hesitated. "They may have died." Or she didn't want them ever to know about this grandchild.

He assumed she understood death, at least in the confused way of a young child.

"Can I have other grandparents?"

The answer, of course, was yes. Somewhere out there, she had a biological father, if he hadn't killed himself with a drug overdose. That father must have parents—who, in fairness, might have loved Abby, too.

His lies had led to a lot of complications, as lies were wont to do.

Still, he smiled at her. "No, just your *mammi*'s parents and your *daadi*'s parents."

She studied *Mamm* and *Daad* with the thoughtful, unnervingly direct look of a child.

"And this"—he decided he'd better clarify all the relationships while he was at it—"is my sister, *mein schweschder*, and my brother, *mein bruder*. All of us have the same *mamm* and *daad*. That makes them your *onkel* Elam and your *aenti* Miriam."

"Oh."

Although she appeared satisfied, he wondered how much of that she had really taken in. It sickened him to think of a three-year-old who had no idea what grandparents, aunts, or uncles were—because she'd never had anyone but an increasingly unreliable mother, and likely abusive men whom he hoped and prayed she had not been required to call *Daddy*.

His mother's eyes were damp, and his father had clamped his mouth shut to suppress what he wanted to say. Luke nodded at him, after which Eli took and released a deep breath, then relaxed.

The two women sat at last, and Luke scooped his daughter onto his lap. His father glanced around then bent his head, the signal for them all to pray.

Although the prayer that preceded every meal wasn't typically spoken aloud, Luke had been making an exception for Abby. How else could she learn their prayers? He held her hands clasped in prayer between his, his head bent over hers, and murmured the words to her. First in English, then German.

O Lord God, heavenly Father, bless us and these Thy gifts, which we accept from Thy tender goodness. Give us food and drink also for our souls until life eternal, that we may share at Thy heavenly table, through Jesus Christ. Amen.

Chapter Sixteen

NICK GLOWERED AT her over the table. So far, his responses had been much as she predicted. She'd had only one slice of pizza, her brother two. She shouldn't have told him about the fundraiser until they were done eating. Now her stomach was in knots.

"Do you even *know* this man?" he demanded.

Trying to stay calm, she said, "No, but I had met his wife. Lydia is a quilter."

"You've met her. Once? Twice?"

She narrowed her eyes at him. "You don't have to mock me. Say what you think."

"All right. This might make sense if the family belonged to our church. But the Amish stay separate by choice. They neither expect nor want your help."

He had to stomp on a tender place, as if he'd found a hidden bruise. Nobody on the auction committee had said, *Why are you getting involved?* but they must have wondered. Nobody had asked why she'd jumped to give so much time to a woman she'd met only once, however sympathetic she felt.

In fact, she hadn't examined herself for an answer to those questions. She'd just . . . offered.

"I want to feel part of the quilting community." That was true.

"All right, I get that," her brother admitted, "but you're going overboard. Donating a quilt or two, why not? But organizing the event?" He shook his head.

On a spurt of anger, she retorted, "Why would I get involved if the family were members of our church, anyway? I hardly know a soul. Everyone rushes out the minute the service is over. Nobody has asked me to join a committee. I don't feel *part* of them. I do feel—" She skidded to a stop. Uh-oh.

The muscles in Nick's jaw tightened, and his hand fisted on the table knife he held. "I *knew* this would happen. That's why you wanted a job with Amish employers, isn't it? Because you'd read about the Amish, and you were convinced they can give you something no one else has. You'd be safe, because they're so peaceful."

"If so," she said with all the dignity she could summon, "it wasn't conscious. I just . . . liked it here. I wanted to stay."

The pity in his eyes seared her. "This is a strange, splinter religion. You know that, right?"

"No!" She half rose to her feet but made herself sink back to the padded seat. "I didn't expect you to be biased. What's strange about them? They've held true to their religious beliefs for hundreds of years. They're not a cult that's broken from contemporary churches. To the contrary. They've refused to let themselves be corrupted by modern ways. They're sincere, Nick. They care about each other, give without a second thought when someone's in need. You tell me why that's a bad thing!"

He blinked a few times. "I'm not saying they're bad."

"Just weird."

"Look at their clothes. They travel by horse and buggy

even though, witness this latest accident, they know how unsafe it is."

"Of course, they're the ones who are wrong, because we should have the right to drive as fast as we want? If we smash into a buggy and kill a few kids . . . hey, has to be their fault, with their backward ways."

He was all but grinding his teeth. "You know I didn't mean that."

"It sure sounded like it." This time, she did slide out of the booth and grab her purse. "I've lost my appetite."

His expression altered. "Don't go, Jul. Can't we talk about this?"

"We just did. You're so afraid I'll join them, you can't see them clearly."

"That's . . . not it." This gentler tone got to her. "I'm afraid you're drawn to them for the wrong reasons."

Clutching her purse in white-knuckled hands, she tipped her head to one side. "And what are those?"

"You know. You imagine that their women are nestled in a cocoon. You'd never have to face the things that frighten you now."

Quaking inside, she took a step back. "Because bad things never happen to them? Like Lydia Graber? She just lost a son, Nick. Even if her husband fully recovers—and he might not—it won't be for months. She's not safe."

"That's why you're doing all this," he said slowly. "Because—" Even he didn't have the nerve to finish. He didn't have to.

Because when she most needed help, she hadn't been taken into the warm embrace of a community of people who genuinely cared.

No, what happened to her scared her friends. As young as herself, they had sidled away, not wanting to confront the horror that could as easily have happened to them. She'd have been alone if not for her parents and Nick. Nobody among the Amish, however cranky and difficult, would ever be alone in that way.

So, yes, that was part of what she admired. The rest . . . she wasn't ready to talk about.

She especially couldn't tell her brother that Luke Bowman was the only man who had ever attracted her. She still didn't believe she was capable of a physical relationship, but at least she'd felt a glimmer of something other women took for granted.

Continuing to back away, she said, "I need to go."

He pushed himself out of the booth. "You haven't eaten—"

"I'm not hungry. I'm sorry. Good night, Nick." Then, yep, she fled again, ashamed to realize she was making a habit of it.

"JULIA ASKS ABOUT Abby," Miriam said, out of the blue. It was almost a week later, a week during which Luke had made excuses when he picked Abby up after work about staying for dinner. Sunday, of course, they'd joined his family, which had included Rose, her husband, and their children. Still shy, Abby had been absorbed by the crowd, but Luke had been able to avoid any really personal conversations with anyone in his family. Arriving this evening, he'd seen that he was hurting his mother's feelings. She'd beamed when he'd asked if they could stay.

Now, after dinner, he and his sister had gone out to sit on the front porch, her in the glider *Daad* had built, Luke on the steps a few feet away. There was no breeze. With this almost the middle of August, the heat was oppressive. Under *Mamm*'s watchful eye, Abby had been engaged by a wooden puzzle. Elam had slipped by a few minutes ago, on the way to meet up with friends at the Kings' barn across a cornfield and a horse pasture from their home. He had yet to be baptized, and therefore could still be excused for drinking alcohol and running a little wild. That's what *rumspringa* was for—to allow Amish youths to have a taste of the outside world before they made the decision about their futures.

Elam, however, hadn't been a teenager in a long time. Most Amishmen were both baptized and married by their midtwenties. He had to be feeling pressure from *Mamm* and *Daad* and Bishop Amos. Luke prayed he didn't see himself following in his big brother's footsteps. Would talking to him do any good?

And there he went, trying to avoid thinking about Julia, but of course Miriam had made doing so unavoidable. "I'm not surprised," Luke said after a minute. "What do you tell her?"

His sister shrugged, giving another push on the porch boards to keep the glider moving. "That she's talking more. I didn't say she still fights the idea of wearing a dress or *kapp*."

He grimaced. This was one subject his daughter would not discuss. He had no idea what lay at the root of her deep resistance. Without his consent, his mother had tried again to stuff Abby into one of the two dresses she'd made, but *Mamm* said Abby had turned feral, all sharp elbows and teeth, kicking and fighting until she'd made her point. Like taking one of the half-wild barn cats and trying to persuade it to wear a dress and bonnet.

The attempt had set back Abby's relationship with her *grossmammi*, he knew, but hadn't had to say after seeing his mother's crimson cheeks. What a child her age wore was a small thing, in his opinion; given her background, building trust was far more important. Once again, perhaps he was responsible for his *mamm*'s fear that Abby would refuse to become one of the *Leit*, the people.

If Julia wore a *kapp*, he had a suspicion Abby would happily do so as well.

What if he asked her—but of course he couldn't do that.

He looked forward even more than usual to the end of the workweek, having two days to spend with Abby, although most of Sunday would be spent at worship. Monday, though, after thoroughly mucking out Charlie's stall, he might take shears and shovel to a patch of blackberries. He'd rather keep working on the inside of the house, but it would be good for Abby to spend time outside. Had she ever rolled down a grassy slope? Climbed a gnarled old apple tree? Looked for four-leaf clovers? If not, it was past time.

When he told Miriam what he was thinking, she rocked for a minute before her soft voice came from the darkness. "Monday? Can I come over? I could pick some blackberries and bake pies. Abby might like helping."

Oh, *ja*, helping she'd like. With a grin, he pictured his already *strubly* daughter with hands and cheeks stained purple. He knew from experience and his mother's exasperation that blackberry stains wouldn't come out of clothes. If he let her wear the unicorn shirt and pink leggings that now had a tear in one knee, permanent purple splotches might persuade even his stubborn child to agree it was time to throw them away.

"I'd like that," he said simply. He could offer to let Julia come out and pick berries, too. With Miriam and her already friends, they'd work happily together in the kitchen. For Abby, it would make for a perfect day.

Inviting Julia to his house wasn't something he could ever do.

After another silence that had allowed him to brood, Miriam said, "Maybe another year, we can start teaching her to quilt. Just a nine-patch first, for her doll—does she *have* a doll?"

"*Mamm* gave her one." He hesitated. "She has a baby doll that came from her foster home, too." The doll's hair, the same color as Abby's, was as big a mess as hers had been when she came. "It's hard plastic and has those eyelids that close and I think it might have said 'Mama' or cried or

I don't know what else, because there's a place on her back for batteries."

"And someone was smart enough to take them out," his sister said with approval.

"Ja." Unseen in the darkness, he smiled.

"Has *Mamm* seen the doll?"

He snorted.

Miriam chuckled, but sounded more thoughtful than impatient when she said, "This isn't like her. I've never seen her impatient. I don't understand."

He told her what he'd been thinking, and after a minute she nodded. "That might be. Except for Rose, none of us have followed the expected path. You leaving the way you did and now you're back but still not marrying, Elam so late to commit, and then there's me. *Mamm* can't understand why I won't marry and start a family as if . . ."

He waited, thinking she might go on without prompting, but when she didn't, Luke asked finally, "Have you talked to her about it?"

"I've tried. She won't understand. Trust in God, I must." Bitterness tinged her voice. "He needed Levi. Refusing to quit grieving, that says I won't accept *Gotte's wille.*"

"Is that true?" he asked gently.

With only a hint of light escaping a crack between the curtains at the front window, he saw her bow her head. "It might be." Her voice was so quiet, he shifted closer to better hear her. "I don't know. I'm just not ready. Or maybe I haven't met a man who can take Levi's place in my heart. Anyway." Now she sounded combative. "Look at you. You're thirty-two years old. *You* haven't married."

"No. But my reasons are different than yours. If I'd married an *auslander*, that would have made my decision to leave the faith final. I suppose a part of me was never sure."

"But you've been back for a year now."

He turned his head to gaze into the night-cloaked yard to be sure Miriam wouldn't be able to read anything on his face. "Maybe, like you, I haven't found the right woman. Making the wrong choice . . ." He hunched his shoulders.

She didn't say anything for a long time. When she did, she surprised him. "Was there ever a woman you considered marrying, when you were away? Like . . . like Abby's *mudder*?"

"No. She and I . . . we weren't . . ." He cursed inwardly, in a way he hadn't in a long while. "I felt sorry for her. She wasn't happy. I think—"

"You think?"

"That something in her home had been very bad. She wouldn't talk about her family at all. She'd been hurt, that's all I know. Running away must have seemed her only choice. She couldn't heal."

"If she'd taken her troubles to God . . . ," Miriam said slowly. She wasn't making judgment, one reason she was the family member he felt most comfortable with.

Still, he agreed. "That's what she should have done, *ja*, but I'd guess that she blamed God, too, for allowing people who should have loved her to beat her or worse." *Worse* was what he believed, that belief reinforced by what Julia had told him.

He cringed at what his sister must be thinking, that he'd taken advantage of a girl like that, but the only way he could defend himself was to betray the truth about Abby's parentage.

Miriam's soft voice came from the darkness. "And yet she held on to her faith. She trusted God enough to trust *you*."

"A man who'd walked away from his faith?"

"I think she'd guessed that you would go back. Or before she died, someone might have told her that you had."

"She wrote a letter," he said abruptly. He hadn't told anyone else. "That's what she said. She believed I was a good man. I'd talked about my family. That's what she wanted for Abby."

A tiny sniffle told him Miriam was crying.

"Miriam . . ."

She flapped a hand. "I'm fine. It's just terrible to think . . ."

"About her childhood?"

"*Ja*, that, but also about what could have happened to Abby. But she'll be all right now, ain't so? Now if we could just convince *Mamm* not to think Abby must change *hurrieder, hurrieder*."

"Faster isn't our way," he agreed, recognizing the irony. The deliberate pace of life, the agonizingly slow discussions before approval was given for any part of modern technology however much it would benefit them, those had driven him crazy when he was young. He'd craved not just the unlimited knowledge but also the fast pace he could see that *moderns* took for granted. Now, he had trouble understanding how he'd endured the rush out there, the ambition, the competitiveness, the drive to be more successful than anyone else, faster than anyone else, whatever the cost.

Once upon a time, whenever a car passed the family buggy on the road, he'd studied it with envy. He'd especially admired the ones built for speed. He hadn't understood then that the speed he'd seen as desirable kept those *Englischers* in it from seeing much of anything they passed. Did they ever even notice the fragile beauty of bloodroot flowers, newly opened? Or the complexity of Queen Anne's lace, or delicate bird's-foot violets? Or the buck half-hidden in the deep shade at the edge of the woods that cloaked the rolling land? Did they know a sycamore from a maple tree? A redbud from a dogwood?

Did they take time to talk to their children as they drove? Or was that another joy lost to the speed of daily life—and to technology that now allowed televisions to operate in cars?

No, he had no regrets at all, which led to the perplexity of why the only woman he could imagine marrying, mothering his children, was an *Englischer*.

* * *

JULIA WAS DISMAYED to see Luke's buggy turning into the alley on Wednesday morning before she'd even set the emergency brake in her car. Worse yet, Luke seemed to be alone.

Well, hurry, then. He'd be relieved if he didn't have to do anything but nod as she unlocked and left him in peace to unharness his horse.

But she had to wait until the buggy passed before she could cross to the back door. He was frowning as his sharp blue eyes examined her so thoroughly, she was left emotionally naked. Why was he bothering? She resented what felt like a silent critique. So, she wasn't at her best this morning. She hadn't recovered from an awful Sunday, ruined by the tension between her and Nick. That was none of his business.

She had the door open and slipped inside before Luke got out of his buggy. Up front, she turned the sign on the front door to Open and sat down to listen to messages, safe in the certainty he wouldn't follow her. He hadn't spoken to her about anything not work-related since that encounter in the hospital, when he'd been forced to allow Abby to interact with her. "Forced" was definitely the right word, given his attitude since.

She heard only silence from the back. Two women were peering in the front window, pointing at individual pieces and oohing and aahing. As she sometimes did, she made a bet with herself; these two wouldn't come in. They just liked to look.

She made the rueful admission that her judgment might arise from her sour mood. Anyway, there was nothing wrong with admiring the magnificent furniture. The women might tell other people, among whom would be one who really was in the market for a china cabinet or a desk.

The door opened behind her just as the two women continued down the sidewalk and out of sight. Bracing herself, Julia turned, pinning on an expression of polite inquiry. It was indeed Luke who approached the side door leading into the office area, handsome enough to disturb her, his suspenders—*gaellesse* in Pennsylvania Dutch—only emphasizing the breadth of his shoulders and the solid muscle in his chest.

"Do you need something?" she asked pleasantly.

His eyebrows twitched. "Only thought to tell you *Daad* won't be here until midday. He is taking a turn to harvest early corn at the Grabers' farm."

"Oh." Didn't it figure he'd undercut her stiffness? "That's good of him. I suppose everyone is doing the same."

"Yes, I'm taking an afternoon on Thursday."

"I see." It was nice of him to tell her, but really, as long as one of the two men was available to answer questions potential customers asked, it didn't matter which.

Only to me, she admitted silently. She liked Eli, but got a tiny thrill every time she talked to Luke.

Even though she also harbored unfair anger at him, because he'd let her fall in love with his daughter and then taken her away—it made it clear that she, Julia, was unclean.

She suddenly became aware that those blue eyes were raking her face and that furrows had formed between his dark eyebrows.

"Something's wrong. You look . . ." His hesitation was long, as if his instincts didn't tell him enough. "Sad" was the word he finally chose.

"How can you tell?"

He shook his head. "I don't know. I can see you've been losing weight, and you can't afford it."

"Gee, that's nice."

Irritation flashed on his face. "That wasn't an insult. It was worry."

"I'm fine. You don't need to worry about me."

Instead of accepting the excuse to retreat, he argued, "You're not fine."

She wasn't. It was as if the walls she'd built to protect herself were crumbling. Luke and Abby had a lot to do with that.

"I had an argument with Nick last week," she blurted. "He used to be my best friend, but we don't seem to see anything the same anymore."

Luke came a few steps closer. Tensing, she would have jumped to her feet, but as tall as he was, that wouldn't really help.

"Which of you has changed?" he asked.

Startled at his perception, Julia hesitated to answer. How could she confide in a man, one who'd initially frightened her—and still occasionally did? The man who had been all but shunning her?

But he'd noticed something was wrong, and cared enough to ask.

"Me," she whispered. "It's me. I just . . . seem to be questioning everything I used to value."

Shocked by her own admission, she thought, *There it is.* It was because of these warm, caring people—even Luke, as remote as he often was—that she'd begun to question how she lived. For all that she'd considered herself a woman of faith, that belief had always been a little . . . smug. She didn't have a personal relationship with God, and she wanted that. So much.

"It's . . . it's partly all of you." Her hand wave was vague, but she thought he understood. "I understand why you came home."

"Is that why you've been learning our language?"

She stared up at him in bewilderment. What was he implying? She wasn't foolish enough to think that fluency in *Deitsh* could make her Amish.

"Miriam enjoys teaching me."

"*Ja*, I know she does." New intensity magnified the effect of his already formidable physical presence. "You might like to attend our service a week from Sunday." One corner of his mouth lifted in what could be a flicker of humor. "Most outsiders are bored and end up with backaches, but you . . ."

She held her breath.

"I think you're different," he said, voice deep.

Julia could not have looked away from him if Nick stormed in the front door that minute. She felt peculiar—light as air, yet short on oxygen.

Was Luke saying what she thought he might be?

Chapter Seventeen

HE MUST BE insane. Confessing that her values were changing didn't mean it had ever crossed Julia's mind to convert to Luke's faith. Unlike those who followed their sister Anabaptist faith, the Mennonites, the Amish made no attempt to convert others. The Mennonites had missions in developing countries throughout the world, the Amish none. Bishop Amos had echoed others when he'd said, "There are many ways to find God. Ours is not right for everyone."

Back in the workshop, Luke was accomplishing next to nothing. He felt foolish to have thought for a minute that she might consider becoming Amish, with all that encompassed.

She would have to move from her apartment. Give up her car, and her a woman who knew nothing about horses, far less harnessing and driving one. Give up her internet and her television and the electronic reader she'd confessed to owning along with all those books. Her vacuum cleaner. Her clothes—although, picturing her wardrobe—that she might not mind so much. Except she would also have to throw away her bras. Did she know that Amishwomen didn't wear them? he wondered.

He was paralyzed, shaken, *ja, ferhoodled*, by a possibility that would never come to pass. It had hit him like a lightning bolt. If Julia converted to the Amish faith, he could ask her to marry him. *He* would teach her what she needed to know, understand her past in a way his brethren and even family couldn't. She'd understand the forces that made him the man he was, too.

She already endangered his heart. Letting himself hope . . . ach, that was foolish.

And what made him think she would agree to marry him in any circumstances? He'd known since meeting her that she had suffered a terrible trauma, that she feared men. That she would likely never welcome a man's touch, a man in her bed. He could be patient, gentle—but could he face a lifetime with a woman who shrank away from him, who lay rigid in bed only because he was in it with her?

Even if she felt ready, who was to say she'd choose him? He might be imagining the tension that stretched taut whenever they were together. If she'd been attacked the way he thought she had, what if he looked like that man?

At length, he forced himself back to work.

Given that he was alone, he chose to do finish work on a dresser, starting with an air sander, powered by the diesel engine he'd fired up first thing that morning. The necessity of concentrating was good; there was always a risk of gouging wood on a nearly completed piece.

Done with that stage, he wiped off sawdust with a rag and then shifted to sanding by hand, using a block and frequently running his fingertips over the wood until he was satisfied that every inch was as smooth as he could make it.

He thought this dresser wouldn't be in the store long. He'd never intended to make a full bedroom set of this design. The lines were almost Shaker in their simplicity, yet with curves subtle enough to fool the eye. For once he'd done no inlay, thinking the grace and function spoke for themselves. He'd used walnut, a hardwood, and he intended the stain to be rich, not quite as dark as walnut had traditionally been stained. He was pleased with the piece, but no more. Doing good work was important, but this work was no better or more valuable than Jacob Schwartz's, when he harvested a field of sweet corn that would sell for enough to feed his family, or Sam Fisher's, when he completed a windmill to bring clean power—God-given power—to a farm or business.

Or Katie-Ann Kline, quietly acknowledged as the finest local quilter for making traditional patterns new again and for her tiny, even stitches. A modest woman, she would say she did her best, but there were many other women as talented. And then she would name them.

Luke wondered how much pride Julia took in her quilting.

By the time his father arrived, he had stained the dresser as well as a rocking chair and two quilt racks. Thanks to Julia's idea, those were selling faster than ever before. The quilt racks didn't take long to build, but the rocking chairs were another story.

He greeted his father and said, "All is well at Sol's place?"

Eli grunted. "Yes, the harvesting is on schedule, but little thanks to me. I was so slow. Lucky that there were other men helping who knew better what to do."

"We can all only help as we're able," Luke said automatically.

Another grunt suggested his *daad* was chagrined at being showed up by younger fellows. Luke hid a smile. Pride was something they all struggled with, one way or another.

"How does it go here?"

"I'm glad of what I accomplished, and Julia said she sold a blanket chest to a buyer in California and a dresser to a man who lives in St. Joseph but drove up here after being told our furniture was especially fine."

Eli nodded, not bothering to deny the truth of that when alone with his son. "California." He shook his head in astonishment. "Doesn't anybody out there make furniture?"

"In factories."

Daad snorted.

This time, Luke openly grinned. "I meant to speak to you. We need more rockers. Do you have any at home that we could bring in?"

"*Ja*, two or three, I think."

Luke suggested the time might be coming when they'd want to hire someone else, but his father pointed out that with fall nearly here, Elam might be able to put in some time building rockers and quilt racks, if nothing else. It would be good because he could work at the shop in the barn at home rather than here. This room couldn't accommodate another worker, and expansion couldn't happen unless a store on either side went out of business—which was possible. One was a real estate office, and these days property was slow to sell in this part of the state.

He saw Julia only when they walked out together at the end of the day. To his relief, she made no reference to their earlier conversation. That evening, he waited for his first chance to unobtrusively speak to his sister. She'd been coming in the back door, and instead he backed her up and stepped out, shutting the door.

"Julia and I talked today." Self-conscious, he tried very hard to make this sound casual while doubting he would succeed in fooling Miriam. "She's interested in attending a worship service. If people believe I suggested it, you know what they'll all think. But you're her friend."

Miriam lifted her eyebrows. "Did you suggest it?"

"I did," he admitted. "She was telling me things I shouldn't repeat, and it seemed the right thing to do, but an invitation coming from you would be better."

Obviously startled, his sister said, "She isn't considering . . . ?"

"Of course not," he scoffed. "When do you remember an
outsider joining us? She's just curious."

She studied him with familiar suspicion, but finally nodded. "I'll invite her. Everyone knows she's learning our
language. With her help on the fundraiser and driving
Lydia around, she'll be welcome."

"Good," he said, satisfied. "Denke."

A mischievous grin accompanied her "You owe me one"
as she slipped past him and opened the door again.

Smiling wryly, he said, "I do."

Thanks to his sister, he was getting off easy. He should
have thought before he opened his mouth—but he was glad
he had.

GRATEFUL SHE HAD over a week before her visit to the
service in the Bowman family's district, Julia had determined to cram the way she had as a freshman in college.

Most of that Sunday was otherwise occupied, of course.
In the morning she went to church with Nick, just as she
had every Sunday since arriving in Tompkin's Mill. What
else could she do? She loved her brother. Following him
home afterward, she even baked a ham and made a huge
potato salad that would give him leftovers for a couple of
days. Their conversation was stilted, both trying not to re-
sume the argument or last Sunday's tension. He didn't say
a word about her Amish employers or friends, and she
didn't talk about the work she'd done for the upcoming
benefit.

Telling herself it was so he wouldn't have a full week to
badger her, she also refrained from mentioning that she
would be attending a different service the next Sunday and
wouldn't be here to cook a Sunday dinner for him, either.

She winced. Pure cowardice, something she'd have to

overcome. She *couldn't* wait until Saturday night to call and say, *By the way* . . .

Miriam showed up unexpectedly at Julia's apartment Monday morning. Luke had dropped her off, she said; he was going to the hardware store and lumberyard for materials he needed to work on his house.

She handed over a heavy book, a copy of the Ausbund, the hymnal used in all Amish worship, from the most conservative branches to the most liberal. She'd forgotten it was in High German until she opened the cover and stared in dismay. Yes, she'd taken modern-day German in college, and then never used it again. That grounding might be helping her learn *Deitsh*, but this—!

"No need to worry," Miriam assured her. "No one will expect you to know our hymns." She explained that a man who had been named as the *Volsinger* started each hymn. "Ours is a cousin of *Mamm*'s—John Mast."

"I'll keep my mouth shut," Julia promised.

"I wish you didn't have to, but . . . we don't sing like . . . like the music you hear on the radio."

"I've read that."

"After the hymns, at least one of our ministers will speak, maybe both, and Bishop Amos, of course. They don't write out what they're going to say, or plan, except the three of them talk it over right before the service."

"The minister at the church I've been attending with Nick reads his sermons. I don't know if he writes his own."

Miriam looked puzzled at the idea that a minister might take his words, however wise and moving, from someone else.

After that, they practiced speaking *Deitsh*, greeting people, saying, "How are you?" and, "I'm well, thank you for having me here today." Miriam also reported that the teenager injured in the car versus buggy accident had been released from the hospital.

"The driver is only seventeen. He went to see Sol to tell

him how sorry he was. Lydia was there. She thought the boy meant it. He's in trouble and may even go to jail. *Englisch* law, you know. He was driving too fast, and he killed someone. Sol forgave him, and the boy cried."

"I wonder if it's real to him yet that David isn't at home with the other *kinder*."

"That might be." She fell silent. "It may not be the forgiveness she stumbles over as much as the loss."

"I understand that."

Matthew 6:14–15 was the linchpin of the Amish faith: *For if you forgive men their trespasses, your heavenly Father will also forgive you. But if you do not forgive men their trespasses, neither will your Father forgive your trespasses.*

Forgiveness couldn't come easily for anyone, but Julia had no doubt that it would lift some of the pain and burden otherwise carried—both for the person being forgiven, and for the one offering the forgiveness.

For the hundredth time she asked herself, if she were to come face-to-face with the man who'd raped and tried to kill her, could she forgive him? Truly, from the heart? Like every other time, she found she just didn't know.

At least forgiveness wasn't an issue for Miriam. Her Levi had died in an accident, from what Luke said. It was the loss of the man she'd loved that she hadn't yet gotten over. Julia's loss had been different—not of a person but rather a part of herself, the confidence that would allow her to lead a full life—but she couldn't deny that she stumbled there, too.

Dear God, help me do better, she prayed silently, before she steered Miriam back to the practice conversations that sometimes had them giggling.

ON SUNDAY, JULIA was to drive herself to the Bowmans' house, traveling from there with Luke's parents, sister Miriam, and brother. The family buggy wasn't large enough to include him and Abby, so they'd make their way on their own. Just as well, he told himself.

To his astonishment, Abby had grudgingly agreed to wear one of the dresses *Grossmammi* had made. But not the hat, as she called it. She shook her head, and kept shaking it.

Even with her passive cooperation, he found that getting her dressed took a lot longer than usual. He'd never had occasion to watch even his much younger sister get dressed, far less help her. How much easier it would be if he had a wife. An Amish wife.

He finally managed to pin the dress in place over her skinny body, feeling like a father who had just managed to secure a diaper on his newborn for the first time, and buckled to Abby's insistence that she wear her saggy, holey pink leggings beneath the dress. Maybe no one would notice. She even consented to the apron, a shade darker than the dress. In fact, she seemed to *like* the apron. Progress was made, thank you, Lord.

Her fine hair acquired tangles every night, especially in back. He'd almost mastered the art of working those knots out without painfully yanking. Then he brushed it all back and achieved a single braid, albeit with fine tendrils already escaping. Finally, he held up the *kapp*.

"You're sure?"

Head shaking, she backed away. "No. No!"

He sighed. "Okay, this time. But all Amish girls and women wear *kapps*. You'll see again today."

Her lower lip pooched out. Luke laughed, scooped her up in his arms, and carried her out to the buggy, where Charlie waited patiently, already in harness.

Once they reached the road, he clucked to the gelding and snapped the reins, asking for a brisker trot than usual. As a former harness racer, Charlie was happy to oblige. Not that they'd be late, but Luke had no doubt his family and

Julia would already be there, and he didn't want her to feel abandoned if Miriam got called to help with the meal, say.

When he turned into the long lane leading to Rudy Brenneman's farm, large by Amish standards, Luke was met by three older boys. They waved him to park in line with as many as twenty other buggies, and after helping Abby down, he left them to unhitch Charlie and turn him out with the other horses. Normally, he'd have been carrying a dish Miriam or his mother had made to contribute to the meal that followed the service, but no one would expect him to have brought food. As it was, he held Abby's small hand in his as they passed the other buggies—and, yes, there was his *daad*'s—and walked the last distance up the lane to the lawn that sprawled in front of a large, two-story white house.

Rudy had built a German-style barn, handsome and roomy, into a slope. The stalls were on the earthen floor, the entry from downhill closer to the road, while the plank floor above at the same level as the house would have been cleared today to accommodate all the members of their church district. He was too late, he saw immediately, to help unload the bench wagon or set up the benches. It wasn't as if he didn't take his turn.

Younger children were running around, women and older girls hustling toward the house with covered dishes or keeping an eye on the children, the men and older boys gathered in clumps to talk.

No sign of *Mamm* or Miriam . . . but there was Eli, speaking with several men of his generation. Surely Miriam and *Mamm* would have kept Julia with them, introduced her to the other women, made her feel welcome.

He had exchanged only a few words with a friend, when movement began toward the open doors leading to the second floor of the barn. Traditionally, married men entered first, sitting toward the front on their side of the aisle, followed by married women and the small children accompanying them to sit on the other side of the barn. Then came the turn of unmarried men and older boys, and finally unmarried women and older girls.

Luke had taken to joining the married men who were his contemporaries, and nobody had objected. Today he hung back, wanting to be able to keep an eye on Julia, who would surely sit with Miriam among the unmarried women. Best if Abby didn't spot Julia until after the service.

Indeed, *Mamm* passed by with her sister and some friends, chattering and not seeing him. He and Abby took their turn among the boys and men who were at least a decade younger than he was, with only a few exceptions like Elam. In fact, Elam saw him and gestured to invite Luke to join him. Luke slid in, lifting Abby to his lap.

His brother's eyebrows raised at the sight of her and he grinned. "*Mamm* will be so happy."

"Except for . . ." Luke tapped the top of his daughter's head.

She lifted her face to glare a warning at him. "No hat!"

"No hat. Today."

Her satisfied nod made him smile and his brother laugh aloud.

That was the moment he saw Miriam and the woman beside her, on a bench across the aisle and only a row ahead of him. Julia stood out with that gleaming hair in a sea of white *kapps*. Both looked his way, Miriam smirking and Julia smiling, her face lit in the way he didn't see often enough.

He'd been surprised in his one, earlier glimpse. She wore a loose, high-waisted dress that fell to midcalf, nearly the same length as the Amishwomen's dresses. He wondered if she'd sewn it especially for the occasion. Out in the world, he'd have expected a dress of that style to have small flowers sprinkled against a background color, but this was a solid fabric in a hue that fell between peach and rust, a good choice with her skin and auburn hair. He felt sure the other women would have approved of the dress. *He* liked seeing her in a pretty color.

Maybe she wore more colors when she wasn't working, but Luke doubted it. She hadn't the day his family helped her move into that apartment, or when he'd seen her at the hospital. A tan dress, though, would have been ugly. He could imagine the women at the fabric store asking what she was buying it for, and gently and tactfully urging her to try this instead.

So far, Abby was making faces at Elam, returned by him. Some of the other boys around them were laughing. Not until a voice was loudly and ostentatiously cleared at the front did they remember where they were and fall silent.

John Mast stood and looked toward the back of the barn to be certain everyone had entered, then announced the first hymn. That one was his choice. The second hymn was always *"O Gott Vater, wir loben Dich."*

O God the Father, we praise You.

His voice, strong and pure, rose alone to the heavens. The others joined in, including Luke. Even as he sang, he glanced toward Julia, wondering what she thought.

The hymns were chanted more than sung, the voices of the faithful blending into a slow, quavering prayer to God. Beautiful in their own way, handed down from countless generations of the faithful before them, Amish hymns were never accompanied by musical instruments. Some would describe them as sorrowful.

As a scoffing boy, Luke had rolled his eyes because even their hymns were sung slowly. Of course they were. Now, he heard less of the sorrow and more of the hope and God's promise of salvation.

Julia wouldn't understand the words, he realized. Why had he imagined she'd be moved by anything about this service?

Abby squirmed, and he adjusted her on his lap so that her head rested against his shoulder. She'd stayed quiet the past two services, but now that she'd found her voice, who knew?

He wished Julia's face weren't blocked by his sister's head and white *kapp*.

Chapter Eighteen

HER BACK DID ache, although she wouldn't admit as much to a soul, and no, she hadn't understood more than snippets here and there of the sermons, and yet . . . emotion seemed to swell in her chest until she wasn't sure she wouldn't burst. It was everything: The astonishing beauty of the voices blending into one, their only purpose to express their faith. The expressions on the faces of the men and women she could see—rapt, joyful, at peace. What rustles she heard were behind her, where the children sat, and children anywhere tended to restlessness. Twice, young women had had to rise and leave with a crying baby or toddler, but now that Julia was standing, she saw that one of them had slipped in again and sat at the very back, holding a now-sleeping girl in her arms.

Julia's language skills had progressed to the point where she'd at least grasped the theme of each sermon, none surprising, although neither of the two men who spoke chose forgiveness as a topic today.

Trust was what the minister asked for. Josiah Gingerich,

Miriam had whispered. He started with one of the best-known psalms.

Yea, though I walk through the valley of the shadow of death, I will fear no evil; For You are with me; Your rod and Your staff, they comfort me.

Reassurance was what Bishop Amos offered, in his powerful voice that vibrated with peace and certainty. Along, perhaps, with a chiding for those who did not trust enough.

As for me, I will call upon God, And the Lord shall save me.

The bishop had concluded with a quote from Isaiah she recognized, as well, reminding the faithful that, in the Lord God, they had an everlasting rock.

Had she ever let herself trust entirely in her Savior? Or had she felt as if He had once let her down, so she didn't dare place any reliance in Him again?

Despite the language barrier, Julia knew in her heart she'd been challenged, and needed to rise to that challenge. Energized, warmed by the knowledge that everyone around her placed faith at the center of their lives, she followed Miriam out of the barn, into the late August heat. She'd heard grumbles about how dry this year had been. Leaves were beginning to turn already, she saw, the glorious colors speaking to her.

A deep voice behind her said, "See who is here, Abby?"

Julia spun around. Smiling rather than somber, Luke held out his delighted daughter, letting her throw herself into Julia's arms as soon as he knew Julia was ready to receive her. He looked so handsome. Well, he always did, but today he no doubt wore his best black coat and trousers over a white shirt. Despite the seemingly never-ending heat, he also wore a black felt hat rather than his more usual straw one.

Abby flung her arms around Julia's neck and clumsily kissed her cheek. "Oh, I've missed you," Julia murmured, kissing her, too. There was someone else she wished she could kiss, but that wasn't possible. And . . . could she really? However friendly Luke's often chilly blue eyes were right now, even if his perfectly shaped mouth tipped up just a bit higher on the right than the left, even if she hadn't felt the least bit of fear when his big hand brushed hers as they transferred Abby . . . he was still a man. A large man with big shoulders and, yes, powerful hands that dwarfed hers, wrists so thick hers looked like twigs in comparison, thighs taut with muscle. A man who could hurt her with a flick of his strong wrist.

The reminder cooled some of her jubilance, but not entirely. Because she'd sneaked a few peeks at him during the service, and seen on his face the peace and certainty she'd sought all her life.

And she had the unsettling realization that, when she'd chosen the fabric for this dress, it was with a subconscious belief that today, among the Amish, she could safely wear something pretty, even feminine. After all, men who lived their submission to God must also be gentle.

Nick had tried to tell her that wasn't true—although the Amish did not come to him or the police in general in cases of domestic abuse or drunkenness, he had seen evidence that they, too, suffered from problems that afflicted every level of society.

How could she be sure Luke didn't hold the willingness to commit violence at a simmer? That he might not have a temper? Who but God knew? He'd been impatient enough to leave the faith in search of something else.

Or was it more powerful that, in the end, he'd chosen to return to his people, willing to humble himself before the members of his church as he asked to be restored to them and to his God?

She blinked, wondering how long the silence had lasted. Abby clutched her, seeming not to have noticed anything, but Luke's smile had faded and his expression had turned quizzical as well as guarded.

"I'm sorry," she said. "It was so much to take in."

If she didn't see him often, she wouldn't have noticed his subtle relaxation.

"Did you understand a word?"

"Of course I did! I missed a lot, too, but I've been working hard with Miriam's help on learning the language, and I know my Bible well enough to recognize quotes."

"Backache?" he teased.

"I'm tougher than that." Her relevant muscles were just . . . underdeveloped. She lowered her voice. "Thank you for suggesting this. I . . . found it really inspiring. I still have goose bumps from hearing the hymns."

Lines gathered on his forehead. "But you couldn't have understood the words to those."

"No, but the sound of so many voices joined into one was extraordinary. I could tell from people's faces that they were sincere, that they were offering praise to the Lord in the best way they could." Unable to read his face, she stopped. "That may sound dumb . . . I mean, I shouldn't assume I know what people are thinking—"

"No," he interrupted, an odd harshness in his voice. "You're right. It's the closest we can come to being one with God."

"Oh." Pierced by a yearning that was nearly painful, all she could think was, *I want that.* Well, there were other ways to find what Luke did in worshipping with these people who, like him, had chosen to block the temptations out there that would distract them from the word of their Lord. There was nothing stopping her from opening her heart in the same way. "Well." Feeling a little awkward, she looked around. "Miriam must be looking for me. I'm supposed to help bring out the food."

He frowned. "You're a guest."

"I like getting to know the other women. And being useful."

He smiled, but crookedly. His mother or his sister would

have said the same. Sitting idle while others worked would be unthinkable. "Then Abby must come back to her *daadi*."

When his daughter's arms tightened around Julia's neck, she laughed. "If I have a little monkey hanging around my neck, I might dump a bowl of potato salad on the bishop's lap, and think how embarrassing that would be!"

For a moment longer, Abby clung before reaching out for her father. "Do you know what I think?" he said. "That this little girl has legs and feet, and can walk."

Abby was giggling as he set her down, and Julia turned toward the house.

SUCH HUNGER HE thought he'd seen. Not for him, of course; she, too, wanted to feel as one with God. Luke thought their Lord had already heard her need and was steering her the direction He thought she must go.

Grimacing, he dismissed what was, after all, a self-serving thought, that just because it had once occurred to him that Julia belonged among his people, that must mean God had the same intention. More likely, Julia had been sent to challenge his convictions.

He led Abby to a section of lawn where some older girls were supervising the younger ones at play. Two weeks ago, she'd declined to join in the fun. He couldn't remember what game they'd been playing, but today a Nerf ball was being bounced off heads and shoulders and backs. Apparently, it was not allowed to hit the ground.

One of the older girls—Rudy's granddaughter, Luke thought—was clever enough to bounce the ball straight to Abby. It glanced off her head, sprang back into the air, and she laughed aloud. When someone directed it right back at her, she stepped forward to connect with it.

Luke slowly eased back. A few times, she looked to be sure he was still there, but otherwise she joined happily in the game, shrieking as she ran about. At the moment, language didn't matter. He thought she was learning more than she realized anyway. But this! To see her play with other children.

He turned his head, glad to spot Julia and see that she had stopped partway across the lawn to watch Abby, too. She smiled. When she looked at him, he wondered if her eyes were damp.

She loved his Abby. Had come to love her while he was still floundering with a decision that violated some of his personal tenets even as he'd seen no other choice he could live with. But each day, he had become more certain that he had done the best thing. He, too, loved this little girl with a fierceness that sometimes startled him. He hoped she'd never have to find out that, in fact, he wasn't her biological father. And why should she? But if it happened . . . a lie was not a strong foundation. He knew that.

He was distracted when Miriam set a platter of fried chicken on a table that he hadn't helped set up, any more than he'd helped unload the bench wagon in the first place.

"Why don't you leave her playing?" she suggested. "She can eat with Julia and me."

"I'll do that," he said. "If she stays happy. I'll make sure she can see me."

"Good." She hurried away, back to the kitchen for another load.

Luke made sure that Abby saw where he was, among a mixed group of men including his younger brother again. And was that a flush on Elam's cheeks after a young woman leaned over his shoulder to fill his glass with lemonade before moving on?

Intrigued, Luke decided it was. Elam was careful not to glance her way until she had moved several places down the table, but when he did, he worked entirely too hard to appear casual. And, yes, *she* was blushing, too.

Luke had to think about who she was. One of those girls too young for him—as most of the unmarried ones were—

she hadn't caught his eye until now. Although she was pretty, he decided, a little unusual with especially dark hair and eyes among a people who tended to blond and perhaps brown hair. And, yes, the occasional redhead.

Without thinking, he turned his head until he saw Julia two tables away, laughing as she poured coffee.

Elam had seen, and raised his eyebrows. Luke mimicked him, nodding toward the girl.

The name popped into his head. Anna Rose Esch. Her family had been new here while he was away, moving from Pennsylvania in search of affordable farmland. He must have met her mother; he remembered talking to the father, Melvin Esch, but what boys they had were Elam's age and younger, so no reason for him to become well acquainted with the family.

Seated two men away from Luke, Elam pretended to dignity and complete indifference to the girl. Luke took a page from his book and tried to be subtle when he checked to be sure Julia was still being treated kindly.

As if most of his church group would consider doing anything else. Ava Kemp, maybe, a sour woman if he'd ever met one, but knowing her husband, Luke could understand why she might be. Sally Yoder had been catty with the other girls when she fluttered around Luke all those years ago, but she had married a solid, good man shortly after Luke walked away from his family and church, and she had four children and carried another now.

As he searched for Julia again, he met another woman's eyes. Rebecca King's. Of course, she came straight to him, hips swaying, and set a hand on his shoulder as she said, "Can I get anything for you?"

He made sure to sound pleasant. "*Nein, but denke.*"

"Your little girl is so sweet. Not so shy now, is she?"

"No, she's gaining confidence," he agreed. "She has *Mamm* and sometimes Miriam when I'm working." He raised his voice slightly. "She even likes Elam."

His brother shot him a look promising retribution. Rebecca laughed, a light, merry ripple, and went on her way. Luke pondered why his instinct was to avoid her. She was pretty enough, if a decade younger than him, just pushy enough to let him see she was interested but not enough to be annoying, well-liked, and yet . . . she was not for him.

He could almost see *Mamm* shaking her head in disappointment.

ABBY SAT SQUEEZED between Miriam and Julia, eating with her usual delicacy. Julia hadn't thought to ask Luke whether her mother was a petite woman, and her daughter simply took after her, or whether Abby may have suffered from malnutrition that might be overcome and allow a growth spurt.

Sitting across the table from them, Sarah Yoder engaged Miriam in talking about the quilt auction and the interest garnered by their fliers and the posting on the quilt shop website. Julia had put both auctions up on the Bowman's site, too, and had answered several questions via email. Ruth had told her earlier that other Amish quilt shops in Missouri as far south as the Ozarks and even up into Iowa had also posted the information.

"Lydia is so grateful," Sarah said. "She has her hands full with Noah home."

"How is he doing?" Julia asked.

They'd been talking in *Deitsh*, and Sarah didn't switch to English. Julia was glad that the other women sometimes seemed to forget she was an *auslander*, and that when she contributed to the conversation, she was fluent enough to be understood, at least.

"Ach, so well! Except he misses David. They were sitting beside each other, you know, just behind their *daad*, talking until . . ." She lifted her hands in a hopeless gesture. "One minute together, the next, David was gone."

"I hope Noah didn't see him."

"I think he did. He cries out at night, Lydia says."

Julia's throat tightened. "I'm so sorry."

Sarah nodded, her sadness showing, but then she said with possibly forced cheer, "Noah has been to see Sol twice now, and that helps. His *daad*'s face looks better, not so swollen, you know, and the bruises are fading."

Julia still hadn't met Lydia's husband. She'd always waited outside his room or Noah's. Since running into Luke and Abby the one evening, Julia hadn't gotten near the waiting room outside Sol's room. And heck, it wasn't as if he was likely to be in the mood to be introduced to a new acquaintance.

Of course, Lydia was here today, as were her two daughters. An *Englisch* neighbor was staying with Noah, Julia had heard. They hoped by the next service he would be strong enough to attend. Friends and family encircled Lydia, not letting her lift a finger or chase after her little girls. The open caring warmed Julia's heart. She felt confident that Lydia wouldn't be deserted, even as her husband's recuperation dragged on, month after month.

Two neighboring church districts were also raising money to help pay the hospital bills, Sarah told them, and the father of the *Englisch* boy who had been driving the car had written a big check to the hospital.

"So good of him," another woman who had been listening in said.

More likely guilt, Julia couldn't help thinking, before realizing how uncharitable she'd been. There was a lot to be said about thinking the best of people.

I'll try, she promised herself.

The entire time she ate, talked to the other women, and cut up food for Abby, she remained disturbingly aware of Luke Bowman. Without even looking, she seemed to know when he wandered from one group of men to another. Twice when she sneaked peeks, his gaze seemed to be resting on her, although she assured herself that, really, he was keeping an eye on his daughter. He worried about her. She'd seen how much. Abby was a lucky little girl, to have a *daad* like Luke. One who didn't care that he wasn't related by blood, either because he had loved Abby's mother—although not in the way of a man for a woman—or because the small girl who was marched into the store needed him so desperately.

Miriam had told Julia earlier that the social worker had dropped by Luke's house Thursday night. Apparently this was the second time she'd come by. Ms. Tanner was a woman who did her job right. Even Miriam had sounded approving, as little as the Amish usually allowed themselves to be involved with *Englisch* authority.

Eventually, Julia went in and helped with cleanup, made welcome instead of being treated as if she were butting in where she didn't belong. When she emerged from the house, she saw that some young women were playing a vigorous game of volleyball, while the young men cheered them on. Abby on his knee, Luke sat a distance away with his father and several other men.

"Oh, have you met my *onkel* Mose?" Miriam asked. "He's *Aenti* Barbara's husband, and you know her. That's their middle son sitting with them, too. Ephraim's wife just had their fourth baby, a little girl. With Down syndrome, but not so bad, and they love her the way she is."

Yes, they would.

As if compelled, Julia accompanied Miriam toward the group sitting beneath a huge old oak tree. The tables no longer groaned with food, but no one had made a move yet to load them back on the bench wagon.

Luke's gaze went right to her, making her self-conscious. Eli smiled at her approach, although his gaze shifted twice to his oldest son.

"Sit, sit," Eli said, moving over to give the two women

room between him and Luke. Julia ended up beside Eli, which was just as well.

She was introduced to Mose and his son Ephraim, and realized she'd worked beside Ephraim's wife, Daniela, in the kitchen. The babies and most of the younger children were napping in several rooms in the spacious house, one woman or another going upstairs to check on them regularly.

Abby, of course, was sound asleep in her father's arms. She'd come a long way, but would have been afraid to be left where she couldn't see him or anyone else in her family.

Or me, Julia thought, except Abby was obviously coming to rely on her grandmother and aunt and didn't need Julia the same.

Julia heard Miriam murmur to her brother, "Your arms must be tired. Do you want me to take a turn?"

He shook his head. "She doesn't weigh any more than a bird."

His hair was growing longer, almost shaggy. Soon his mother would be able to give him the haircut that would make him truly look Amish. Julia couldn't decide how she felt about that.

"Does anyone know where Elam is?" Eli asked. "I see Deborah with her dishes, which means it's time for us to go."

"Oh!" Miriam jumped up and went to her mother to take a basket and a casserole dish. Julia started to get up, too, but Eli laid a hand on her arm.

"No need. You've done enough today."

"Everyone has been so nice, and it was a wonderful meal."

"Glad we are that Miriam asked you," he said.

Julia hoped she wasn't imagining the irony in his voice—and the glance he gave Luke.

Who diverted his father by saying, "I'm surprised Elam didn't bring his own buggy today. How else can he drive his girl home?"

Eli chuckled deeply. "She's not his girl yet, and she never will be if he keeps hanging back. Other fellows are courting her, too."

"The Esch girl?"

"*Ja*, that's the one. The right girl makes a coward out of any man, ain't so?"

All the men present laughed heartily, Julia feeling as if she wasn't meant to hear this—and very aware that Luke alone had not laughed.

Chapter Nineteen

"A LITTLE HIGHER," Julia directed the two Amishmen standing on a pair of ladders and holding a long slat in place between them. She tipped her head to one side and then the other. "Six inches? No, a little more . . ."

Without a word, they obediently edged the wide slat upward until she said, "There! That's perfect." One did the bracing while the other tapped in a nail, after which they looked at her for approval. "That's great."

When they placed two other nails and climbed down, she asked them to put others up at the same height. They would be used to display queen-size quilts the full length of this wall inside the grange hall. Men and women both worked throughout the hall, arranging racks and temporary rods and slats on the walls so that quilts of all sizes could be viewed before the auction started. She wasn't the only non-Amish person present, thank goodness; two other ardent quilters she'd met at A Stitch in Time had also volunteered, bringing their husbands along.

One group unfolded chairs and set them up in long rows

with a center aisle. A low stage had been stored in an out-building and hauled in for the auctioneer, along with a po-dium. This auctioneer would not use a microphone.

The woman telling her had chuckled. "Not that Jerry needs one. Ach, that boy always had a loud voice. You wait and see."

The second auction of fine furniture, crafts, antiques, and more was being set up in a large barn less than a quar-ter mile away. Parking would be in a field in between. Ta-bles selling food would be outside both the grange hall and the barn so that people going to only one of the auctions would still have a chance to buy an on-the-fly meal and goodies to take home, too.

Because of her bookkeeping experience, Julia would be one of those handling checkout. Since there'd be no com-puter or fancy program to handle the auction, she didn't think any particular expertise would be required. Amish businesses in many cases accepted credit cards, but not to-night. They'd take checks, but cash would predominate. Tens of thousands of dollars' worth of cash. Apparently, *Englischers* who attended Amish auctions and fundraisers knew to bring their wallets stuffed with bills.

Ruth bustled up. "*Ja*, that looks good. Do you want to start hanging quilts?"

"As soon as the men are done."

"A few curious people have already poked their noses in. Always some of those, there are."

Julia laughed. Her mother had held garage sales a few times, and invariably people—probably dealers—would show up at the crack of dawn expecting an early peek.

"Are dealers likely to come?" she asked.

"To look maybe, but not to buy. They like to get quilts cheap, when no one else is bidding against them."

That made sense.

Looking at the boxes full of gently folded quilts, she said, "Ocean Waves first," and found she was talking to herself.

The men had moved on, but left the ladders. Another woman Julia didn't know, perhaps her own age, saw her lifting the first quilt from a plastic tub and hurried over. "I'll take one side."

"Thank you. I'm Julia Durant."

"*Ja*, I saw you Sunday. I'm Mary Brenneman. Abe's Mary."

Julia nodded even though she didn't have any idea who Abe was. They were in the same church district as the Bowmans, which was identification enough. She was doing reasonably well at remembering people she'd met, but large Amish families meant that no more than a dozen last names were shared by nearly everyone in the county, and favored first names like Mary and Rachel and Daniel and Jacob popped up confusingly often.

Julia carried a bagful of clips up the ladder with her. They'd hold the quilt to the slat for this temporary display. She wouldn't want to use them for more than a few hours, since the weight of the quilt pulling against the clips could damage the fabric. This should be fine, though, she decided, once they'd secured it. Obviously, this group of women had held similar auctions before, and knew what they were doing.

She and Mary worked quickly and in harmony, getting nine quilts hung. Six other queen-size quilts and two king-size were being hung behind the stage. Full- and twin-size were on the far wall, or draped over bedsteads or quilt racks. The Bowmans, father and son, had also donated six quilt racks, although she knew their inventory was getting low. These would be auctioned off halfway through the afternoon.

She itched to see the setup for the other auction, where Eli, Elam, and Luke were helping. They had agreed to close the store today, hanging a sign on the door suggesting potential customers come to the auctions, a bold map providing directions.

Not all the stores on the main street were closed today, but most Amish-owned ones were. Their entire focus was on raising money for one of their brethren. Julia hadn't heard even a hint that anyone worried about lost revenue.

She and Mary wandered around to admire quilts throughout the hall, her new friend talking about the makers, almost all of whom she knew. There were a few exceptions, including old quilts. They stopped to admire a nineteenth-century Texas Star quilt and a crazy quilt in red and purple velvets that were only slightly faded. Mary had made two quilts, one full-size and one crib, both gorgeous, and she admired the ones Julia admitted as her own.

Eventually Julia couldn't resist the good smells coming through the wide-open doors and went out to buy lunch before the rush of people arrived for the auction. She threw caution to the winds and had a pierogi followed by a gooey slice of shoofly pie. Wouldn't you know, she was wiping her chin when a deep, amused voice said, "Tastes good, does it?"

She wrinkled her nose at Luke and Eli, who had stopped by the picnic table. "You know it does. Deborah made this, didn't she?"

Eli laughed. "She cooked all day yesterday and got up early to start again this morning. Pies, cakes, chili, cinnamon bread."

"I love cinnamon bread. Is it being sold at the bake table?"

"*Ja*, but you'd better move fast."

"I'll do that. Once I can heave myself to my feet."

Both men laughed. Luke asked if the crew working here were ready for the sale, and said at the barn they were well on their way, too. Food wasn't to be set up by the barn until later, though, so they'd decided to get some lunch.

Luke said, "Unless you're needed, why don't you wait and keep us company?"

Startled, she managed an "Oh. I can do that."

Eli returned a few minutes later with a sausage smothered in chili, Luke with a pierogi like she'd eaten.

"I hope word got out," Julia worried. A few cars were bumping their way across the field, directed by teenage Amish boys, but not enough.

"We'll be busy," Eli said placidly. "You'll see. They're just starting to arrive."

"Except for the nosy early birds."

"We had those over at the barn, too," Luke agreed. "One generous fellow offered to buy a dining room set right then and there, for about a third of its value, and thought we'd be smart to take his offer because then we could use the space for something else."

"Did he know he was talking to the furniture maker himself?"

The skin beside Luke's eyes crinkled with a smile. "Not until I thanked him kindly, but said no. I suggested he bid on it, but I don't think he hung around."

Eli shrugged. "Trying to get a steal." His tone was more tolerant than Julia felt.

In truth, many bidders at a charity auction were hoping for a steal. They could help a good cause and still get something they wanted for less than value. But if enough people came, some of the quilts and furniture might go for well above value.

"Look at the traffic now," Luke murmured.

She swiveled on the bench. "Oh, my. Oh, I can hardly wait!"

The two men clearly thought she was funny, but she didn't mind. She'd never done anything like this before. In fact, she'd spent too many years enmeshed in fear to extend herself for the sake of others.

Well, that was going to change.

LUKE WAS SURPRISED when his father made no comment about Julia at all as they walked back across the field, dodging slow-moving traffic.

Both worked for another couple of hours, allowing themselves to be directed by those organizing the auction. Looking around at last, Luke judged that they were very nearly ready. Given how much effort Julia and Miriam had put into the quilt auction, he wanted to watch part of it.

Not seeing his father, he shrugged and slipped out, only leaving word where he'd gone.

The field was almost completely full with row upon row of parked cars. If most people stayed, and more arrived for the evening auction, they might have a problem.

Even before he reached the hall, he heard the auctioneer working the crowd. "I have sixteen hundred, sixteen hundred. You know you want this quilt. If you don't want to go a hundred, I'll take a raise of fifty. What's fifty dollars?" Pause. Triumph. "I have sixteen hundred and fifty now. Who'll go seventeen hundred?"

Luke knew that voice. Jerry Ropp, one of Luke's first cousins. Four or five years younger than Luke, Jerry had talked eagerly about becoming an auctioneer by the time he was fourteen or fifteen, to his father's disapproval if not the bishop's. It seemed he'd achieved his dream.

And today, who could dispute that he did good work?

Luke smiled. Outsiders said the Amish didn't change, but they were wrong. And glacially slow change was fine with him, now that he'd lost his youthful impatience.

The room was jam-packed, the rows of folding chairs full and spectators or bidders lining the walls. Conversation hummed even while the bidding went on. By the time he stepped inside, the quilt had sold to buyer number two hundred two for seventeen hundred and fifty dollars. Jerry had eked out another hundred and fifty there by the end, and every little bit helped.

Luke decided to stay by the open doors, given the heat and closeness in here.

With barely a pause, volunteers had hung another quilt behind Jerry, and he'd started his patter already. This one wasn't an Amish quilt. The colors were downright garish, the patches deliberately uneven. An old quilt, maybe?

The bidding started briskly and rose fast.

"Seventeen hundred, I have . . . eighteen hundred, now nineteen. Who'll give me two thousand?"

Luke had just seen that Julia was here at the back wall watching, close enough he'd look unfriendly if he didn't acknowledge her. Keeping his distance would be smart, but she could tell him how the event was going. He knew she'd donated quilts, and hoped they had sold for good money. He hadn't closed the ten feet between them, though, when a man said, "Ugly, that one is, but old, Jerry says."

Amos must have come in right on Luke's heels.

"It is ugly," he agreed. "Who would want that on his bed?"

"I don't think anyone would use it. It's supposed to be from 1890," the bishop said. "It's put together with fancy embroidery."

"Twenty-three hundred . . ."

One of Jerry's assistants waved and gestured at a raised bid card.

"Twenty-four . . ."

Amos shook his head.

"It's for a good cause," Luke said piously. "We must be grateful to whoever donated this . . . this . . ."

Amos finished his sentence. "Crazy quilt. That's what it's called."

Both listened until the quilt finally sold for twenty-seven hundred dollars.

"Ah," Amos said, straightening. "This next one is Miriam's. I heard her telling someone earlier."

It was a crib quilt, a pattern that looked like the pinwheels he'd seen at fairs. This one was yellows and greens and blues, made for a boy, he guessed. Miriam made many crib-size quilts, he had noticed, claiming she liked to try new patterns, pick out new fabric, and the smaller size kept her from getting bored. But he wondered about his sister, still mourning the man she'd loved, refusing to consider marriage, seemingly fixated on turning out quilts for other women's babies.

This one went for nine hundred dollars. Luke thought that was a good price for a crib quilt, more than Ruth charged for the ones in her store.

In the brief lull, Amos gazed keenly at Luke and said, "I've meant to talk to you, to tell you what people have been saying."

Luke hoped he didn't noticeably stiffen. *"Ja?"*

"People think it's *wunderbaar* what a good *daad* you are, and you a single man." There seemed to be a delay up front, so the bishop wasn't drowned out, much as Luke might wish that would be so. "They say how lucky Abby is that the *Englisch* woman found you. Looks like Miriam, I've heard people say, and her eyes the same color as yours."

The lie almost choked him. He managed to say, "She's so small for her age. I worry."

"Your *mamm* and sister are not tall women."

"That's true. Miriam was so pudgy, though. Do you remember?"

"Ja, but she was given the best from birth. Your Abigail will catch up, God willing."

Luke nodded.

"That's all I had to say." Amos glanced toward the front. "Looks as if they're ready to start again, ain't so? What a blessing so many people came to buy." He mentioned finding someone else he needed to speak to—had Luke seen Isaac Kemp? No? Ach, he must be here somewhere. Amos mixed with the crowd and was out of sight in a moment.

Nothing could have stopped Luke from turning to see if Julia was still there, so few feet away.

She was, and something in her expression told him she'd heard Amos's every word—and her *Deitsh* was good enough now for her to have understood it. Julia, the only other person who knew that Abby did not have his blue eyes or look like Miriam, because she wasn't related to either of them.

Her lips parted . . . and then pressed firmly together.

Needing to clear his head, he turned his back on her and the continuing auction, walking out.

LUKE AVOIDED JULIA through the evening. She knew it was deliberate; a couple of times he turned abruptly and went the other way when he saw her.

It hurt her feelings, of course, but she knew why he was doing it. She must have assumed the corporeal form of his guilty conscience, like Charles Dickens's ghost of Christmases past. Did he think she was trying to hunt him down to issue a lecture?

No, he couldn't believe that. It was just his guilt making him uncomfortable with her, because she was the only person who knew what he felt and why.

A magnificent bedroom set Luke and Eli had donated was the final item to be auctioned off that evening. As exhausted as she was, Julia wanted to see what it went for.

She knew from the inlay that it was Luke's work. His father's was as fine, just . . . different. A little more traditional, maybe.

Hoping to get away before the crowd, she stood at the back of the barn. Sweat trickled down her spine and stung her eyes. There were too many people packed in here, and the diesel-operated portable lights didn't help. Miriam and Elam joined her just before the auctioneer asked for an opening bid.

"We've made so much more than we could have hoped for." Miriam sounded dazed. "Did you see how much Katie-Ann's Postage Stamp quilt sold for?"

Her brother rolled his eyes. "You've told us three times."

Julia had seen, all right. Five thousand dollars. She hadn't been surprised, though, because of the extraordinary

work involved in piecing the incredibly tiny squares—and
the flow of the colors. The full-size quilt had been a mas-
terwork, and three bidders had fought until the very end.

Miriam was right; they had earned far more in the quilt
auction, and Julia thought this one as well, than she, at
least, had dreamed. She felt . . . blessed to have had a part
in it, however small.

Tuning in, she heard the auctioneer say, "We have an
opening bid of seven thousand dollars. Will somebody give
me eight—?"

Somebody would. And nine and ten and eleven thousand. Julia thought her mouth fell open at some point.

She'd compared the Bowmans' prices with those of furniture stores online that sold Amish furniture, and thought
Eli and Luke ought to ask more. Much of the Amish furniture out there was beautiful in a classic way—mission, for
example—but didn't compare to the pieces Luke crafted,
using the sheen of finely finished wood in imaginative ways
that still spoke of the generations of Amish furniture makers before him.

At eighteen thousand dollars, the room fell silent but for
Jerry Ropp. She marveled that he hadn't lost his voice by
now. The two remaining bidders didn't speak as they lifted
their bid cards. The woman with one of the men whispered
something to him just before he held up his number again.

Nineteen thousand.

Twenty.

The entire room broke into spontaneous applause at
such a staggering addition to the night's total.

The shake of a head, and the lucky bidder would be paying twenty thousand dollars and, no doubt, shipping for his
glorious bedroom set.

To the roar of additional applause, Julia slipped out into
the strikingly cooler air of evening. Hurrying away from
the barn, she hoped she could escape before the mob. She
was desperate to flop down on her bed and maybe not move

for two days. Her entire body ached. She wasn't sure she'd ever been on her feet for so many hours before. Or cared so much for the result.

Just before she plunged into almost complete darkness, a young Amishman approached. "I can help you find your car."

She didn't know his name, but felt sure she'd seen him Sunday. He had the friendly, earnest expression on his face she'd come to expect from the Amish she'd met.

"I know where I parked, but . . . would you mind walking me to my car?" she asked. "It's awfully dark."

"*Ja*, I'm happy to." As they set out down the first row of parked cars, he asked eagerly, "Did it go well in there?"

"*Very* well. Extraordinarily well." Julia could still scarcely believe it. She told him about the bedroom set and enjoyed hearing his voice crack when he repeated, "*Twenty* thousand?"

"Twenty."

"I wish I'd seen that." He was quiet, following her as she slipped between two monster SUVs to the next row. Then he said quietly, "David was a friend of mine. He would have hated to see his *daad* and *bruder* so hurt."

She wanted to turn and hug him, but he wouldn't accept that, not from an *Englisch* woman he knew only because she'd been a guest at one church service.

"No," she said, just as softly. "I hope he was watching."

"*Ja*."

Neither said another word until she found her car, unlocked it, and thanked him. Once she'd climbed in and locked the doors, she watched him disappear in seconds.

Her hand shook as she put the key in the ignition. What had she been thinking, heading out alone like that? What if the boy hadn't seen her and she'd met up with somebody in the darkness? She was never that foolish. Never.

With her lights on, she drove slowly the short distance to the country road that would take her into town. Bump, bump, bump, and then she reached smooth pavement.

Tension curled in her stomach.

That boy who had walked her to her car might have been sixteen years old. Boys that age assaulted women. She'd only been nineteen when it happened to her, and she'd always wondered if he was another student.

Yet tonight, it hadn't occurred to her to worry about the boy.

Was Nick right, that she'd made a huge assumption about the Amish? Was that what drew her to them?

No. It was so much more than that. So much that today had epitomized. The generosity and the warmth and the faith, in all meanings of the word.

Really, when she got to the old schoolhouse–turned–apartment building, she was too tired to be afraid crossing the short, well-lit distance to the back door, or when waiting for the elevator in the deserted foyer, and, finally, letting herself into her own apartment. She heard tinny voices from a TV next door, and the knowledge that another person was nearby kept her calm as she peeked in each room and closet and under her bed. She didn't go out at night often, for a good reason.

Teeth brushed, she lay between cool sheets and thought, *I've changed*. She wasn't as fearful—she had, after all, set out alone. But it was more than that. Some of it was daily routines. She couldn't remember the last time she'd turned on her new television, or even her stereo. She quilted, and read newspapers and books. She was cooking more from scratch, too, and liked the results even though she'd never be the cook Luke's mother was. Her own food was good enough, though, that she was pretty sure she'd gained weight. Not a lot yet, but . . . she didn't know how she felt about it.

Sunday . . . she'd *liked* wearing a pretty color and feeling the airy fabric swirl around her legs when she walked.

She hadn't let Nick cow her, either. No, their conversation hadn't been face-to-face, but she made him accept that joining the Amish in worship was something she wanted to do.

She'd become more confident even as her life seemed . . . simpler.

And Sunday, she'd liked knowing that, whenever she looked around, Luke Bowman was watching her.

Chapter Twenty

TUESDAY MORNING, LUKE arrived to find he was the first. *Daad* was to be a little late—he'd gruffly conceded that he needed to pull out whatever rocking chairs he had stored in his barn workshop.

He frowned. "I suppose there might be a few quilt racks, too."

Luke knew his father hated making those. Luke didn't like wasting his time on them, either, even though they brought in a steady source of revenue. They felt too much like assembly-line work to him.

Julia came in the back door not five minutes later, her big handbag over her shoulder, a pie cradled in her hands.

"Apple," she told him. "I figured I'd share so I didn't eat the whole thing myself."

"Your brother wouldn't help you?"

Her expression dimmed slightly, but she smiled. "I made two."

"Ah. I'll look forward to sharing your pie when we stop

for lunch." He told her why his *daad* had been delayed, and she nodded and took a few steps past him.

Then she stopped and turned back. "I wanted to say how fabulous it was to hear the price your bedroom set brought at the auction."

"But only a small part of the whole," he pointed out.

"I know that, but—" Julia laughed. "I really didn't mean that in a 'you brought in more money than anyone else' way, you know. Just . . . it was exciting. And it got me thinking."

He waited.

"Well, you should consider raising some of the prices here in the store and online. Especially now that more orders are coming from other parts of the country. We don't have to depend on what people locally can afford."

"But what if the people here can't afford to buy anything then?"

"I know you're right, it's just that I've done some looking online—" She broke off. "Never mind. I'm being competitive, aren't I?"

Her chagrin stirred his sense of humor. "That might be."

She blew out a puff of air. "Forget I said it."

He let her take a step before he spoke to her back. "You heard what Amos said to me, didn't you?"

Julia stopped but didn't turn around for a minute. When she did, she looked troubled. "I couldn't help it, but it's none of my business."

He hesitated. "Will you set down the pie so we can talk?"

"I'll never say anything."

"I know you won't." He took the pie from her and placed it on the butcher-block countertop that ran one length of the room. "I saw your face. You think I shouldn't have claimed to be her father, don't you?" Was he too mealy-mouthed to say *lied*?

It would seem so.

Her nose was red enough that he thought it might peel.

In helping with the auction, she must have spent too much time outside. He wanted to touch that sore place gently—and perhaps trail his fingers down her creamy cheek and jaw. This new tension stretched tight even as he couldn't let go of his original worry, especially since her hesitation made him think she would hold back.

The color of her eyes seemed to deepen, perhaps because of what she saw on his face, but then she took a deep breath. "Since you asked," she said with obvious resolution, "I think it's going to eat at you. People will always look for Abby's resemblance to you and your family, you know. And . . . what if she gets hurt and she needs a transfusion?"

"My blood is O positive, which is the most common. Hers might be, too. If not . . . I can say it must be the same as her mother's."

She didn't say a word.

No, she let him rerun what he'd just said. He closed his eyes. "I've been plotting future lies to support the big one I already told. I didn't know I was doing that."

"Admitting the truth will get harder the longer you put it off."

He groaned. "But . . . what about Abby? When she finds out I'm not her *daad* . . ."

The compassion in Julia's beautiful brown eyes weakened his knees. "She doesn't have to know now. You can tell her when the time is right, just as people do who have adopted a child. She's old enough that she might remember living with her mother and . . ."

"The men who came and went," he said grimly, finishing what Julia didn't.

"Yes. Why would she resent the fact that you took her in? By then, she'll feel so loved, not being your biological daughter shouldn't matter so much."

"What I fear most," he admitted, "is that Bishop Amos will believe we should look for Beth's family, give them a chance to know their granddaughter."

Her forehead crinkled. "How would he be able to do that?"

"Our bishops write to each other often. They spread news and discuss ideas before they take action on them. The chances are good that Beth was raised here in Missouri or in a neighboring state. If Amos wrote to others, asking about a family whose daughter had run away from home and never come back, who was old enough to have had a child . . ."

"You believe he'd do that even though you oppose it?"

Luke could tell she didn't understand that. She'd gotten to know many of the Amish on the surface, including him, but, like most outsiders, would struggle with the most basic tenet of their faith.

"Obedience is our way," he explained. This was part of what he had run away from himself. The part he sometimes still found hard. "I shouldn't be raising myself so high as to think my judgment is greater than his."

"But Abby's mother wanted you to raise her."

"He may agree she had the right to make that decision, but he might not, too. We don't know why Beth left the *Leit*. Maybe she left because of a scandal of her own doing."

"You don't believe that, do you?"

"No. She didn't act as if she cared what happened to her."

"If she lived or died."

"*Ja.*" Remembering still pained him. She remained Amish enough to refuse even to consider suicide, but there were other ways. "For Abby, she might have tried. I don't know."

"If she was a drug addict . . ."

"They don't make good choices," he agreed, unable entirely to articulate what his gut had said about her. That's what worried him—that he wouldn't be able to find the right words for Bishop Amos, either.

"Luke." Julia astonished him by taking his hand and squeezing it. She would have taken hers back, but he held on, feeling the connection between them that defied practicality. Cheeks flushed, she said, "What I think doesn't matter. I meant it when I said I'll never tell anybody. I only worry that the lie separates you from your family and people. And God. Does He understand?"

This time, when she wriggled her fingers, he had to release her slim, cool hand. He wondered if he'd managed to keep everything he felt from his face. Or were all his doubts, all his emotions, laid bare? He thought they might be. A painful lurch in his chest felt like he'd been kicked by a horse. He wanted to step forward and gather her in his arms, lay his cheek against her head, close his eyes and do nothing but breathe her in, warm himself and soak in her strength.

Of course, he could do nothing of the kind.

"Thank you," he said hoarsely. "You've asked good questions. I'm lucky that, of all the people who might know the truth, it's you who does."

Watching her retreat, cheeks crimson now, he was shocked to find how much he meant that. Julia was a good friend to him right now, even though he wished that she could be more. What she thought of him mattered, as much as the respect of his bishop and his family did.

The difference was that none of them would understand why he hadn't told the truth from the beginning, while she did. Part of that was because she was an outsider who'd seen beggars in bus shelters and prostitutes on corners and addicts slumped in doorways. *Daad* and Amos, doing business with the *Englisch* as they did, were more worldly than many of the Amish, but they didn't see the kind of *Englisch* he'd gotten to know as he scraped out a marginal existence in a major city while he worked hard to get enough education to move to a decent place. If they had, they might understand better why Beth had to have been desperate to choose that existence over whatever she'd left.

Standing alone among the tools of his trade and half-built furniture, Luke felt a warm mantle of comfort, as if Julia's arms had closed around him in fact. If he chose to perpetuate his lie . . . she would understand that, too, he believed. Know he had valid reasons—and that he'd made the decision he had for the good of the little girl he already loved as his own—not selfish ones.

No, he didn't have to worry about Julia's judgment because she was on his side.

Hearing a neigh out back, he guessed his father had arrived. He'd have to go out and help *Daad* unload.

But first . . . Luke bowed his head and spoke from his heart.

I need Your guidance, Lord. You know I've gone astray before. Help me see the right way now. Help me know what You would ask of me.

LUKE WAS EXCEPTIONALLY quiet when he and his father came up front midday to have slices of her apple pie. Eli watched him with worry in his eyes, but they both exclaimed over the pie.

"Deborah would say this is as good as hers," Eli insisted.

Julia wrinkled her nose at him. "Deborah would say that because she's a modest woman who would never claim to be the best cook in Tompkin's Mill. I'm happy as long as you're enjoying it."

"If only we had a few scoops of ice cream," Luke said, although since he was currently scraping his plate clean with his fork, she couldn't see that he'd missed it so much.

Both he and his father had second slices, although she couldn't see how they'd put that much away on top of the lunch Deborah had undoubtedly sent with them. She hoped they weren't forcing it down to please her . . . but the pie *was* good, if she did say so herself. The apples were just tart enough, she'd used the right amount of sugar and cinnamon, and baked it exactly long enough.

"Nick will probably eat his pie in two sittings," she said ruefully.

"We could take care of this pie in only one sitting," Eli suggested, a twinkle in his eyes. "Divide that last piece, we could."

"That's mine for dessert tonight," Julia said firmly, covering the pie and moving it to the desk.

They laughed, Eli admitting that he wasn't sure he could have taken even one more bite.

Luke thanked her, his eyes darkened to navy, his expression unreadable, and accompanied his father in back.

She twiddled her thumbs and finally pulled out a book to read, since traffic in the store was next to nonexistent today and she hadn't sold so much as a quilt rack. The only useful thing she did all day was carry two racks down the block to A Stitch in Time to restock their inventory, and promise that Luke would bring them another rocking chair when he came to a good stopping point.

If he did, she didn't see him, but probably he'd gone out the back and down the alley—especially if he wanted to avoid her. And why wouldn't he? Julia winced at the memory of how . . . how *self-righteous* she'd undoubtedly sounded. Who was she to talk? She'd never in her life faced a dilemma like his. Humble himself utterly, bow to God's will as his bishop interpreted it . . . or protect the vulnerable little girl he loved? In fact, when she thought about it that way, she wasn't sure he hadn't done the right thing in the first place.

Maybe she should tell him so—but she knew better.

What had that last look he'd given her meant?

A too-familiar ache reminded her that she'd never know, because he and she could never really even be friends. Remember that chasm separating them?

Midafternoon, Miriam burst in. "I'm so bored! Nobody is shopping today! I thought we could have a language lesson."

"Nobody is coming in here today, either, not since this morning when people just wanted to talk about the auction."

"Us, too. So . . . how do you say, 'There's nobody here.'"

"We're here," Julia objected, before reciting, *"Sis niemand do."*

"Why are you so stubborn?"

Julia laughed. *"Ferwas bischt allfatt so schtarrkeppich?"*

"Put it on the bill."

"Duh's uff die rechning."

On and on. Some of the sentences Miriam drilled in her seemed a little silly. When would she say, *I planted an acre of potatoes*? But she might say *planted* or *potatoes*, she decided, and the verb tense applied elsewhere, too.

Ruth had told Miriam not to bother coming back, so they continued until closing. They all walked out together, Miriam having driven with Eli that morning. As usual, they went their way, Julia hers, with a mood dip now common at the end of her working days.

LUKE WRESTLED WITH himself for two entire days. It took him longer than it might have, because when he was working with wood, he couldn't afford to let his attention wander, and much of the rest of the time he needed to stay in the here and now for Abby's sake.

She took more attention these days as she gained confidence. He couldn't count on her staying put where he left her, that was for sure. She wanted to go out and feed Charlie, or scrape the wallpaper, or play hide-and-go-seek both indoors and out. She was fast reaching the point when she needed friends her age, not just his relatives. Sunday, he would look around and think which of those children lived near his house, or his *daad*'s. Most Amish children didn't start school until they were six, but it was important she had regular playtime with other children.

He wouldn't think about any possibility that had her living elsewhere, not going to school here at all.

From the minute he saw that Abby had fallen asleep, that was when he agonized. What if the bishop said this? Did that? What if he felt Luke must be chastised by a period of shunning?

Worst of all, what if Amos insisted on trying to find Abby's family?

Not until Thursday evening did Luke understand that trust was his real issue. He must trust in the wisdom of his bishop and, yes, in God's will. Thinking Abby could depend only on him *was* taking too much on himself.

Friday morning, he told both his parents that he had to stop after work to speak to Bishop Amos before coming to pick up Abby.

"I need to talk to both of you, too," he told them, not liking the worry he was causing, but unwilling to explain yet.

Their faces appeared drawn, but all his mother said was, "Then you'll stay for dinner?"

"That would be good. Thank you."

Crouching in front of Abby, he hugged her goodbye with more than usual fervor. When he released her, she pulled back to gaze into his eyes as if in search of secrets. *"Ich liebe dich,"* he said, and she rose on tiptoe to kiss his cheek before darting away.

Walking out of his parents' house, he felt both love for his daughter and a sense of peace.

"WHY DON'T WE talk outside?" Amos suggested. "I wouldn't mind walking instead of more sitting."

Hearing the women's voices from the kitchen, Luke said, "I'd be glad to do that."

Not until they were strolling across well-tended lawn

sloping gradually upward from the house to an extensive grove of walnut trees did Amos ask, "What troubles you?"

"Does nobody who isn't troubled come to talk to you?"

"Not often," the older man said drily.

Luke was ready to have this over with. "I told you and everyone else a lie," he said flatly. "I thought I had good reason, but I was wrong."

Amos stopped and faced him, his gaze penetrating. "Does this have to do with Abigail?"

"What else?"

"I have sometimes wondered—" He shook his head. "No matter. What is the lie?"

"Abby is not my biological daughter." Something loosened in him once the words were said.

"I think you need to explain."

They resumed walking, skirting a double line of raspberry vines, pruned and tied up. A lanky brown dog joined them, tail swinging, but demanded no attention. Cicadas were in full throat.

"Her mother put my name on the birth certificate," Luke said. "She told people she wanted Abby to come to me after she died. She and I had known each other, but not that way. I felt sorry for her." He told the bishop about the sad, frantic girl desperate to find someone to love her. "I tried to help her, but I'd see her often for a few weeks and then she'd disappear when she met another man. I suspected she was using drugs, but didn't know for sure. When the social worker found me and told me about Beth's later years, I knew I'd been right."

Amos made an acknowledging sound. He stroked his beard, as Luke had seen him do before.

"I knew Beth had been raised Amish, too. That gave us a connection from the first. But she absolutely refused to tell me where she'd grown up or the names of her family. She wouldn't speak a word of *Deitsh*. I never knew for certain if hearing it would sting because of what she'd lost, or if she hated everything she'd come from."

Luke told him about Beth's letter, begging him to raise Abby as his own. "I think I may have been the only person she met after running away whom she trusted. That was partly because I'd been raised Amish, too, but also because I talked about my family and sisters and brothers. I told funny stories, about times I'd hurt my mother's feelings or *Daad* lost patience with me. She must have heard about the love I'd taken for granted. In her letter, she said she wanted for Abby what I'd known." The last thing she'd written was, *I love her, I do, but I look at her and know how I've failed her. You're not a man who would ever fail anyone who depends on you. I wish I could have trusted myself to you.*

"So she either had no family left, or she didn't want her parents to have her daughter."

"That's what I think." Luke wondered how much the bishop knew about the terrible things human beings could do to each other. Possibly not much, but it had occurred to Luke that terrible things happened among any group of people. Amos might well have had to deal with families where cruelty or a sick form of love or alcohol or drugs had done damage. He wasn't a man to gossip. "I had the impression that Beth hated herself, that she felt shame or worse. That she thought her body was all she had to offer a man."

Amos's mouth tightened. "The social worker believes you are Abby's father."

"Yes. I let her think that I could be."

"As you let us think."

Luke rolled his shoulders. "I'm sorry. Abby was so traumatized. I was afraid for her, and in my arrogance thought I had to protect her."

"From anyone who might suggest we look for her real family. That's what you fear, ain't so?"

The sun had yet to drop over the wooded ridge that backed Amos's land, but when Luke looked around, he saw that the color of the sky had deepened with the first shades of violet.

"Yes. The lie has eaten at me—" Julia's words, but true. "I don't want to live a lie. I need to be honest with God, with you, and with my family."

"And Abby?"

"I can talk to her when she's older. She would misunderstand if I said now, 'I'm not your father.' I am her father in the ways that matter most. I will always be."

"I've seen that," Amos said slowly. "What if we were to find her family, talk to them?"

"If they went to *Englisch* court, they could sue for custody and win."

"If they are Amish, they wouldn't do that."

"No, but what if their bishop said to you, 'The loss of their daughter left a hole in the lives of this couple. Only their granddaughter can fill that. This Luke Bowman stole that little girl.'"

"But we have the birth certificate. We have the letter Abby's mother wrote, giving her child to you."

We. Never had a word been so heartening. Amos was allying himself with Luke, saying, *I will help you protect her.*

"It could cause trouble," he said nonetheless.

"*Ja*, that is possible," Amos agreed. He resumed walking, and Luke caught up with his longer stride. "May I read that letter?"

"It's in my buggy."

They turned around and started back toward the house, neatly painted white as most Amish houses were. Luke knew that the fields were farmed by Amos's youngest son, who lived in a small house on another part of the property. It had been built early in the nineteenth century, long before the Civil War, and had been long vacant when Abraham and his wife Rachel had decided to scrub it out and make it a home again. As a good Amish housewife, she'd have tolerated no shades of the past.

"You haven't told your parents yet?" Amos asked as they approached the buggy.

"No." Luke ran his hand over Charlie's side and patted his sleek rump before reaching beneath the seat cushion and taking out the precious letter.

The bishop unfolded it and read in silence. When he handed it back, his expression showed pity. "I, too, wish she had let you help her," he said heavily.

"I shouldn't have moved without finding her," Luke said. "She wouldn't have been pregnant yet, but that doesn't excuse me."

"Would she have let you take care of her?"

Luke squeezed the back of his neck. "She refused any help but a meal now and again, and a small amount of cash. I tried to give her a hundred dollars once, and she refused it. Twenty was the most she'd take."

Amos laid a hand on Luke's shoulder. "I think this is guilt you should not have to carry. We can do no more than try."

He nodded, unable to speak.

"In the end, the blessing is that she accepted what you offered," Amos said. "Not for herself, but for her daughter. And I believe she was right. That is a trust you will never betray."

Luke was close to tears.

"I regret the fear that kept you silent, but I understand it. Turning back to the ways you grew up with hasn't always been easy for you, has it?"

"I would have said it was, until—" He couldn't finish. And that had been arrogant, too.

"Abby was brought to you."

"Yes." And his father had hired Julia, but he couldn't, *wouldn't*, say that.

"You're a good man, Luke. I will trust what your heart tells you, and Abby's *mamm*'s wishes. They could not be clearer. We will not speak about her other family again, unless something changes."

"*Denke.*" Incredulous, Luke felt the dampness on his cheeks.

Amos smiled. "Go home and tell your *dochder* that you love her."

No promise was easier to keep. "I will."

Amos felt no need to say anything else. He simply walked away, going around the side of the house to the back door. Using the front door wouldn't occur to him. Family didn't, except for rare, special occasions.

Luke wiped his cheeks with his shirtsleeves before untying his gelding, getting back in the buggy, and turning for his childhood home.

Chapter Twenty-One

❖◆❖

UNUSUAL SILENCE SEEMED to have a weight as Luke sat on one side of the kitchen table, facing his parents on the other side, the two men with fresh-poured cups of coffee. Once again, he struggled to find the right words.

Miriam had packed earlier this evening to stay with Rose until the baby was born, which left Elam to entertain Abby out of earshot. He'd set Abby on his shoulders and taken her outside to pet the animals and round up the chickens. Back in her leggings and one of her pink shirts, to *Mamm*'s dismay, Abby had bounced and drummed her heels on her *onkel*'s chest. Elam laughed, although Luke understood that he hated always being shut out of important talks. He wasn't even the youngest. Yet Luke had the sense that their parents treated Miriam, two years younger, as an adult in a way they didn't Elam, perhaps because of the depth of seriousness in her that belied her years.

At twenty-five, he was a man, but at home it seemed he would remain a boy. In most Amish families, as the youngest son, he would take over the farm when his father retired. But here there was no farm, and Elam didn't want to be a furniture maker.

Luke had been thinking about that. Even after buying his own place, he had enough money from his years working in the outside world to buy some good farmland, if Elam was sure that's what he wanted.

Running a hand over his now bristly jaw, he grimaced. There he went again—this time, thinking about his younger brother to put off the moment he must disappoint his parents again.

But there was no avoiding it. No fancy words to wrap it up in. At last he said bluntly, "I haven't been honest with you. Abby is not my daughter."

His parents didn't so much as blink for long enough to make him twitch. If his father's expression changed at all, it was to become stern.

Mamm was the first to speak. "Not our *kinskind*?"

"I hope she still will be. But by blood . . . no." He explained, as he had to the bishop, about his attempts to befriend Beth, her destructive lifestyle, how he had lost touch with her and never known she was pregnant.

"You didn't share a bed with her," *Daad* said. It wasn't exactly a question.

"No. I would not have. I felt sorry for her. Because we'd both been Amish, I felt that helping her was right."

"So why did the social worker say Abby was your daughter?" *Daad* asked.

Luke explained that, too. About the birth certificate and the letter from Beth and the frightened little girl who looked so much like her *mamm*. And his thinking that at last he could do something for the sad woman who wouldn't take his help, and for this little girl who had no one else.

His father wanted to know what Amos said. He was quiet after Luke told him.

"Did you think we couldn't love her if we knew she wasn't related to you?" *Mamm* asked.

"I never thought that. I'm sorrier than I can say that I lied to you. I took it on myself to protect Abby, thinking I was the only one who could."

His father turned the coffee mug around and around, never lifting it to take a sip. "What changed your mind?"

His first instinct was to lie again. Deeply ashamed, Luke told them the truth, although that, too, would worry them.

"Julia. She knew."

"Because she was there when Abby came," Eli said slowly.

He shook his head. "I think I had to tell someone. She cares about Abby, and was willing to listen. Talking to her seemed . . . safe."

"Because she's not one of us."

"Yes."

They waited. His parents were good at that. Their children never succeeded in keeping a secret from them for long.

"At the auction, she overheard Bishop Amos talking to me, saying people think Abby looks like Miriam and that she has my eyes. I could tell Julia was thinking something she didn't want to say. So I asked her Tuesday, when I got to work. She said the lie would keep eating at me, making me hold myself back from my family, friends, and God. That it would get harder to tell the truth the longer I waited." He paused. "I knew she was right. I should have trusted all of you, not taken that decision on myself."

They talked for another twenty minutes. Once, Elam started to open the back door, saw their expressions, and retreated with Abby. When he opened the door the second time and poked his head in, he said, "Abby wants to go home. She's getting sleepy."

In fact, she was rubbing her eyes and visibly drooping.

Luke pushed back his chair and stood. "It's been a long day for her. Come to your *daadi*, little one."

She cast herself from Elam's shoulders into Luke's arms with complete faith that he would catch her. Which was as it should be. As he knew his Lord wouldn't let him fall, when the time came.

"Tell Elam what I said." He nodded at his brother. "Thank you. When you have a chance, let's talk. I had an idea that might appeal to you."

His brother stared at him in outrage. "You're not going to tell me? *Anything?*"

"Not tonight. Sorry, *bruder.*"

JULIA WAITED WITH increasing anxiety for Luke to tell her what decision he'd made, and what if any outcome there'd been to his admission. It wasn't as if he owed her anything, but he had to know she worried about Abby. What if she was taken away from Luke and sent to the people whose daughter had run away and refused even to name them? What if they were as horrible as Luke feared?

She was still torn over whether she should have kept her mouth shut. For Luke, she still thought honesty was best. For Abby, Julia wasn't so sure.

Wednesday came and went. Thursday the same, then Friday. Her tension rose. He made no effort to get her alone, gave her no significant looks.

She was also very conscious that this was a church Sunday. Nobody had suggested she attend again, as why would they? Visitors didn't come back over and over. Her presence might even have made some people uncomfortable, especially those who had next to no contact with *Englischers.* Many women, especially, never worked outside the home, and therefore had little reason to interact with outsiders. Then, there she was, head uncovered, with her faltering *Deitsh,* acting as if she belonged.

She had offered to come into work early Saturday morning so that a shipping company could pick up a dining room set being transported to Jackson Hole, Wyoming. The man at the shipping company said importantly that the wife of the couple who'd bought it was a well-known actor, that she'd won at least one Emmy Award, but Julia didn't recognize the name. She didn't follow the awards shows. At most, she might read in the paper about which movie won the Academy Award for Best Picture in a given year. Usually, she hadn't seen it.

The truck was to arrive before eight. All she had to do was let the men in and show them the right furniture to wrap and transport. This wasn't a company they commonly dealt with, because the buyers had hired them.

Following her suggestion, the truck pulled up in front, temporarily blocking most of the street. Air brakes squealed, giving her a minute's warning. She hurried to the front door and unlocked for the two men, who wore matching navy-blue uniforms.

"Good morning," she said with a smile. "You're right on time."

"We do our best." The older of the two men looked friendly. At five foot ten or so, with a little extra weight around the middle and graying hair, he made her feel comfortable.

The younger man assessed her in a way that would have bothered her if they'd been alone, but within minutes, the two men were carefully wrapping the china cabinet, chairs, and table.

"Nice-looking furniture if you can afford it," the older man said.

"I can't," she admitted, "but now that I've seen the extraordinary work that goes into every piece, I think if anything the Bowmans are underpricing their furniture."

"Underpricing?" The young guy twitched a price tag on a glass-fronted display case. "You'd think this was made out of solid gold."

"But it's beautiful, you must admit," she countered.

He snorted. "I thought the Amish didn't bother with anything fancy."

"They make most of this furniture for *Englischers*, not their own people. Even so, they think first about function. Drawers slide like silk, the proportions are never awkward, and most of the furniture would blend with antiques or more modern stuff."

"Quite the little saleswoman, aren't you?"

Coming from him, it didn't sound complimentary, but the older of the two called brusquely for help, and in a surprisingly short time they were gone.

Since the store wouldn't open until nine, she locked the door behind them and turned to go back to the office.

Luke stood not twenty feet away, his expression grave.

Startled, she exclaimed, "You're early."

"I got here a little while ago. I don't like you meeting strange men by yourself."

She blinked. "It's part of the job."

"It shouldn't be." He sounded uncompromising.

"They were completely professional."

"Were they? It didn't seem so to me. I'm not sure that one likes the Amish."

"I doubt he's ever met one," she retorted. "My impression is that he doesn't like rich people. He may haul things for them, but he resents them."

Luke visibly turned that over in his mind before nodding. "That may be. He was right about one thing, though. You are very good at selling our furniture. *Daad* knew what he was doing when he hired you."

Naturally, she blushed. A woman who tried to travel under the radar didn't garner many compliments. "I've never tried selling anything before. Your furniture is so well made and beautiful, too, I don't have to work very hard to sound enthusiastic. I don't think I'd be very good at it if the product was cheaply made or I suspected it would disappoint the buyer."

"You wouldn't stay in that kind of job." He sounded certain, as if he believed completely in her integrity.

"No." She twined her fingers together. She'd sworn she wouldn't ask about the thing with Abby, but they were alone unless Eli had come with Luke but stayed in back. Even then, they weren't likely to be immediately interrupted. "Did you talk to your family?"

"I did." He gestured toward the office. "Let's sit down, shall we?"

As anxious as she was to hear what happened, she was standing just inside the plate-glass window, visible to any passerby. She nodded and hurried past him and behind the counter to take a chair.

He strolled after her, already having shed his coat, if he'd started the day with one, as well as his hat. His hair showed the print of the hat brim until he shoved his fingers through it. Instead of taking a chair, he half sat on the long counter, one booted foot braced on the floor.

"I went to Bishop Amos first and told him the truth, then my parents. I need to thank you for your advice. You were right—keeping such a secret bothered me more than I let myself realize. Letting myself trust in God, telling the truth, has released the poison that was eating at me, as you put it."

"I didn't say poison," she objected.

His mouth curled. "No, but that's what you meant, isn't it?"

"Sometimes I expect you to say, 'Ain't so?'"

His eyebrows quirked in that way they had. "I'm reverting to my childhood speech patterns. Before, I tried hard to rid myself of any hint of an accent, never mind the peculiar way we structure sentences."

"It's not peculiar, it's natural. German has a different structure than English. And even if *Deitsh* is a dialect—"

He held up a big hand and laughed. "No need to be so fierce! You're right. But you know as well as I do how people out there perceive anyone different."

"It's human nature. Don't the Amish look askance at anyone who's different than *they* are?" she countered.

"We do."

They looked at each other.

"Are you in trouble?" she asked.

"No more than I should be. My parents were hurt. *Mamm* thought I hadn't trusted them to love Abby if she wasn't my biological daughter. *Daad* . . . I think he thought when I came home, there'd be no worries."

"There weren't, were there?"

He made a sound in his throat. "I told myself there weren't. It never occurred to me that accepting the humility I chafed against as a teenage boy was easy only because I hadn't been challenged. I bought a house and land that pleased me, enjoyed the work here with *Daad* and the remodeling I started on the house. Everyone seemed glad I was home. Now, I think I was full of myself. Why wouldn't I be able to handle everything?"

Why not, indeed? Luke had to be brilliant to have worked in an esoteric area of the digital world, and starting with only an eighth-grade education. He'd adapted to an entirely different way of life, wiped his speech clean of any trace of an accent. He seemed competent at everything he did. The only time she'd ever seen him look helpless was when Abby rejected him at first. Well, and because he'd probably never helped a little girl get dressed, or tucked one into bed—although that might not be true, Julia thought, given that he had two sisters, at least one of them younger. Surely the older kids among the Amish helped raise the younger.

What had disrupted his certainties? That was easy.

"And then Abby was brought to you."

His mouth opened . . . but then he closed it, as if thinking twice about whatever he'd been about to say. His voice was a little huskier than usual when he said, "She disrupted my life, all right."

"In a good way, as it's turned out."

His expression softened. "In a very good way. She is still not an easy child—"

Julia laughed softly. "Is she wearing Amish dress all the time yet?"

He made another of those sounds. "Only some days, and she absolutely refuses to wear a *kapp*. A hat, she persists in calling it."

"She wouldn't understand what it means."

"No, but there's something else, I think." He shook his head. "I don't know. My hat doesn't bother her. It's the idea of putting one on herself. Or else . . ."

"She's just being contrary?"

His grin flashed. "That's possible."

Julia laughed again, happy just because Luke was so relaxed and truly talking to her. Her heart hurt when she thought about Abby, but not as it would if she'd never known what happened to the little girl she'd become so unreasoningly attached to so quickly. At least she knew Abby was healthy and happy . . . and speaking again to express her wants.

Too, there was always the chance Julia would see her again. She'd loved having Abby beside her at the fellowship meal, teasing her and helping her eat as if . . .

I were her mother. Her mamm.

Oh, yes, this pang was a strong one.

"You miss her," Luke said, his tone odd.

She looked into his vividly blue eyes and realized he'd seen everything she felt thinking about Abby. It was disconcerting, having someone able to do that.

"I do. There's something about her . . ." She trailed off. Love of any kind wasn't always logical, was it?

"Yes." Kindness and something more softened the often hard set of his mouth, altered the lines that would only add character with the years. "There is something about you, too." He spoke in a low voice, husky. "You know that, don't you, Julia?"

He wasn't talking about Abby anymore. Did he mean *himself*? Could he have feelings for her . . . ? It was so hard to believe.

She felt strange, her face hot, the rest of her cold and shivery. "No," she croaked. "I'm ordinary. Not—"

He shook his head. "I can't believe you haven't noticed. Abby wasn't the first person to disrupt my life. You were."

"Me? But . . . you didn't want to hire me."

He slowly pushed off the desk, rising to his full height. "I was afraid of what might happen if you were around all the time. I was right to be afraid, Julia."

Her breath came faster. Unable to stay sitting when he towered over her, she stood, too, only that brought her much closer to him. So close, she had to tip her head back to see his face. Some of her symptoms felt like fear, but not quite.

"Julia," he said. Whispered.

At the same time, he wrapped his hands around her upper arms, squeezing gently. And then his head bent, slowly, so slowly he must be giving her a chance to withdraw. But . . . how could she? This might be her only opportunity to know what it felt like to be tempted.

His lips touched hers, brushing them softly. Coming back again. Somehow, her hands had come to be grabbing him, her fingers clenched on the strong muscles that ran between his neck and shoulders. The next touch of his mouth was firmer, more sure.

She quaked.

He lifted his head, his eyes blazing. And then he closed them. "I can't do this. I'm in a fight with myself, but there is no excuse—"

His hands dropped from her arms and he took a step back, bumping into the counter, and him a man who was never clumsy. She lost her hold on him, too. They stared at each other, Luke seeming as shaken as she felt.

Luke Bowman had kissed her.

I was right to be afraid, he'd said. Of how he felt about *her*. Was that possible?

"I hear *Daad*," he said suddenly. "I must go—" Almost past her, he stopped. "Did I scare you? I never thought . . ."

Slowly, wonderingly, Julia shook her head. "You didn't scare me."

"That's good. But I should not have done it. I'm sorry, Julia."

A man had kissed her, and she not only hadn't been afraid, but enjoyed it. How could that be?

Because she trusted Luke on a level so deep, she'd been able to let go of the fear that had crippled her so long? The same man who was backing away, his expression tormented, his regret palpable.

A moment later, he disappeared into the workshop. Julia dropped into her chair, and pressed her hands to her cheeks.

Had he just opened a window for her, allowing her to see beyond the walls she'd built around herself for protection? Or had he allowed her only a glimpse before he slammed it closed again?

She had been foolish enough to fall in love with a man who might be tempted by her, but would never let himself act on it again. That he'd done so this once must have shocked him, violating his beliefs and the commitment that was central to his life.

One of the things she loved about him was the strength of that commitment, the bone-deep values that had pulled him back to the Amish.

Anguish poured through her. Luke would be better off if she quit her job, cutting off their friendship and all other possibilities. That would be the best thing for him, the loving thing for her to do.

She bent her head in prayer, reaching for the God who

had sustained her through all her trials. "Help me under-stand why I came here if this is how it ends. Is leaving how I can make everything right?"

She'd believed God led her here, but now, confused, she wondered if she'd really listened to Him at all, if He hadn't had an entirely different purpose.

Chapter Twenty-Two

SOMEHOW LUKE GREETED his father in a voice that must have sounded normal, because *Daad* didn't seem to notice anything was wrong. He rummaged among the chisels, mumbling under his breath because he couldn't immediately lay his hand on what he wanted.

"I wouldn't have just set it down," he grumbled. "Do you have—?"

Luke silently pointed to a chisel sitting in plain sight on a bench.

His father opened his mouth, closed it, picked up the tool, and went to his workstation.

Luke sat with his back to his father and stretched out a measuring tape across a slab of elm. He didn't see the promise in the wood or the uncompromising marks on the tape. Instead, he saw Julia, her cheeks colored, her lips soft, her lashes rising slowly to show him dazed brown eyes with sparks of gold.

How could he have ever allowed himself to lay his hands on her? Worse yet, to kiss her? Yes, he had battled the desire since the day she came in to apply for the job. He tried to comfort himself that God didn't demand perfection, only that men and women learn from their mistakes.

Except . . . this hadn't felt like a mistake, which made it a greater one. Julia had drawn him in every way from the beginning, but he'd foolishly let himself think they could be friends, that he could accept her counsel, protect her, without ever giving in to temptation.

Examining the depth of his feelings for her, he saw that if he hadn't accepted baptism, he might have chosen her. That rattled him to his foundations, or the earth might even have suffered a tremor. Still, he followed where these thoughts led him.

Then, he could have maintained his relationship with his family, at least. Now, if he walked away for the sake of a woman, he would be under the *meidung*. He might never see his parents or brother and sisters again. He wouldn't be invited to their weddings, or hold any new nieces and nephews when they were born.

And what about Abby?

That he was even asking himself such things stunned him anew. He knew the answer, he'd known it all along. God must come first in his life, followed by family and his brethren. His word was worth nothing if he abandoned everything else that mattered for Julia.

Perhaps he'd weakened after she came to their church service. Her presence had awakened him to hope, to the possibility that she might join the Amish. *But how likely is that, really?* he asked himself grimly. She'd said nothing about coming again, never mind speaking to the bishop. This wasn't like converting to Catholicism from being a Baptist, anyway. The Amish didn't save their religion for Sundays; they had made hard choices to keep that faith at the forefront of their lives. Hard choices especially for the women, his familiarity with the *Englisch* world told him.

What modern woman would take a step so drastic?

No, he couldn't let himself hope. He had to apologize again and then avoid her to the best of his ability. He couldn't ask her to leave the job, not after she had worked so hard to make a place for herself here, and even increased sales with her ideas and computer know-how. That wouldn't be fair to her; the problem was his.

His thoughts took a sideways jump. He prayed that she hadn't lied about not being afraid of him when he grabbed her that way. Having her get to her feet, stand so close to him that he could smell her soap and maybe her skin, his mind had clouded. He hadn't thought at all. It scared him a little that she had such power over him. He asked himself again whether God might have brought her into his life as a test. If so, he had just failed.

"Working hard, I see."

He jerked at the sound of his father's voice coming from right behind him.

"I was thinking. I've changed my mind about what I want to do with the elm." Another lie came with shocking speed to his tongue.

No, not a lie; it was true that he'd had second thoughts at seeing the especially fine grain in this wood after the order arrived yesterday from one of their suppliers.

"I thought you planned while you were sleeping. You don't usually sit here and stare into space."

"Something just didn't seem right."

His father rested a hand on his shoulder and said quietly, "That happens."

He could only nod and pray *Daad* was still talking about work.

"Did the dining room set get off all right earlier?"

"*Ja*. It was almost all loaded when I got here. Julia said she didn't need me, but I could tell one of the two men made her uncomfortable."

"Then we won't leave it to her to meet strangers like

that again. I wouldn't want Miriam doing anything like that."

"No." Julia might be mad, but Luke could never erase from his awareness the knowledge that she had been hurt and was afraid of men.

Except, of course, he'd done just that when he snatched her to him and kissed her.

Ashamed, he pushed back his tall stool and said, "I'll check on the horses and maybe go for a walk. That might clear my head."

His father met his gaze with kindness. "Is this to do with what you told us last night?"

"No. Just some confusion, nothing to worry about."

He would make very sure his parents never had to worry about his commitment to his faith again.

His decision might be made, but his chest felt as if it were being crushed.

ELAM CAME TROTTING from the back door of their parents' house even before Luke had reined Charlie to a stop.

Thumbs stuck jauntily under his suspenders, he grinned up at his brother. "I thought I made trouble around here, but me, I'm a beginner compared to you."

Luke opened the buggy door and got out. "*Mamm* and *Daad* told you, then."

"Ja. *Mamm* went to see Rose and Miriam today to tell them, too. She didn't want them surprised Sunday along with everyone else."

"You think everyone will know by tomorrow?"

"Of course they will," Elam said cheerfully. "You know what the bishop's wife is like."

Maybe Amos would have kept to himself what Luke had told him. But Luke knew better. Forget Twitter. *Mamm* had speculated that Amos made use of his wife's propensity for gossip to keep his flock informed. Unfortunately, that made sense.

"As long as nobody says a word about it in Abby's hearing."

"Who would do that?" his brother asked simply.

Luke nodded a concession. Nobody would want to upset a three-year-old girl.

"What did you want to talk to me about?" Elam tied Charlie to a post, not as if the gelding would have gone anywhere. Already, he stood hipshot, patient. He knew the routine.

"Dinner isn't close?"

"No. You're not staying?"

"Not tonight." Hiding his turmoil all day had been hard enough. He didn't need to sit under his parents' discerning eyes and pretend everything was fine. "Walk with me," he suggested.

They didn't go far, only to a bench that *Daad* had built to encircle an old maple behind the house. It was rarely used; how often did *Mamm* slow down long enough to sit and watch the birds or feel the sun on her face? Miriam was no better. If Elam dared relax so visibly, someone would be sure to decide he could do a chore.

"How is the job going with Willard?"

"It's good," his brother said. "I might do some things differently than he does. He's not interested in bothering with a cover crop, for one."

"What else would you do?" Luke asked with real curiosity.

"If it were me, I'd grow crops for the organic market. It's big now among *Englischers*, you know."

"I noticed that."

"Getting certified organic doesn't take such big changes, since we don't use most of those poisons anyway that you read about. Any crop will sell for a better price, then. I like the idea anyway, of caring for the land that way and being sure the food I produce is safe to eat." He bent to pick up a twig, which he began to break into increasingly tiny pieces.

"Why am I talking about such things? Willard will never listen. Unless I join a new settlement where land is being divided up . . ." He shrugged.

"My idea has to do with this. Not a new settlement," Luke amended. "I wanted to be sure you hadn't gotten bored with your job and were thinking of trying something else."

"No, I'm lucky Willard hired me. I've never liked being stuck inside. Hard work outside is best, growing things, helping trees produce their best fruit, seeing crops prosper." He shook his head as if embarrassed. "I know that was never what you wanted."

Luke grimaced at being reminded what—whom—he wanted, but he said, "You know I have plenty of money left from my job in computers."

Elam looked at him. "No, I never thought—" His mouth tightened. "I asked *Daad* for a loan. The store is doing well enough, he could afford it, but he isn't convinced I'm serious. He was disappointed I didn't love furniture making. As far as he's concerned, I'm flitting from thing to thing. By my age I should know what I want. When I say that I do, he doesn't believe me."

Luke had heard enough to suspect that Elam needed more respect from their father than he'd been getting. He did say, "You haven't been baptized."

"No," his brother mumbled. "What difference would it make? It's not as if I like to party. But here I am, still living at home. I almost took a job on a construction crew so I could travel, but that's not work I want to do, either. *Mamm* complains that I'm not married, but how can I court a woman when I can't afford to support a family?"

"*Mamm* and *Daad* would be glad to let you live in the *grossdaadi* house."

"I know they would." Elam flung the bits of twig away in a jerky, near-violent gesture. "I should accept gladly, but I can't."

"You think *Daad* won't see you as a man until you go out on your own."

"Am I wrong?"

Luke pondered that. *Daad* probably wasn't as impatient and condescending as Elam believed, and Elam's restlessness and refusal to accept help betrayed a level of childish resentment. Yet Luke's sympathy went to his brother. *Daad* would never understand that he was part of the problem. Luke's own relationship with his father had been contentious before he walked out. *Daad* had had no choice but to see him as a man when he returned. They'd been able to skip the stages in between.

Funny, when their father was a good man, kind and supportive, not pushing Miriam too hard or harboring a grudge about Luke having rejected his upbringing for so many years. Yet he could be blind, too, and especially where this youngest son was concerned.

To his brother, Luke said diplomatically, "I think you and *Daad* have been butting heads for too many years. It makes it hard to see someone in a new way, isn't it so?"

Ain't so was what he'd been thinking. Because of Julia.

He had to quit seeing her in his head, hearing everything she'd said to him.

"What I was thinking is that I can loan you the money to buy a farm. Once you're established, you can start making payments to me. There's no hurry—I know it will take time. I can help with other expenses, too. You might need horses, a tractor and other equipment, chickens or cows or . . ."

Elam stared at him, the expression on his face making Luke's chest ache in a different way. The hope was so powerful but also fragile, as if he feared the offer could vanish in an instant, pop like a soap bubble.

"You mean that? You can afford it?"

"I can. I wish I'd thought to do it sooner. I suppose I listened too much to *Daad*."

He, too, knew how it felt to want something desperately that you knew was out of reach.

"I've saved almost twenty-five thousand dollars," Elam said unexpectedly. "Enough maybe for a down payment on a place, but with so much to do before I sell a first crop, I wouldn't be able to make monthly payments soon enough to satisfy a bank."

"That's a lot to have saved," Luke said, impressed.

Elam had his eyes on a shimmering dream. "I hear some *Englischers* out on Frampton Mill Road are planning to sell their place. It has rich soil, and a fine orchard already." Eagerness had him talking faster and faster. "It needs work—they've let it go these last years. I hear their kids aren't interested in farming and the old man can't keep up anymore. It would be perfect."

"It might go high at auction."

"They may list it with a real estate agent."

"What if we were to go take a look and talk to them?"

Excitement blazed in Elam like an internal fire, so hot Luke could have warmed his hands.

"Don't count on this place. We may need to settle for a more modest piece of land," he cautioned.

His words banked the fire, if only slightly. "*Ja*, even if they want to sell their farm equipment, it's nothing I could use."

Luke smiled. "They may be glad to meet a young man who will take care of their land the way they want."

Elam grinned and bounded to his feet. "I wish we could go now!"

"Monday," Luke suggested, standing, too. It was time he and Abby started for home, especially since he'd have to make dinner.

"Do we have to tell *Mamm* and *Daad*?" asked Elam.

"No. If you want to, that's fine. Otherwise, let's wait until we find the right place.

"You don't know what this means to me."

Luke clapped him on the back. "I think I do."

He had to stretch his legs to keep up with his slightly

shorter brother, who all but flew toward the house. If he couldn't stop himself from glowing like a kerosene lantern in the dark, *Mamm* and *Daad* would notice right away.

"YOU'RE NO FUN anymore," Miriam declared. "You never make a mistake."

In her deep depression, Julia wondered how fast she'd forget what she'd learned if she moved back to Cleveland and never used *Deitsh* again. Her high school German had dwindled in no time until about all she could do was count to ten—although faint memories of what she'd learned back then were helping her learn the High German of the Bible and the *Ausbund*.

And why was she bothering with *that*?

If she was going to give her notice to Eli, she ought to do it. Instead, she'd dragged her feet over the weekend. Maybe she could find another job locally and not have to leave for good. She could stay friends with Miriam, couldn't she? And many of the quilters she'd gotten to know. In fact, yesterday she'd spent the day at a quilting frolic, with nine Amishwomen and her working on a wedding quilt for Sol Graber's youngest sister, whom Julia had never met. No matter; she agreed with the others that the loss and grief the family had suffered was good reason to do something nice for a young woman who might be doubting her decision to marry while her brother was still hospitalized, her nephew barely out of bed on crutches.

Everyone teased the grandmother who'd pieced the quilt, saying she'd chosen the classic Fruit Basket pattern in hopes the couple would be "fruitful." Smiling slyly, she denied it, saying only that she hadn't wanted to subject the young man to a flowery design.

"Girly," Julia said in English, and watched them all think about that. Renewed giggles trailed around the room.

It had been a lovely day. Lydia Graber had come, looking

much more relaxed. Sol was doing so much better, she said, regaining his spirit. With *Gotte's wille*, he'd be driving his own team to plant their fields by spring.

Now she said to Miriam, "I don't do nearly so well when people are talking fast. And when there are a bunch of people, and they talk over each other . . ."

"Oh, ach, that will come!" Her smile was beautiful. "You must spend more time with us."

To Julia's horror, tears burned in her eyes. No, no, no! But faster than she could blink them away, Miriam saw her.

"I said something wrong." She had switched to English.

"No, I swear. You didn't."

"Then . . . then what?" Miriam asked, worry in eyes that were the very same color as her brother's.

"Nothing. Really. I must have gotten out of bed on the wrong side."

Miriam didn't buy it. "Was it the quilt frolic at Gloria's? If somebody wasn't welcoming . . . !"

Julia smiled at her friend's fierce defense. She had more in common with Luke than Julia had known.

"No, truly. Everyone was nice. Lydia asked that I be invited, you know, since I drove her to the hospital regularly."

"Oh." Miriam settled back in the chair. "Then what?"

"It's . . . I've been looking at my life, that's all. Wondering if I belong here. My parents want me to come home, and Nick and I have been quarreling, which makes it hard when he's my only family here, so I don't know."

"I can see why it would upset you to be . . . be bumping heads with your *bruder*."

She didn't seem to have even noticed she'd used a *Deitsh* word while otherwise speaking English. The Amish often did that, Julia had noticed, even Luke, for all his fluency in English. Likewise, they used English words while speaking *Deitsh*. Of course, the old Germanic dialect didn't *have* words for many modern objects and ideas, and the Amish had simply incorporated the English words.

"I don't suppose Ruth has a job opening," Julia said impulsively. "Sometimes I don't think your father really needs me full-time."

"But he talks so highly of you! He says sales are growing because of you, your work on the website and your ideas for promotion and your friendliness with people who call or come into the store."

More pangs, because Julia loved her job. Thus the foot-dragging. She also smiled at the idea that it was her "friendliness" responsible for greater sales. "Well, compared to how your brother probably greeted customers . . ."

Miriam giggled. "Does he glare at them?" She made an awful face in mimicry.

"Sometimes."

"I don't want you to leave Tompkin's Mill. I think you might be my best friend now. You understand how I feel when my Amish friends don't."

Tears overflowed again. Julia leaned forward and gave Luke's sister a hug. "You're my best friend, too. But . . ."

Miriam scowled. "But what?"

Did she have to say this? "You're Amish and I'm not. I . . . haven't made any good friends who are *Englisch*. Some quilters, but they're all older and married. With you . . . I think there's only so far our friendship can go."

"I hoped you might be thinking about joining us."

Julia couldn't believe what Miriam was saying—well, what it sounded as if she was saying. "Joining you?"

"Converting to become Amish. I thought when you came to worship with us . . ." She broke off, unusual lines forming on her forehead. "You were thinking about it, weren't you? Not just curious about us?"

Julia couldn't seem to draw a breath. Join the Amish? She'd flirted with the idea, but never taken it seriously.

Was it really possible?

Chapter Twenty-Three

❖◆❖

"I WAS WRONG?" Miriam whispered.

"No. Not wrong. I just . . . never thought . . ."

"Thought what?"

"That I *could* do it. *Do* outsiders convert?"

"Not often, but sometimes. You know Anna Rose Esch? The girl my brother was making sheep's eyes at? Her mother's family is Italian. Anna's *mudder* grew up on a farm, not a city like you, but she met Melvin and said that her home was with him."

"Didn't, oh, the bishop expect more than that?"

"Oh, *ja*, of course. She had to study to become Amish, learn the language, show that her faith was genuine."

Julia felt absurdly as if Luke's harness horse had kicked her in the head. Or maybe the hot Missouri sun had finally felled her.

Nick had worried when she first came that she might get sucked into the "cult," but she'd rolled her eyes even as she increasingly came to admire the Amish she got to know.

Even as she fell in love with Luke—she couldn't lie to herself, she'd been that foolish—she hadn't ever stopped and thought, *I could become Amish, too.*

"I . . . have to think about this," she said. "It would mean a huge change for me. It's one thing for someone like Luke, to go back to a familiar way of life because your faith calls you, but for me . . ."

Hadn't her faith called her here? Not just her faith, but God? Nick admitted he'd chosen Tompkin's Mill almost randomly after looking at any number of small towns across the country for the right kind of job opening. If he hadn't chosen this one, she might never in her life have set eyes on a black buggy pulled by a smooth-gaited Standardbred horse, or a flock of women in pretty colored dresses, their heads covered by *kapps*. She might not have felt the soaring joy of hearing the Amish talk so matter-of-factly about forgiving even the most brutal of their enemies.

She might have continued huddling in her apartment in Cleveland, afraid to venture out after dusk, to date, to encounter new people.

Miriam squeezed her hand. "I understand. I know that Bishop Amos would be glad to talk to you about what you'd have to do."

"Yes. Of course." Still dazed, she knew she really did need to let the idea settle inside her, make herself examine what she'd be giving up—and what she'd gain.

And part of that must be knowing that just because Luke had admitted to being attracted to her didn't mean he was in love with her or would consider marrying her. She might, in fact, have to watch close-up as he married another woman who would become Abby's mother.

A dry voice seemed to murmur in her ear, *If you do this, it must be because you want to place God first in your life, and for no other reason.*

Heeding that voice, Julia said softly, "And we know that

all things work together for good to those who love God, to those who are called according to His purpose."

Miriam's smile radiated peace. "Romans."

Julia bit her lip. "Will you . . . not tell anyone that we talked about this?"

"*Ja.* This decision you must make with your heart. You don't need anyone trying to influence you." She added impishly, "Except for me, of course."

Julia laughed and leaned forward to hug her friend.

LUKE COULDN'T THINK of any good excuse why it would be better if he were to drive separately to work that day.

That made it more difficult for him to speak with Julia alone, which of course was part of his goal. Still, he knew he owed her an apology. An explanation.

The moment came on Thursday when *Daad* realized he'd forgotten the lunch *Mamm* packed for them. He rushed out to the buggy to look, but came back shaking his head. "Getting old, I am. I'll go out and buy lunch for us."

They decided on burgers and fries, easy and quick, and a treat because it wasn't a meal they often had. Eli went out through the front so he could ask Julia if she'd like him to bring her a meal, too.

Luke waited. He thought he heard voices, then silence. Now was the time. When he stepped through into the showroom, it was utterly quiet and appeared deserted. Had Julia gone with his *daad*?

But her head suddenly appeared above the counter, and he realized she'd been bent over.

Sounding embarrassed, she said, "I dropped something, and . . ."

He nodded and walked over to stand on the customer side of the counter. Best to have something between them.

"I wanted to apologize again for the other day. I know

better than to touch you that way. I can't get involved with a woman who isn't of my faith. Then what did I do but act on impulse. I have no excuse." He paused. "I hope you won't be uncomfortable with me."

He absolutely couldn't tell what she was thinking. Her beautiful eyes had become opaque. No gold shimmered in them.

After a moment, she said, "I understand. Don't worry about it, Luke."

Was that an acceptance of his apology? He thought so. He should have been more relieved than he was. He considered telling her that he'd keep his distance from now on, as he should have from the beginning, but didn't think it was necessary. Instead, he asked awkwardly, "Did you put in an order with *Daad*?"

She might have been talking to a complete stranger. "No, I resisted—" Her eyes widened. *Temptation.* That's what she'd almost said. "I brought a lunch from home."

"Well, then . . ."

The smile she cast his way was pleasant, one she might give a passing stranger on the sidewalk. He hated it. And then she turned her attention to the computer monitor as if he weren't there.

As he retreated to the workroom, Luke rubbed his chest, feeling as if he'd been left with a crack in his breastbone.

Friday he made an excuse to his father and went out to the alley, then around the corner to the real estate office that was right next door to the store.

Elam hovered out front, relief blooming on his face when he saw Luke. "See?" he almost whispered. "They have the listing. There's a picture in the window."

Luke studied the photograph, thinking it wasn't nearly as good as Julia could have done. Maybe real estate would sell better around here if the photos online told people how beautiful this part of northern Missouri was, with rolling hills, flourishing woods that were spectacular with autumn colors right now, an old covered bridge over Tompkin's Creek, not to mention the remnants of the mill that had given the town its name. Plenty of rivers and creeks, too, with good fishing.

This picture was of the house, which was a mistake, too. Nobody would buy this place unless they wanted the land and the two old but solid barns. Elam was right; work would have to be done on the fencing, and one of the barns needed a new roof. The fact that fields had been left fallow this last year or even longer was a good thing, resting the soil for new crops.

The house would be good for a family, though, a lot like Luke's. Two stories, with a fine deep porch stretching across the front. The listing here, hanging in the window, said there were four bedrooms and a den, two bathrooms, and a separate dining room. No garage, which *Englischers* wouldn't like. Of course, Elam would have to ask to have the power lines removed and then do the same conversion Luke was doing in his house. There'd be no big hurry, though, once he had the appliances hauled away and replaced by ones that ran on propane.

The price was exactly what Don Carter had told them it would be. He'd seemed pleased by their interest, told them he'd be right happy to sell to an Amishman because they took such good care of their places.

"All shipshape," he said with a nod. "I hear even when you get old you have help with that."

"We do," Luke had agreed, seeing the sadness on this man's face because his grown children hadn't come to lend a hand.

Now he and his brother walked into the office, causing the small bell tied to the top of the door to tinkle. A man in polyester slacks overhung by a belly that strained at the buttons of a white shirt emerged from the back, seeming astonished by the sight of them.

"How can I help you gentlemen?" He eyed Luke. "Aren't you one of the Bowmans next door?"

"I am. I work there with my father. Elam is my brother, but a farmer instead of a furniture maker."

He was pleased when Elam took the lead from there. "I might be interested in the Carter farm on Frampton Mill Road. I've been looking for something like it."

Interest sparked in the agent's face. "Well, now, I have a couple of similar properties available, too."

He opened his laptop and showed them photographs of those places, too. One Luke dismissed immediately; the barn was caving in, and he saw no indication there was so much as a small creek or pond nearby. The other wasn't as fine as the farm the *Englischers* were selling. Luke thought it over-priced, which was probably why it hadn't been snapped up by an eager young Amishman. It seemed to be good land, though, and the real estate agent—Ken Reimer—pointed out a stream curving through the pasture. It appeared someone had dammed it up at one time, enough to create a pool big enough for children, at least, to take a dip on hot days.

Elam had his heart set on the other, but he carefully studied the information on this place, too.

"Do the owners live there?" he asked.

"No, it's been vacant for several years now. I think they expected to get an unrealistic amount of money for it. No-body has even looked at it in a long time. They might be more open to an offer now."

Elam squared his shoulders. "I'd like to look at it as well as the Frampton Mill Road farm."

"Now?" Ken Reimer pushed back his chair.

"No, both of us must get back to work. Would we be able to see them in the early evening? Six o'clock, maybe? Otherwise, we might have to wait until Monday."

And Elam hated a delay of even a few days, Luke knew. Waiting for the property to actually get listed had been hard enough for him. What if someone else came along and snatched the prize right out from under his nose?

Well, if it was another Amishman, he'd be chagrined but accepting. Maybe not so much if the buyer was *Englisch*.

"This one"—Ken stabbed a finger at the more run-down property—"we can look at anytime. Let me call the Carters."

So they waited while he did.

"Yes, two young Amishmen," he agreed, his gaze going to them. "You already spoke to them, did you? What would you say to six o'clock tonight?" After an *uh-huh* or two, he hung up. "They'd be happy to have you come out today. Er, shall I drive . . . ?"

"Best if we meet you there," Luke said. "It's not so far between the two places. A mile?"

"Fine, fine." He heaved himself to his feet and held out his hand. "I'll look forward to seeing you at the Carters' house at six."

Elam shook first, then Luke.

Well pleased, they walked out.

In the alley, Luke asked, "Do we tell *Daad* what we're up to now? Or should I make an excuse to be late to pick up Abby?"

"I told *Mamm* that I wouldn't be there tonight for dinner. She assumed I'd be meeting friends. It's up to you what you want to say."

"I'll imply something the same." He could buy a burger and fries again on the way out of town. "I can pick you up at Willard's. He won't mind if you leave your buggy there for a few extra hours, will he?"

"No, I'm sure he won't. *Denke*. That would be good." Elam's sidelong glance held nerves. "Can you afford so much money?"

Buying either farm outright would decimate Luke's savings, but he felt confident his brother would pay him back over time. It helped that Elam's substantial savings meant he could handle initial expenses, from equipment to seed to living costs. Besides, Luke was making plenty of money for his needs—in part, because of Julia.

"I can," he said. "So long as you start making payments when you're able. And yes, I know it will be a year or two before that becomes possible."

"Denke." Elam flung his arms around Luke for a quick, hard embrace. *"Denke."*

He took off down the alley.

Luke almost called a reminder that he would be picking him up, but didn't bother. As if his little brother would forget.

IT HURT, NOT to see Luke except in passing. Given that his face was always expressionless, Julia tried for the same. The first time she needed one of them to come up front to talk to a customer, Luke didn't even turn his head.

"Can you take this one, *Daad*?"

Eli didn't seem to think anything of it, but the third or fourth time she either had a question or needed one of them to come out to the display room, he gave his son a long, thoughtful look before agreeing.

Julia gritted her teeth. She had to make a decision. She couldn't bear to stay if she wasn't going to commit herself to joining their faith. This hurt too much.

When she was alone, she thought about almost nothing else. Every ramification ran through her mind, starting with how her family would react.

Nick had already made his opinion clear with his belief that her attraction to the Amish faith was "crazy." And maybe it was. She was looking from the outside in at them. What if the view was different once she'd committed herself? What if she resented giving up so much she took for granted?

Within twenty-four hours of her talk with Miriam, she was panicking.

She hadn't given a thought to the day-to-day practicalities, starting with where she would *live*. Her apartment was obviously unsuitable. Most Amishwomen lived with family until marrying. Would somebody take her in as a boarder? Or rent her a *grossdaadi* house not needed for a few years?

Oh, and what about transportation? So far, her knowledge of horses was confined to which parts of her lunch Charlie and Polly enthusiastically shared. She'd ridden in a buggy only the once—from the Bowmans' house to the home where the Sunday service had been held, and then she'd been enclosed in the back seat, unable to see much ahead.

She'd never so much as sat on a pony or horse, and certainly not harnessed or steered one. Brushed one. Didn't they need their hooves cleaned out? Even if she learned the basics, she'd be scared to death to take a horse and buggy out on a road shared with cars.

If she could stay close enough to town to walk . . .

But the idea of walking by herself any distance made her shiver, too, especially once dark started coming earlier. She'd sworn never to let herself be vulnerable again. Her new apartment was the first one ever where she hadn't immediately had a second and even third dead bolt installed.

Would she be able to keep her job? See her parents? Fly . . . no, not fly, they'd have to visit her here. What if one of them had a health crisis and needed her? What if . . . ?

What if, what if, what if.

To even be considering this, she must be off in the head, for sure.

Yet as freaked out as she was, the quote from Romans drifted through her head that night as she lay on the edge of sleep.

And we know that all things work together for good to those who love God, to those who are called according to His purpose.

The voice was deep, calm, welcoming.

* * *

A WEEK AFTER his apology, Luke struggled to hide his anguish from his family. Fortunately, he didn't have to hide it from Julia; he'd perfected the art of avoiding her.

He'd stayed for dinner at his parents' only two nights this week, which meant more grocery shopping and cooking, but Abby didn't seem to mind. She wasn't unhappy anymore to be left with her *grossmammi*, but he hadn't heard a delighted giggle from her all week, either, or seen her light up the way she had when she spotted Julia in the hospital waiting room or at the Sunday service.

It seemed he wasn't the only one grieving for what couldn't be.

Tonight they had chicken in a barbecue sauce and corn on the cob, a favorite of Abby's. She loved gnawing on the cob even after the kernels were gone. She'd lost a front tooth this past week doing that. This evening, neither had said a word in ten minutes, when she looked at him.

"*Daadi*, is Julia gone?"

His heart sank. Gone? "Out of their reach" wasn't an explanation she'd understand.

"What do you mean by 'gone'?" he equivocated.

She held his gaze. "Like Mommy."

"Oh, little one. Come here." Hurting anew, he pushed his chair back and held out his arms.

Abby scooted off her booster seat and chair and trotted around the table to him. He scooped her onto his lap and hugged her.

"No, Julia isn't dead. She isn't gone forever, like your *mamm*." He ought to explain that Beth was waiting in heaven to see Abby again, but was afraid he'd only confuse her. "Julia still works for your *grossdaadi* and me. I see her most days." He took a breath. "But she isn't Amish like we are. She worships at a different church, dresses differently than we do, drives a car, and uses electricity."

Face thin and anxious, she said, "So did *Mammi*."

"*Ja*, I know. But your mother asked me to raise you the way she and I were both raised, putting God at the center of our lives. Julia—" The words stuck in his mouth, because he thought Julia did that. She wasn't so different from him when it came to the important things. "It's best if we stay apart from people who don't share our beliefs. Sometimes that's hard, when you love someone and can't spend time with her."

His daughter tucked her head against him and didn't say anything for a long time. He closed his eyes and reveled in her slight weight and the trust that brought her to him so readily. He would forever be grateful to a merciful God who knew she needed him—and that he needed her.

"I liked playing with Julia," Abby said sadly.

"*Ja*." He heard his hoarseness. He had liked spending time with her, too. So much so, he had moments when he asked himself if he'd made the wrong choice. He'd been so sure this path to God was the right one for him, but no matter his determination, he wavered every time he thought about her.

But faltering wasn't his way, either. The Amish had never chosen the easy path, but rather the rockiest because each carefully chosen step made them think of what their Father asked of them.

"I'm sorry," he whispered to this small child who couldn't understand the battle he fought with himself or the reason for it. Yet he knew that time spent with Julia would hold his daughter in the *Englisch* world when his whole intention was to immerse her in a faith and a lifestyle that had deeper meaning, that would enrich every day of her life.

And still he felt as if he were being wrenched two ways, with the possibility he'd be torn apart.

Chapter Twenty-Four

❧◆❧

LUKE DREW CHARCOAL Xs on pale wood that would be the side of a drawer. He always did, even though it was probably unnecessary. Still, the small amount of extra time kept him from ruining a piece of wood if he had a moment of absentmindedness when cutting out the dovetail joints he used for every drawer.

The door into the store proper opened. His hand stuttered. Out of the corner of his eye he saw Julia but didn't raise his head.

She didn't look at him, either. "Eli, may I speak to you for a minute?"

His *daad* had been placing a board on the table saw, but he said, "*Ja*, certain sure."

The minute the door closed behind them, Luke sat up straight, the charcoal stick dropping from his hand. What could this be about? Had he made working here uncomfortable enough for her that she would quit? He could have been more pleasant, more cooperative, while still keeping his reserve. If she left—

He felt sick.

There were plenty of other things she might want to talk about. A bookkeeping or delivery problem, or she had another idea to increase their sales. A customer mad about something; that happened. In that case, she *should* turn to one of them.

Except, he knew she'd never come to him again.

He stared down uncomprehendingly at the dark Xs he'd drawn on a row of boards. *Daad* would return any minute. Whatever she wanted would be nothing of significance.

If she left them—

The door opened. Luke glanced up. His father was alone, two small furrows deep between his eyebrows.

"Is something wrong?" Luke asked.

"No, no, Julia asked for a few days off, that's all." Yet he looked perturbed. "To go home and see her parents."

"Is one of them sick? She hasn't been away for more than a few months."

Daad shook his head. "She didn't say, if that's so."

"She must miss them."

"I couldn't tell if she was happy to be going home or not."

If not, why would she go?

She hadn't been happy *here* these past two weeks. He'd seen that. What if she intended to job hunt while she was in Cleveland? And look for an apartment, as well, so that she could move back where she came from, near her parents?

He was responsible for her unhappiness. But what could he do?

"How long will she be gone?" This was Tuesday, the beginning of their workweek.

"She will fly to Cleveland on Thursday, stay for the weekend and be back at work Tuesday or maybe Wednesday."

Maybe. Luke didn't like the sound of that. If Julia left Tompkin's Mill for good, how would he explain it to Abby, when she equated "gone" with "dead"?

He shrugged. "So, not even quite a week." If she came back at all. "We can manage."

His father narrowed his eyes at him. "I don't understand that QuickBooks she's using. But you do, ain't so?"

He did, but had decided to avoid computers altogether once he came back. That part of his life was over. "If we save receipts and invoices, she can catch up in no time once she's back. You know how far behind we were when we hired her."

"*We* hired her?" *Daad* snorted. "*You* had nothing to do with it."

"You're right. So why are you worried?"

Daad only shook his head and went back to the table saw.

Luke had a suspicion they shared the same worry: that she wouldn't come back at all, or only long enough to work out a notice.

Not seeing her daily might be best for him . . . but the idea of not catching at least a glimpse of her when she arrived every morning, of knowing she wasn't just up front if he needed to see her, made him feel as if he were driving a car again, so fast he'd never make the curve ahead. Yet the brake pedal slammed to the floorboard under his foot without slowing the looming disaster.

A groan escaped him, but his father wouldn't hear over the whine of the table saw.

JULIA HADN'T HAD to check a bag, so once she passed the last security checkpoint, she looked around for her parents. Dad should be at work, but she knew he'd take the time off to meet her. Even knowing she had Nick to depend on in Tompkin's Mill, they hadn't liked it when she called to let them know she'd gotten a job and intended to stay.

Oh, she dreaded the upcoming conversation, but she'd save that for this evening, not spoil the reunion.

"Julia!" Beaming, Mom hurried toward her. "Honey, I'm so glad you decided to come home, even if it's only for a few days." She flung her arms around Julia, who let go of the handle of her suitcase to return the hug.

Barely an instant later, Dad wrapped them both in a comforting embrace. "I missed you," he murmured in her ear.

Her eyes stung. Here she'd run away from them, and she was about to cry because she was so glad to see them. The hug, the familiar smell of the cigars her father occasionally indulged in, the rumble of his voice and Mom's warm cheek pressed to hers all made her feel as if she'd come home.

Yet she knew that, no matter what, she couldn't. She had to forge a way herself, not lean on her parents forever.

Her father hadn't cried, but she and her mother both had. Laughing, sniffling, they both wiped at damp cheeks.

"Mama Santa's for lunch?" her father said.

On a burst of pleasure, she said, "I'd love that." Her family had always considered the pizza at Mama Santa's, in historic Little Italy, the best in the city. "Maybe when I go back, I should take Nick a pizza."

"Will you buy a seat for it?" her mother teased.

Over a salad and pizza, Julia told them more about her job and the auction she'd been involved in planning, and her mother bragged about being asked to sit on the board of trustees for the enormous Cleveland Public Library system. She was already president of the Friends of the Library for their local branch. Dad, as usual, was quiet, saying only, "Nothing new," when she asked about his work as a water engineer.

Nick, of course, wasn't nearly as informative about his life as they'd have liked. They wanted the scoop from Julia, but she had to tell them that, if he was seeing a woman, he hadn't told her.

"I do think he likes his job," she said. "I get the feeling he's surprised himself by being good at the politics part. Keeping the mayor and city councilors happy while reshaping the department by training and example. You know Nick. He likes being in charge."

Maybe, it occurred to her, he'd taken after their mother more than Dad, a civil engineer who tended to be laid-back and unambitious about rising to a supervisory position. As he said, why would he want a change when he liked what he did and made a good living doing it? In contrast, Mom, a librarian, had risen to co-director of public services for the entire Cleveland Public Library, part of the leadership team of the system.

Huh, Julia thought. *Maybe I'm more like Dad.* And why was that a surprise?

Dad did decide to go into the office for a few hours. At home, Julia excused herself to take a nap, since she was exhausted after getting up at the crack of dawn for the hair-raising drive to Kansas City to catch the morning flight to Cleveland.

She got up to help her mother cook and get dinner on the table. Sharing the kitchen like this brought back good memories. They hadn't been any different than Miriam and her *mamm* putting dinner together, doing a domestic dance perfected over many years. For a busy professional woman, Mom had been a good cook who loved to bake in particular when she had the time.

Once Dad was home and they sat down at the table to eat, Julia smiled at her parents. "Neither of you ever put your job ahead of Nick and me. I think I always took that for granted. I feel so lucky to have had you."

"Thank you for saying that." Her father set down the fork he had barely picked up. "Now why don't you tell us what you came home to say?"

Mom said indignantly, "Bob! Can't we eat first?"

He raised his eyebrows.

Julia, too, set down her fork and took a deep, preparatory breath. "I've become good friends with many of the local Amish in Tompkin's Mill. I attended one of their worship services. I'm . . . giving serious thought to converting."

Whatever they'd expected, this wasn't it. Obviously speechless, her parents both gaped.

AS WAS OFTEN the case these days, Elam came out to meet Luke before he'd pulled Charlie to a stop by the rail halfway between the barn and their parents' house. At least everything going on with Elam distracted Luke from his other worries.

His brother launched in the minute Luke descended from the buggy. "There was a message for me at Willard's phone shanty this morning. The closing is set for Wednesday."

"Good. That's fast." It had to be because they were paying cash. "You're still planning to give the Carters two weeks to move out, aren't you?"

Elam nodded. "I hope they don't have trouble. I thought I might stop tomorrow and ask if they can use any help. For heavy lifting, you know."

"I'd be happy to help them, as well. That's a kind thought, little *bruder*."

Elam grimaced. "I think the time has come to tell *Mamm* and *Daad*."

"I agree. Shall we do it now?"

"This is a good chance, since it's just the four of us. Well, and Abby, of course, but she won't want to contribute her thoughts about my move."

Luke chuckled. "No, she won't. *Daad*, now . . ."

"Maybe I shouldn't have kept it to myself for so long."

"Maybe not—but this way, you've kept the debate to a minimum. It's almost done."

Elam swallowed. "That's so. Are you planning to stay for dinner?"

"I wasn't, but if *Mamm* has enough . . ." He shrugged.

His brother gave him a "get real" look. On any given

night, the dinner their mother had ready could easily accommodate a family of eight who happened to drop by.

Walking into the house with his nervous brother, Luke wondered what Julia was doing right now. Having dinner with her parents? Most likely. He'd never thought to ask what they did for a living. Her talk of being "smothered" suggested they loved her dearly. He, too, would have a hard time letting a wounded child of his—even an adult one— fly free of his protection.

Unlike most Amish fathers, he didn't like the idea of his daughter—or daughters—getting married at only seventeen or eighteen years old. No, twenty would be a minimum, and he would want to be absolutely certain in his own mind that any man who asked to marry his daughter was the right one.

Moderns might scoff at that attitude, but he suspected Julia's brother would be on Luke's side. For all the good it would do either of them, given the willfulness of teenagers. *He* certainly hadn't listened to his parents at that age.

Abby stood on a step stool helping her *grossmammi* snap green beans. The apron wrapped twice around her pooled at her feet. When she saw her father, she said, "*Daadi*, see? I'm cooking."

"I do see." He lifted her up, gave her a big kiss, and set her carefully back on the same step. "Now I know to have you help me make dinner at home, too."

She glowed with pleasure at the idea. Luke thought ruefully that he might be sorry he'd introduced it, because her help would slow down any effort to get dinner on the table quickly. But *Mamm* had always encouraged her kids to help, from the time they weren't much more than toddlers—they set the table, went to the pantry or cellar for a jar of applesauce or stewed cabbage or whatever she'd decided she had to have. Even the boys had husked endless ears of corn during the season, picked and cored apples, whatever needed doing. He wouldn't be able to cook now if his mother hadn't taught him so early he didn't know he was learning.

Luke asked if he and Abby could stay, and was told that he shouldn't have to ask such a question.

He hid a grin. Both men hung their hats on pegs on the wall and washed their hands at the sink. Elam grabbed silverware and set one end of the table while Luke pulled out the chair where he usually sat.

He could hardly wait for the fireworks to begin.

Daad had a canny way of knowing when dinner was about to be served. Tonight, he appeared at the exact right moment, looked surprised to see Luke lifting Abby up beside him, and took his own place.

Luke frowned a little. "Without Miriam here, you're having to do too much, *Mamm*. I can help—" He started to rise.

"Pfft! If I'm such an old woman I can't cook dinner for my own family, I should go sit out on the porch in a rocker and drool."

He laughed at her and relaxed back onto his chair.

The stroganoff and noodles circled the table, followed by bowls holding cooked green beans and pickled beets, a basket of sourdough biscuits making the rounds last. He took small servings for Abby and generous ones for himself. It might be smart to shovel his food into his mouth to make sure he didn't end up going away hungry if *Daad* reacted badly to Elam's announcement. Anger would certainly frighten Abby.

Across the table from him, his brother served himself, too, but Luke could tell his mind wasn't on the food. Elam had always detested pickled beets, yet had just plopped a spoonful on his plate.

Once everyone had their food and had begun eating, he said, "I have news."

"Don't tell me you've quit your job at Willard's," his father said disapprovingly, confirming Luke's belief that it was past time for his brother to get out from under *Daad*'s thumb.

Elam's chin rose. "I plan to give him notice tomorrow."

"What?" That was both parents.

Picking up on the atmosphere, even Abby looked from face to face.

"I'm buying a farm. Luke is loaning me the money. The closing will be Wednesday, and then it'll be mine."

"You mean, it'll be Luke's," *Daad* said harshly.

Time to speak up. "No," Luke said, going for peaceful. "I trust Elam to pay me back in time. I consider this an investment, one I can well afford. I like what he intends to do with the good land he chose, and I'll help him as he's been helping me with my house."

Elam shot him a grateful look.

"What if you decide you don't like farming, just as you didn't like furniture making or building buggies?"

"Building buggies was nothing but a summer job when I was just out of school, *Daad*. And I've always wanted to farm, you know that. I went to work for you because I thought you needed me."

His calm maturity silenced their father, if only for a minute.

Eventually the conversation came around to where this land was, and whether the house was livable. Elam's excitement converted their mother, for sure. *Daad* was a tougher nut to crack. Still, even he was impressed, first when Elam told him how much money he'd managed to save on his own, and then when he learned that the *Englischers* had decided just this week to leave their farm equipment as part of the property instead of selling it themselves. Elam would have the mechanized equipment auctioned off and then use the money he earned to buy what he needed.

He talked of his plan to grow organic crops, his knowledge of what he had to do to get certified and how he would control pests clear evidence of the research he'd done.

Mamm finally said, "You'll be able to start a family."

Luke grinned wickedly at his brother. "She's right. Although how will you get a girl when you're so *blaid* with the pretty ones?"

Calling him "bashful" did not go over well.

Elam's eyebrows flickered and he shot back, "Perhaps I've been following my big brother's example."

Their father burst out in laughter. "*Blaid! Ja, ja*, that's it. Now we know why neither of our sons is married, Deborah."

Luke wished that were his problem.

EVERY CONVERSATION WITH either of Julia's parents ended up back on the subject that preoccupied them—and her, of course.

She'd be helping her mother fold laundry, when Mom would burst out, "Are you *sure*?"

"I'm not sure. You know that. I'm exploring the possibility," she'd repeat patiently, because she couldn't blame them for being freaked out at the idea of their only daughter joining a religious group they'd never encountered outside brief news snippets or fiction. "But, Mom, it's not like a . . . a convent, or a cult where I'll disappear. You can visit whenever you want. I'd just be restricted when it comes to visiting you because the Amish don't fly. I think bus travel is okay, but—" *No, no, don't remind her that I'd be traveling in Amish garb.*

"But *why*?" her mother wailed at least twice a day.

Julia struggled to put all her inchoate longings into words her parents, churchgoers who were genuine believers but didn't lean on their faith the way she did, could understand. She didn't like to remind them of her rape, but found herself talking some about her sense that truly forgiving her assailant might make a difference to her recovery.

"Do the Amish tolerate spinsters?" her mother asked another time. "Isn't that how they'd think of an unmarried woman?"

"I have no idea, but of course they do. They really aren't so different from us, Mom. They've chosen to hold themselves apart from the world so that they can live their faith. Is that so bad?"

"Sometimes I think neither of my children will ever marry or give me grandchildren," her mother said dolefully.

Julia's lips parted, but admitting that she'd fallen in love with an Amishman would lead them astray. After a moment, she said, "I might marry among them, Mom. I admire men who place God and family ahead of worldly ambitions."

Sharp-eyed, her mother said, "Your father does, you know. You don't have to go looking among a religious sect."

Julia was growing to hate that word, but she had to face it: that's how most outsiders thought about the Amish. Although not so much their neighbors or, in the case of A Stitch in Time and Bowman & Son's Handcrafted Furniture, their customers. It was people who'd never carried on an actual conversation with an Amishman or -woman who couldn't get past the fact that they dressed differently from contemporary Americans and insisted on sticking with horses and buggies even on roads built for speeding cars.

Julia realized she didn't much care what outsiders thought. A measure of her tension left her at that moment. She did care what her parents and her brother thought. Otherwise . . . think how quickly she'd lost touch with the friends she'd left behind here in Cleveland. They had tended to be work friends, or fellow quilters, but without proximity the ties had frayed quickly. Because she'd feared taking any risks at all, her friendships had always had limitations. She'd never gone out dancing or drinking with friends, rarely went to any evening event like a concert or play, and didn't fly off for sunny weekends in the Bahamas, either. She had lived independently by eliminating as many risky behaviors as possible.

I really have changed, she thought in wonder, and it wasn't only because she hardly ever turned on the TV or had gotten bolder at sharing her ideas on the job. The important change had been her refusal to hide behind multiple dead bolts, and to walk into the late-evening darkness to find her car.

She almost smiled, thinking about Psalms 23:4. She'd turned to it so often, but knew now she'd never fully *believed*.

Yea, though I walk through the valley of the shadow of death, I will fear not evil; For You are with me; Your rod and Your staff, they comfort me.

Now . . . the increasing depth of her faith had given her the courage to open herself to life again. And to take a step no one even in her family—maybe especially in her family— would understand. The certainty it was right for her felt as firm as bedrock.

Chapter Twenty-Five

Nick scowled even as he let Julia in his front door. He knew.

She had a "well, duh" moment. Why hadn't it occurred to her that in her alarm Mom would have called him right away, probably Thursday evening after the dinner-table discussion? She'd have been mad he hadn't warned her about his sister's foolishness, and wanted his take on the whole thing besides.

Not, Julia thought, that she could have won either way. If Nick had had any suspicion of how serious she was about this, *he'd* have called Mom or Dad to give them the heads-up and demand they talk Julia out of her idiotic scheme.

"Hi, Nick," she said with extra cheeriness. "It's nice to see you. Mom and Dad looked great. Mom may have retired, but she's not letting that slow her down."

The look he gave her combined annoyance and rueful amusement. "It's pretty obvious that Mom's just figured out another way she can run the whole show. Next thing we know, she'll be president of the board of trustees. If they have such a thing."

"They must, but I have no idea what it's called."

"Julia . . ."

"Can we work at getting dinner on the table before we argue? I'm starved."

After a miserable drive from Kansas City, she'd gone to her apartment to leave her suitcase but not even stopped to change clothes before coming straight here, per brotherly demand. She was rumpled, her hair falling out of ties, and she was tired. Not like there was a choice unless she'd wanted to take a hop on a small plane. Naturally, she was white-knuckled behind the wheel in city and busy freeway traffic.

I might not be driving at all for very long.

Great—except she'd be petrified the first time she took a horse and buggy out on her own, too.

Could she buy a decent horse and buggy for the money she'd get selling the used car she'd bought such a short time ago? She didn't have a clue what either cost.

Dinner was pretty much a repeat of the first evening with her parents, except Nick wasn't surprised.

"I just don't get it. You can be friends with any of the Amish without joining their church. You've got a nice place to live, a job you claim to like."

"I can keep the job. Unmarried Amishwomen often hold jobs. But if I were ever to marry, I'd be happy staying home to raise my children. I'm not . . . driven like you are, Nick. I never have been."

"Never?"

She knew what he meant, didn't even mind his raising the subject. "Never," she repeated. "Even before the assault, I didn't know what I wanted to major in. I vaguely thought of aiming for graduate school to become a librarian, prob-ably just because Mom was one and talked about it, plus you know how big a reader I am. I was enjoying college, but mostly because I felt like I was finally an adult. Out on my own."

Even Nick smiled at that. Living in a dorm and taking classes, all paid for by your parents, didn't qualify you as an adult, not by a long shot.

"Nick." She reached across the table and touched his hand. He turned his over and clasped her hand. "When I'm with the Amish, I feel as if I've come home. I don't know why that is, but it's that simple. Would it really be so bad? I'd stay local, and we could see each other whenever we want."

"Could we?"

"Well, we wouldn't be going to church together."

He sighed.

"You'll still love me if I do this, won't you?"

"Blast it, Julia! Of course I would. I just can't help feeling . . ."

Surprised by his tone, she asked, "Feeling what?"

He ran a hand over his head. "That this is my fault. If I could have caught that lowlife—"

She blinked. "I wouldn't be drawn to the Amish? Um, I don't quite see the connection."

"You could have healed," he said roughly. "It's as if you couldn't. You got stuck partway."

"That may be true, but don't you see? I *am* healing now. I'm starting to let go of my fears. I even—" Whoa! Not somewhere she wanted to go with her brother.

His eyes narrowed, seeing past her defenses. "You even what? Tell me, Julia."

Oh, why not? she thought recklessly.

"A man kissed me, and I enjoyed it. I wasn't scared, Nick. Do you know what a miracle that is for me?"

He leaned forward, his gaze more piercing yet. "What man?"

"Not your business."

"*Who?*"

She grinned at him. "Don't be nosy. And really, it

doesn't matter anyway. What does matter is that it happened. I'm shaking off the past, Nick. Can't you be happy for me?"

"It was your boss, wasn't it? That Luke Bowman. I saw the way he looked at you."

Hope stirred in her, because even at the beginning, she'd been aware of Luke, and able to tell he was equally aware of her.

But she only rolled her eyes. "Not telling you."

"Humph."

Julia waited.

A slow change came over his face. The skin crinkled beside his eyes, and his mouth lifted into a crooked smile. "Yeah," he said gruffly. "I can be happy for you. I just don't want to lose you."

Naturally, tears sprang into her eyes. She had to grab her napkin and blow her nose. Her smile trembled when she said, "You won't. I swear you won't."

"Okay." He shoved back his chair and came around the table, still holding on to her hand. He tugged her to her feet, too, and then bent to press an astonishingly gentle kiss to her forehead.

If she wasn't mistaken, he'd just given her his blessing.

Of course, he couldn't resist saying, "You know, you don't have to do this."

Julia laughed.

LUKE REINED HIS gelding into the alley Tuesday morning. Julia's familiar car wasn't there.

He often beat her here, he told himself. There was no reason to worry yet. He knew he was here earlier than usual, and didn't bother pulling out his pocket watch. *Daad* was probably still sipping his coffee at home.

She'd be along, or maybe she'd left a phone message apologizing and saying she'd be back tomorrow.

But the bands constricting his chest didn't loosen.

Even hoping this way was flat-out stupid, but how could he help himself? And *that* scared him. He had a big problem where she was concerned. What, he imagined if he kept scrabbling until his fingers were bloody and his nails torn, he'd find a solution? There was only one within his power, and he knew it. When he returned to his faith, this vulnerable yet strong and compassionate woman was part of what he'd given up. He just hadn't known it then. Was he now to say, *No reason I can't toss that commitment aside*?

From long practice, he removed the harness quickly and slung the collar over the fence rail. Freed, Charlie shook his head vigorously, sending his lush black mane and droplets of sweat flying. Luke tossed some hay into the manger and topped off the water before crossing the alley to the back door.

Inside, he stopped, painfully aware of the silence. He shouldn't have driven himself today; it would have been better if he arrived with his father. Luke had made an excuse because he'd feared he couldn't hide his increasingly bleak mood from his father. *Daad* had the gift of reading him all too easily.

He put his bagged lunch in the small refrigerator and prepared to start work. His concentration ragged, he'd been remarkably unproductive this past week. He'd quietly put that handsome slab of elm away in the timber room, given that the right idea for what to do with it refused to gel in his head.

Thinking he heard a car engine in the alley, he turned to face the back door and waited, not breathing. Sure enough, a key scraped in the lock, and the door swung open. Julia stepped in, her fiery hair backlit by the morning sun, her gaze going straight to him. She looked . . . as disturbed as he felt.

It was the first time in weeks he'd let himself openly stare at her. "You're here," he said inanely.

"I told Eli I'd be back to work today."

"Or Wednesday, he said."

"That was just in case . . ." She shook her head.

"You look tired." He should have kept his mouth shut, pretended not to notice.

She hadn't moved since she set eyes on him. "I am," she said quietly. "The week was . . . hard."

"But you were home with your parents."

"I know." This twisty little smile hurt to look at. "They had dreams for me that will never happen. I hoped they'd understand, but they don't."

What did that mean? He shouldn't ask; he should get to work and let her go out front and start on hers. She'd probably need all day to catch up.

But something alien overcame him. This much he could have: the answer to a question that had haunted him from first meeting her. "Will you tell me what happened?"

Obviously startled, she said, "You mean, with my parents?"

"No. Why you seem sad when you think you're alone and don't have to pretend. Why you dress as though you want to be invisible. Why . . ." No, he couldn't ask why she was afraid of him.

Really, he hadn't needed to ask the question at all. He knew the answer, just not the details. How would learning those details help?

She looked away for a minute. Said, voice low and scratchy, "I thought you weren't talking to me anymore."

"I shouldn't." His hands were knotted in fists, he realized, and with effort loosened them.

"When I tell them, people look at me differently."

"Tell me anyway."

She made an odd sound. "Oh, why not. What do I have to lose?"

Her resignation intensified the ache in his chest.

"I was raped, then beaten. I . . . we think he was trying

to kill me. He came close. I was in a coma for two days. I remember parts of it, but not the end, and not his face. The police believe he was someone I knew, or at least would have seen around. They wanted me to identify him, but how could I?"

In so few words, she'd said so much. Luke wanted in the worst way to put his arms around her, but it wasn't hard to tell from how she held herself, arms tight to her body, that she wouldn't welcome any touch. Telling him had thrown her back to the worst moments of her life.

No wonder she was afraid of men.

And he didn't dare touch her anyway.

"He was never arrested," he said hoarsely.

She shook her head.

"How old were you?" Not a child, he prayed.

Gazing toward the far wall, not him, she said in a low voice, "Nineteen. It was the summer between my freshman and sophomore years in college. I was subletting an apartment because I'd taken a job for the summer with the financial aid department. I came home after being out with friends, and I forgot to lock the door. Or . . . that's what they think. He didn't have to break in." Her desperate gaze returned to his. "The police kept drilling on that. Had I invited somebody? Or hinted that I might welcome him?"

"No." Luke took a step toward her. "You know none of that is true. And if it was, so what? Flirting isn't an invitation for a man to rape you and hurt you."

Her shoulders hunched, and once again she averted her eyes. It might not be conscious, but more than ever she was trying to shrink, to disappear before his very eyes. Guilt seized him. *He* had done this to her. What had he been thinking? That it would help her to relive an event so horrible, she would forever carry the wounds? Or had he merely been indulging his curiosity?

No, he could absolve himself of that. His need had gone deeper than that.

"Julia." Her name sounded as if he'd scraped it over gravel.

She said suddenly, "I hear your father. I have to get to work." She rushed toward him, compelling him to step aside, and yanked open the interior door. Before he could so much as turn, she was gone.

He stood stock-still, filled with rage and so much else on her behalf. Even if she'd lied about hearing his father coming, Luke knew she wouldn't want him to follow her.

In that minute, his faith in a loving God was shaken to the point of breaking. Had that vicious attack been God's *will*? Luke wasn't sure he could bear to think so.

Panting, each breath harsh, his entire body shaking, Luke imagined trying to forgive the monster that had hurt her.

No, God asked too much.

INCREDIBLY GRATEFUL TO see the pile of work waiting for her, Julia booted the computer from its nearly weeklong rest and immersed herself in bringing the accounting up to date. Along the way, she noted which pieces of furniture had sold so she could remove them from the website, if they'd been on there. She'd have to tour the showroom, too, to look for additions she needed to photograph.

Of course, her mind wandered.

She'd had no problem last night telling her brother she wasn't going to satisfy his curiosity, so why hadn't she done the same with Luke? This was the guy who'd pretended she wasn't there for something like two weeks. Why hadn't she pulled out the tried and true and said, *Not your business*?

She blinked a few times and focused again on the columns of numbers showing on the monitor. She couldn't let herself think about that strange interaction with Luke. Not now.

Twenty minutes after she'd begun, Eli popped out to welcome her back. No surprise, she didn't set eyes on Luke again the rest of the day. She and Eli left at the same time,

Eli not commenting on his son's early departure, her not asking about it.

Only later, trying to will herself to sleep, did Julia try to picture the expression on Luke's face as she'd told him her story. All she knew for certain was that he'd felt something powerful. Surely not rage. How would that be compatible with his beliefs?

Not disgust, either; he'd been insistent that none of what happened was her fault. Remembering that much gave her comfort. Her parents and Nick had said the same, as had the counselor she saw for nearly a year once she was able to drive herself again. But with the police, there'd always been an undertone. She'd heard other rape victims say the same.

One careless moment, her arms full when she'd gotten home, and it was her fault she'd been assaulted.

She looked toward the faintly lit rectangle of her bedroom window and had a puzzled thought. In the past, she felt dirty when she told someone about the worst thing that had ever happened to her, knowing he or she would never see her the same again. This time . . . she'd felt almost cleansed, as if telling Luke had allowed her to let go of subterranean emotions she didn't even like to acknowledge.

Or maybe it wasn't Luke at all. Maybe in examining her relationship with God, she had found some peace.

Her heart felt . . . warm, as if it contained a glowing coal. Of course she could forgive the man who'd attacked her! she realized in astonishment. All she'd ever had to do was let go of her anger and resentment. She'd blamed him for all her fears, all her anguish, but she might have been freed much sooner if she had done as God asked of her and forgiven a man so troubled. Wanting him to be caught so he didn't hurt other women, that was different. But what she'd done was allow him to tower over everyone else in her life, casting a shadow so dark, she hadn't been able to find the sunlight.

Or hear God's voice. Psalms 27:1 said it best: *The Lord*

is my light and my salvation; Whom shall I fear? The Lord is the strength of my life; Of whom shall I be afraid?

And yet she'd let herself fear so much.

The most astonishing peace swept through her, as if that glowing coal in her chest spread warmth until even her fingers and toes tingled.

Dear Lord, she prayed, *if vengeance is needed, I trust that to You. I pray that the rapist was never caught because he never did such a terrible thing again. I pray he horrified himself, and in seeking to forgive himself, found You, and some peace.*

Tears stung her eyes, but felt good, too, as if needed to complete the cleansing begun by answering Luke's questions and seeing the power of his response.

By forgiving her attacker, she dismissed him from the dominance he'd held over her life ever since.

Julia drew in a deep breath that expanded her lungs to an extent that dizzied her. The man whose face she couldn't see receded in her mind, became small and faraway, a last glimpse seen in the rearview mirror as she accelerated down a highway. No longer important.

She wished she could tell Luke how she felt, but that would have to wait.

At peace with her decision, she knew what she had to do tomorrow.

Chapter Twenty-Six

❖✦❖

WEDNESDAY EVENING, LUKE fed himself and Abby, then chose to go out and attack the blackberries in the pasture again. For the past day and a half, he hadn't been able to do anything but battle the rage and anguish inside his head and heart. He needed to throw his body into this fight, too, however symbolic that might be.

As *strubly* as ever, pigtails sagging, the old blackberry stain on her sacky unicorn T-shirt, Abby sat cross-legged on a blanket just on the other side of the board fence where she could see him and he could see her. Snatching up occasional bunches of grass, Charlie had evidently decided to stay away from Luke, who was inexplicably tearing thick roots from the ground, bleeding from innumerable scratches on his arms. In this fight at least; he had an opponent that didn't hold back.

It might be exhaustion that had begun to mute the savagery of his emotions. Physical exertion was good that way.

He could not go back and save Julia from the horror done to her so many years ago. If her brother and the other police hadn't been able to find and arrest the man, Luke had no hope of hunting him down now—assuming his deepest beliefs would allow him to do such a thing.

As he groaned and straightened his back, a faint sing-song voice came to him. He looked to see that Abby had lifted one of her faceless Amish dolls to show the horse, who'd stuck his head between the rails to touch the doll with his muzzle. Was Abby talking to Charlie, or just singing?

Luke stopped in his labors, leaning against the shovel he'd planted hard in the soil. Some of his anger lifted at the reminder of how far that frightened little girl had come. When he opened his heart to her, she had done the same to him, and was healing from her painful beginnings before his very eyes.

I could heal Julia, too, if I were given the chance, he thought.

The chance he'd have only if he left the Amish and most of the people he loved. He'd read scripture last night after tucking in Abby, and for all his anger known that he trusted in God.

Blinking sweat out of his eyes, he accepted that vengeance was not his to take. Forgiveness . . . that would come, too. Given his faith, he had to trust that it would.

Several cars had passed on the road since he started working, as well as two buggies. Those he'd noted, recognizing the horses and therefore knowing who was driving them.

Now another came down the road, not from town but going toward it. He shaded his eyes against the setting sun. He knew that horse, too, Bishop Amos Troyer's mare Finola, distinctive with her flashing white socks worn only on her front legs.

He automatically checked again on his daughter, to see her patting Charlie's nose. The gelding nickered, but as Luke watched, pulled his head back through the fence and raised it, staring toward the road. When the buggy turned into Luke's driveway, his horse trotted and then cantered to meet it and race it along the fence line.

Puzzled, Luke picked up his shears and carried the shovel with him, too, as he crossed the short distance to the gate. When he closed it behind him, Abby jumped up and ran to him.

Sweaty, dirty, and bloody, he took her hand rather than lifting her to his hip, and led her to where the buggy had come to a stop. Finola and Charlie were snorting and nickering to each other now as Amos climbed out of his buggy.

"Friends, I think," he said, nodding toward the horses.

"Have they ever met?"

"Shared pastures on Sundays, maybe." He smiled at Abby. "I'm glad to see you. Watching your *daadi* work, were you?"

Shy, she hid behind his leg.

"Has something happened?" Luke asked.

"*Ja*, something I had hoped for, but still came as a surprise."

Amos loved to be cryptic to draw out the suspense. He'd only get worse if Luke revealed his impatience.

The bishop smiled. "I had a visitor. We talked for a long time." His eyes stayed keen on Luke's. "An *Englischer*, who wishes to join the Amish."

An *Englischer* who wanted to become Amish? That happened so rarely—

For an instant, the world seemed to stop. The beat of his own heart was all Luke heard.

"Julia?"

"Julia?" Abby whispered.

But the bishop looked at Luke, not at the child who loved the same woman.

"*Ja.*" This smile was incredibly kind. "I had the feeling she hadn't told anyone except your sister."

If so, Miriam had some explaining to do.

Luke shook that off. "Did you agree?"

"Why would I not?" Amos spread his hands in acceptance. "She already speaks our language with great proficiency for someone who only started learning a few months ago. She knows the Bible well. She convinced me that she believes the Gospel and is prepared to forsake sin and put on true righteousness and holiness. By luck, I have classes scheduled to start soon."

Luke came near to falling to his knees under the force of an explosion of joy and hope.

"I need to see her," he blurted.

Bishop Amos smiled. "I thought you might want to. That's why I came to let you know."

Luke looked down at his daughter, who would like to see Julia almost as much as he did—but that reunion could wait. "Will you take Abby to my parents?"

"I expected to do that, too. What do you say, little one? Will you go for a ride with Amos?"

Luke crouched down and looked into her eyes. "Please. Amos will take you to *Grossmammi* and *Grossdaadi*'s. I will come and get you soon."

She was confused, but he didn't let that dissuade him. He bundled her into Amos's buggy, gave her a big kiss on the cheek, and closed the door.

"I need to harness Charlie—"

Amos stopped him with a hand on his arm. "A smart man would clean up and change his clothes before he asked a woman the question I think you want to ask."

It was all Luke could do to glance down at himself. "You're right. I can take that much time." He held out a hand and said simply, "*Denke*, Amos."

They shook, and Amos got back in his buggy and steered his mare in a sweeping circle and back down the driveway.

Luke ran for the house.

*   *   *

JULIA STARED AT the page and realized she didn't remember any of what she'd just read. She was too restless, too—she didn't even know what to call it. She was going to do this. Her life would change drastically . . . but not right now. This was still her apartment. Who would know if she turned on the TV? Her digital clock would wake her in the morning in time to go to work. She'd drive her car to get there.

When would all of this change? Abruptly, between one night and the next, or gradually over the course of weeks?

She was driving herself crazy.

"I have to do something," she said aloud.

Quilt. What else? Unfortunately, her mind could still roam free while she quilted, since her hand knew so well what to do. Still, that would engage part of her attention. Plus . . . quilting was one thing that wouldn't change, except that she'd no longer have the benefit of electric lighting.

She'd recently pieced a wall hanging with buildings of different sizes and shapes, including a steepled church, different pitches of roofs, interspersed with trees, evergreen and deciduous. To do the hand quilting, she stretched the quilt in a large hoop instead of the frame in her spare room. Picking up where she left off, she began to quilt a picket fence in the frame below a row of houses.

At a knock on the door, her hand jerked. Who on earth . . . ? Surely not Nick, come to renew his disapproval.

She set down the hoop and went to the door, with its tiny peephole. Pulse racing, she looked through it . . . and saw Luke. His hair was wet and disheveled. Stubble showed on his angular jaw. As she watched, he knocked again, firmly.

Why was he here?

Julia made herself close her eyes and take a few deep breaths before she undid the dead bolt and opened the door. "Luke, is something wrong?"

He walked in, crowding her back. Eyes intense, he said, "Why didn't you tell me?"

"Tell you what?" How could he have already learned . . .

"Bishop Amos came by to say you'd asked to join us."

"Oh. I had no idea he'd do anything like that." She was wringing her hands together. Her gaze lowered to his arms. "You're injured!"

With a glance down, he said, "Only scratched. I was cutting back blackberries." He shook his head as if rattling his brain into place. "How long have you been thinking about this?"

"I . . . would you like to sit down?"

His jaw flexed. "No. I don't think I can make myself sit right now."

Her knees felt so weak, she wasn't sure how long *she* could keep standing.

"Answer my question."

"You're being a bully."

He let out a huff that might have been a laugh. "You had to know I was torturing myself."

"I . . . no." Torturing himself? Sometimes she'd imagined, but . . . "I talked to Miriam a few weeks ago. Until then . . . well, it hadn't occurred to me that I *could* convert. I mean, I hadn't seen anyone who talked as if they'd had any other kind of life. Miriam told me that you don't proselytize, but that occasionally outsiders do join you."

"I almost asked if you'd consider it, but it's such a big change, I didn't think there was any chance," he said gruffly. "It will be like jumping back a hundred—no, two hundred years in time. No horseless carriages for us. It will mean giving up so much." He gestured, as if to encompass her entire apartment, or maybe her world.

"You're trying to talk me out of it?"

"No. Only . . . hoping you're being realistic, that this isn't a rainbow that will vanish when you reach for it. If you change your mind again, I don't know how I'd—"

The intensity wasn't just in his eyes, but in his voice, too. How he'd what?

"Julia." He reached for her hands. Pried them apart, then wrapped them in his much larger ones. "I told you I was in a fight with myself."

Breathless with what might be hope, she said, "I didn't know exactly what you meant."

"That I gave thought to walking away from the *Leit*, if that was the only way I could have you."

Shocked, she made herself meet those glittering blue eyes. "You wouldn't do that."

"I wouldn't have wanted to. But . . . seeing you, never able to say what I need to . . ." His throat moved. "I didn't know if I could bear it."

That's what he'd almost said a minute ago. That he might break if she gave *him* hope and then snatched it away.

She returned the clasp of his hands. "I was going to quit my job."

"What?"

"If I made the decision not to convert. I didn't know if I could stand seeing you every day, either. It . . . hurt."

"I never wanted to hurt you," he said in a low, raw voice.

"If I'd wanted my life to stay the same, I shouldn't have taken the job. Those first few days, you scared me and made me feel things I never have."

"You scared me, too," he admitted. "That's why I didn't want *Daad* to hire you. From first sight, I knew what a temptation you'd be."

"It wasn't just, oh, that I reminded you of what you'd given up when you came home? As if one part of you still longed for the kind of women you knew before?" She hadn't even known she carried that worry until the words came out of her mouth.

But Luke was almost smiling as he shook his head. "No. If so, I'd have been out of luck. You're nothing like most women I met out there. But I do like knowing that you understand the man I was in the *Englisch* world will always be part of me. I can never go back and be who I might have been if I'd never left the faith. You see all of me, don't you?"

"Yes." Why was she so close to tears, when she was also happier than she'd ever been in her life? "Just as you'll understand why I can't remake myself instantly. I'll bumble around and offend people and . . ."

"Why would anybody be offended? You're a devout, compassionate woman who is doing something extraordinary. They'll want to help you adjust." He paused. "You'll have me to help you."

THAT SOUNDED LIKE he was offering friendship, not more. They couldn't marry until she'd been baptized anew—assuming she had been as a baby—but that didn't mean they couldn't make promises.

Yet somehow Luke found himself seated after all, with Julia needing someone to answer her many questions.

"It felt like a letdown, coming home. You know? I talked to Bishop Amos, but then I could have spent the evening watching television. I don't want my commitment to be questioned, but I'll need to find someplace to live, and . . . and someone to help me make dresses. And can I keep banking the same way? I'll need to learn how to drive a buggy, and harness a horse, and—"

Luke laughed and captured her hand again. He loved the feel of it, fine-boned, with smooth skin but for the calluses left by the quilting needle. The fit was perfect, making him think of a dovetail joint.

"We'll ask my parents if you can live with them," he suggested. "You know them well already, and *Mamm* would love to guide you. Abby and I can eat dinner there every night so we can spend time together. Once Rose has her baby, Miriam will be there, too."

"Oh. Do you really think . . . ?" There was the fragile hope that always moved him.

"I really think. *Mamm* will be so happy. She hasn't understood why I haven't married." Ach, there, he'd said the word. But he decided to finish answering her torrent of questions first. "She loves to sew. You will not need to harness a horse or drive yourself for a long time, although we'll teach you. If you want to keep working for *Daad* and me, you'll ride to work with us each day."

The hope on her beautiful face was now blinding, as if the sun had crested the horizon and spread glorious color across the sky. Basking in it, he said, "You will marry me, won't you, Julia?"

"If you're asking me—you're *sure*?"

"I'm more certain than I've been about almost anything else in my life." Peace washed through him, smoothing away the jagged emotions that had kept him on edge for months. "Do you know how happy Abby will be to find out you're to be her *mammi*?"

Suddenly her eyes were awash with tears. "I can't wait. I fell in love with her right away."

"I could tell." He smiled crookedly. "And with me, too?"

Tears still hanging on her dark eyelashes, she squeezed his hand hard. "With you first. You must have known."

More soberly, he said, "At first I hoped for both our sakes that wasn't true. But I haven't been able to deny how much I love you. It was as if"—he looked down at the seamless clasp of their hands—"you were perfect for me."

"With only one big problem."

He hesitated, knowing this was something they had to talk about. "Not one. Two. You were not Amish, and I frightened you when I stood too close to you."

She bowed her head. "Now you know why."

"Yes." With his free hand, he lifted her chin. "I will be as patient as I need to be. Amish don't make vows often, but this one is important."

"A few times I dated," she said, sounding choked, "but I always ended up panicking. Especially if the man tried to kiss me. But when you did, there wasn't even a hint of the old fear. I've always known I could trust you." Cheeks pink, she finished, "I don't think you'll need very much patience at all."

"God was with us when you walked into the store that day," he muttered—and then he kissed her again, as he'd done a hundred more times in his imagination. Her lips were soft, accepting. Eager.

No, he didn't think he'd need much patience, either . . . except that they had to wait until they could be married.

When he told her Amish weddings were commonly held after the harvest, November being a popular month, she nodded and said she'd read that. He continued, "You must be baptized first, but Amos thought that wouldn't take so long with you already speaking our language and so familiar with the Bible. I think November would be a fine month for our wedding."

She did cry a little when she told him about her talks with her parents, who had been upset, and her brother, who surrendered with less fight than she'd expected.

Swiping away the tears with her free hand, she said, "My parents will come around when they see I'm happy. I'm sure they will. And they'll love Abby. They both want grandchildren."

"My parents already have several, and they still want more," he said, smiling broadly. Heart full, he looked down at her. "Will you come with me tonight, to *Mamm* and *Daad*'s? We can tell them and Abby, too."

Nerves showed in her eyes. "But it'll be late . . ."

"Why don't you pack a bag," he said gently. "You can sleep in Miriam's bed, or my old bedroom. Tomorrow when it's light, we can come for more of your things. We can eat dinner together every evening, drive to work together, go home to Abby together every day."

"A step toward my new life," she said slowly.

"A big step," he agreed gravely. "Is it too big a one?"

This smile lit her from within and made his heart swell until he wasn't sure his rib cage could contain it.

"No." She pushed herself up and kissed his rough cheek. "It's just right. Give me five minutes, and I'll be ready to go."

When he carried her suitcase out four minutes later, leaving her only to bring an enormous tote bag filled with an unfinished quilt and a wooden hoop, she didn't even look back.

Epilogue

❖◆❖

"This is the kitchen, *Mammi*," Abby said softly. She held tight to Julia's hand. "*Daadi* says he'll add more cupboards if you want them."

Julia smiled down at the daughter of her heart. "You can tell *Daadi* that I think there are plenty."

A smothered chuckle came from just behind her. Luke was sticking close. Probably looming, but now she enjoyed having him close, knowing he'd use any excuse to rest a hand on her shoulder or back, or run his knuckles softly over her cheek.

This was Julia's first visit to the house that would soon be her home. Deborah had decided they would have *middaagesse* here today, once the tour was over. Not just lunch, but something like a picnic, although Deborah insisted there must be tables and chairs.

"It would be foolish to get grass stains on our dresses!" she'd declared, not seeing the amused glance exchanged by Miriam and Julia.

The two of them were already outside setting food on

one of the tables Luke and Eli had hauled from the house. Elam had been assigned the task of carrying chairs out. He was too busy admiring the walls in the dining room to pick up even the first chair.

His voice carried to the kitchen. "I worked my fingers to the bone on these walls."

Also in the dining room, his father just snorted. Luke laughed.

Beneath Julia's feet, the sycamore wide-plank floors gleamed. That was really what Luke had wanted to show off, she knew. He, his *daad*, Elam, and friends had sanded and finished the wood both upstairs and down in preparation for Luke to bring her home as his wife. She'd have worried about the wear and tear that normal family life would put on them, except in the Amish way he'd made sure that original flaws in the wood and even some later damage, like burns, remained. Like all the work he'd done on the old farmhouse, he'd retained the character, instinctively avoiding perfection.

That said so much about the man she loved, Julia's heart ached anew and she thanked her heavenly Father for the countless blessings that now enriched her life.

Eli and Deborah had welcomed her with open arms. Of course, Bishop Amos had told them that Luke had gone straight to her that evening, but she believed their joy was real. She knew Abby's was.

She bent to say, "Show me your bedroom, Abby."

The little girl turned. "Can I, *Daadi*?"

He gently tugged one of the ties dangling from her organdy *kapp*, a miniature version of the one Julia now so happily wore, too. "Of course you can."

Then he laid a hand on Julia's back in that way he did. His eyes had darkened. "You can see our bedroom, too."

Our. Once that word would have struck terror into her heart. No longer. After all the *wunderbaar* kisses they had shared these past weeks, how could she be afraid anymore?

"I can," she said, almost primly. "But we'd better hurry. I hear another buggy. It must be Rose and her family." Two *kinder* already, and now the new *boppli*.

So much family. Knowing her parents and Nick planned to attend the wedding had completed her happiness.

Smiling, she started up the stairs.

Home.

About the Author

The author of more than ninety books for children and adults, **Janice Kay Johnson** writes about love and family—about the way generations connect and the power our earliest experiences have on us throughout life. An eight-time finalist for the Romance Writers of America RITA Award, she won a RITA in 2008 for her Superromance novel *Snowbound*. A former librarian, Janice raised two daughters in a small town north of Seattle, Washington.

Ready to find
your next great read?

Let us help.

Visit prh.com/nextread

Penguin
Random
House